Praise for the novels of Debra Webb

"A hot hand with action, suspense and last, but not least, a steamy relationship."
—*New York Times* bestselling author Linda Howard

"Debra Webb's name says it all."
—*New York Times* bestselling author Karen Rose

"Compelling main characters and chilling villains elevate Debra Webb's Faces of Evil series to the realm of high-intensity thrillers that readers won't be able to resist."
—*New York Times* bestselling author CJ Lyons

"A well-crafted, and engrossing thriller.
Debra Webb has crafted a fine, twisting thriller to be savored and enjoyed."
—*New York Times* bestselling author Heather Graham on *Traceless*

"A steamy, provocative novel with deep, deadly secrets guaranteed to be worthy of your time."
—*Fresh Fiction* on *Traceless*

"Debra Webb's best work yet. The gritty, edge-of-your-seat, white-knuckled thriller is peopled with tough, credible characters and a brilliant plot that will keep you guessing until the very end."
—*New York Times* bestselling author Cindy Gerard on *Obsession*

"Interspersed with fine-tuned suspense...the cliffhanger conclusion will leave readers eagerly anticipating future installments."
—*Publishers Weekly* on *Obsession*

"Webb reaches into our deepest nightmares and pulls out a horrifying scenario. She delivers the ultimate villain."
—*RT Book Reviews* on *Dying to Play*

Also by Debra Webb

MIRA Books

Shades of Death

The Blackest Crimson
No Darker Place
A Deeper Grave

Harlequin Intrigue

Faces of Evil

Dark Whispers
Still Waters

Look for Debra Webb's next novel

THE COLDEST FEAR

available soon from MIRA Books.

For additional books by Debra Webb,
visit her website at www.debrawebb.com.

DEBRA WEBB

A DEEPER GRAVE

mira

mira

Recycling programs
for this product may
not exist in your area.

ISBN-13: 978-0-7783-1993-1

A Deeper Grave

www.MIRABooks.com

Printed in U.S.A.

This book is dedicated to all the amazing men and women who risk their lives every day to protect and serve the communities of this great nation as officers of the law. Though many of my fiction novels include members of law enforcement who are not good guys, I know that in real life these bad folks are the exception and not the rule. Thank you for all you do to keep us safe.

A
DEEPER
GRAVE

Only on the edge of the grave can man conclude anything.

—Henry Adams

One

Fern Parker turned up the volume until the music vibrated in her earbuds. She closed her eyes and tried to pretend her parents weren't right down the hall screaming at each other. Ever since they moved into this shitty house in this shitty neighborhood all those two ever did was fight. It didn't matter that she and her brother had lost nearly all their friends or that they couldn't even go to the mall or any damned where else without being pointed at and whispered about. The worst part was moving to a new school. Fern hated the place, she hated the other kids and she hated the teachers. All her parents cared about was proving who was the guiltiest.

She hated them both. Hated her life.

Fern pressed her lips together and squeezed her eyes shut a little tighter. God, she wished she had some weed. Maybe she'd have some later. *He* had bought it for her before. Last time it was beer. A smile softened her lips. He was so damned hot.

Maybe tonight they'd have sex. He'd pretended not to want it as much as she did, but she knew. He was only trying to be a gentleman. Older guys were like that. She didn't care that he was older. He was watching out for Fern and her family like a guardian angel. No one else cared.

He deserved something for all his trouble. Besides, Fern was tired of being a virgin. Tonight she was going to be bad. Just let her parents try getting in her shit for being bad. "I hate you both," she muttered.

Something touched her arm and she jumped. *Sage.* Her crybaby little brother.

"What do you want?" she demanded, removing an earbud. He scared the crap out of her sneaking around like that. She should have locked her door.

"Can I sleep in your bed?" He stared up at her with those puppy dog eyes all shiny with tears. You'd think he was five instead of ten.

Hard as she tried not to care, she regretted yelling at him and for one second she almost said yes. She loved the little brat even if he made her so mad sometimes. He always got scared when their parents argued. Then she remembered the guy she'd promised to meet after her parents crashed. No contest.

"Get out of here!" She snagged her brother by the arm and escorted him into the hall. "Leave me alone," she warned.

"Pleeease," he whined.

"Go away!" Fern slammed the door in his face.

She felt bad again for about a second. He was

her little brother and she loved him. She'd gotten in seriously deep shit sticking up for him. Her school record was ruined. She rolled her eyes. Who cared? It wasn't like she was going to Harvard or Princeton now the way her father had always promised. She'd be lucky to get into a state school with financial assistance.

Her whole fucking life was falling apart and it was *their* fault. She glared at the wall that separated her bedroom from her parents'. The whole city knew the awful things they had done. All the jerks who'd ever pretended to be her friends had turned their backs when the government seized their home...*froze their assets*. A sixteen-year-old girl shouldn't even have to know about those things much less be living them.

It wasn't fair. Her parents had ruined her life. She and her brother would never recover from their bullshit.

Frustrated, Fern stormed from her room and down to the kitchen. Maybe she'd see if her father still kept a stash of beer in the garage fridge. She didn't bother turning on a light. The layout of the house wasn't that complicated. It was maybe a fifth the size of the home she'd grown up in. This place sucked in every way.

A quick twist of the dead bolt and she slipped into the garage. At the fridge, she opened the door, light spilled out around her and she spotted the Budweiser. She smiled and reached for one. Standing in the vee the open fridge door made, she twisted off the top and took a long, deep swallow. Something stung her neck. She jerked. Swatted at whatever it was. The half-empty bottle of beer hit the concrete, shattering and splashing foamy liquid over her legs.

"Shit."

Before she could step away from the mess, an arm locked around her waist and a hand closed over her mouth. She told herself to struggle but her muscles wouldn't work. The light from the fridge faded to darkness.

"Good night, princess."

Two

Montgomery, Alabama
Thursday, October 20, 7:35 a.m.

Detective Bobbie Gentry adjusted the temperature on the dash. Last week it had hit better than seventy degrees every single day. As if the weather gods suddenly woke up and realized it was fall, last night's low abruptly dipped nearly to freezing. Football weather, her father had called it. Her husband, on the other hand, would have picked up their little boy and swung him around, announcing that the cooling temps and changing colors of the leaves meant it was time for the fair to come to town.

Except those happy moments wouldn't happen this year. James was dead. Their son, Jamie, was dead. And her folks had passed away years ago.

Bobbie was alone.

The good news was she had come to terms with the reality of her life…at least to some degree. Dying wasn't her first thought when she woke up or whenever she thought of her little boy. Her heart no longer threatened to stop beating when she recalled her husband's voice, or his touch or that sexy smile. At some point in the past few weeks she had stopped counting the days since her life, for all intents and purposes, had ended.

She was alone, but she was learning to live with it.

"I don't need a babysitter."

She slowed for a traffic light and glanced at the detective in the passenger seat of her Challenger. "No one said you did, Bauer. Besides you'd do the same for me."

Asher Bauer stared out the window, refusing to meet her gaze. "I dunno where you get the idea that I'm a nice guy."

Bobbie tapped her fingers on the steering wheel. They'd had versions of this discussion numerous times before. Typically Bauer was a charming, keep-everybody-laughing kind of guy—unless he was in a mood. When he was in a mood, he considered himself the scum of the earth and wanted nothing to do with anyone. Like now.

"Maybe I think you're a nice guy because you brought me flowers every week when I was in the hospital and in rehab." She sent him a knowing look. "That was a lot of flowers."

"Holt made me bring 'em."

"Yeah right. Holt had nothing to do with those flowers and we both know it."

Sergeant Lynette Holt wasn't the type to suggest flowers. She barely remembered to order an arrangement for her wife when their baby was born.

Bobbie wished she could turn off whatever switch had been tripped over the weekend. Last Friday Bauer had been psyched, looking forward to a trip to T-Town to watch the Crimson Tide play Texas A&M. It certainly hadn't been the game. The Tide had crushed the Aggies. Maybe he and his date had a fight. Of course Bauer would deny he'd been on a date. Whether he called it a date or not he'd taken a female companion to the game in Tuscaloosa. They'd no doubt partied and fooled around. And, apparently, parted on less than amicable terms. He'd been in a mood since.

"I get my Mustang back this afternoon," Bauer said, totally ignoring the flower comment. "You and Holt don't need to worry about picking me up after today."

"That's great. You'll feel like a free man with your wheels back."

Bauer grunted in response. Three weeks ago he'd left for work and barely made it a mile when another driver T-boned him. Beyond hefty damages to his beloved car, he'd sustained nothing more than a mild concussion. The fact that he hadn't had a drink since around ten the night before ensured he was stone-cold sober at the time of the accident— another lucky break. Bauer had spent the required seventy-two hours on medical leave before returning to work and for whatever reason he'd chosen not to get a rental to use while his car was in the shop. Holt had told him to take one of the Crown Vics but he'd played off the suggestion.

Bobbie wondered if he'd been afraid to get behind the wheel again so soon after the accident. Sometimes even people who took the most daring risks could get scared. She had asked him and he'd promptly disregarded the question in that same aloof manner he used to make people think he was arrogant. But he wasn't. Bauer never talked down to anyone and he kept his troubles to himself. Case in point, even after two years Bobbie still didn't know why his fiancée had committed suicide. Not that she could fault him for keeping certain things close.

We all have our secrets. She had plenty of her own.

"You make your meeting last night?" She braced for a sarcastic response. Asking an alcoholic if he'd gone to his AA meeting was tricky.

"Has a cat got an ass?" He raked his fingers through his hair and then stretched his neck from side to side. "Holt said if I missed a meeting I was going on leave."

No cop wanted to be forced off the job, but Bobbie agreed with Holt's edict. Bauer's drinking had become more and more of a problem over the past year. He'd hit the wall a couple of months ago and started sneaking a drink at work when the pressure was on. Holt had ordered him to get his butt to Alcoholics Anonymous. He hadn't argued. Apparently the accident had driven home the message that he needed to get his act together on and off the job. Bobbie figured he had realized that he might have avoided being hit if he'd been more alert rather than hungover. He hadn't said as much, but a few of his comments hinted at the idea.

While Holt had taken some time off with her new baby, Bauer had been without a partner so he and Bobbie had worked together for a few weeks. Howard Newton—Newt—had been Bobbie's partner since the day she made detective. Seven years. He'd been like a father to her. His death two months ago had left her reeling. She missed him something fierce. Always would. But life moved on whether you were ready for change or not. September fifteenth a new detective had transferred in from Birmingham and Lieutenant Owens, the Major Crimes Bureau commander, promptly introduced him as Bobbie's new partner. Holt and Bauer had been partners for nearly a decade. It was only right that the new guy was assigned with Bobbie.

Like every other aspect of her life this year, finding balance with a new partner hadn't been easy. She'd lost so damned much. Until recently she'd spent most of her time wishing for just two things: vengeance and death. She hadn't expected to accomplish one without the other, and yet here she was.

No looking back.

"You got food in the house?" she asked, her voice sounding loud after the long span of silence. "We could go shopping after work."

Bauer made a disgusted sound. "Like I said, I don't need a babysitter."

As much as she understood his frustration, she couldn't deny being grateful that someone else was the object of the team's scrutiny and concern these days. She'd done her time and endured more than her share of sympathetic looks and queries as to whether she was okay. *Okay* was something she might never again be, but she was moving forward. One slow step at a time.

She said, "I'll take that as a yes." She hadn't noticed any weight loss. Obviously the man was eating. The dark circles under his eyes suggested he wasn't sleeping as well as he should. Still, every sandy-brown hair was in place and he was dressed as if he was headed to a magazine cover shoot rather than the morning briefing.

Bauer exhaled a big breath. "I'm good, that's all anyone needs to know." He paused for a couple of beats. "I appreciate the offer, but I can do my own shopping."

Bobbie braked for another traffic light. This time she turned to him. "I get it and I'll gladly stop nosing into your business on one condition."

He gave her an eye roll. "And what might that condition be?"

"If you need someone, you'll call me. Deal?"

He made an impatient face, but he nodded his agreement. "Deal. Now get off my back."

"You got it." The light changed to green and she nudged the accelerator. Since she hadn't exactly set the best example of reaching out to friends for help, she appreciated that Bauer didn't mention as much.

He unclipped his cell from his belt, checked the screen and answered, "Morning, Sarge. What's up?"

Unless Holt had decided to check up on him, there was a call. Bauer grunted in response to whatever the sergeant was saying. Bobbie concentrated on driving, tension working its way into her muscles. The city of Montgomery had been pretty quiet the past two months. The serial killer known as the Storyteller had wreaked havoc for a few days back in August but he was in hell now where he belonged.

Bauer ended the call and tucked his phone away. "We got two bodies over on the corner of Westminster and Woodmere. Devine is already on the scene. You can drop me off at CID and head that way."

"Any details on what happened?"

"She didn't tell me a whole lot. She was bringing me up to speed on a case in her neighborhood that blew up again last night."

"The domestic abuse case?" Bobbie had a bad feeling about that one. The couple lived only two doors down from Holt. Every time there was a flare-up between them it was worse than the last. Holt had, unfortunately, let the escalating situation get personal for her. *Like you have any room to talk, Bobbie.*

Some things were personal.

Bauer nodded. "That's the one." He moved his head from side to side. "I don't get why women stay in that shit."

Bobbie didn't, either. Not really. Although she had to admit that her own experience with being abducted, raped and tortured had changed her in ways she hadn't expected, so she tried not to judge anyone else. Talk was cheap until it happened to you.

"How about you drop me off at the scene?" she

suggested. "When I'm done there, I'll hitch a ride with Devine."

Bauer didn't answer as she slowed for a U-turn.

"Any witnesses? Who found the bodies?" she asked, not wanting to give him time to come up with an excuse for why he couldn't drive her car to the Criminal Investigation Division offices.

He shrugged. "Don't know about any witnesses. Holt said the housekeeper found the bodies." Bauer reached for the coffee he'd abandoned in the cup holder and knocked back a slug. "She did say it's some creepy shit though."

"I guess I'll find out."

Creepy was relative. After what she'd gone through with the Storyteller, very little surprised Bobbie. Still, adrenaline pumped hot and fast through her veins. There was a lot missing in her life. No matter that she'd stopped the monster responsible for that loss, the emptiness remained. Being a cop was all she had left. She worked hard to stay on her toes and to maintain focus. Being a cop was her life.

The case was all that mattered.

Westminster Drive
8:30 a.m.

Detective Steven Devine waited on the sidewalk outside the tri-level brick home now surrounded by yellow crime scene tape. The lawn was neatly kept with lush green shrubbery and large trees. The house was situated in a typical middle-class suburb in an older, quiet neighborhood. Any vehicles the owners drove were either gone or hidden away in the garage.

Bobbie waved to Devine, then greeted the officer maintaining the perimeter as she ducked under the tape. The presence of two Montgomery Police Department cruisers as well as that of the coroner's van had drawn neighbors outside. So far Bobbie didn't see any sign of reporters, which suited her just fine. She'd had her fill of the media over the past ten months. Be that as it may, as soon as word about the homicides hit the grapevine the newshounds would appear. Generally they weren't far behind the coroner's van.

"Morning, Bobbie," Devine said, his good old Southern boy smile in place.

He was a couple of years younger than Bobbie's thirty-two. Tall, lean and reasonably attractive with the kind of calming blue eyes that stirred trust, particularly in female witnesses. He kept his dark hair cut regulation short and his tailored designer suits professionally pressed. More important than all the outer trappings, his history as a homicide detective in Birmingham was impeccable. So far Bobbie couldn't complain.

"Morning. What do we have inside?" Bobbie headed for the front door.

Devine's long legs easily kept up with her hurried stride. "Husband and wife are deceased. The bodies appear to have been staged. Sixteen-year-old daughter and ten-year-old son weren't home.

The housekeeper says they frequently stay with friends."

"We need to confirm the location of the children ASAP." Worry tied a knot in her gut. If the kids were home at the time of the murders there could be more bodies showing up soon.

"Got someone working on that," Devine said.

Bobbie frowned. "Is this a murder-suicide?"

"No, ma'am." Devine paused at the door, his hand on the knob. "If you watch the news or read the papers you're familiar with the vics, Nigel and Heather Parker."

Bobbie doubted there was anyone in the state who hadn't heard about the two. The identity of the victims added a whole new dimension to the investigation. Nigel Parker had apparently spent the past several years attempting to emulate the notorious Bernie Madoff. The wife, Heather, had started her own Ashley Madison–style service to accommodate her husband's high-powered clients as well as the who's who in the state of Alabama. The feds believed Heather had been using pillow talk to help her husband swindle his clients. Both empires had recently begun to crumble. Nigel's diverting and skimming had been uncovered and Heather's "little black book" had somehow landed in the hands of a national tell-all rag of a newspaper. Even the governor's name had appeared within those torrid pages.

"So what are they doing here?" Bobbie surveyed the neighborhood a second time. The Parkers owned one of those luxury estates over on Bell

Road. Most likely the feds had seized their property. Or maybe the family was simply attempting to live incognito.

"According to Mrs. Snodgrass, their longtime housekeeper, the reporters, the threatening calls and letters got to be too much. This is one of the rental properties Parker owned under a shell company so they moved here."

Bobbie had caught a couple of clips from the FBI's recent press releases on the local couple who'd made national headlines. In addition to Nigel Parker having received numerous death threats, shots had been fired at his home on at least one occasion. A homicide investigation involving high-profile victims was a nightmare case for any police department. Literally hundreds of potential persons of interest would have to be combed through. Not only would a lot of time be unavoidably wasted, the feds would be poking their noses and two cents' worth into every step.

"We'll have no shortage of persons of interest to interview and all sorts of help from the FBI." The reality sounded worse when she said it out loud.

Devine chuckled drily. "No doubt. There're plenty of folks who wanted to see this guy get his." He jerked his head toward the street. "Uniforms are canvassing the neighbors. Coroner arrived about fifteen minutes ago. Evidence techs are processing the house one room at a time. I put in a call to Special Agent Hadden. Had to leave a voice mail."

"Good." Devine was meticulous, played by the rules and needed no prompting to get the job done—all of which made his initial action this morning completely out of character. "Why didn't you call me when you first arrived on the scene?" Fair question. He'd clearly been here an hour or so.

"You had to pick up Bauer," he offered. "Holt said she'd let you know."

Frustration inched its way up her spine. Bobbie suspected the sergeant had her own reasons for not taking this one herself. Between the baby, new nightmare neighbors, and her need to keep Bauer on the straight and narrow, Holt was spread a little thin. Still, Bobbie would rather not see a crime scene after six or so other people had already walked through it.

"In the future," she said as she pulled gloves from her jacket pocket and dragged them on, "you call me first regardless. No exceptions. Got it?"

Devine nodded. "Got it."

"Let's have a look then."

Bobbie let that particular tension go. Her new partner had garnered plenty of homicide experience in Birmingham. No reason for her to worry about him handling the scene properly. It was the principle of the thing. She was his partner. He should have called her.

Over the past month she'd been impressed by his work ethic. Since he was single he was completely focused on the job. It was also nice that he didn't try using the fact that he was a man to prove he was better at every turn. With his criminal justice degree from Western Illinois University and eight years on the force in Birmingham he'd already turned down the offer of a promotion to sergeant. And if his stellar credentials weren't enough, he'd showed his softer side when he made the lateral move to Montgomery to be close to his elderly aunt. The aunt had no remaining family beyond Devine and his parents. Since his parents had a prestigious medical practice in Birmingham, a move would have been problematic. With no complicated ties, Devine had decided he'd rather relocate to Montgomery than see his aunt sentenced to a nursing home. How often did someone his age make such a big sacrifice?

His lapse in judgment this morning aside, he was a good partner.

But he would never be Newt.

Inside, the house wasn't permeated with the usual smells related to violence. No bloody metallic odor, no hint of gunpowder in the air, but there was the lingering essence of death—that distinct uneasy impression that something bad had happened here. The living room, dining room and kitchen were one large open space. The furnishings likely cost more than the house. Every throw pillow was in place, every knickknack and piece of art expertly arranged. Two evidence techs were going over the space. Even the tiniest fragment of trace evidence could make all the difference to the case. Fortunately, MPD had a damned good forensic team.

A staircase went both up and down from the west side of the main living area, creating the three levels. The house sported '70s style paneling, popcorn ceilings and parquet wood flooring.

She imagined the Parkers hadn't lived this modestly in several decades, if ever.

"The laundry room, a bathroom and a small den are next to the garage down there," Devine said, indicating the seven or eight descending steps. "Three bedrooms and two baths are up."

"Let's see the bodies."

Devine pointed to the second floor and Bobbie followed him up the carpeted stairs. She had a look at the first bedroom they passed. The purple walls were plastered with posters of rock bands and rap singers. The open doors of the closet showed a wardrobe of mostly black. Unlike the order she'd encountered so far, discarded jeans and sneakers were scattered across the floor. The laptop on the desk was open and displaying a stream of photos showing teenagers drinking beer and smoking God only knew what. Sweat formed on Bobbie's skin as she crossed the room. The sixteen-year-old daughter's bed was still made. Wherever Fern Parker was, she apparently hadn't slept here. Maybe last night she'd decided to run away with a friend. Sixteen-year-olds were prone to impulsive behavior.

"Let's put the laptop into evidence." No one wanted to believe a child was capable of murder, but it happened.

"Yes, ma'am."

While Devine called a tech up to the girl's bedroom, Bobbie checked the closet and dresser drawers. She took a look behind the curtains and spotted what she had hoped not to find. Damn. Few teenagers went anywhere without their phones. "This may be her cell phone."

Devine joined her at the window. He blew out a breath. "Damn. I missed that."

Bobbie examined the phone. No text messages, no emails. "That's why we always take a second look." Even the best detective wasn't infallible.

Devine reached for the phone. "We'll start calling her contacts list now."

Bobbie moved across the hall. The boy's room was located opposite the sister's. Blue walls and loads of Legos set the theme for the space. Shelves were crammed with books and superhero action figures. Bobbie reminded Devine to take the boy's laptop into evidence, as well. If the younger Parker had a cell phone he hadn't left it behind. Like the sister's bed, this one hadn't been slept in, either.

Down the hall the bathroom was clear. Bobbie hesitated at the open door to the parents' bedroom. The room was elegantly decorated, the furnishings unquestionably from their former residence. The massive bed took up most of the floor space. Bobbie entered the room and moved closer to the bed. Both victims had been marked with what appeared to be blood on their foreheads. Heather was marked with an *A*, likely for *adulteress*. Nigel's forehead bore a *T*, probably for *thief*. Both appeared to be sleeping peacefully but the ashen skin and blue lips belied the facade of serenity. Heather's long blond hair spread across her pillow. She wore a lacy black nightgown. Nigel's brown hair was tinged with gray along the temples and looked as if it had been neatly combed after he was placed in the bed. His upper torso was bare. A cream-colored silk sheet was turned down at their waists.

Bobbie drew back the covers to reveal the rest of their bodies. Heather's gown hit the tops of her thighs. Her husband wore paisley print silk boxers. Beyond the strokes of blood on their foreheads, there was not a single speck of blood visible on the vics or the linens, no immediately observable physical injury. Not the first defense wound on their hands or arms.

Devine joined her at the bedside. "Brace yourself for what you'll find under those high-end nightclothes. It's been a day or two since I saw anything this bizarre."

"Has the coroner given any preliminary conclusions on cause of death?" Her partner hesitated and she shot him a look. "I'm hoping your hesitation and that look on your face isn't about *me*."

Like everyone else, Devine knew her history. *Poor Bobbie had been broken to pieces by a depraved killer who destroyed all that she loved.* She still saw the looks and the questions in the eyes of some. *Had time and all the surgeons and shrinks been able to put Bobbie back together again?* She might never be the same woman again, but she was damned well as good or better at being a cop.

He shook his head. "It's me." Her partner passed a hand over his face. "The victims were taken to the garage. Based on the blood and...other stuff left behind down there that's where the murders took place."

Bobbie considered the couple posed in their bed. Heather was average height and had a slim build, but her husband was tall and likely weighed a good one-seventy-five or -eighty. The killer had to be strong enough to handle getting the bodies down to the basement, and then back up to the bedroom again. Otherwise they had two killers on their hands.

"Each vic," Devine continued, "was disemboweled through a horizontal incision to the abdomen." He tugged the waistband of Parker's boxers down just enough to show a neat row of sutures. "All the organs were removed, including the lungs and heart. After the killer was finished, the incisions were closed, the bodies washed, dressed and placed as you see them now." He gestured to the woman. "Hers is the same."

A year ago Bobbie's first inclination would have been to wonder what kind of sick animal would do something like this. Now she knew the answer all too well, so instead she asked, "Were the victims conscious during this procedure?"

"Don't know yet. If so, there's no indication of a struggle. The arterial spray patterns suggest their hearts were still beating at the time the primary incisions were made."

Jesus Christ. "What tools did he use to do his work? Were they here already or did he bring them with him?" Her voice was steady when she spoke though her heart pounded a little faster. Cops weren't expected to be immune to this kind of horror, but Bobbie's actions were still under the microscope. She couldn't afford the slightest outward indication of being shaken. "Are the organs still here?"

There had to be one hell of a mess in the garage.

"Whatever he used, he took it with him. I found a couple of steak knives in the kitchen but nothing that would do this with any efficiency." Devine glanced at the victims as if he hated to discuss what was downstairs in front of the couple, and then he looked Bobbie straight in the eye. "The organs are here. He—whoever did this—took a bite out of each of the hearts."

Bobbie surveyed the Parkers once more. Something about the MO felt familiar. Hadn't she read about a similar case maybe eleven or twelve years ago? "We'll need impressions made from the bite marks if possible."

"Dr. Carroll mentioned that already," Devine said.

"Seppuku." The word rolled off the tip of Bobbie's tongue as the old headlines flashed through her mind.

She had been in college—a sophomore if she remembered correctly. A serial killer had disemboweled his victims in a manner similar to the technique used in the Japanese samurai honor code ritual. The gruesome ceremonial death was carried out against those who, in his opinion, had shamed themselves. The killer had chosen victims from the local headlines—in Chicago maybe—who were suspected of gross wrongdoing. Bobbie vaguely recalled one had been a hedge-fund manager who stole from his clients—not unlike Nigel Parker. Another had been a teacher accused of having sex with two of her students—one of whom committed suicide during the trial.

"Wait." Devine touched his forehead as if he'd experienced an epiphany, as well. "I remember that case. But the Seppuku Killer executed himself—" he shrugged "—ten or so years ago. He fell on his sword right in front of the detectives who'd cornered him."

"His only shame was in being caught." More of the details from those gruesome murders filtered into Bobbie's thoughts. Like these, his victims had been posed in their homes or offices. She turned to her partner. "We should have a look at that case. I think he was active in the Chicago area. This may be a copycat."

"I'll make a call to Chicago PD."

"Excuse me, Detectives."

Bobbie's gaze shot to the door where a uniform—Officer Leslie Elliott—waited. The younger woman looked pale despite her mahogany complexion. "You found something?"

"Officer Elliott," Devine offered before she could answer, "was following up on the Parker children's whereabouts."

Elliott nodded. "The boy didn't show up at his friend's last night. They haven't heard from him since yesterday afternoon. We just called the six contacts in the girl's phone and not one of them has seen or heard from her since around ten last night."

A new rush of cold slid through Bobbie's veins. "Where's the housekeeper?"

"She's on the back deck," Devine said. "She didn't want to stay in the house."

"Talk to her again," Bobbie told her partner. "Since we can't confirm the kids are okay we need to issue Amber Alerts. The killer may have taken one or both." As Devine hurried from the room, Bobbie glanced at the other woman. "Good work, Elliott. Why don't you show me to the garage?"

The officer's shoulders squared and she nodded. "This way."

Downstairs in the family room Devine had ushered the housekeeper back inside and the two were now seated on the sofa. Face crumpled in pain, Mrs. Snodgrass glanced at Bobbie as she and Elliott moved through the room. Bobbie wished she could provide some reassurance about the children, but at this point there was no way to know what to expect.

Best-case scenario the two had run away and hidden somewhere. Worst case…the killer had taken them.

A short hall at the bottom of the second set of stairs led past the laundry room–bathroom combo and a small den before exiting into the garage. As soon as Bobbie opened the door to the garage the stench of blood and feces had her holding her breath. In the two-car garage a refrigerator, its door ajar exposing the soft drinks and beer inside, stood in the storage area to the left of the steps. The paneled walls had been painted white long ago, age making them appear more off-white. One overhead light, a two-bulb fluorescent, flickered lending an eerie feel to the space.

A Mercedes SUV and BMW sedan were shoehorned side by side. Bobbie walked around the short wall that separated the parking area from the storage space. The first thing she spotted was the arterial spray on the dingy white wall. Streams of blood ran all the way down to the floor like crimson tears. Dr. Lisa Carroll, the coroner, was crouched near a large pool of blood.

"Be careful of the glass." Carroll pointed to the fridge. "A beer bottle was dropped there. We haven't gathered up the pieces yet."

Bobbie glanced at the shattered brown glass. "I guess our perp got thirsty."

"I imagine he did," Carroll agreed. "This definitely took some time."

Carroll and Bobbie had attended Booker T. Washington High School together. They'd never actually been friends, but Bobbie was happy to hear the younger woman had accepted the position left open by the retiring coroner last month. It was a part-time job and most of the doctors in the area didn't want to steal the time out of their busy schedules. Carroll was hardly more than five foot two and probably didn't weight a hundred pounds soaking wet. Back in school she'd been a wallflower and pretty much stayed to herself. Hard work and relentless determination had won her numerous scholarships. Bobbie wondered why a woman so focused and driven had chosen to be a general practitioner rather than a surgeon or some other specialist.

Carroll exhaled a big breath. "Well, everything appears to be here."

Bobbie surveyed the pile of organs stacked in the center of the blood. Partial shoes prints were visible near the edge of the wide coagulating puddle. Before she could ask, Officer Elliott said, "The evidence tech took photos of the shoe prints, but they're smudged." She pointed to where the prints abruptly disappeared about two feet from the pool of blood and other bodily fluids. "Detective Devine and I concluded that the killer probably took off his clothes right there."

Bobbie agreed. The pattern of smudged prints and the smears of blood suggested as much. The killer had planned these ritual-style murders down to the last detail, brought fresh clothes and a bag for the stained ones. No question about premeditation.

"The shower in that bathroom we passed—" Elliott hitched her thumb back toward the direction they'd come "—is as clean as a whistle but one of the tech's checked the drain. The killer must have cleaned the bodies there and took a shower before he left."

"I'm sure Devine also told you about this," the coroner said.

Bobbie turned to Carroll who held a heart in her hand. She pointed to an obvious chunk that had been bitten from the organ. "He mentioned that, yes." Damn, what a mess. "Do you have an estimate on time of death?"

Carroll blew her black bangs out of her eyes. "I'm going to say somewhere around midnight based on body temperature and the stage of rigor the bodies have reached. That said, I haven't examined them as closely as I'd like. I felt this—" she gestured to the blood and body parts "—needed to be addressed first."

Bobbie understood. "Thanks. I'll check in with you later today." She turned back to Elliott. "Let's have a look at that shower."

As Bobbie followed the officer back into the house her cell vibrated. She pulled it from her belt. If she was lucky it would be about the kids. *Let them be safe.* "Gentry."

"Detective Gentry, this is Lawrence Zacharias."

The name didn't ring a bell. If this was another reporter or writer who'd managed to get her number she was going to have to break down and take a new one. Enough was enough. She was not selling her story. "How can I help you, Mr. Zacharias?"

"I represent Dr. Randolph Weller. I'm certain you're aware of who he is."

Hearing the name disrupted Bobbie's equilibrium. She stalled and propped her hip against the washing machine to brace herself. She held up a hand for Elliott to give her a moment. Elliott turned her back and pretended to study the shower. Bobbie appreciated the gesture.

Randolph Weller, also known as the Picasso Killer, was one of the most prolific serial killers alive today. In addition to being a vicious murderer who'd killed his own wife and buried her in the backyard, he was also a celebrated psychiatrist. Other than the fact that he was in solitary confinement in an Atlanta federal prison for his crimes, Bobbie knew little about the man save one stunning fact: he was Nick Shade's father.

Had something happened to Nick? Her pulse accelerated into overdrive. Memories of the enigmatic man who'd helped her survive that final showdown with the Storyteller whispered through her. She hadn't heard from Nick Shade since that day in the cemetery...the same day Newt was buried. Bobbie felt confident the serial-killer hunter the FBI preferred to pretend didn't exist was on the trail of another murderer no one else had been able to catch. As strange as it seemed, considering they'd worked together for only a few days, she missed him. An unexpected bond had developed between them.

Didn't matter. Nick Shade was long gone.

"Detective?"

"Yes." Bobbie hated the uncertainty in her voice.

"Dr. Weller would like to see you."

If he'd announced that Weller was Santa Claus she wouldn't have been more surprised. How would Weller even know she existed? She supposed it was possible he'd read about how she'd survived the Storyteller.

Wait, she understood now. Weller probably had some way of following Nick's work. If so, he would know Nick had helped her end the Storyteller's reign of terror. God knew they'd both been all over the news back in August.

"Detective, are you still there?"

Bobbie straightened, curiosity overtaking the

uncertainty. "I'm sorry, Mr. Zacharias, I'm a little confused. Why would he want to see me?"

"He insists that it's imperative he speak with you in person as soon as possible. It's about his son, Nicholas."

When Bobbie hesitated yet again Zacharias added, "Dr. Weller believes Nicholas is in grave danger."

Three

Bobbie had left for Atlanta as soon as she and Devine had found the missing boy. Ten-year-old Sage Parker had been hiding in the attic. The closet in his parents' bedroom had a full-size access door that opened onto additional floored space over the back porch. He claimed he hid there a lot lately and last night he'd fallen asleep in the dusty, too warm space. Last month when the shit hit the fan in the news and his parents started screaming at each other all the time he'd found solitude in the attic among the boxes of stored Christmas ornaments and toys he and his sister once played with together.

Finding the boy alive and well was the only good news they had so far. Sage had no idea where his sister was. None of her few friends had seen her and, according to those same friends, she currently had no boyfriend. Fern Parker had vanished. Bobbie hoped she had taken off as teenagers will sometimes do when angry with their parents. The alternative didn't leave much hope for her survival.

Other than being hungry and a little dehydrated from spending twelve hours hidden in the heat of the attic, Sage was unharmed. He insisted he hadn't heard or seen anything. Bobbie wasn't so sure the kid was being completely honest. She'd pushed as hard as she felt comfortable and he'd stuck with his story. After dinner his parents had begun their usual routine of screaming profanities at each other and his sister had gone into her room, slamming the door in his face. Eventually his parents had taken their screaming match back downstairs and Sage had sneaked into their bedroom and through the closet to the attic. The child admitted he hadn't wanted to go to his friend's house because he worried about his parents and sister, but he couldn't bear the screaming so he hid. He'd fallen asleep and hadn't awakened until he heard the sirens, then he'd been too afraid to come out of hiding.

Bobbie had ridden in the ambulance with him to the ER. The physician on call had suggested Sage stay twenty-four hours for observation just to ensure he was okay. His mother's sister who lived in Nashville had been called. She'd arrived before Bobbie left for Atlanta. Bobbie hadn't told Sage his parents were dead. She'd left that painful business to his aunt. To ensure the boy's safety, a uniform had been assigned to his room. The FBI was sending one of its agents to serve as part of his security detail as well.

Poor kid had no idea what lay ahead of him. His

entire world had been shattered. There was no way
to save him from the hurt of learning to live without his parents. At the moment though, the most
pressing concerns were keeping the boy safe and
finding his sister. If the killer learned a possible
witness had survived his killing spree he would
want to rectify that oversight.

After the boy and his aunt were settled into a
room at Baptist Medical, Bobbie had hit the road.
She'd arrived at the prison nearly forty minutes
ago and had been pacing this small waiting room
since. Her patience was quickly running out. She
should be back in Montgomery looking for Fern
Parker and whoever killed her and Sage's parents.

Bobbie stopped her pacing and shivered as if a
cold wind had passed through her. Not so long ago
she'd been in the precarious position the Parker
children were in. The serial killer she had survived had wanted to finish what he'd started. She
clenched her teeth and dropped into the nearest
chair. No one was going to get to that little boy or
his sister—assuming they could find her and the
bastard didn't have her already—as long as Bobbie was breathing.

Devine had conducted face-to-face interviews
with the teenagers on the short contacts list in
Fern's cell phone. According to those few, there was
a long list of newly *unfriended* teenagers on Face-
book and Instagram who should be interviewed as
well. The feds had already pushed their way into
the homicide investigation and were interviewing
potential suspects who had been wronged by ei-

ther Nigel Parker or his wife. The FBI's involvement was understandable since the Parker fraud case had been theirs. If Fern had been abducted they would be lead on that aspect of the case. Special Agent Michael Hadden from the Montgomery field office would work as a liaison between the MPD and the agent in charge, Ronald Vincent, of the Parker case. Hadden promised to provide any names of persons of interest the MPD didn't have in an effort to ensure all bases were covered.

Bobbie had tasked Devine as liaison with Hadden. Chief Peterson had made it clear that his detectives and the Montgomery Police Department would remain lead on the investigation until the homicide aspect of the case was solved. According to the chief, Special Agent Vincent, who'd come all the way from New York, hadn't been too happy about it but he'd let it go quickly enough. As much as Bobbie wanted to focus solely on who had decided to use a dead serial killer's MO, her top priority was to find Fern.

The possible motives for the murders were easy enough to deduce. Both Nigel Parker and his wife had made serious enemies. Nigel by stealing from his clients; Heather by having affairs with at least four of those married clients and arranging secret lovers for many more of her husband's friends. Fern was the big question mark in Bobbie's mind. If the killer was levying vengeance, what had the girl done to deserve to be taken? What was her shame? Or was she simply in the wrong place at the wrong time, ending up collateral damage? Until she was found all they had was speculation.

"Detective Gentry."

Bobbie pushed aside the troubling thoughts and focused on the tall man dressed in a guard's uniform who had entered the waiting room. When she'd arrived she had gone through the usual routine of signing in and then turning over her handbag, badge, weapon and all other personal items the same as any other visitor. Eventually she had been sequestered to this small private room.

"That's me." She stood, smoothed a hand over her jacket. She felt more than a little naked without her department issue Glock at her waist and the backup piece she kept strapped to her right ankle. She'd left her backup piece as well as the knife she carried in the trunk of her car. Leaving her Glock in the car was out of the question.

"I'm Malcolm Clinton. I apologize for your wait. The warden had to approve your visit and he was in a meeting when you first arrived," the guard explained. "Apparently Mr. Zacharias failed to mention that you're a detective."

"No problem. Can I see Weller now?" Another zing of anticipation rushed through her. The two-and-a-half-hour drive from Montgomery had given her plenty of time to come up with a number of questions she wanted to ask the infamous doctor. She had every intention of requiring his cooperation if he wanted hers.

"Yes, ma'am." Clinton gestured to the door. "This way. We have certain procedures as you likely know. The inmate will be fully restrained during your visit and there will be two guards outside the door. If at any point you feel uncomfortable or if an issue with the inmate arises, all you have to do is call out and the guards will assist you."

Bobbie had visited her share of prisoners, mostly in county lockup. A federal prison like this one was a first for her. "I understand."

She followed Clinton along the somber corridor, the hair on the back of her neck standing on end. As much as the knowledge that Randolph Weller was a sadistic killer sickened her, she wanted to know all she could about Nick. If he was in trouble, she owed it to him to help in any way possible. He was the main reason she was still breathing. On top of saving her life, he had helped her to see a life beyond the vengeance she had wanted so badly.

Gaylon Perry, aka the Storyteller, had murdered nearly two dozen people and no one had even come close to figuring out who he was much less catching him. Nick Shade had learned more about the psychopathic serial killer than anyone else. After discovering one of the victims had survived, Nick had come to Montgomery to wait for him. Like Bobbie, he had known the Storyteller would be back for her—the one that got away. Nick was the only reason she had survived that showdown.

"Let the guards know when you're done," Clinton said, drawing her attention back to the present. "You're not to touch him or pass anything to him. He'll undergo a full cavity search after your visit."

Bobbie had no desire to get any closer than necessary. "Does he have visitors often?" The answer didn't really matter, she was curious about one particular visitor.

"The only visitors he has are the two agents from the FBI who show up every week or so."

"His son doesn't visit?"

If Clinton was surprised by her question he kept the reaction to himself. "In nearly fifteen years his son has been here only once and that was about two months ago." The guard eyed her for a moment before unlocking the next door. "Are you working on a case that involves Dr. Weller somehow?"

Under normal circumstances visitors for a serial killer like Weller would be strictly controlled. Based on the attorney's call Weller was evidently allowed some amount of leeway for his ongoing cooperation with the FBI. Bobbie wondered what other privileges the monster had managed to negotiate. As much as the idea sickened her, every cop understood the value of a good source.

Under the circumstances she saw no point in concealing her reason for the visit. "His attorney, Mr. Zacharias, called and asked me to come. Apparently Weller has a message for me."

Clinton's gaze narrowed. "You are aware that Weller is a psychopath who murdered forty-two victims, including his own wife?"

"I'm aware of his crimes," Bobbie assured him.

"Before being incarcerated he was a highly respected psychiatrist," the guard went on. "Let me be frank with you, Detective, you cannot trust him in any capacity."

"Don't worry. I learned that lesson the hard way." Sometimes she didn't even trust herself. Like now. Her hands shook when she had no reason to be afraid or even nervous for that matter. She squeezed them into fists.

Apparently satisfied with her answer, Clinton opened the door and waited for her to go ahead of him. As he'd said, a guard was stationed on either side of the interview room door. Bobbie thanked him and before she entered the room where Weller waited she took a breath. Once she opened the door and walked in, she didn't hesitate.

"I'm Detective Bobbie Gentry." She paused a few feet away from the chair on her side of the table standing in the center of the room. "You requested a meeting with me."

Randolph Weller's arms were manacled to the belly shackle at his waist. Beneath the table his ankles were chained together, and then to the floor. The table was long and narrow. A chair sat on either side. Four other chairs waited at the south end of the reasonably large room. There were no windows. Only the unforgiving glare of fluorescent lights illuminated the space.

Bobbie didn't wait for Weller to speak as he seemed satisfied to study her for the moment. She took the final few steps, pulled out her chair and sat down directly across from him. She had Googled Weller and read all she could find on the investigation that took place fifteen years ago after his own son turned him in. Weller's gray hair had receded with age. Unflattering lines carved across his forehead and creased his mouth. His skin was ashen from the lack of sunlight, but it was his eyes that disturbed her the most. Deep, dull hazel that looked more gray than hazel, like the headstones in the old cemeteries back home. Those eyes hadn't stopped analyzing her since she entered the room.

"Please accept my sincerest apologies for staring," he said, his voice deeper than she'd expected and oddly soothing. "You are a remarkably beautiful woman."

Bobbie barked a stiff laugh. "I'm sure you didn't ask for this meeting to flatter me. What is it you have to tell me?"

"I can see why my son became so obsessed with you."

Bobbie kept her jaw locked tight, opting not to respond in word or expression. If he wanted information about her and Nick's relationship, he could ask his son.

Who are you kidding, Bobbie? The two of you barely know each other.

Images of Nick's hands on her skin flickered one after the other through her mind, making her pulse react.

Weller smiled as if he'd read her mind. "Your eyes are simply incredible, Bobbie. May I call you Bobbie?"

Her heart abruptly stumbled. Another serial killer had been fascinated with her eyes... *I couldn't resist you.* "I'm not here to make small talk with you, Weller. You said Nick is in danger. Explain your concerns and I'll do what I can to help."

Weller stared at her for long enough to have her wanting to shift in her seat. She refused to let him see that he unsettled her the slightest bit. The man was far too perceptive and decidedly *different* than she'd anticipated. His voice wasn't merely deep it was elegant, like dark, rich silk. His brilliance was as well-known as his heinousness and yet even the way he sat, despite being shackled in that generic chair, gave him an air of sophistication. There was something about the set of his mouth that reminded her of Nick and she loathed the idea that anything about this psychopath did so.

"Bobbie Gentry." He seemed to savor her name as if tasting a new wine. "Don't tell me, let me guess. Your father had a crush on the lovely country music singer with that same name? You have the trademark long dark hair and the exquisite high cheekbones."

Evidently he intended to get around to what he wanted to tell her about Nick in his own time. Considering his only visitors were FBI agents who wanted to pick his brain, she imagined he hoped to indulge in the rare opportunity to socialize. She could waste time fighting him or just play along.

"Actually, Gentry is my married name. My husband and I used to laugh about the irony since I can't carry a tune in a bucket."

"Your *dead* husband."

Bobbie flinched. He knew damned well her husband was deceased. "I'm confident you're aware he was murdered by Gaylon Perry."

"Your mother died when you were such a tender age," Weller went on without responding to her comment. "Is that why you spent more time at work than at home with your own child? Did you want to protect him from the kind of pain you suffered when you lost your mother?"

Fury ignited so fast inside her she barely stayed in the damned chair. "I won't play head games with you, Weller. Say what you have to say or I'm gone." *Bastard*. Snippets of her life before a monster just like this one had stolen it sifted through her mind.

"Now, now, Detective. Surely you can do me the courtesy of showing respect. After all, you're the reason my son will likely die sooner than later."

Her traitorous heart did another of those stuttering stumbles. "You keep talking about how much danger he's in yet you're not telling me anything. I can't help Nick unless I understand the potential danger."

"For years he lived in the shadows," Weller began, his voice low, his gaze distant. "I suppose I inspired his need to rid the world of my kind, one killer at a time."

"It's nice to know your perceptive powers are as keen as ever, Doctor." She poured all the contempt she could summon into the words. The bastard murdered Nick's mother and allowed him to believe she'd abandoned him. Damn straight his actions motivated Nick to become the hunter he was.

"Touché, Detective."

She waited for him to continue when she should be back in Montgomery looking for a missing girl and interviewing persons of interest in a double homicide. Her gut twisted at the idea that a ten-year-old boy was now an orphan and his sister could very well be dead or dying. No matter that the job was all she had, sometimes she hated it. More than anything, she hated the sadistic killers like the one seated less than three feet away.

"Nick has always been particularly careful not to get involved on a personal level." Weller sighed. "Until *you*. Now he has dug himself a deeper grave than even he knows." He paused for effect. "Since I'm quite certain he won't listen to me, I'm hoping he will listen to you."

Bobbie considered his words for a moment. "Who do you believe has targeted him?" Despite her efforts to control her respiration, her heart beat faster and faster as she waited for his response. The list of questions she'd intended to ask had vanished. She could only think of how she might possibly help Nick.

"I doubt you're aware of what I'm about to share, and I'm certain our fine friends at the FBI will be quite interested in hearing." He glanced up at the camera in the far corner. "I'm certain they're listening even now."

Bobbie didn't have to wonder. An inmate like Weller wasn't allowed a private conversation except with his attorney. He was too smart not to know this. Whatever he had to say, he wanted those listening to hear.

"Like any other community, professional or personal," he began, "there are communications between those who share, shall we say, an admiration for the art of death."

"Like murdering your wife and burying her in the backyard?" Bobbie bit her lips together. The words had burst from her mouth before she could stop them. She knew better. She'd been a cop long enough to understand how this worked. Antagonizing the man wouldn't help her gain any ground with him.

His gaze was razor sharp when he met hers. "There are things I'm not proud of, Bobbie, and the crude manner of her death is one of them. If I could do it over again, it would have been far more civilized."

Jesus. What a twisted piece of shit. "I'm sure your son would appreciate the sentiment." The barb was intentional this time.

Ignoring her remark, he went on, "There is a council of sorts. An esteemed group of highly educated overachievers. The Consortium they call themselves." The beginnings of a smile touched his lips. "At one time I was quite revered among its members. Sadly time changes all things."

"A consortium of serial killers." It wasn't a question. She just wanted to make sure she heard him right considering her head had started to spin at the mere concept.

"Correct. They share the occasional weekend conference. Primarily to discuss territorial issues and the need to clear up a situation that might pose a threat to one or more of their members."

"Like Nick."

"Precisely. He's taken several high-level killers out of the game in the past decade or so. The Consortium has reason to be concerned."

"They want to stop him."

"They *will* stop him," Weller corrected with a succinct nod.

The certainty in his words sent a spear of ice deep into her chest. "How do you suggest I prevent that from happening?"

Delight or something on that order twinkled in his eyes. Bobbie was immensely grateful Nick had gotten his dark eyes from his mother. This man's were utterly soulless and far too seeing.

"You would sacrifice yourself toward that end?" The idea seemed to amuse him.

"I'm a cop," she returned, "it's what I do."

"I'm not quite sure you comprehend the scope and magnitude of what I'm conveying to you, my dear Bobbie."

"Why don't you break it down for me then?" A blast of fury had her clasping her hands in her lap. She would not permit him to see how easily he rattled her.

"The Consortium is made up of the world's most cunning and manipulative minds. They haven't been caught for a reason. They take great care in every move. They cultivate connections that contribute to their success. Absolutely nothing is left to chance. They cannot be stopped."

Bobbie wanted to laugh at the absurdity of the conversation. She wanted to get up and walk out. Somehow, she couldn't do either. How was she supposed to help Nick from a danger she couldn't measure much less find?

"Then why bother telling me?"

"Nick needs to see that he cannot win. It is imperative that he give up this quest and disappear before they find him."

Bobbie shook her head. "He'll never do it."

"Then you must help him see the error of his thinking."

"I have no idea how to reach him." She had the number he'd used to call her but she'd never attempted to contact him. She imagined he changed numbers frequently. "How am I supposed to get a message to him?"

"Now," Weller said, smiling as if she were a child and had just said something completely foolish, "the answer to that question is one you already possess. The message was relayed to both you and my son this very morning in a rather unoriginal however gruesome manner."

Now she understood. "Seppuku."

"Well done, Bobbie," he conceded with a nod. "The Seppuku Killer was the first Nick took out of play."

"The Seppuku Killer committed suicide." Even as she said the words, she understood the man staring at her was privy to something she was not.

"The FBI had been looking for him for years," Weller countered. "An anonymous tip gave the authorities his location. He merely made the choice to take his life rather than face the consequences of his lifestyle."

"If Nick provided the anonymous tip, why would he leave a killer armed?" The Seppuku Killer had been holding a samurai sword when the police arrived. Nick would never send the police into a trap.

"My son almost always gives his prey the option of taking their own lives or facing prosecution."

Before she could respond, he added, "He has never taken a life. That's why he left the military and never pursued a career in law enforcement."

"He won't risk taking a life under any circumstances for fear of becoming anything like you." She hadn't intended to say the words aloud, and judging by the look on Weller's face she'd hit the nail on the head.

"He'll come to you, Bobbie. He will want to protect you. The Consortium has waited a very long time to find a weakness it can manipulate to reach him. *You* are that weakness."

Before she could summon a response, he added, "Understand that they will show no mercy. He will suffer greatly before he dies."

Dread or uncertainty—maybe both—expanded in her chest, but she refused to let him see it. Instead, she tossed the ball back into his court. "What plan of action would you propose I take to stop them?"

"You cannot possibly. All you can do is stop *him*. He will listen to you. He will do whatever necessary to protect you."

Bobbie shook her head. "I'm afraid you've overestimated our relationship. We hardly know each other."

"I know my son. In all these years he has not allowed himself to draw so close to anything or anyone...until you."

She'd heard enough. Bobbie stood. "If I can reach him, I'll pass along the warning."

She turned away from Weller's too-seeing eyes and headed for the door. She needed air. The very scent of the bastard on the other side of the room was making her feel ill.

"Make no mistake, Detective Bobbie Gentry."

She paused at the door and slowly faced him once more.

"Do not romanticize your relationship with my son. However desperately he wants to be a hero, there will come a day, soon I fear, when he will be forced to kill. When that time comes he will learn the deep, dark secret he has denied for so long."

Rather than give him the satisfaction of a response or a moment longer to analyze her, she turned her back and banged on the door.

"Once he has experienced taking a life," Weller continued.

She didn't want to hear another word. She pounded on the door again. "I'm done in here." *Open the damned door.*

"He will not be able to resist killing again and *again*."

Weller's warning followed her out the door.

Gardendale Drive
10:30 p.m.

Bobbie slowed to a walk as she turned up the sidewalk to her house. D-Boy rushed to the front door ahead of her and waited, panting, tongue lolling after the long run. Bobbie stepped up onto the stoop and jammed her key into the lock. Before opening the door, she reached down and scratched the animal behind his ears. "Good boy."

The brindle pit bull had belonged to a former neighbor. The single mother and her children had moved last month and she'd happily agreed to let Bobbie have the dog. For the most part Bobbie had been taking care of him since the day he moved into her neighborhood, and now he belonged to her. The first order of business had been a trip to the vet for a checkup and for shots. She had learned that he was two years old, had no health problems and showed no signs of abuse. Every evening since bringing D-Boy home she had worked with him, teaching him simple commands of obedience. So far he was an attentive student and a quick study.

Inside the door she silenced the security system and listened to the sounds of the place she called home. Though the day had seen a high of sixty degrees, it was only about forty outside now. The absence of the steady hum of the air conditioner left the house silent. The vague scent of scrambled eggs and butter from the breakfast she'd prepared that morning lingered in the still air. The security system was another new addition. The chief had been so happy when she had it installed that he'd insisted on paying for the first year of service. Rather than argue with him, she'd surrendered to his need to be the protective uncle. She'd learned over the years to choose her battles carefully.

Ever patient, D-Boy stared up at her. "Go ahead,

boy," she said, giving the animal permission to have a look around. Once he'd padded through the two bedrooms and one bath, he trotted to his water bowl in the kitchen. The first night she'd brought him home he'd watched her check the house and he'd been performing the duty himself since.

Nick had told her in August that she needed a dog. At the time she couldn't possibly have allowed anyone or thing into her life. As if she'd spoken the thought aloud, D-Boy hustled back to where she stood. Water dripped from his mouth as he studied her expectantly. He was accustomed to her full attention in the evenings. Her unexpected trip to Atlanta had disrupted their routine.

Bobbie smiled. "I could use a drink myself, buddy."

Door locked, she headed to the kitchen and grabbed a bottle of water. D-Boy followed close on her heels. She checked his food and water bowls and then she latched the doggie door she'd had installed in the back door. Though she doubted anyone would get beyond the door with D-Boy in the house, no need to leave an open invitation. A quick shower and she intended to hit the sack early. Today had been a long one and tomorrow was stacking up to be even worse.

Her thoughts ventured to the meeting with Randolph Weller. The man was pure evil. How had such a sick bastard created a son his complete opposite?

He will not be able to resist killing.

Bobbie refused to believe that DNA made monsters as some believed. Maybe the twisted genes passed along tipped the scales in rare cases, but she rejected the idea that it started there. Every person was unique. No matter that Weller was a killer, that didn't mean his son would be one any more than her mother's singing like an angel in the church choir gave Bobbie the ability to carry a tune.

Weller might be an expert on human nature but he couldn't see the future.

She flipped on the hall light as she made her way to her bedroom. At the door to the spare bedroom that had until recently remained empty, she paused. D-Boy glanced back at her and waited. Seven or eight boxes sat in the room, a couple of them open. The familiar ache that started deep in her chest was one she was reasonably certain would be with her the rest of her life.

The boxes contained important *things* from her old life that she couldn't bear to part with. Her son's favorite blanket. Her husband's beloved vintage Foo Fighters T-shirt. Photo albums and videos. The locket that had belonged to her mother and her mother's mother before her. The folded flag from her father's funeral.

Bobbie Sue Gentry was thirty-two years old and those few boxes, about two feet by two feet each, represented the best of her life to date. *Her old life.* She couldn't live that life anymore, couldn't be that woman. Most people didn't understand. Sometimes she thought Bauer might, but maybe not. Those boxes were all that remained of her early history, her marriage and her family.

She turned away from the door and continued on to her bedroom. Her old life was dead and buried. Her penance for survival was to carry on. Why not devote her life to being the best cop she could be? Perhaps one day it would include something more than her job, but not now. The idea that she could even conceive such a notion was relatively new and still a little hard to swallow.

She was a work in progress.

Bobbie removed her backup piece and the ankle holster and placed both on the bedside table. The knife she kept strapped to her left shin landed there next. She'd stopped carrying a stun gun tucked into her bra. The one she'd owned had ended up in evidence and she'd never bothered to claim it or to buy another. She didn't need it now. She toed off her sneakers and peeled off her sweat-dampened clothes.

With a pair of clean panties and her backup piece in hand she padded across the cold wood floors toward the bathroom. D-Boy followed. She flipped on the bathroom light and he took his position outside the door. She smiled. He was a good guard dog.

She went inside, closing and locking the door behind her. With her .22 on the closed toilet lid, she turned on the shower and waited for the warm water to make its way from the water heater at the other end of the house. Her face was flush from the three-mile run. She'd gained a little weight the past couple of months. Not a bad thing, according to the doc when she'd had her required department physical last week. With her forefinger she traced the thin, barely there line that looped around her neck. The nylon hangman's noose she'd worn for three weeks had left a gruesome scar. She'd had plastic surgery to remove it in hopes of preventing the inevitable stares and questions from everyone she met.

As steam started to fill the air, her fingers trailed down her chest, tracking the scars. So many scars. Her palm flattened on her belly. Below her waist her right thigh and calf were riddled with ugly marks from *him* and from the surgery to repair the damage he'd wielded. Bauer teased her about being the bionic woman with all the hardware in her leg. She angled her head and peered at the reflection in the narrow full-length mirror behind her.

She read the words tattooed on her back, the meaning curdling in her gut.

Over and over she cursed herself for the path she chose to take.

The pain a reminder of those devastated for her sake.

The Storyteller had tattooed those lines on her flesh. Her *story*. She could have had them removed but she needed to look at them every day. She never wanted to forget. Just thinking about the psychopath who had tortured and raped her for better than three damned weeks made the bones in her right leg ache. The Storyteller had left a trail of bodies, including her husband's, across the southern United States over the past thirteen years. He was the reason her little boy was dead. The bastard might never have been caught except that having a victim survive to identify him had marred his record and he hadn't been able to resist coming back to correct that anomaly. Bobbie had been that victim and she'd been waiting for his sorry ass to return. Images from those final moments in that dilapidated shack in the woods flashed one after the other through her head.

She'd made sure he got what he deserved.

Her choices were the reason she would never hold her baby again. She would never make love with her husband again. Her old partner would never call her "girlie" again. She stared at the long scars on the backs of her wrists. At first she had wanted to die, too.

She exhaled a heavy breath, only then realizing how thick and damp the air in the room had grown. *No looking back.*

She climbed into the shower and let the hot water sluice over her weary muscles. Tomorrow and the day after and the day after that she would do all in her power to be the best cop possible.

The image of Nick Shade edged into her thoughts. Her hands stilled on her skin, body wash slipping away. She wondered where he was. If Weller wasn't playing some sadistic game, Nick was in danger.

Tomorrow she would try to reach him.

She hurried through the rest of her shower and quickly dried off. On second thought, why wait until tomorrow? Why not call him now? If the number he'd used previously was still in service, they could talk tonight. *Now.*

Wrapping the towel around her body, she grabbed the .22 and left the steamy bathroom, headed for her bedroom. D-Boy trotted after her. Her cell was already vibrating loudly in the quiet room. She reached the bedside table and grabbed it up. Devine's name flashed on the screen. She couldn't pull the charging cord loose and hold on to her towel, so she bent forward to answer, pinning the towel with her forearm. She placed the .22 next to the knife once more.

"What's up?" Her pulse thumped a little harder with anticipation. There could be a break in the case or another murder. Anticipation fired through her. Maybe Fern Parker had been found.

"I didn't wake you, did I? Damn. I just realized how late it is."

"No, no. I was in the shower." Bobbie dropped onto the side of the bed. "What's going on?"

"I've spent the past six hours going back through what we have. I've called every name on Fern's contact list again and then called every person suggested by anyone on that list. For the last two hours I've focused on the parents. Despite all that work I'm left with nothing more than a couple of new names. I want to go over them with you. Do you mind? My mind is racing with possibilities on this damned case. I don't think I'm going to sleep again until it's over."

"Sure." Bobbie pushed the wet hair back from her face. She was always ready to talk about the case. This was the first homicide she and Devine had caught as partners. "Let's hear 'em."

"Wait, how did your appointment go?"

Bobbie cringed. She'd told her partner she had a doctor's appointment. "Good," she lied. "I have to wait for some of the test results, but I'm sure they'll be fine."

"Nothing like having the doc give you a clean bill of health."

Thankfully he moved on to the names he wanted to discuss. Bobbie felt guilty for lying to her partner but sometimes it was necessary. As soon as she and Devine had finished she would call Nick.

She owed him more than she could possibly hope to repay.

Four

Nick Shade waited in the darkness for another full minute. The shotgun house he'd been watching for the past two weeks was dark. The woman who called the place home was always in before dawn. Like a vampire, she didn't make public appearances during daylight hours.

He had been tracking the Executive Executioner for two months. Finding her had been a little trickier than he'd estimated. The Big Easy was the forty-year-old former schoolteacher's preferred hunting ground. She'd left victims all the way from Houston to Tallahassee, but New Orleans apparently held some significance for her. It wasn't her hometown though. Adele Pratt was from Jackson, Mississippi. She had been a daddy's girl all the way up to the day he'd dropped dead in his office. Her father had been a low-level ad man at a major firm where he worked ridiculously long hours in an attempt to keep the boss happy. Adele had been murdering ruthless businessmen like her dead daddy's boss for nearly a decade.

Nick reached above his head and stretched his back. He'd been waiting and watching for hours, day in and day out. It was almost time. His prey was on the verge of taking her next victim.

Adele Pratt didn't know it yet but she was finished.

For the first thirty years of her life she'd never shown the slightest reported penchant for violence, and then one of her students shot herself right in front of Adele. Something happened to her in that moment when a fifteen-year-old decided she couldn't deal with her demanding and ironically high-level executive father for a moment longer. Adele's family hadn't heard from her since that day. They all thought she'd gone off somewhere and taken her life. But that wasn't the case. Nick had found poor, sweet, reserved Adele. She had been busy giving all those demanding men like her father's old boss and her former student's father what she believed they deserved—a truly nasty death after hours of slow torture.

She had lured in her latest prey and, if she followed her usual MO, tomorrow night she would make the kill. Oil tycoon Race Cashion had no idea what a lucky man he was. Adele, aka Alana Jones the Executive Executioner, was about to retire permanently.

The day's thick humidity had eased a little with the darkness, but the air was still far too suffocating for Nick's liking. Halloween was approaching and the city had spent the entire month celebrating death in all its grim beauty. Nick stood and stretched again. The rocking chair he'd vacated eased back and forth once, then twice. The elderly man who lived in the house Nick used for a vantage point was sleeping off his nightly drunk. He generally started around five and by ten or so he was down for the count. Nick had to give him credit, he had good taste. The bourbon he inhaled night after night was some of the best the average man could buy and likely exhausted the biggest portion of his retirement check. Each night Nick tucked ten bucks into the coffee can over the stove. The old guy had cut a hole in the lid and used the can like a piggy bank where he kept his change. By the last week of the month the mound of quarters, nickels and dimes was probably all he had left. This month when he removed that lid he was going to have a nice surprise. It was the least Nick could do for the use of his back porch.

He picked up his backpack and slipped across the narrow yard, using the overgrown shrubbery for cover. There were a few preparations he needed to make before Adele returned home. He approached her back door, listening for any sounds of trouble. Picking the ancient lock was too easy. People who renovated historic homes should never rely on the security of a century-old lock. He silenced the alarm and then reset the system with the code she'd written on a sticky note and stuck to the wall above the keypad. It wasn't that Adele was too dumb or flighty to recognize the recklessness of leaving the code in plain sight. Not at all. The woman was highly intelligent. She simply wasn't afraid.

Maybe she really wanted someone to come in and end her misery.

The house was quiet. Adele didn't own any pets and she never had company. No friends, not even her targets were allowed in her home. Nick had searched the place thoroughly and discovered the photographs and trophies from her kills. During that thorough search he'd memorized the layout of the interior, which allowed him to move about inside now without the aid of light. The back door entered into a small laundry room, which led into a long narrow hall. Beyond the two doors in that hall, one leading into a bathroom and the other to the master bedroom that had once been two bedrooms, was the remaining space that served as the kitchen, dining, and family room. If the lady of the house followed her usual routine, she would arrive home shortly and take a bath. After a long soak in the tub she would go to bed.

Adele lived lavishly. Fine clothes and jewelry and a top of the line Lexus. The men she murdered supported her in high style and they had no idea they were paying their own murderer. Nick removed his backpack and started to unzip it when the purr of her luxury sedan broke the silence.

She was early. He shouldered his backpack and took a position in the elaborate bathroom. Down the hall the key turned in the lock with a concise click. As soon as the door swung inward the alarm began its urgent warning. She entered the code, silencing the system.

Her soft laughter filled the air. "You are too wicked," she teased.

Nick stilled. Was she speaking on her cell phone?

"You bring out the devil in me." The male voice was deep and slurred.

Nick swore silently. He recognized the voice—Race Cashion. Had she moved up her timeline? Why deviate from her MO and bring the man she intended to murder here? Maybe she had a little something extra planned for Cashion. Nick mentally ran a couple of adjustment scenarios and decided on an alternate plan of action of his own.

More playful back and forth echoed through the house. Cashion was obviously inebriated. Adele's actions didn't make sense. She never murdered a victim in her home. Like a fox she hunted and slept alone with the two being mutually exclusive. Maybe tonight was about a last-minute opportunity to milk this kill for more money—retirement money perhaps. Whatever the case, Nick's task had just grown considerably more complicated.

Adele led her prey to her bedroom, not turning on a single light. Suited Nick fine. His eyes had already adjusted to the darkness. He spent the next fifteen minutes listening to frantic, drunken sex. When Cashion muttered something about the bathroom, Nick readied to put him out of commission.

He moved soundlessly to the side of the door as it opened. Cashion shoved it closed as he reached for his dick. Nick closed one hand over the man's mouth and simultaneously wrapped an arm around his throat in a sleeper hold. Cashion struggled for three or four seconds, but he was far too wasted from the alcohol and physically spent from the sex to put up a real fight. Nick lowered his naked, unconscious body to the floor and eased back to the door.

Adele would be waiting. To deviate from her usual pattern was not unheard of, but to commit the murder where she lived was risky. Perhaps she was ready to move on, adopting another alias and home. Or maybe she had sensed someone was watching her and decided to act out of character just to see what happened.

Nick opted to wait and let her come looking for her lover.

A full minute elapsed before she called out her lover's name. When Cashion didn't answer she flipped on the light in her bedroom and came to the bathroom door, pushing it open. She stood naked in the open doorway staring down at the man.

"Fucking useless bastard," she grumbled as she moved toward him.

Nick slipped behind her and she stalled, her body going rigid as his shadow fell over her.

"Hello, Adele."

Before she could whip around and charge him, he grabbed her and pulled her against him, one hand closing over her mouth.

She kicked and elbowed frantically as he carried her back into the bedroom. She squirmed and twisted, but her slight frame was no match for his. On the bedside table he spotted the hypodermic needle she used to disable her victims. These days more serial killers than not used drugs on their victims. The ease of purchasing injectable drugs on the internet or even on the streets made their work far less complicated. Clearly she had planned to finish Cashion tonight. As if she'd read his thoughts, she stilled in his arms. It wasn't necessary to be a mind reader to know what she was thinking, but he wouldn't use the drug on her. The risk of overdosing was far too great. Adele wasn't getting off that easily.

"When did you notice you were being watched?" he asked, curious. He dared to loosen his hold on her mouth.

"I didn't." She inhaled a big breath, her breasts moving against his arm. "Yesterday my neighbor thanked me for the money I'd been leaving in his coffee can."

Nick laughed. That was what he got for trying to help the old guy out.

"Who hired you?" she demanded. "Let me go and I'll pay you twice whatever you're being paid."

Keeping a firm grip on her, Nick moved toward the bed. She squirmed, elbowed and kicked in earnest. "I'm afraid," he said between her attempts to head butt him, "you can't afford me." He tossed her on the bed.

"I could scream," she warned as she tried to scramble away.

"You could—" he snagged her easily "—and the police would likely be summoned. Then I'd have to show them all those trophies you've kept from your kills."

When he started to cover her mouth once more she clamped her teeth down on his hand. He growled and yanked his hand away. As he shouldered off his backpack, she fought even harder and spewed curses. He manacled her slim wrists in one hand and kept her pressed against the mattress with his forearm as he fished for the duct tape in his pack. He grabbed the edge of the tape with his teeth and pulled.

"Bastard," she muttered. "What are you? Some sort of bounty hunter?"

"Not exactly." He flipped her onto her belly. She tried to squirm away, but he held her in place. He wrapped her wrists tightly in duct tape, binding them together. She muttered more curses against the pillow as he ripped off another length.

He reached for her legs. She quickly spread them apart and arched her butt upward. "Don't you want some of this before you do whatever you came here to do?" She laughed. "They all want it so badly until they realize just how much it's going to cost them."

"No, thanks." He pulled her legs together and bound her ankles tight despite her wiggling. With her arms and legs secured, he rolled her onto her back and readied to place a strip of tape over her lips.

"Who are you?"

"No one you know."

Nick pressed the tape over her mouth while she

glared at him. Then he rolled her to her side and wound several layers of tape around her neck. He pulled her calves toward her back, forcing her body into an arch, and then wound more of the tape around her ankles, effectively hogtying her. She groaned and grunted and struggled but couldn't move more than an inch or so without choking herself.

That would do.

He returned to the bathroom as Cashion was struggling to his feet. Nick put him down again. "Tomorrow you'll understand that this was the luckiest night of your life."

Nick bound Cashion as he had the woman in the other room. When that was done he went to her walk-in closet and removed the faux drawer that hid her keepsakes. He brought the photos and the trophies into the bedroom and spread them around her on the satin linens. No matter how she pleaded when the police arrived the photos and newspaper clippings would tell the tale.

Nick used her cell to call 9-1-1. He gave the operator the address and left the phone line open as he tossed it onto the bed. Three minutes later he was in his car and headed away from her street. He hadn't driven a mile when blue lights barreled past him heading toward the scene he'd left behind.

Tomorrow the Executive Executioner's capture would fill the headlines, print and electronic. Nearly a dozen homicide cases would be solved.

One less serial killer to take lives.

Nick pondered the other names on his ever-growing list. His cell vibrated before he could decide on his next hunt. He dug the phone from his pocket and checked the screen. The name gave him pause.

Malcolm Clinton.

He'd only met Clinton on one occasion and that had been two months ago. Clinton was a guard at the prison where Randolph Weller resided in far better circumstances than he deserved. For an agreed-upon fee, Clinton had promised to call Nick with the names of any visitors beyond the usual FBI profilers who wanted to pick the monster's brain. This was the first time Clinton had called. The idea that his father hadn't had the first visitor who wasn't FBI in all that time made Nick inordinately happy.

Or, even better, maybe the bastard was finally dead.

He accepted the call. "You have an update for me." His pulse reacted to the anticipation pumping through his veins.

"Yes. Dr. Weller had a visitor this evening. I had to pull a double shift so I couldn't call until now."

"I'm listening."

"It was a woman his attorney called for him. A detective from Montgomery."

Tension slid through Nick.

"Detective Bobbie Gentry," Clinton said.

"How long did she stay?" Why the hell would Bobbie visit *him*? Nick couldn't fathom any reason she would visit Weller.

"Not more than fifteen minutes. She seemed a little distracted or unsettled when she left."

Nick glanced at the time on the dash. "What time was this?"

"About five thirty."

"Thank you." Nick ended the call before Clinton could say more. He tossed the phone onto the seat. "What're you up to, Bobbie?"

He'd kept up with her since he left Montgomery. As hard as he'd tried to forget her, he could not. She showed up in his dreams when he slept and in his thoughts when he didn't. He'd learned Bobbie had a new partner, a Detective Steven Devine. Nick had done a thorough search of Devine's background and found nothing troubling except that he was single and close to Bobbie's age.

The idea of her spending long hours each day with the guy grated on Nick. He'd watched her interactions with Howard Newton—the partner she'd lost. The bond had been palpable. Would she forge that same sort of bond with the new guy? Wasn't that what cops did?

None of your business.

He shook off the thoughts. He had more pressing concerns. Why would she visit Weller?

There had to be something going on. He'd been mostly out of touch the past forty-eight hours. When he closed in on his prey, it was important that he not be distracted. Even a major homicide case wouldn't explain why Bobbie would go to Weller. Whatever had happened, it had to be specific to a serial killer she believed Weller would know, and even then the FBI would likely insist any questions be funneled through their channels.

Nick glanced at his phone and resisted the temptation to call her. Five or six times in the past two months he'd pulled out the one video of her he'd kept and watched it just to hear her voice. The video had been made before her abduction by the Storyteller. She'd been in the backyard with her husband and child—the husband and child the Storyteller had stolen from her. Nick kicked himself every time he watched. What kind of fool was jealous of the life a dead man had lived? And yet, Nick watched the video over and over, the life depicted in those captured moments making him yearn for things he could never have.

"This is your life," he reminded himself. There was no need to pretend otherwise. Feeling sorry for himself wouldn't get the job done.

Nick made the trip across town to the low-rent motel he'd been staying at since his arrival in New Orleans. He backed into the parking slot directly in front of his door. Inside, the dark room smelled musty but it was cool and quiet, two things he required on a hunt. He closed the door and turned on the light.

The reports and photos he had gathered on the Executive Executioner lined one wall. He knew many things about Adele. Where she was born, where she'd lost her virginity, how she lured her prey. His research was always in hard copy. He didn't have to worry about a housekeeper stumbling upon his work since he always made an arrangement with motel management. He cleaned up after himself and picked up fresh towels and linens at the front desk. There was some risk using this method but not nearly so much as leaving electronic tracks for his friends in the FBI to follow.

Now that the hunt was done, he would pack up his research, drive to some place well outside the city and burn the whole lot. But first he had to know why Bobbie had visited Weller.

He opened his laptop, entered the passcode and then searched the news for the Montgomery area. The first headline to top the Google search gave him the answer.

Seppuku-Style Killings Take the Lives of Wealthy Montgomery Couple

He read the story, noting that Bobbie was the lead detective on the case. According to the reporter's inside source, the murders were carried out in the same MO as the Seppuku Killer from the last decade. Had to be nothing more than a copycat. But Bobbie having shown up to visit Weller after being assigned the case was far too big a coincidence to ignore.

Nick closed the laptop. If someone was trying to send him a message, he or she had known exactly how to get his attention.

He would shower, grab a few hours of sleep, and then he was going to Montgomery.

To Bobbie.

Five

Baptist Medical Center
Friday, October 21, 7:00 a.m.

Bobbie watched Sage Parker sleep. According to the uniform who'd just gone off duty, the boy had a bad night. Nightmares had disturbed his sleep. Bobbie's heart went out to the child. No matter that his aunt had arrived yesterday to be with him, he was alone in a way every child feared. Both parents had been taken from him in one fell swoop; his sister was still missing. Every hour that passed diminished the expectation of finding her alive.

When she was twelve years old Bobbie lost her mother, but she'd had her father. Her father hadn't passed away until she was in college, but his sudden death had been extremely difficult to accept. Not because she had loved him more than she had her mother, but because his death had been like losing her history. There was something intensely painful about losing the roots that bound you to this life. Sage Parker's pain had only just begun.

She sighed, resisting the impulse to sweep a lock

of light brown, very nearly blond, hair from his forehead. Freckles dotted his nose and cheeks. His fingernails were dirty from playing the way little boys play. Digging in the dirt and pocketing rocks were two of his favorite things to do, according to his aunt. He was a climber and had the broken collarbone to prove his fearlessness. He would need all the courage he owned to get through the next couple of years. His parents were gone, murdered. He'd have to leave his friends and all that he knew and move to Nashville, assuming his aunt was willing to take him, and start over again.

Then and there Bobbie silently made two promises to the kid. She would find his sister and she would get the person or persons responsible for devastating his life. His parents, no matter their sins, deserved justice. Sage deserved the ability to move forward without looking over his shoulder or wondering for the rest of his life.

Marla Lowery, his aunt, appeared at the door, her coffee cradled in both hands. Bobbie stood and, with one last look at the boy, walked toward the door.

"I thought I'd get some breakfast while he was resting," Marla offered in explanation for her absence.

The officer on duty when Bobbie arrived had told her as much. The FBI agent had taken a break, as well. "I'm sure you're exhausted." Bobbie flashed a smile at the new uniform who'd come on shift a few minutes ago.

Marla peered into her coffee cup. "I've been thinking about what you asked me."

Bobbie gestured to the hall and moved away from the door of Sage's room. She preferred not to have him overhear anything that might upset him more than he was already. When they were a couple of yards away, she asked, "About Fern?"

Marla nodded. "My oldest said Fern has been at war with several students at her old school. She was…" Her voice stalled and her lips quivered. "Receiving a lot of hate messages on social media."

Marla had three children, all girls. The oldest was about the same age as Fern. "How long have these problems with the other kids been going on?"

Based on her social media accounts, Fern had a love-hate relationship with most of her friends the past few months. She had made quite a list of enemies. Bobbie had interviewed her principals and teachers at both the old school and the new one. The sixteen-year-old's recent behavior was completely at odds with the rest of her school experience. She had always been a straight-A student. Her teachers loved her, or at least they had until the real trouble started about three months ago. Fern's behavior became erratic and angry outbursts were suddenly the norm. Her grade-point average slipped. She started to dress and speak differently as if she wanted to be someone else.

"My daughter said Fern confided that the school was threatening to expel her."

Bobbie had learned as much from the school counselor. "Was there anyone in particular Fern couldn't get along with?"

Marla shrugged. "I have no idea. I really can't

believe she changed so much. Six months ago she was the sweetest, most thoughtful girl you would ever meet. And so smart. Suddenly she was sporting all those body piercings and wearing black and using horrible language. I can't imagine what happened to make her turn so rebellious and mean-spirited." Her lips trembled and tears welled in her eyes. "Or maybe I can. God only knows what the kids have suffered with what their parents have been going through. I'm ashamed to say we've only seen them twice in the last year. Heather and Nigel were always so busy and then all the legal trouble started." She shook her head. "I shouldn't have allowed that much time to pass between visits."

"We all get busy sometimes," Bobbie offered. "You spoke to Heather regularly?"

"One of us called the other every three or four weeks. She never even hinted there were problems at home…beyond what's in the news obviously." She frowned. "Fern's problems at school couldn't be the reason for…*this*. These are children we're talking about." Her lips worked for a moment before she managed to say the rest. "You don't think Fern or one of her classmates had anything to do with their deaths."

Fern was missing. There was no sign of forced entry into the Parker home and no indication of foul play related to her disappearance, both of which didn't look good. On top of that the girl had issues at home and at school. She wouldn't be the first teenager to murder her parents, but Bobbie was relatively certain the killer wasn't Fern or one of her friends. As true as that was she wasn't prepared to pass along those conclusions yet. The bottom line was the students Fern angered had parents. There were few things more ferocious than a parent determined to protect his or her offspring.

"In truth it's too early to say. We'll operate under the assumption she's a victim until we have evidence to suggest otherwise," Bobbie hedged.

Randolph Weller's words rang in her ears. She ignored that warning voice. She had an obligation to conduct the investigation of this case the same way she did all others. Weller's input would not be a part of the process until she had reason to believe it held merit. The whole idea of a consortium of serial killers was over the top to say the least. She hadn't decided whether or not he was playing her somehow.

"Six months ago I would have said there was no possibility Fern would be involved in anything like this." Marla glanced at the door of her nephew's room. "Now, I don't know." Her gaze rested on Bobbie's once more. "Is it true that Heather was running a...*sex* service of some sort disguised as a dating service?"

Bobbie wanted to tread carefully there. "This investigation has a lot of unknowns, ma'am. We're nowhere near ready to say who was doing what. Give us time to get the facts straight before we pass them along to you. Frankly, that aspect of the case is more the FBI's purview." The pain in Marla's expression prompted Bobbie to add, "We both know that sometimes people do things they don't want to do for reasons we might not readily see or understand."

"The FBI questioned me about Nigel." Marla shook her head as if trying to deny the ugliness. "I can't believe he robbed all those people. We've known him for twenty years and he always seemed so nice. Heather never said a word." She drew in a deep shuddering breath. "I'm just glad our parents didn't live to see this."

Bobbie understood Marla meant the illegal activities the Parkers were allegedly involved in and the vicious murders, not to mention a missing child. Whatever the age or the circumstances of death the truth was no parent wanted to survive a child. She knew this better than most.

A scream rent the air. Bobbie whipped around and rushed toward Sage's room, her hand on the butt of her Glock. The uniform stationed at his door was already at his bedside.

As soon as Bobbie's brain assimilated the fact that the boy was okay, she analyzed the scene. A male dressed in scrubs, a nurse she presumed, stood back from the end of the bed, his hands out to his sides, patient chart on the floor as if he'd dropped it. A plastic caddy that contained a blood pressure cuff and other medical tools sat on the foot of the bed. Sage was curled into a protective ball as close to the headboard as he could get, the sheet pulled up to his chin.

"I just need to take his vitals," the obviously shaken man said, looking from Bobbie to the uniform.

"Let's see your badge," Bobbie ordered.

Marla hurried around the bed to comfort her nephew. "He's been doing this since I got here. Every time a man enters the room, he gets upset."

Thomas Brewer, LPN. Bobbie compared the photo to the man whose face was a couple shades paler than the one in the photo. A match. She passed the badge back to him. "Why don't we have a female nurse take care of him?"

Brewer bent down and picked up the chart. "I'll make a note in his chart. I don't know why they didn't do that already if this happened before." He reached for the caddy and Sage gasped. His aunt made soothing sounds and smoothed his ruffled hair.

Bobbie nodded to the officer. He followed Brewer into the corridor and returned to his post. "You don't need to be afraid, Sage. We'll keep you safe."

Brown eyes peered up at her. "That's what my daddy said."

Bobbie moved closer to the bed. She chose her words carefully. "Did something scare you before what happened while you were in the attic?"

He dropped his gaze to the sheet but he nodded. "The other day I was at home alone and someone came in the house."

Bobbie's instincts nudged her. "This is very important, Sage. Can you remember what day this happened?" She found herself holding her breath as she waited for his answer.

"Monday. Mrs. Snodgrass does the grocery shopping on Mondays. I was supposed to be at school." He shrugged skinny shoulders. "There was a big test and I forgot to study."

"So you decided to stay home?" Bobbie understood that feeling. After her mother died, she'd felt the need to hide from the big things like a test at school and the birthday party down the street. Her mother had always taken her homemade cookies to neighborhood parties. Bobbie hadn't wanted to tell anyone who asked that her mother couldn't bring cookies because she was buried in the graveyard by the church.

"But, Sage," his aunt protested, "you've always made honor roll. You've never been afraid of a test." Marla looked to Bobbie and shook her head, tears glistening in her eyes.

"Has someone at school been bothering you?" Bobbie remembered that part, too. Kids could be so damned cruel. *Who you gonna tell, Bobbie Sue? Your momma's dead.* She could imagine the things said to Sage about his parents considering the exploits the news channels and social media had been reporting. His mother had likely been called a whore and his father a thief. The image of the letters painted on their foreheads swarmed in front of Bobbie's eyes. Poor kid. The trouble had just begun for him and his sister—if she was still alive.

Sage nodded, but kept his gaze lowered. "Jacob Cook was calling my mom names. That's why my sister was fighting with his sister all the time. A bunch of people were being mean to her and me." He looked up at his aunt. "Is that why she ran away?"

A hit of adrenaline detonated in Bobbie's veins. "Do you think your sister wanted to run away?"

Sage shrugged his skinny shoulders. "She promised she wouldn't leave me. She said she'd take care of me if our parents went to prison. I guess she changed her mind."

Bobbie and Marla exchanged a look. "Don't worry about your sister. I'm certain she didn't run away from you. We'll find her," his aunt promised.

Bobbie gave him a nod and a promise of her own. "That's right and I'll make sure Jacob Cook never bothers you again." She had a feeling Fern's recent behavior was not about drugs or some other self-destructive behavior. It was survival for her and her brother. "Tell me about what happened on Monday."

"I was in my room building a Lego fort when I heard someone in the kitchen. I thought my mom had come home for lunch so I sneaked into the attic. I knew I'd be in big trouble." His eyes grew rounder with each word.

"Are you sure it wasn't your mom?" Bobbie's pulse hammered with mounting anticipation. The sooner they had a break in this case the better. One theory was that the killer had staged the scene to muddle the investigation. If that wasn't the case and this copycat was a serial killer, they could have more bodies all too soon, Fern Parker's being one of them.

Sage nodded. "It was a man. He came into my parents' room. I could hear him."

"Could you see him?" Bobbie held her breath.

Sage shook his head no. "I only know it was

a man 'cause I heard him cussing. He said bad words."

Bobbie asked, "Did his voice sound like your father's or like mine?"

"You're a woman," he said with a frown. "His voice sounded like my dad's, but it wasn't my dad. He said stuff like this—shit, damn it!" he repeated in an extra deep voice, and then he winced. "Sorry, but that's what he said."

"That's okay," Bobbie assured him. "Anything you tell me will be a big help. Are you certain you didn't see him in your parents' room?"

The boy nodded. The killer may have been laying out his game plan. Since the Seppuku Killer had murdered victims whom he considered to have shamed themselves, the Parkers' recent notoriety was likely the motive for their murders. But what about Fern? There was no record of an abduction or a child victim in the Seppuku case. Not that Bobbie had found, anyway. Copycats often deviated somewhat from the original MOs but this one was quite a giant step. The range of vile things the killer may have done to Fern checked off in Bobbie's head, made her stomach knot. *Don't let that girl be dead.*

Sage jumped. Bobbie snapped her attention back to the present and followed his gaze to the door. The agent had returned and he and the MPD uniform were talking to a man in a white coat. She recognized the pediatrician in the lab coat and her heart rose into her throat. *Charles Upchurch.* Dr. Upchurch had been her little boy's doctor.

She steeled herself for the encounter. She

couldn't keep avoiding the people who had known her before. "Don't worry, Sage. Dr. Upchurch is a friend of mine. I know him really well. You don't have to be afraid. Okay?"

The boy nodded, still looking uncertain.

"Have your aunt call me if you remember anything else. It's really important that you do, okay?"

Sage nodded again, this time with obvious eagerness.

"Call me if you need anything," Bobbie said to the aunt.

Since Marla already had Bobbie's cell number, she moved into the corridor to speak with Dr. Upchurch. The hospital needed to ensure Sage was cared for by females for the duration of his stay and MPD would have to get female officers here to keep him secure. The more comfortable he was, the more likely he would remember something that might help the case.

Upchurch recognized her and smiled. "Bobbie, it's good to see you." He thrust out his hand. "How is…?" His voice trailed off and his expression fell as his mind filled in the events of the past year.

"Good to see you, too, Doctor." She gave his hand a shake, then jerked her head toward the room. "Sage is having some anxiety with male strangers. I assured him he was safe with you, but…just so you know."

"Got it." Upchurch nodded. "I'll see that the rest of his stay is comfortable. We're running a few more tests just to be sure he's okay. He vomited a couple of times last night but those incidents may have been related to anxiety."

"Let me know," Bobbie urged.

When the doctor remarked that she looked well, Bobbie thanked him and excused herself. She stepped a few feet away from the room and made the call to Lieutenant Owens to bring her up to speed on the Parker boy's needs and what he'd told her. A female officer would replace the one on duty ASAP. After ensuring the officer on duty understood the new arrangements, Bobbie couldn't get out of the hospital quickly enough. She took the stairs and headed for the maintenance exit to avoid the reporters loitering in the visitors' parking lot. Plowing through the crowd and fending off their questions would be pointless. She had nothing she was authorized to share just yet. Fern's picture was in every paper, on the internet and on the television news. Hotlines had been set up for callers who might have seen or heard anything useful. Marla Lowery had gone on the local news and offered an urgent plea for help as well as a reward for any information about her niece.

As true as it was that the passing hours lessened the likelihood of finding Fern still breathing, Bobbie intended to stay focused on the idea that she was alive out there somewhere and needed to be found.

Her right leg protested the hustle down the flights of stairs. The pain was a consistent reminder that she was lucky to be alive. She opened the door into the morning sun and headed across the asphalt to where she'd parked her car amid the vehicles belonging to hospital employees. The man leaning against her Challenger stopped her in her tracks and very nearly stopped her heart.

Nick Shade. The stranger who'd made such an impact on her at a time when she believed her life was over.

The blue button-down shirt stretched over his broad shoulders, sleeves rolled up his muscled forearms, the well-worn jeans hugged his body. He wore black work boots as usual. His dark hair was a little shorter, not quite touching his collar now. The way he watched her as she approached startled her all over again, the same way it had the first time they met. There was just something about those dark eyes…as if he could see her thoughts, could sense her feelings.

"Good morning, Detective."

That voice. His voice had haunted her well before he showed up at her door to tell her to stay out of his way in the hunt for the Storyteller. She hadn't known at the time, but he had visited her in the hospital while she was in a coma recovering from her first encounter with the Storyteller. She'd been at her worst, refusing to fight for her life. She'd wanted to die. *Come back, Detective Gentry.* His words had somehow drawn her back to the land of the living.

She smiled, couldn't help herself. "Morning." What was he doing here? She hadn't gotten around to calling him. "You're about the last person I expected to run into today."

He straightened away from her car. "We need to talk. Do you have a few minutes?"

Devine was back at CID lining up today's interviews. She had a few minutes. "Sure."

"Take a ride with me."

She nodded. "All right." He led the way to a mid-size black Chevrolet truck. Beyond the illegal tint on the windows, the vehicle was fairly nondescript. "What happened to your car?"

He opened the passenger-side door for her. "I trade frequently."

She opted not to mention that the routine was in all probability a smart move considering he hunted serial killers using methods that skirted the law more often than not. "Where're we going?"

He slid behind the wheel. "No place in particular."

As he pulled away from the hospital's rear parking she studied his profile. Nick Shade was an attractive man and…as damaged as she was. He, too, had survived a ruthless serial killer—his own father. She doubted either of them would ever have a normal life. At least she had experienced a glimpse of what a real life was supposed to be. She would cherish those memories the rest of her days.

Would Nick ever allow himself to have that?

"You look good."

His deep voice drew her back to the present. "Thanks." It had taken her a long while to be able to accept a compliment. "You, too."

Silence settled between them as he drove. Back in August they'd spent a lot of time exactly like this, driving and hoping they would find a lead that would break the Storyteller case. Nick had been there for her during those shattering days before and after her partner's death. God she missed Newt.

As if he'd read her mind, Nick asked, "How's Carlene?"

He did a lot of that, too. Read her mind. "She's okay. She sold the house and moved to Nashville to be near their oldest daughter who just found out she's pregnant. Carlene's really excited about being a grandmother." *Newt would be so happy.* Bobbie swallowed at the lump in her throat.

"Tell me about this new case. The Seppuku copycat."

So that was why he was here. His father's warning echoed in her ears. She should tell him...*in a minute.* She wasn't sure how he would react when she announced that she had visited Weller. They hadn't discussed the connection between him and Weller. Instead of dropping that bomb, she gave him the details of the double homicide on her plate. "We have a survivor, the son. And hopefully the sister. She's still missing."

"This case is why you went to see *him*?"

So he knew. She didn't know why she was surprised. Nick Shade missed nothing. "No—at least not that I was aware. His attorney called and insisted that I come."

Nick braked for a light. He turned to her. "You know who he is."

His statement was not a reference to Randolph

Weller's infamous reputation as one of the most prolific serial killers alive today. "I do."

He stared at her for five endless seconds. "Why did Weller want to see you?"

Bobbie braced herself against the stony look in his eyes. From the moment she discovered his father's identity she instinctively understood that there would be no love lost between the two, and for good reason. "He wanted me to warn you."

The light changed and Nick looked away, moving forward with the flow of traffic. "Why didn't he have his lawyer call me?"

"He said you wouldn't listen to him." Bobbie took a deep breath and gave him the rest of the details. "I stared at my phone for hours last night." When she should have been sleeping, she kept to herself. "I planned to try and contact you today."

"You have my number," he said without looking at her. "What stopped you?"

Was he angry or disappointed that she'd done what she thought she had to do? Instead of responding to his question, she said, "He suggested the murders were a message to you. That these organized serial killers—he called them the Consortium—are coming for you. He's concerned they'll try using me as a way to get to you." She stared out the window and said the rest. "That's why I hesitated before calling. I didn't want you to come to Montgomery."

I knew you'd come.

He pulled into the parking lot of a convenience store. "You couldn't hope to stop me."

Bobbie stared out the windshield at nothing at

all. "Weller could be manipulating us." She'd come to a number of conclusions last night and that was one of them. Anything was better than the idea that a group of serial killers working together had decided to take Nick out. "He's desperate to be a part of your life."

"You give him too much credit," Nick argued. "He's far too cold and controlled to feel desperation."

"Maybe." Could a psychopathic serial killer love anyone but himself enough to feel desperation? Bobbie wasn't sure.

"I'll look into it."

"You'll look into it?" She wanted to shake him. "There are people out there plotting your death and all you can say is that you'll look into it?" Frustration and no small amount of exhaustion made her voice sharper than she'd intended.

His glare turned fierce. "This has nothing to do with you, Bobbie. It would be best if you stayed out of it."

She opened her mouth to set him straight when her cell phone interrupted. She snapped it free of her belt. "Gentry."

"We have a serious lead," Devine said, his tone eager. He hesitated, then asked, "You okay?"

"What lead?" she demanded, ignoring his question. She glowered at the man next to her. Who the hell did he think he was?

"I just picked up the coroner's preliminary report," Devine explained.

Bobbie started to demand why the hell she

hadn't been informed that the report was ready when Devine went on. "The knife used on the vics is consistent with a double-edged blade six to ten inches long. Judging by the striation marks, the blade has a distinct pattern Dr. Carroll is trying to track down."

Bobbie reached for calm. "I'll meet you at the office in half an hour."

"Ah…you might want to come now," Devine argued. "I have the name and address of one of Parker's enemies—one he cheated out of a couple million bucks."

Bobbie was about to remind him there were several of those when he added, "This guy collects rare Japanese swords and daggers. And he's suddenly planning a trip out of the country, as in he's booked on a flight out of Birmingham this afternoon."

Anticipation shoved the frustration and exhaustion aside. "I'll be right there."

Six

Greystone Place
9:00 a.m.

Bobbie surveyed the spacious den that was actually a gallery. Three of the four walls were lined with glass cases containing hundreds of knives and swords. Some of the instruments were longer than others, some sported ornate handles and sheaths. Each was labeled with the era and style of weapon.

If Mark Hanover wanted to conceal his proclivity for instruments of death potentially similar to the one used in the Parker murders, his housekeeper hadn't gotten the memo. She'd answered the door, listened carefully through Bobbie's introduction and then led them directly to this room to wait. Strange, to say the least.

Speaking of strange, Bobbie had wanted to ask Nick how he'd found out she visited Weller. Someone at the prison was likely keeping him informed. Nick avoided her question about whether he was in Montgomery for a few days or only passing through. She wanted the opportunity to tell him how much she appreciated what he'd done for her. What he did for so many others. When he was here before there hadn't been time and she hadn't been in the right place emotionally to adequately convey her appreciation.

"I've never seen a collection this extensive, not even in a museum."

Bobbie turned to her partner. There was a lot she didn't know about him, particularly when it came to personal tastes. She knew he wasn't married, wasn't in a serious relationship and had no desire for kids. His family was from old money and, according to Holt, he was the sole heir to his elderly aunt's estate. Her husband, the Colonel, had died when Devine was just a kid. He was named after the man. All of which explained his expensive suits and the pricey Porsche Panamera he drove.

Bobbie grunted a noncommittal sound to his remark about the collection. It wasn't that she had anything against people with money. Her husband's family had been quite wealthy. Having wealth flaunted like this was something she could live without. She supposed a man of means had a right to whatever hobby he could afford. Her shrink reminded her every other week that she needed a hobby.

That was another thing about her choice to return to the land of the living. In order to keep her job, the chief—her godfather and pseudo uncle—had insisted she agree to counseling for however long the department psychologist deemed necessary. The last few weeks she had decided maybe

Debra Webb

it wasn't such a bad thing since, much to her surprise, the doctor offered a decent number of valid points she hadn't wanted to see before. She was trying harder these days to be honest with herself and to keep an open mind. Her new attitude was paying off. Recently, the shrink had lengthened the time between her appointments to two weeks instead of one.

She was stronger, physically and mentally, which was a good thing. *Better to nail the bad guys.*

On cue, the towering mahogany pocket doors slid open and Mark Hanover entered the room. The slim-fitting suit was no doubt made from the finest fabrics available, the shoes were certainly hand-tooled leather. He was younger than she'd expected, early to midfifties maybe. His dark hair was peppered with just enough gray to look distinguished. His face, on the other hand, was as smooth as the day he was born. Good genes or Botox? Her money was on the latter.

"I apologize for keeping you waiting," he announced as he looked from Bobbie to Devine and back. "I'm Mark Hanover." He thrust his hand toward Bobbie first.

"Detective Bobbie Gentry," she said as she placed her hand in his. His shake was firm and quick, his palm cool and dry. Bobbie gestured to her partner. "Detective Steven Devine."

The two men shook hands next. Hanover seemed to hang on to Devine's hand a beat longer than necessary. Devine flinched and drew away. Bobbie considered what little she knew about Hanover. His marriage to one of the city's socialites had ended last year. Considering the way he watched Devine, maybe his sexual interests ran to something more than his wife was willing to tolerate.

"Please—" Hanover indicated the pair of leather sofas that faced each other in the center of the room "—make yourselves comfortable. How may I be of service to the MPD this morning?"

The two men waited for Bobbie to be seated first. When they had settled, she began, "I'm sure you've heard about the Parker murders."

Hanover gave a somber nod. "Tragic. Simply tragic. Especially the girl. Who would take a child?" He shuddered visibly. "As unfair as it is the sins of the father can at times carry over to the children."

Bobbie wondered what sins this man kept hidden. If her father had said it once he'd said it a thousand times: *people don't get that rich and stay that way without a few skeletons in the closet.* "We're hoping Fern is still alive."

"Of course," Hanover agreed. "I'm more than happy to help. I support numerous fund-raisers and activities for children. Please let me know if there is anything I can do. Perhaps a larger reward?"

"Thank you. I'll let the department's liaison know you'd like to help." Bobbie explained, "We're interviewing all who had business dealings gone wrong with Mr. Parker. Your name is on the list."

Hanover's eyebrows reared up his forehead in an unflattering expression and then he pursed his lips and shrugged. "Since I lost more than most of his other clients, I suppose it's reasonable that

I would be a suspect. Perhaps your top suspect," he suggested.

"Person of interest," Devine corrected. "You and many others are persons of interest."

"I see," Hanover acquiesced, his smug expression giving away his amusement. "I expect that's the less threatening of the terms." His tone was openly condescending, the words directed at the younger man.

Bobbie watched him carefully. He was completely relaxed and enjoying the interview. "You're quite the collector of—" she indicated the room at large "—daggers and swords."

"I am, indeed." He glanced around the enormous space. "My father started the collection when I was a child. We spent several years in Tokyo. I attended my first five years of school there." As if to emphasize the point he added, "*Chosen-teki nado no yona jokyo wareware wa-chu ni jibun jishin o mitsukemasu.*"

Bobbie exchanged a look with Devine who appeared annoyed and said, "I assume that was Japanese."

Hanover gave a nod of acknowledgment. "I said, 'What a challenging position we find ourselves in.' Wouldn't you agree?"

Bobbie had friends who'd majored in international business in college. Learning Japanese and Chinese was considered beneficial for those who wanted to make their mark in the Asian market. She wasn't surprised Hanover was proficient in one or both.

Was he trying to impress them? "You lost a couple million dollars to Nigel Parker's Ponzi scheme."

"I did." He leaned back and draped one arm across the back of the sofa. "If you're asking me if I murdered Nigel and his wife and took his daughter, the answer is no. As much as it pains me to lose money, I have plenty more where that came from."

"Were you a client of his wife's?" Might as well cut to the chase. Maybe the man's divorce was about his inability to stay faithful. His personality certainly left something to be desired. Bobbie wasn't particularly fond of braggarts.

Hanover smiled and glanced directly at Devine before responding. "As much as I enjoy beautiful women, frankly, I would have been far more likely to be involved with Nigel than his wife."

You guessed that one right, Bobbie. "You're the only one of his clients who owns rare daggers and swords."

He cocked his head and studied her, more of that amusement sparkling in his eyes. "What are you suggesting, Detective Gentry?"

"We aren't suggesting anything, sir," Devine responded before she could. "We'd like to examine your collection."

Her partner leaned forward as he spoke, his expression and tone daring the other man to deny them access. Did these two know each other? This was the first time she'd noticed her partner's inability to avoid a pissing contest. She'd certainly never had him speak over her as if she weren't in the room.

"We can get a warrant," Bobbie pointed out, looking from one man to the other. There was no need to play games.

Hanover turned his full attention back to her. "That won't be necessary, Detective Gentry." He stood and fastened the center button on his elegant suit jacket. "Examine my collection to your heart's desire." He touched a finger to his lips as if he'd only just recalled a relevant detail. "While you're at it, perhaps you can find the century-old dagger that was stolen from me last month. I'm certain the officer who came to the house filed a report." He squared his shoulders. "Now, if you'll excuse me, I was in the middle of preparing for an urgent business trip."

Bobbie stood. Devine did the same. "Mr. Hanover, I'm afraid there may be a problem with your planned travel."

Hanover scrutinized her for another long moment, whether it was curiosity or irritation in his eyes Bobbie couldn't say for sure. "You look like your mother."

Taken aback by the unexpected statement, Bobbie flinched before she could school the reaction. "Excuse me?"

"Your mother," he repeated, "she was an amazing woman."

Bobbie opened her mouth to question him when her phone vibrated. She checked the screen. Holt. "Excuse me." She looked to Devine. "I have to take this call. Make sure Mr. Hanover understands the situation regarding travel."

While Devine explained to Hanover that his travel plans would have to wait, Bobbie stepped away. "What's up?"

"We have another homicide," Sergeant Lynette Holt said before shouting at someone in the background to get some more uniforms on the scene. To Bobbie she said, "I need you here. Now." She rattled off the address.

There were still a couple of questions she wanted to ask Hanover. "We're interviewing—"

"Just get over here," Holt growled. "We may have a connection between this one and the Parker murders."

County Downs Court
10:30 a.m.

Bobbie showed her badge, then ducked under the crime scene tape and hustled up the sidewalk. Devine had dropped her off and would move on to the next name on the Parker client list. Since none of Fern's friends had panned out it was time to focus on enemies of the parents. Devine would also follow up on the robbery Hanover claimed to have reported last month. The guy was an odd one, that was for sure. She'd flat out asked Devine if he knew Hanover and he insisted he had never met the man. It was possible her partner had only been reacting to Hanover's blatant sexual overtures.

That was the thing about having a new partner. It took years to learn all the ins and outs of a person's personality and to build the kind of trust she and Newt had shared. God, she missed him.

Bobbie tugged on a pair of gloves before entering the front door of the ranch-style home. Holt and Bauer were scheduled to help with the interviews of POIs in the Parker case today. A new homicide had taken priority. She glanced around the living room. An evidence tech was busy dusting for prints, another was checking the camera he'd used to photograph the scene. The coroner's van was out front so Dr. Carroll was here somewhere. Holt appeared in the passageway between the living room and dining room.

"This way." She motioned for Bobbie to follow her.

Bobbie trailed down a long hall after her sergeant. Doors to three bedrooms and a bathroom stood open. The first two bedrooms were sparsely furnished. Like the living room, the rooms were neat. No indications of a struggle or any sort of trouble. "How many vics?"

"One."

"Any witnesses?"

"Nope."

The final bedroom on the right was their destination. The smell of coagulating blood and feces was thick in the air. Asher Bauer and the coroner stood on either side of the Caucasian male, early to midtwenties, hanging from a rope attached to a hook that had been mounted overhead in the middle of the room. The pool of blood soaked into the carpet beneath the victim was clearly most of what had once been in his body. Along with the deep crimson puddle was the feces and urine that had evacuated his dying body as well as certain body parts. *Damn.*

"Slade Manning," Holt announced.

Bauer cleared his throat. He looked a little green around the gills. Bobbie could see why. The vic was naked and he'd been castrated. His genitals lay in the middle of the coagulated mess on the carpet. Bobbie glanced behind her and noted the arterial spray on the wall. She grimaced. *Damn.*

"His heart was still beating when he was castrated," Carroll said, drawing Bobbie's attention to her.

"Man," Bauer said with a scowl, "this is seriously fucked up."

Bobbie couldn't agree more.

"The rest was helped along by gravity," Carroll continued with a gesture toward the victim's ankles. "The posterior tibial arteries were opened up to speed things along. Whoever did this wanted him to bleed out as completely as possible."

Bobbie shifted her attention to Holt. "How is your vic connected to Nigel Parker or his wife?"

"Don't know for sure yet," Holt said. "Manning was single. He was a star football player at Auburn his last two years of college but never got picked up by a pro team. Two former girlfriends accused him of abuse but never followed through with the charges. Ruined his pro aspirations but kept his record clean."

"Neighbors say he was a quiet guy," Bauer said, picking up where his partner left off, "who grilled out with his work friends occasionally. He had a steady stream of ladies. No complaints about him

from anyone questioned so far." He hitched his
thumb toward the closet door on the other side of
the room. "He liked to dabble in S&M. Lots of sex
toys and kinky outfits. The hook in the ceiling was
probably part of his repertoire. *Was* being the operative word." He shuddered and put a protective
hand over his package. "Man."

"So there isn't a connection to the Parker case?"
Bobbie was totally confused. It wasn't like Holt to
demand a command appearance when Bobbie was
already on another case. Bauer's expression warned
there was something more. One of the three in the
room needed to spit it out. She didn't have all day.
"What?"

"Do you know this guy?" Holt asked her.

Bobbie shook her head. "Never seen him before."

"The killer left you a message on his back,"
Bauer explained.

Bobbie held his gaze for one endless moment
before she made her way around the puddle of
bodily fluids and parts to view the victim's back.
The scars on her own back burned as if the cruel
words had been tattooed there yesterday rather than
ten months ago. She stared at the dead man's back.
The words written in what appeared to be red lipstick took a moment for her brain to assimilate.

Do I have your attention yet, Bobbie?

Something like defeat sank deep into her bones.
Weller was right. Whoever was doing this planned
to use Bobbie to get to Nick.

"There's more of that lipstick on the sheets." Holt gestured to the bed. "Suggests he wasn't alone."

The sheets were rumpled. Bobbie moistened her lips and asked the coroner, "Any sign of sexual activity on the bed?"

"More than you'll find in most low-rent motel rooms," Carroll said.

A couple more knots twisted in Bobbie's gut. "Are we thinking whoever was in bed with him, presumably wearing red lipstick, is the killer or another missing person?"

Holt shrugged. "Can't say yet. All we know for sure is that whoever did this knows you somehow."

"If your evidence techs are finished," Carroll said, shattering the mounting tension, "I'd like to take him down now."

"Bauer'll give you a hand," Holt said, her tone as somber as the coroner's. Bauer glanced at his boss as if he'd rather she suggested he commit himself to rehab. Holt ignored him and said, "We need to talk, Bobbie."

The numbness expanding through her limbs made Bobbie's movements stilted as she followed Holt back down the hall, through the dining room and kitchen, and out the back door. They both spent a moment drawing in some much-needed fresh air before peeling off the latex gloves they wore.

"I'm assuming that since this nut job used the word *yet* in his message that the Parker case is related."

"We haven't found anything to suggest the Parker murders were committed by someone who wanted to get my attention." Bobbie's stomach clenched, mostly because she knew her words weren't entirely true. Weller had warned her. Nick had basically confirmed the threat by showing up. *Shit*.

"Go back over the scene at the Parker house. Make sure nothing was missed. We'll work on finding out who was here with Manning."

"You haven't found any personal effects belonging to anyone besides Manning?"

"Not one damned thing." Holt planted her hands on her slim hips. "I have to tell you, I've got a bad feeling about this."

Bobbie couldn't discuss Weller's warning with her, at least not yet. The cop part of her felt guilty for holding back but she owed it to Nick to talk this out with him first. "I'll have Devine meet me on Westminster and see if we overlooked a message somewhere. I'll need a ride."

Holt nodded. "Have one of the uniforms take you."

Bobbie hesitated. "How's the baby?" Holt and her wife, Tricia, had named their baby after Newt. They called him Howie. He would have appreciated the gesture. Everyone who knew him missed him immensely.

Holt rubbed at her forehead with her arm. Bobbie felt a trickle of sweat slip down her spine. No matter that it was the middle of October and not even noon, it was far too warm. Or maybe it was the message on the dead guy and the possibility of a second missing person making them both sweat.

"Howie's good." The sergeant exhaled a big

breath and locked gazes with Bobbie. "I mean it, Bobbie, if there's anything I should know, I need you to tell me sooner rather than later. I don't want a repeat of...what happened before."

Guilt sat a little heavier on Bobbie's shoulders. "Got it." The words were bitter on her tongue.

Holt held her gaze for a moment, weighing Bobbie's response. "All right. Get over there and see what you can find."

Bobbie nodded. If she opened her mouth again she might not be able to keep holding out. Holt had backed her up during those final minutes in that damned shack where the Storyteller had taken his last breath. Bobbie owed her better than this.

But she owed Nick Shade more.

Westminster Drive
2:30 p.m.

The burger Bobbie had eaten on the way here threatened to swell into her throat as she entered the Parker home. It would take a major cleaning to extinguish the smell of death that had filled the house. Cold, dead flesh had a distinct odor—an odor that clung to walls and draperies and carpets well after the bodies were taken away. The metallic scent of blood and the unmistakable smell that was far too much like that of raw steak from the gutting the victims had suffered would take a serious chemical cleaning to dispel.

"Where do you want to start?" Devine, hands

in the pockets of his designer trousers, stared at her expectantly.

"I'll start in the garage if you want to take the attic." She was burning up already. She wanted no part of the attic.

"Sure thing." He readied to remove his jacket.

Bobbie hesitated before heading to the garage. "Had you and Hanover met before this morning?"

Devine laughed. "You asked me that already, and—" he shook his head "—the answer is still no. But I did get the distinct impression that he would like to know me better."

"It sure looked like he was flirting with you or daring you somehow."

"No kidding." Devine shook his head and held out his arms. "I'm sorry, but do I look gay?"

His offended expression made her shrug. "I never really thought about it."

Sullen, he tugged at his tie. "I guess I should ask Bauer."

"Maybe," Bobbie agreed. "I'm going down to the garage." She flashed him a weary smile. "Have fun."

Except for Fern's room the house was far too clean to have been home to a teenager and a ten-year-old boy. Bobbie couldn't help wondering how much was the housekeeper's doing and how much was the killer's. He'd damned sure cleaned that bathroom, leaving nothing more than a residue of the blood from his victims in the drain. More irritating, there was nothing she could really put her finger on as being wrong. As she passed through the kitchen Bobbie checked the oven. Spotless.

So weird. Did they eat takeout every night or was the housekeeper that damned on top of the cleaning?

Tugging on a pair of gloves, she moved down the steps to the lower level. When she opened the door to the garage the lingering stench of decomposing human organs and waste assaulted her. This was one area where the killer had left a hell of a mess. A remains removal service had cleaned up whatever the coroner's office and the lab had left behind. Still, the smell was brutal. Maybe Devine had gotten the better deal in the attic.

Bobbie walked the space, checked under and inside the vehicles. The ceiling was clear. The walls, other than the areas closest to where the murders had occurred, were clear. The only evidence left behind was the arterial spray on the walls and the dark stain on the concrete that would require stain block and a couple of coats of paint.

If the killer had a message for her, why hide it?

Her cell vibrated and she removed it from her belt. Coroner flashed on the screen.

"Gentry."

"Bobbie, this is Lisa. Sergeant Holt asked me to have a second look at the Parker bodies."

Their autopsies were scheduled for next week. The bodies were being transferred to the state lab later today. Montgomery wasn't set up for autopsies at this time. There was never enough money. The only reason the autopsies were happening next week was the pressure from the feds.

"Did you find something?"

"Sorry. Nothing new."

"Thanks for checking. Wait," Bobbie said before ending the call. "Is there a way to determine if the murder weapon used on Manning was the same one used on the Parkers?"

"It might be difficult to establish," Carroll said. "With the Parkers he cut through a significant amount of tissue. The incisions made in Manning's body won't give us as much to look at pattern-against-tissue wise, but I'll do what I can."

"Thanks. Let me know." Bobbie ended the call and surveyed the garage once more.

Heather and Nigel Parker were dead. Slade Manning was dead. Of course there was always the chance the two cases were completely unrelated. Either way, the red lipstick found at the Manning scene suggested he might not have been alone in the house at the time of his murder and that he may have known his murderer.

The day was far from over and already the weight of it was bearing down on Bobbie. Did they have two missing persons now or two more bodies out there waiting to be found?

Seven

They were going to need a bigger case board.

In the conference room turned command center Bobbie stood back and surveyed the notes she had added to her side of the whiteboard. Photos of the victims in the Parker case were taped on the board. She had added details beneath each one. Next to the photo lineup was a list of thirty-eight persons of interest with motive to want one or both dead. Beneath Fern's photo was the list of known enemies provided by her friends.

Holt capped the marker she held. "I've found no connection so far between Manning and the Parkers." She exhaled a weary breath. "Even the message to you can't be tied to the Parkers beyond the theory that their murders are what the killer meant by *yet*."

"We do have another missing female," Bobbie reminded her.

"Un-fucking-fortunately," Holt muttered.

A decade old VW Jetta had been found on the

street about a block from Manning's house. After having the vehicle unlocked, a purse and cell phone belonging to Vanessa Olson were found in the trunk. Her final text had been to Manning letting him know she was there. The time stamp showed she arrived at his residence at midnight last night. Carroll put Manning's time of death at about 2:00 a.m. Olson was a no-show today at the gym where she worked as a fitness coach. Bad news any way you looked at it.

Bauer and Devine were conducting interviews, attempting to make a dent in the growing list of POIs. Manning's as well as Olson's friends and family had been added to the list that seemed to be growing longer by the hour. So far there wasn't a single common motive for wanting any one of the three dead. Not one of those interviewed who knew the Parkers knew Manning or Olson. The Parkers were known by many of Manning's and Olson's friends but only through what they'd seen or read in the news.

"The manner of death is different." Bobbie tapped the marker she held against her chin. "They have no friends or relatives in common that we've found. They lived in different neighborhoods. Manning was not married and had no children. Olson is twenty and single."

"That leaves us with the theory that this is a copycat who's reenacting murders committed by high-profile serial killers who're already dead or incarcerated. Based on the note at the second scene we can assume that for some reason he's attempting to impress you or to lure you into his fucked-up game."

"Yay me," Bobbie muttered. Carroll had called half an hour ago. She couldn't determine if the same weapon had been used on Manning. The tissue where the incisions were made on Manning's body wasn't thick or dense enough for the blade to leave sufficient striation.

At first Bobbie hadn't recalled a case involving the Manning MO but a quick search of a couple of databases, including ViCAP, and an exact match popped up. The Pretty Boy Killer. The killer, Lewis Wilton, sixty, had a lethal scorn for popular younger men. Wilton had spent his youth being the hotshot high school football star hoping to play college ball and to eventually move on to pro ball. Right after graduation a freak car accident had basically castrated him—rendering him incapable of having an erection—and damaging his right hip so badly that his football aspirations were over. On top of all that his fiancée dumped him. Eventually he finished college and became a high school history teacher and coach. Twenty-five years later after murdering six young men, recent graduates about to launch their college sports careers, Wilton was caught with his seventh victim hanging much as Manning had been. His bitterness and envy had festered, triggering a plunge into the violent psychopathy from which killers were born.

Bobbie would need Nick to confirm, but it made sense that Wilton was another of his takedowns. The idea that whoever was behind these murders, maybe this Consortium Weller mentioned, could keep dropping bodies for God only knew how long was not lost on her.

You definitely have my attention.

She couldn't keep Weller's warning under wraps much longer.

"We know the Parkers were chosen because of their alleged crimes," Holt noted, surveying the faces on the board. "That's in keeping with the sort of victims the original Seppuku Killer had chosen. Manning fits the profile for the Pretty Boy Killer for the most part, except his football career extended into college rather than ending in high school. The question is, what's the connection to you? Did our killer or killers become obsessed with you because you beat the Storyteller? Does he see you as some sort of challenge?"

"Sucks to be me right now," Bobbie said, avoiding the question. Guilt stabbed at her again. She had to talk to Nick soon.

The victims are counting on you, Bobbie.

She would not let the victims or their families down. If there was any truth to Weller's warning, was there really no way to stop this so-called Consortium? A nameless, faceless evil that could be anyone anywhere?

Hanover's offhanded comment echoed amid the other worries whirling in her head. How did he know her mother? Why did his announcement that he did feel somehow threatening? Before Bobbie could add any more questions to the mounting list her cell vibrated, dragging her attention away from the troubling thoughts. She hoped Devine and

Bauer had found a lead. Or maybe Nick wanted to talk. When she was done here she intended to call him if she hadn't heard from him.

Uncle Teddy.

My office. Now.

Her groan of frustration had Holt demanding, "What?"

"The chief wants to see me." She should have known this was coming.

"Go. We've done all we can for now." Holt checked her watch. The face was big enough for Bobbie to see that it was past seven already. Holt's wife had given it to her after the baby was born. *To remind you of all you're missing with each passing hour.* "I'll check in with Bauer and see where he and Devine are with the interviews."

"See you tomorrow." Bobbie turned to go.

"One more thing, Bobbie."

She hesitated and glanced back at her sergeant.

"We're a team," Holt reminded her a third time. "I don't mean to keep beating a dead horse, but no secrets this go-round."

Bobbie nodded.

Only one.

Montgomery Police Department
320 North Ripley Street
7:35 p.m.

Chief of Police Theodore Peterson stood well over six feet. For a man who'd passed sixty a while ago he still carried himself like the star football player he'd been at the University of Alabama back in the day. He and Bobbie's father had been best friends. They'd grown up together, married the same year and served side by side as cops for better than two decades. When her father died, the chief had tried to step in and be a father figure for Bobbie. As much as she loved Uncle Teddy, Newt was the one who had eventually felt like a second father to her.

Then again, maybe she'd pushed the chief away because of the job. No one liked a teacher's pet in school and the same applied on the job. Bobbie went to great lengths to see that not a soul in the department could accuse her of capitalizing on any perceived favoritism from the chief or his office. There were a few who might make the occasional remark about nepotism, but not one could back it up.

Bobbie shifted in her chair. She'd been sitting in front of his desk for five long minutes. When she'd arrived, Stella, his administrative assistant, had told her to go on in. The chief had been on the phone so Bobbie had waited quietly. A full two minutes ago he'd ended the conversation and still he hadn't so much as acknowledged her presence.

Finally, he laid down the pen he'd been using to make notes and looked up at her. "Dr. Sanger says you're doing great. He's very pleased with your progress."

Really? Had he seriously called her in his office to discuss what her shrink had to say? *Play the game, Bobbie.*

"I feel great," she said. Those words were what he wanted to hear. She knew this. She also knew him well enough to understand there was more.

He braced his forearms on his desk and clasped his hands. "Tell me about these two homicide cases and the missing women."

"Lieutenant Owens didn't brief you?" That was like asking if the sun would come up tomorrow. Of course the Major Crimes Bureau commander had briefed the chief. The question directed at her was his way of segueing into what he really wanted to ask.

Since he continued to glare at her without uttering a word, she answered the question that was really on his mind. "I don't know any of the victims. I have no idea who killed them or why the person or persons responsible left a message for me on Manning's back. Fern Parker is still missing and now we have a new missing person, Vanessa Olson. I don't know her, either." When he would have spoken, she forged on. "Nothing is going on in my personal life that you don't already know about." That last part wasn't entirely true.

"You left work early yesterday."

Now there was a statement she hadn't seen coming. "I had a doctor's appointment."

"Are you ill?"

"It was a female checkup."

He nodded. "I see."

Every woman comprehended the power of that statement. Tell a man you had female issues and he was ready to change the subject faster than you could blink. She did need to have one of those. The doctor's office had called her six or seven months ago to remind her to schedule an appointment but she'd never bothered. Physicals and routine exams were not something a woman who wanted to die thought about adding to her calendar.

But you didn't die, Bobbie.

She would make the appointment—as soon as these cases were solved.

"Joanne said she spoke to you about putting your house on the market."

Joanne Rogers was the sister to Sarah, the chief's wife. *Deceased wife.* Her aunt had been in a nursing home until her death a few weeks ago. Aunt Sarah stopped recognizing Bobbie or anyone else except on rare occasions ages ago. Her death was a bittersweet end. Sarah Peterson had been a wonderful woman. She'd taught Bobbie many of the things a mother usually taught a daughter. Bobbie had always hated dressing up. She'd been too much of a tomboy. When the cutest boy in her class had invited her to junior prom, she'd wanted to go so badly it hurt. But Bobbie Sue knew nothing about wearing high heels and makeup. Her daddy didn't have a clue how to help a seventeen-year-old deal with becoming a woman. Aunt Sarah had given her a crash course. No matter that Sarah and Teddy Peterson weren't related to Bobbie by blood, they had always treated her like the daughter they never had. As frustrating as that connection could be for her career on occasion, she loved the man waiting patiently for her answer. They just didn't always see eye to eye.

"I'm thinking about it," Bobbie admitted.

The house had been sitting empty for nearly a year. Only in the last couple of weeks had she worked up the courage to box up the things she wanted to keep. She supposed it was time. She couldn't bear to live there. The home represented a life that no longer existed. She couldn't go back. A fresh start was the smart way to go. *Did that make her a coward?*

"You can't keep living in that Gardendale dump." The chief leaned back, resting his hands on the arms of his chair. "You deserve better, Bobbie. It's time you realized as much."

The shrink repeatedly told her the same thing. To some degree she had come to terms with the idea that James's murder and Jamie's death weren't her fault. James had been murdered by the Storyteller. Their little boy had died trying to escape the slaughter. Bobbie was only guilty of doing her job—maybe too well. Still, it was difficult not to feel remorseful about surviving and moving on.

"I've been looking for something new. Something manageable and in a neighborhood near work." It was true. She'd even talked to Bauer about it. She couldn't live in an apartment building like his, though. D-Boy needed a yard. The dog was the first step in allowing herself to commit to another living creature and she wasn't going to let him down.

Peterson nodded. "I'm glad. I want you to be safe and happy."

She knew this. Both he and Sarah had always been there for her. "What about your happiness?" She wasn't the only one who needed to move on.

He looked away. "I'm fine."

Sarah had been diagnosed with Alzheimer's around ten years ago. She hadn't lived in their home in two years at least. He had to be lonely. "The best leaders lead by example," she reminded him. "How can you expect me to move on with my personal life if you don't."

He held her gaze for a long moment. "I spoke with LeDoux."

The name echoed through Bobbie, hitting those dark places she preferred not to think about anymore. The Storyteller had damaged him, too. LeDoux didn't have the physical scars Bobbie carried but he had scars nonetheless. "How's he doing?"

"He claimed he's fine, the same way you always do."

Bobbie ignored the off-the-cuff accusation and waited for him to admit why he'd really spoken to Special Agent Anthony LeDoux. For six years, from the time a victim had been left on his front doorstep, LeDoux had been point on the Storyteller case, but it wasn't until after Bobbie's escape that the killer's identity had been uncovered. His return to Montgomery had drawn LeDoux into the same darkness as Bobbie.

"Why did you call LeDoux?" She had a sneaking suspicion the answer was one she didn't want to hear.

"Actually, he called me," the chief said. "He heard something about you and thought I should know."

Tension trickled through her muscles. "I haven't

been involved in any high-profile cases since August. Why would he hear anything about me?"

"Let's not play games, Bobbie. You and I both know that someone is targeting you again. The media focus on you for the past year may have drawn the attention of those who enjoy doing others harm."

"The same can be said for the whole team," she argued. "All our faces were in the news. LeDoux's, as well." *And Nick's*, she didn't add.

"I haven't seen anyone else's name written on a dead man's back," the chief countered.

"Are we going to do this again?" The whole conversation sounded like a rerun of two months ago when the Storyteller was wreaking havoc in the city. When would the chief stop trying to protect her? She could take care of herself.

"You show me proper respect and I'll do the same."

Bobbie stood. "Yes, sir."

He pointed to the chair she'd vacated. "I haven't told you what LeDoux said."

With a sigh she hoped conveyed her impatience, Bobbie lowered back into the chair. She didn't need a crystal ball to know what was coming next. *Damn it!*

"Surely you're aware the FBI monitors certain high-value prisoners. Particularly those who provide intelligence on a regular basis."

Her stomach sank. She opened her mouth to explain and he held up a hand to stop her.

"You left early yesterday to drive to Atlanta for a visit with Dr. Randolph Weller."

And there it was.

"Don't bother denying it," he interjected before she could rally an explanation. "The entire conversation was recorded and played for LeDoux and he passed it along to me. My question is why would you not tell me about this, Bobbie? Do you somehow believe our personal relationship exempts you from following the rules?"

He was angry. The flicker of fury in his eyes was telling enough, but his posture had gone ramrod straight and his words hit their mark.

"I was stunned by the call from Weller's attorney," she admitted with a halfhearted shrug. "I had no idea what he wanted from me but my curiosity wouldn't allow me to ignore the summons. So I went."

He motioned for her to continue, his frustration and anger making the movement stilted.

"So much has happened today that I hadn't gotten around to telling you." He couldn't deny she had a valid point there.

"Weller warned you that his son was in danger. He asked you to contact him. Have you spoken with this Nick Shade?"

No matter that Nick had been instrumental in saving her life, the chief still referred to him as if he were some *thing* rather than a person. "I'm hoping to have a discussion with him soon."

In her opinion the brief meeting they'd had this morning didn't count. They'd hardly talked about what the chief wanted to hear. *Just another white lie.*

"If you talk to him—if he comes into my jurisdiction—I want to hear about it."

Bobbie nodded. "Whatever you say."

"Do not force me to waste resources by adding a surveillance detail to you," he warned. "Keep me informed or I will do just that."

She sure as hell had no desire to have a cruiser following her around again. "I'll keep you informed."

"LeDoux mentioned the FBI is taking a harder look at Shade, which may explain why Weller is concerned." The chief watched her closely as he continued. "They're following up on some of the serial killers who've been murdered in the past decade or so. They think Shade may be a killer rather than the hero he would have you believe he is."

Outrage charged through Bobbie. "LeDoux knows that isn't true. He would be dead—I would be dead—if not for Nick Shade."

"All I'm saying is that you need to watch your step, Bobbie," he warned. "Three people are already dead. Two young women are missing. This city doesn't need to be caught in the crosshairs of a battle between Nick Shade and the FBI."

Bobbie feared this battle was something far bigger than the chief or the FBI understood. Evidently LeDoux hadn't mentioned the Consortium. Why would he keep that part a secret? Maybe it was time Bobbie reminded LeDoux that if a war between Nick and the FBI was coming he might want to keep her on his side.

"Is that all?"

The chief lifted one shoulder in a resigned shrug.

"Go. But," he qualified, "do not ignore what I'm saying to you, Bobbie."

She started to turn away but she hesitated. "What do you know about Mark Hanover?"

The chief blinked. "Why would you ask about him?" He executed another of those negligible shrugs. "Is he somehow involved in the Parker case?"

"He is," Bobbie confirmed. "He lost a great deal of money. When Devine and I interviewed him today he mentioned that he knew my mother." She played his words over in her head. "It was strange."

"He's an unpleasant man, Bobbie. Your mother, your father, Hanover, we all knew one another growing up but we ran in different social circles. That hasn't changed to this day. Take anything he says with a grain of salt." A frown furrowed across his brow. "Did he say something that made you uncomfortable?"

Bobbie shook her head. "It wasn't really what he said. It was how he said it."

"He's very good at making others uncomfortable. He's not someone you want to know."

Bobbie had gathered as much. With another warning to watch her back echoing in her ears, she made her way out of the building. It wasn't that she never ran into anyone who knew her mother. There was just something accusing or insinuating about Hanover's remark.

She would be talking to the arrogant SOB again.

Eight

Asher shifted in his seat. He'd spent way too much time in this car today. They still had a long way to go on the list Holt had given them, but they'd made some decent headway. Dozens of calls had come in on the hotline about the two missing women, Fern and Vanessa, but none of the tips had panned out so far.

He looked over at the man behind the wheel. "We should call it a day. Showing up at doors at this hour doesn't go over well. People complain."

Devine didn't answer. Just stared out the window.

"Hanover was telling the truth about the break-in," Asher reminded him.

Devine finally tore his attention away from the mansion across the street. Asher could tell he had a major hard-on for this rich dude.

"He's daring us," Devine growled. "He feels untouchable. Above the law."

Something about this guy hit a personal chord with Devine. "You have a history with Hanover?" Devine had family in Montgomery. It was reasonable to think he might have run into this guy at some point in his life.

"History." Devine made a sound in his throat. "That's a good way to put it, I guess."

Asher laughed. "Bobbie will kick your ass for keeping shit from her," he warned the new guy. "You don't even want to know what Holt will do."

"He was one of the adults who volunteered with the youth camp for the underprivileged," Devine said as if Asher had said nothing and then he fell silent for a moment. "He probably still spends two weeks out of his summer helping to organize and execute the youth camp for the poor children of Montgomery. I was barely old enough to meet the criteria and my aunt insisted I attend. Sons and daughters of the more prominent families were expected to take a less fortunate kid under their wing and set a good example. Be a friend and a guide through the two-week outdoor adventure." He made a sound in his throat, not quite a laugh. "It was an adventure all right. I was just a kid…"

Oh, hell. "Man, you don't need to tell me this shit." Asher held up his hands stop-sign fashion. "You should tell Bobbie. She's your partner."

Devine stared out into the darkness again, his attention on the multimillion-dollar estate lit up like the capitol building. "She won't understand." He turned back to Asher. "You understand. Imagine being raped when you're nine years old by a grown man—a pillar of the community, someone the people who should have protected you looked up to."

"Fuck." Asher shook his head. "I don't want to hear this, man."

"I couldn't tell my aunt. She believed Hanover and his family were above reproach. The bastard was a Boy Scout leader."

"Damn." How fucked up was that? Asher didn't know why he was surprised. He was a cop, plus he wasn't oblivious to the national headlines. People hid behind respected positions and did crazy shit all the time.

Devine leaned back in the seat. "How many other kids has he touched? He would have raped that girl—the one I was assigned to guide that summer—if I hadn't stepped in."

Asher frowned. "And neither of you ever told?"

"Never. She died from leukemia a few years later."

"That story is seriously sick."

"Everyone always thought Hanover and his father were above reproach. Still do."

"Maybe his father did shit to him. Maybe that's why Hanover messed with you." The bastard Gaylon Perry who'd killed Bobbie's family had been victimized by his father—a man of the cloth no less.

"I want to get this guy," Devine admitted. "He needs to go down."

Asher smiled in spite of the disgusting subject. "All this time I thought you were some kind of straitlaced by-the-book fucker."

Devine turned his head to look at him, a faint smile on his face. "I am. Most of the time. I'd put the past behind me, you know. I didn't spend the summer with my aunt anymore as a boy, but I still visited. In all those years I never ran into him. When I saw his name on the POI list something snapped inside me. The memories wouldn't stop haunting me. My face pressed against that rough wooden floor...the pain. Him grunting like a pig. Sweating. Me crying like a baby."

Anger burned through Asher. Kids should be protected. What the hell was wrong with people? "Whether he has anything to do with these murders or not, we can shake him up a little. Make him sorry for what he did to you."

Devine turned to Asher. "I should have told my aunt." He exhaled a weary breath. "I guess I thought if I didn't I was protecting her from the ugliness. If I'd told my parents they would never have allowed me to visit her again. I couldn't let that happen, especially after the Colonel died. She needed me. Still does. I'm the only one who cares enough to see that she is taken care of the way she deserves."

"Protecting the people we love can hurt sometimes." Asher suddenly wished for a drink. He'd been sober for twenty-one days. He didn't want to screw that up.

"Who were you protecting?"

The question startled him. "What do you mean?"

Devine shrugged. "I've heard the rumors about your fiancée but I don't believe what they say."

Asher didn't give a damn what anyone said. "I don't want to talk about it."

"Wow." Devine laughed drily. "I tell you my darkest secret and you can't share what everyone in the department but me seems to know."

Asher hardened his jaw. His first inclination was to tell the guy to fuck off. He didn't do kumbaya moments. Let Devine be just another fellow cop who thought Asher was a piece of shit for cheating on his fiancée and causing her to want to die.

But he couldn't do it.

"I didn't cheat on her."

Devine didn't say anything, just listened.

"We were planning our wedding." His heart started to pound as he recalled those days. She was so happy. "We wanted to start a family right away, so she stopped taking her birth control pills. She was so excited. We both were."

"Did she discover she couldn't have children?"

Asher shook his head. "Worse. She found out she had stage-four ovarian cancer. The docs said they could remove everything, give her chemo and buy her some time. The cancer was too advanced to offer any decent chance of survival."

"Damn." Devine scrubbed a hand over his jaw. "I feel like a dick for feeling sorry for myself."

Asher waved him off. The guy had no way of knowing. Asher hadn't told anyone. "She decided to die on her terms. She wanted to save me and her family from watching her suffer a slow painful death. So she climbed into the tub with a bottle of wine and sleeping pills and went to sleep. She left a note for me and one for her family."

"She must have been very brave."

Asher nodded. "She was."

"Sounds like you still miss her."

"Every day." Asher blinked at the burn in his eyes. He damned sure wasn't going to cry in front of the guy no matter what he'd shared. "Every day."

"We should find a bar and get hammered." Devine smacked the heel of his hand against his forehead. "Shit man, I'm sorry."

"How about we do something better?" Asher suggested.

"Name it." Devine started the engine. "I'm ready."

"Let's question some of Hanover's friends again. Make him feel the pressure. Cast a little shadow on his image."

"That's the best idea I've heard all day." Devine shifted into Drive.

Asher decided maybe he liked Devine, after all. You had to hand it to a guy who could go through that kind of trauma and not turn out totally fucked up.

Still, Devine would never be able to fill Newt's shoes.

Nine

Bobbie had dark brown hair and pale skin that refused to tan, but Dr. Lisa Carroll had her beat by a mile with deep black hair and skin so light it was almost translucent. Back in school, the boys the future doctor had ignored and the mean girls who picked on her had nicknamed her Morticia Addams. Carroll had been quiet with few friends. She graduated as valedictorian and won every damned scholarship imaginable. She and Bobbie had never actually been friends, more like acquaintances surviving the brutal teenage years.

"I'm sorry I couldn't meet with you sooner," Carroll apologized again as she led Bobbie through the lobby of her small clinic. "It took me hours to catch up here." She shrugged. "People have appointments, they expect to be seen."

"No problem."

Bobbie had done some checking when she heard about Carroll taking the coroner position. Never married, no kids. Like Bobbie, work appeared to be her life. She had refused to go into practice with anyone else. She wanted to see all patients whether they could pay or not and she didn't want anyone's permission to do so. Rumor was she had turned a large storeroom at the back of her clinic into a mini apartment to avoid rent or a mortgage.

"You'll have to overlook the mess. I need to catch up on my filing." Carroll stepped into an office no bigger than the cubicle Bobbie had at CID. "Just set those on the floor and have a seat." She gestured to the chair flanking her desk, the seat stacked high with patient charts.

"Thanks." Bobbie moved the stack to the floor and took the seat.

Photos of children, patients Bobbie decided, lined most of the wall space. The rows of smiling faces were interrupted only by a narrow space for a small bulletin board. Announcements and business cards were thumbtacked to the board. A filing cabinet with drawers too full to close all the way stood in one corner. Aside from the mounds of files on the doctor's desk, there was a huge mug filled with pens and pencils and one framed photograph. The photo was Carroll and her parents. The coroner's freshman year, as best Bobbie recalled. Her parents had been killed in a car accident the next year. Losing their parents at an early age was another thing they had in common.

Carroll cleared a space on her desk for the file she dug from one of the smaller stacks. When she'd opened it, she looked up at Bobbie. "I can't tell you much. I do a cursory examination, draw a few blood, urine and tissue samples to send to the lab, and send the bodies to one of two places—a funeral home or the state lab—depending on the circumstances of death."

"There was a serial killer, several years ago, the Seppuku Killer," Bobbie explained. "He injected his victims with fentanyl and then murdered them the same way the Parkers were murdered." Something had kept the Parkers and Manning from fighting their attacker. Had to be a drug.

Carroll nodded. "You're thinking this killer used it as well."

"I am. You can test for that, right?"

"You can. First thing in the morning I'll call the lab since I've already sent the samples I collected. It'll take some time. They're always backed up but I can try and sweet-talk my contact there. I'll have a look at the bodies once more before they're picked up to see if I can find any injection sites."

Bobbie was regrettably very much aware of how long it could take to get test results from the state lab. "I appreciate it." She fought a wave of weariness. She needed to eat and shower. She was beat. "You checked on the Parker boy today?" Dr. Upchurch had called Bobbie to let her know that Carroll had offered to drop by the hospital and follow up with Sage.

"He's doing really well, considering. Dr. Upchurch mentioned you'd rather he not be released today. I assume it's okay to sign off on his release tomorrow? You know those pesky insurance companies don't like patients staying any longer than necessary."

"That works." Pesky insurance companies were something else Bobbie was well aware of. Her months of rehab had come with loads of insurance issues. "As soon as he's released we're planning to move him and his aunt to a safe house until we determine whether or not he's in danger."

The feds were picking up the tab for the safe house, which was actually a suite at the Renaissance downtown. Lieutenant Owens had ensured an MPD officer would be posted at the room along with two FBI agents assigned to the boy's protection detail.

"Your partner, Detective Devine," Carroll said, "is convinced the unusual pattern made by the blade used on the Parkers is significant. One of the evidence techs—Andy—took extensive photos of the wounds."

Andy Keller was the best. He was also determined to spend time with Bobbie. She agreed to dinner occasionally. He'd done her far too many favors to ignore his requests. She only wished she could make him understand that being friends was the most she could offer him or anyone else. The image of Nick Shade pushed into her thoughts. *Not meant to be.*

"You never know what piece of evidence will make the difference," Bobbie said. Devine could be onto something. She thought of Hanover with all his swords and daggers. Whatever Hanover's game she had to separate her personal feelings from the job. Not always easy. Particularly since the man seemed to know how to hit just the right spot for a reaction.

"You know—" Carroll closed the folder and braced her arms on her desk, drawing Bobbie from the troubling thought "—I remember what you did in junior high."

"I hope I won't be too embarrassed." Bobbie was relatively certain Carroll wouldn't be interested in hearing what she remembered.

"You kicked Shane Culver's butt for calling me names." Carroll smiled. "It's the only time I ever felt like I had a real friend and I barely knew your name."

Bobbie smiled, something she did a little more of lately. "I never could abide a bully."

"I wasn't surprised that you became a police detective." She gave a nod. "The job suits you."

Bobbie appreciated that the other woman didn't mention the more recent appearances in the newspaper. "Thanks."

Carroll's face clouded with regret and Bobbie realized she had not dodged that bullet. "What happened," Carroll said carefully, "was…unimaginable. Your courage and strength amaze me."

If only she was as strong and courageous as everyone seemed to think. Bobbie gave Carroll a nod and stood. "Let me know what you find. I won't hold my breath on the test results."

"I'll push them as hard as I can," Carroll assured her.

They didn't speak as they made their way back

to the front entrance. When Carroll had unlocked and opened the door, Bobbie said, "Thanks again."

"Anytime."

As Bobbie walked away she heard the locks click into place behind her. Considering the stack of files on her desk, she imagined Carroll would be burning the midnight oil. Bobbie would be doing the same thing no matter how exhausted she was.

She climbed into her Challenger and started the engine. She had the case files Devine had sent her on the killers their perp appeared set on copying. Whoever had executed three people and abducted two others in the past forty-eight hours had familiarized himself with the MOs and signatures of the killers he wanted to imitate. The abductions were a big deviation. Neither the Seppuku Killer nor the Pretty Boy Killer had taken victims without killing them right away.

Whatever reason this killer or killers had for taking Fern and Vanessa, Bobbie hoped like hell they could find them before the bastard carried out the next step in his plan. Maybe there was more to those two killers than could be found in the reports. When she spoke to Nick she could get the whole story from him. She remembered the wall of information he'd gathered on the Storyteller. He would know far more than any of the databases or case files she could explore. This morning he'd confirmed that she had the right phone number. When she got home if he wasn't there waiting for her, she would call.

As she drove, her mind drifted back two months

to all the times he had showed up at her house in the middle of the night. She'd been so focused on having her revenge against the Storyteller she hadn't wanted Nick's interference. She'd told him more than once to stay away. How else was the Storyteller supposed to get close to her? Nick had refused to go away. As much as he had wanted to get the Storyteller for his own reasons, he'd been determined to keep Bobbie safe. She sure as hell hadn't cared whether she lived or died…as long as the Storyteller died first.

Turning onto Gardendale, she slowed. As always the house at the end of the street was lit up like a beacon in the darkness. Javier Quintero's place was the farthest thing from a safe harbor as could be found in any neighborhood in this city. Quintero and his gang ran the organized illegal activities on this side of town, but no one could prove it. It was as if the man had an inside source within the department that kept him one step ahead of the law. Bobbie wanted to hate Javier but she couldn't. He'd done her a tremendous favor two months ago and, sadly, she owed the man. One of these days he would call in that marker. She supposed as long as it wasn't illegal she would reciprocate.

She pulled into her driveway and shut off the engine. Guilt immediately settled on her shoulders. Though he had food and water and access to the backyard, she felt bad she'd been gone fourteen hours. Poor D-Boy. At least he was no longer chained to a porch as he'd been with his previous owner.

Her cell vibrated against her side as she climbed out. *Don't let it be another body.* She didn't immediately recognize the number but the out-of-state area code was a familiar one. "Gentry."

"We need to have a conversation, Bobbie."

Special Agent Anthony LeDoux. Bobbie bit back the immediate response she wanted to hurl at him. "No kidding."

"I would have thought you'd learned something from your last involvement with a serial killer."

Bobbie jammed the key into her front door and gave it a twist. D-Boy waited for her on the other side. She scratched him behind the ears. "I think we both learned something." She shut off the alarm system and locked the door during the ensuing silence. LeDoux shouldn't dish it out if he couldn't take it.

"I thought we were friends, Bobbie. Why didn't you call me when Weller contacted you?"

"Don't try the guilt thing with me, LeDoux, you started this." There was absolutely no reason for him to call the chief and tell him about her visit to Weller. "You could have called *me*."

"I'm trying to help you, Bobbie. You can't go visiting an asset of the Bureau's without having your name pop up in places it shouldn't. If I hadn't called Chief Peterson, someone else would have. I was able to frame the situation a little more to your advantage."

Bobbie suspected there might be some truth in his words. "So why didn't you mention the rest?"

She tossed her keys onto the table next to the

door and toed off her work shoes. As tired as she was, she should change clothes and go for a run. The nightly ritual went a long way in keeping her sane. She'd been letting other things get in the way too often lately.

"Your chief doesn't have clearance."

Shrugging out of her jacket as she made her way to the bedroom, Bobbie laughed. "But I do?"

"Weller was properly reprimanded for violating the terms of his agreement with the Bureau. This is the second time he's crossed the line. He's skating on thin ice." LeDoux made a sound that failed the definition of a laugh. "He should have been exterminated years ago."

She hung her jacket in her closet and moved to the bed. "What was the other violation?" She placed her Glock on the bedside table, then crouched down to loosen the ankle holster.

"Your friend Nick Shade visited him back in August when Perry was in Montgomery. He asked the old man for help."

Bobbie stilled, her fingers on the belt at her waist. "Weller is his father, why would his visit be a violation?" She held her breath as she waited for LeDoux's answer. She could think of one very large reason—Weller had murdered his mother and Nick had been the one to out the heinous serial killer.

"He can visit his daddy—not that he ever has—but Weller isn't allowed to pass along information, particularly information about criminals or crimes he hasn't even shared with the Bureau."

"Information about another serial killer?" Bobbie's heart was pounding. Nick had told her he was going to a source for information on the Storyteller. Had he really visited his father for the first time just to help her? Or maybe he'd wanted to stop the Storyteller that badly. Either way, the impact of that news shook her.

"I'm afraid I can't say. Why don't you ask your friend the serial killer hunter?"

Bobbie bit back the response she really wanted to make. LeDoux had nothing to do with Weller or this case. Why was he suddenly involved? "What's going on, LeDoux? Why are you a part of this? And what is this so-called Consortium?"

Silence filled the line once more. Images of the time she and LeDoux had spent chained in that desolate place crashed through her mind. It was a miracle either of them had gotten out alive. Others hadn't been so lucky.

"Like I said," LeDoux answered finally, "I'm trying to help you. He's using you, Bobbie. We don't know why just yet, but that's the only thing you can be sure of. This business about a consortium of serial killers is bullshit. It doesn't exist."

"I don't need you trying to protect me, LeDoux." She endured enough of that from the chief. She was a highly trained, seasoned detective. She could take care of herself. She pulled the clip loose from her hair and tossed it aside.

"We have to stick together against them, Bobbie. They're not like us… Shade is not like us. You shouldn't trust him, either."

"How can you say that after the way he saved

both of us?" The man was unbelievable. Frustrated, she headed for the kitchen. She needed to eat. D-Boy raced ahead of her, hoping for a treat.

"Just be careful, Bobbie."

She opened her mouth to demand what he had to do with any of this since he'd ignored her the first time she asked, but the man leaning against the counter in her kitchen temporarily stole her ability to speak.

Nick Shade.

"I have to go," she said to LeDoux. The agent was still ranting at her when she hit the end call button. "Hey," was all she could think to say. D-Boy sat at his feet as if Nick was his long-lost master.

"What does LeDoux want?"

Bobbie considered lying but he would know. Nick could read her like an open book. She suspected he could do the same with anyone. "He told the chief about my visit to Weller."

"LeDoux doesn't want you to get yourself killed." Nick gestured to the paper bag on the counter. "I thought you might be hungry."

Out of habit she started to deny his assessment but her stomach rumbled and her mouth watered.

"Thanks." She propped against the counter and reached into the bag. Chicken sandwiches and chips. She passed one of the sandwiches to him. "I guess you heard about the latest homicide." It wasn't a question. Nick Shade had connections.

"The Pretty Boy Killer was my fourth hunt." Nick peeled the wrapper from the sandwich. "Apparently he isn't going in any particular order."

Bobbie swallowed the first bite and resisted the urge to moan. "I remember headlines about the Seppuku Killer, but not the other one."

"The Seppuku Killer had a higher body count and his victims were headline makers, like the Parkers. You would remember him."

Since their earlier conversation was interrupted, she still didn't know his thoughts on Weller's story. "LeDoux says the Consortium doesn't exist."

"He's right." Nick sank his teeth into his sandwich instead of saying more.

She needed way more than that. Why would Weller make up a shadowy organization to explain the threat to Nick? How would such misleading information help her keep Nick out of danger? "Then he's baiting you," she reasoned. *Using me.*

"It's working."

Nick was Weller's son but he was also responsible for his arrest. Maybe this wasn't about protecting Nick. After all, could a psychopathic serial killer really love anyone? Weller's reaching out to Bobbie and the murders could very well be about vengeance. But why wait all these years?

"Do you think Weller is behind the murders somehow?"

His dark gaze settled on hers, searching, analyzing as if her every thought and feeling were right there in front of him. "I'm not certain yet what his involvement is."

She moistened her lips and reached for the courage to ask the questions that had burned in her brain since the day Nick left. "Was he…a good father *before*?" She shrugged, knowing the words weren't coming out right. She wanted to know more about Nick. He certainly knew everything about her. "I mean did he appear to be a good father? Did he go through the expected motions? Teach you how to play baseball? Take you fishing?"

Nick finished his sandwich and wadded the wrapper into a tight ball. "He was average, I guess. Though he didn't do sports. My mother took up his slack when it came to outdoor activities." He shrugged. "He came home in the evenings. Listened to whatever my mother and I wanted to talk about over dinner. He was patient."

The memories visibly confused or unsettled him. "The details you recall don't fit with what you know he is."

He braced his hands wide apart on the counter and leaned against it, then shook his head. "He didn't miss the important events at school. He always did exactly what he said he was going to do. I have no memory of hearing my parents argue." He looked away. "And then one morning she was gone. He said she left during the night. Some of her clothes were gone. Her purse and jewelry. We never heard from her again."

The pain in his voice was one Bobbie recognized all too well. She could imagine the little boy trying to be strong, hoping to hold on to his father's approval after his mother had vanished. Had his father—the heinous serial killer—held him and promised him everything would be okay?

"You were a kid. Ten years old? Who took care

of you while he was at work?" When her mother
had died, her aunt Sarah had picked her up from
school and did many of the things her father
couldn't do because of work. "Did you have any
other family to help out?"

"Just the two of us. He moved his office to the
house and I came home every day to a parade of
patients, one every hour like clockwork."

Bobbie had read that before his downfall Weller
volunteered several hours a week at the very prison
where he now resided. Even then the FBI and other
law enforcement agencies had relied on his superb
insight and opinions. How ironic. The very man
whose opinions waxed so brilliantly about the sub-
jects he evaluated had been committing shocking
murders right under their noses. She studied the
man who had been the little boy living with the
most evil monster of all. How had he survived?

"Don't waste your sympathy on me, Bobbie." His
voice was low, quiet and far too knowing.

"You spent all those months feeling sorry for me
and I can't feel sorry for you," she countered. Nick
had visited her in the hospital after she escaped the
Storyteller. Bobbie didn't actually remember, but
his promise to stop the serial killer who'd stolen her
life had found a place deep inside her and lodged
there. "Don't even try to say you didn't."

Hell, the whole world had felt sorry for her.

"Most of the time what I felt was respect and
admiration."

The confession took her by surprise. She decided
to take the compliment for what it was and move

on. "Are you planning to stay in town for a while or are you just passing through?"

He'd ignored her when she'd asked him the same question this morning. As much as she feared the danger was all too real and that it would have been better if he hadn't come, she couldn't deny being glad to see him or that she hoped he stayed. She hadn't expected to feel this...*attraction*...to him or anyone, for that matter. She'd spent so long being angry and sad and filled with the need for vengeance she'd thought she couldn't feel anything beyond those three painful emotions. *He* made her feel...*more*. What the more was remained unclear at this point but she wanted to explore whatever it was.

"Do I have a choice?"

She wanted to insist that of course he had a choice. He could disappear and never look back, rendering any efforts by this killer—whoever the hell had sent him—pointless. But he wouldn't do that. He would stay and fight and protect her, damn it.

"I suppose not." She thought of the two missing women and said, "There was a major deviation from the MOs of both the Seppuku and the Pretty Boy Killers."

"The Parker girl is still missing?"

Bobbie nodded. "A woman who was with Manning when he was murdered is missing, as well."

"Is there anything at all that connects the two?"

"Not that we've found so far."

He drew back and reached for the bottle of water on the counter.

"If Weller is behind all of this, why would he reach out to me?"

"He's curious about you, I imagine."

"Why?" Every part of her stilled in anticipation of his answer.

His gaze locked on hers and the ability to breathe vanished. "Because I've never allowed a personal involvement before. He can't stand not knowing what you are to me."

She held her breath. "And what is that?"

He downed another swallow of water before resting his gaze on her once more. "Someone who means a great deal to me."

She managed to draw air into her lungs despite the tightness in her chest. "You think he would really send a killer after his own son?"

"Yes."

It was a simple word, only three letters. It was the utter certainty and complete lack of emotion in his voice that levied a kind of devastation that she couldn't fully quantify.

"Okay." She squared her shoulders. "I should tell the team what we're looking at."

"You should. LeDoux needs to push Weller for answers."

Bobbie glanced at the clock. She hadn't realized how late it was. "Tomorrow will be soon enough, I guess." She shook her head to try and clear it. "So, are you staying at the Economy Inn this time?"

The memory of that wall in his room where he'd

compiled all he had learned about the Storyteller quickened her pulse. Would he do the same this time? More important, would he allow her to be a part of it? Damn it, she was a part of this. She would not permit him to leave her out.

"If they have a vacancy. I haven't checked."

One, two, five seconds lapsed. "My couch is vacant."

Inside, she cringed. Friends did that, though, right? He needed a place to stay; she had an empty couch. It was the right thing to do. Besides, the proximity could help keep her in the loop.

"How can I refuse such a generous offer?" A smile tipped one corner of his mouth.

His smiles were so very rare even the ghost of one was startling. "Good." She nodded, repeating the word over and over in her head. This was good. She could keep an eye on him if he stayed at her place. "First one up feeds D-Boy and lets him out."

Still sitting at attention near Nick's feet, the animal swept his tail back and forth over the worn floor at the sound of his name.

Nick gave the dog's head a rub. "Glad to see he has a good home."

She smiled. "A friend suggested I get a dog."

For another of those long lapses of silence they held each other's gaze. The foolish need to reach out to him nudged her, but neither of them was ready for that. Maybe they never would be. They were both so broken.

"Well…" She drew in a deep breath. "I should call it a night. There's an extra house key in the

drawer by the stove. The code for the security system is Newt1. You'll find a pillow and blanket in
the hall closet." She nodded. "Good night."

She turned her back and headed for her room.
If she could just get inside and close the door she
might be able to avoid hugging him or something
equally embarrassing. She was tired and vulnerable. Never a good combination.

"Thank you."

She hesitated, told herself to keep walking.
Couldn't. Slowly, she met his gaze once more, her
heart pounding hard enough to fracture her sternum.

"For what?"

"For caring enough to drive all the way to Atlanta and face the monster who stole *my* life."

Ten

Lynette Holt stared out the open window. The breeze was a little chilly but she needed to be able to hear. Sound carried in the darkness. She could make out the drone of the traffic on Atlanta Highway. Tonight, though, her attention was tuned in far closer to home. A second ago she'd thought she heard the Sheltons yelling, but she hadn't heard the noise again. Maybe if a helpless baby weren't involved she could let it go. Let the other neighbors continue to call it in and allow the chips to fall where they may. But the baby prevented her from pretending it wasn't her problem.

She already had far too much hanging over her head at work. Three dead, two missing. Not one decent lead. Thankfully she had Bauer under control. But then there was Bobbie. Damn her, she was hiding something and Lynette knew it.

"Are you ever coming to bed?"

Lynette jumped. She hadn't heard Tricia come into the room. "Sorry. Did I wake you?"

"The cold spot on your side of the bed woke me." Tricia sat down on the sofa next to Lynette. "You can't force the woman to make the right choices."

Lynette understood Tricia meant Olivia Shelton, the woman two houses away whose husband abused her every day of her damned life. Lynette fully understood she couldn't make the woman do the right thing, but she couldn't stand idly by and do nothing, either. She was an officer of the law. She had a sworn duty to serve and to protect.

Olivia and Wesley Shelton had become a sore spot between Lynette and her wife. The younger couple and their six-month-old daughter had moved in three months ago. The first few weeks they had been quiet, like the rest of the neighbors on the block. Then the fighting had begun. Screaming and crying and name-calling. Neighbors had called the police on numerous occasions. A week ago a representative from every home on the block had showed up at Lynette's door to demand action.

She was doing all in her power, which wasn't a hell of a lot since Olivia Shelton wouldn't cooperate. The woman wore bruises like most women wore jewelry and black eyes more often than not. But she refused to press charges or to move to a shelter.

"I can't do nothing," Lynette reasoned, knowing the words were falling on deaf ears.

"You're too close to this," Tricia argued. "When you feel compelled to step in, call Bobbie or Asher.

This is too personal. For better or worse or until their lease is up they are our neighbors."

Tricia was right. Lynette comprehended that fact, but every time she thought of a baby living in the hell that bastard raised nearly every night she wanted to storm down there and kick his no-good ass. But there were laws that protected pieces of shit like him the same as they protected the innocent. Unless the wife filed a complaint or filed for a restraining order, there was little Lynette could do.

"I'll talk to Bauer. Maybe he can help with this." Lynette was at her wit's end.

Tricia reached out and caressed her cheek. "You are a good cop, love. You care deeply. But you can't save everyone."

Lynette felt herself smile for the first time today. "I think having a baby made you smarter."

"They do say cells from the baby stay with the mother for decades, making her stronger and healthier. Maybe smarter, too."

Lynette wrapped her arms around Tricia and held her close. "You were already brilliant."

"You're pretty smart yourself." Tricia kissed her cheek. "So is everything settling down with the new guy?"

"Yeah. He's working out better than I expected." Steven Devine had somehow managed to impress everyone on the team. Except maybe Bauer, though Lynette thought he might be coming around.

"You worried about Bobbie again?"

Lynette contemplated the idea for a moment. She opted not to mention her suspicions about Bobbie having secrets. Tricia would only worry and hound Lynette about the issue. "Actually I'm feeling good about where Bobbie is these days. She's much stronger and she even smiles and laughs once in a while."

"This new case isn't stirring up any old issues?"

"Maybe a little, but she's holding her own." *Maybe if she'd just come clean there wouldn't be any issues.*

"Good. You're always happier when your team is happy."

Lynette smiled. "And when I'm happy, you're happy. Is that it?"

"Definitely."

They laughed. When the laughter faded their mouths found each other's. They hadn't been intimate since Howie was born. Suddenly they couldn't touch each other enough. Lynette's heart beat so fast she couldn't breathe. God, she needed this.

A scream two houses away fractured the moment.

They stilled, neither ready to pull away.

The yelling and cursing started next.

And then Howie began to wail.

Eleven

Fern would give anything if she could go home. Tears streamed down her cheeks. Her little brother needed her. Now she was probably going to die and he would be left all by himself to deal with their parents' shit.

She'd been so mean to him…slammed the door in his face. How could she have been so mean?

Her fingers hurt from trying to dig her way out of this fucking black hole. She'd dug and dug at the hard dirt walls. The only thing she'd accomplished was breaking her damned fingernails. Not that it mattered. A dead girl didn't need fingernails.

She'd awakened this morning—or maybe it wasn't morning, she couldn't be sure—to the sound of another, older girl being shoved in through the door. Light had spilled in for a moment making her squint. The man with the mask had taken her, too. Vanessa, the new girl, didn't know him, either. Fern shuddered. What was going to happen to them? If he was planning to ransom them, he was shit out of luck. Her parents were broke. She didn't know about Vanessa's.

As mad as she was at her parents, she felt bad that they would be so worried about her. A sob tore past her lips. She wanted to go home.

"Don't cry. We'll get out of here."

Fern drew her arms tight around herself. "He's going to kill us."

"He's going to try," Vanessa said. "But I'm not going down without a fight. You with me?"

Fern licked her lips and nodded, then remembered the other girl couldn't see her in the darkness. "Yes. I'm for sure with you."

"How long have you been here?"

Fern shrugged. "I don't know. It was Wednesday night when he drugged me and brought me here." She hoped she got the chance to hurt him—whoever the hell he was.

"Today's Friday. It's probably the middle of the night by now. Maybe even Saturday. Have you had any food or water?"

"He threw in one of those big thirty-two-ounce bottles of water when he left me here. I guess he doesn't want me to die until he's ready." Her throat ached. "I ran out just before you got here." Fern held back the sobs. She should have rationed the water. Now they would both shrivel up and die from thirst.

The rustle of clothing told Fern the other girl had gotten up.

"I can reach the opening but it won't budge."

"Yeah, I tried that, too. When I first got here." The door was like a hatch to a hole in the ground.

There was an old creaky wooden ladder that led up to it. She had tried over and over to shove it open.

Vanessa sat down on the dirt floor again. "Okay, for now we're stuck here so let's take some steps to make sure we stay healthy."

Fern wasn't sure how they could do that.

"If you need to use the bathroom, go over into the far corner and try to cover up your waste. You know, like a cat."

"Okay." Fern hated to tell her but she'd already had to do number one and number two, more than once. She had done it in the corner but she hadn't covered it up. They'd both felt their way around the walls looking for shelves or anything that might be stored in here, but the place was nothing but dirt and a couple of old boxes. A rectangular cave in the ground.

*A grave...*a deep grave.

"You think he'll come back?" Fern asked. He didn't have to come back, he could just leave them. He hadn't dropped any water or food into the hole when he shoved Vanessa inside.

"I don't know, but the Girl Scout motto is to be prepared. We couldn't exactly prepare for this, but that doesn't mean we can't work with what we have."

Fern bit her lip, then asked, "What do we have?"

"Each other." A flame flickered in the darkness and Vanessa smiled at her.

Fern's heart leaped even as her eyes squinted at the sudden brightness. "You have a lighter!"

Vanessa nodded. She let the flame go out. "I smoked some weed with a friend of mine before…"

Fern knew what she meant. Before that fucking monster had come after her.

Vanessa flicked her lighter again. "Let's see what's in those boxes back there."

Twelve

It was still dark when Nick leashed D-Boy and stepped outside. The scent of burning wood from a fireplace or a woodstove somewhere nearby lingered in the cool morning air. He took his time walking the neighborhood. As night grayed into dawn he noted little or no change from his last visit. Like before most of the lawns needed attention. Three or more vehicles were parked in the yards of the small homes. Like a game of musical chairs, tenants had come and gone, moving back and forth between this neighborhood and other similar ones in the city. Rent and deposits were cheap, background searches were ignored and credit checks were not required. As he'd anticipated, most of the residents appeared to be in bed. It was Saturday, after all.

D-Boy hesitated and stared through the chain-link fence that stretched across the yard where Quintero and his thugs resided. Judging by the empty beer cans and liquor bottles scattered over the porch, there had been one hell of a party last night on this end of the street. Nick doubted the neighbors complained. They were all too afraid of Quintero, which was how he continued to conduct his illegal business without fear of law enforcement.

Nick wondered if Bobbie would ever return to the home she'd shared with her husband. Miles away from this neighborhood, minivans and SUVs filled the garages while professionally manicured lawns showcased the middle-class homes. Bobbie Gentry had been happy there—even if she hadn't been like the other wives. She was a cop who chased bad guys 24/7 while the others shuttled their offspring to dance class or soccer practice after work. Bobbie's husband had happily filled in all the blank spots she left behind to protect and serve.

A knot formed in his gut and Nick cursed himself again for being envious of a dead man. It wasn't so much the man, but the life he'd shared with Bobbie. The chances of Nick having a wife and kid were less than zero. He would never take such a risk even if the opportunity presented itself. He would never put someone he cared for in that position. There were far too many targets on his back. Far too much risk of passing on the evil in his DNA.

Besides, like Bobbie, he was too focused on finding and stopping monsters. On being the hero, some would say. Nick wasn't a hero. He'd never been a hero. At twenty-one he'd been a self-centered kid who wanted to have fun and still survive college with a passing grade-point average and a marketable job skill. When his world shattered, he'd become an angry jerk who wanted nothing but revenge. Then the regret and sense of responsibility for the forty-two murders committed by his father had descended squarely on his chest. He'd felt the crushing soul-deep guilt for not protecting his mother—for not seeing what his father was. For being a blind, self-centered shit. Reason told him a child couldn't possibly see through the mask Weller had worn. Still, he'd hated himself for being too young not to see…too naive not to sense the malevolence.

Then he'd grown angry all over again at the realization of what he could not be. He couldn't be a cop and remaining in the military wasn't an option for fear he might be in a position one day that required he take a life. How could he risk taking a life and turning into what his father was? Two months ago the sadistic bastard had asked him if he'd "felt it yet"? Nick had wanted to tear off his head and reach down his throat to rip out his heart.

Because he had felt it.

For the first time since he chose the path of hunter, stopping the sadistic serial killer he'd hunted hadn't fulfilled the ravenous urge inside him. Finding Gaylon Perry, aka the Storyteller, hadn't been enough. He'd wanted to kill him. He had wanted it more than he had ever wanted anything in his life. He'd pretended not to feel it. He'd told himself he only wanted to find and stop him.

That he wanted to protect Bobbie and any other potential victims.

But it was a lie. He'd yearned to watch Perry die.

His most recent hunt had ended successfully without the overpowering desire to kill his prey. If he was lucky, what happened with the Storyteller was an anomaly. An unexpected reaction related to his feelings for Bobbie.

Yet another reason he should be keeping his distance.

He'd caused enough pain here already. Nick was the reason at least three people were dead and two were missing. Whoever Weller had sent, the son of a bitch had taken those lives to lure Nick back to Montgomery.

He would find the missing women. He would make the bastard who took them pay. The glitch would be in accomplishing his goal while keeping Bobbie safe. Weller clearly understood that she meant something to Nick and he would attempt to use that weakness. Whatever the cost, Nick could not allow that to happen.

D-Boy led the way back home. He didn't so much as glance at the house where he'd lived two months ago.

"You're one lucky fellow."

D-Boy looked up at Nick as if he agreed.

The sun peeked above the trees as he skirted the yard next to Bobbie's, slipped through the gate and made his way to her back door. Unless his instincts had failed him, there were no eyes on them at this time. But the threat would be close. Using the key

Bobbie had given him, he unlocked the door. He listened for a long moment before stepping inside. The smell of freshly brewed coffee told him she was up, but the lack of sound suggested she had returned to her bedroom to prepare for the day.

He tucked the key into his pocket and locked the dead bolt on the inside. Until he was done he would hang on to the spare key. Staying so close was a double-edged sword. His presence drew the danger toward her, yet if he stayed away she was far too vulnerable. Like before, she preferred to ignore any potential threat and charge into the fray.

Bobbie's instincts were better than average, but she couldn't conceivably grasp what she was up against when it came to Weller. No matter the case files she read or even the crime scene images she viewed, she couldn't possibly reconcile what he was with the facade he presented to her. Only firsthand experience could fully expose the kind of evil he was, and few survived that experience.

D-Boy whined, drawing Nick from the troubling thoughts. The animal stared up at him as if he had forgotten something very important. He spotted the large plastic bin on the floor next to the water bowl and empty food bowl.

"Time for breakfast, is it?" He transferred a scoopful of kibbles from the bin to the bowl and D-Boy dug in. He patted the animal on the back. Nick's craving for caffeine had him finding the right cupboard and retrieving a mug. Before he turned around he felt more than heard Bobbie enter the room. Mug in hand, he turned to face her. "Good morning."

She grunted. "We'll see. Tell me why Weller would send someone to lure you to Montgomery and then warn me you were in danger. It seems counterintuitive."

Nick was so accustomed to seeing her in trousers and a jacket for work, the jeans and T-shirt surprised him. She looked relaxed. His gaze swept over her lean curves. She looked good. When they'd first met, those attractive curves had been subtler, and inside she'd been so shattered that it hurt to look for too long into those pale blue eyes.

"What does he want from you?" she asked when he didn't answer her first demand. She took the mug from his hand and shoved it under the drip spout of the single-serve coffeemaker. Next she popped a pod into the machine, set it into action and looked to him for the answers he wasn't ready to share.

"I don't know what he wants." He should step away from her. This close the lavender scent of soap on her skin was distracting.

"Does he want revenge?" She passed him the mug of steaming coffee and prepared to brew herself another cup.

"Possibly." Nick spent little time wondering anything at all about Weller. The sooner he was dead, the better.

"A man who would go to such extremes to get your attention must have a strong motive." Bobbie held the mug to her lips and blew on the hot liquid inside.

Nick looked away and sipped his coffee. He could close his eyes and draw every line and angle of her face in his mind. "You forget who he is," he warned, setting his mind back on the subject at hand. "For Weller taking a life is as simple as tossing out an unwanted pair of shoes or flipping a light switch."

Even as a child he had sensed something was not as it should be with his father. Years later when he'd come home early for spring break and found him in the process of creating art from the bodies of the two men he'd butchered, that same sensation had settled deep in his gut the instant he'd parked in the driveway. Nick had climbed out of the car and entered the house, calling his father's name in the deafening silence. Then he'd gone to his studio. Painting had been his father's hobby, his passion. He'd said it soothed his soul. Growing up, whenever they traveled, art museums were always on the agenda.

The art Nick found him creating still haunted him whenever he closed his eyes.

"Have you considered that after all this time he might want you to suffer the same fate you created for him?" She abandoned her coffee, her attention fixed solidly on Nick. "LeDoux said the feds are taking a harder look at you. Maybe Weller is setting you up for a fall. Maybe that's what this is all about."

"Maybe." Nick wasn't prepared to offer more.

Far too much was still unknown and she was already in too deep.

"Why don't you talk to someone at the FBI or confront Weller?" She went to the fridge and had a look inside.

"The FBI knows who I am and what I do." He shrugged. "As for Weller, we don't talk."

She withdrew two cups of yogurt and offered one to him. He shook his head and she stuck the extra cup back in the fridge and closed the door. "You talked to him back in August." She prowled in a drawer and found a spoon.

"He told you about my visit?" Nick didn't know why he was surprised. Weller wanted to make her believe he had his son's best interests at heart. Whatever his game, it wasn't about anyone's interests but his own.

"Nope." She licked the yogurt off the spoon.

His gaze followed the move.

"You sure you don't want some?" She pointed at the cup with her spoon.

He shook his head again.

"Why didn't you tell me he was the source you went to see back then?"

"He was only one of several. Would it have mattered?"

She ate another spoonful of yogurt. "Probably not."

He concentrated on finishing his coffee. There was more she wanted to ask him. He could feel her anticipation. "Who told you I'd visited him?"

"The guard mentioned it when I was there." She

stared at her spoon to avoid his gaze. "Last night LeDoux said something about you going to see him the last time you were in Montgomery."

He didn't doubt one of the prison guards answering a detective's questions about Weller's visitors. What he did doubt was LeDoux's purpose for mentioning Nick's visit. *Is that more of your jealousy talking, Shade?* Somehow he had to get this possessiveness he felt toward Bobbie under control.

She lifted her gaze to his once more. "Did Weller begin drawing away from you emotionally after your mother was gone?"

Nick set his coffee cup aside and crossed his arms over his chest. The idea that he'd just made a classic defensive move wasn't lost on him. "The real question is, was he ever emotionally engaged with me?"

She lifted one shoulder in a shrug. "Was he?"

Nick considered the concept for a moment. As much as he didn't want to think about those years, he understood she wouldn't let it go. He remembered sitting on his father's knee and having him say good-night at bedtime. His mother would help Nick ready for bed, but before tucking him in she always took him to his father for a good-night pat on the back. He remembered smiles and nods of approval. Kind words. Patience. Never hugs or kisses, nothing so intimate.

"To a degree, I suppose." It bothered Nick to admit that he and the bastard had ever connected on any level.

"He may have maintained a certain distance to protect you."

Anger stirred at her gullibility where the bastard was concerned. Weller was an expert at cloaking himself in what he wanted others to see. "I have no desire to talk about him."

"Is there any way around talking about him?" She tossed her spoon in the sink and her empty cup in the trash. "He's the one who issued the warning."

"Tell me what your team has gathered on the case." Nick took his mug to the sink and rinsed it out. She could be right. There might be no way to avoid discussing Weller, but he'd had enough for now.

"We're interviewing the people who were close to or worked with the victims. An Amber Alert was issued for Fern Parker. A missing vulnerable adult alert was issued for Vanessa Olson. We've entered both into the NCIC. We have a hotline set up with a full-blown media blitz ongoing. The feds are doing their part. We're following up on the murder weapon. Dr. Carroll, the new coroner, noted a distinct pattern made by the blade used to open the abdomens of the victims. One of our evidence techs is working on nailing down the specific pattern. It could turn out to be a waste of time, but it's all we have at the moment." She massaged her temple as if an ache had started there. "The two abductions are the big sticking points. Why deviate so dramatically from the MOs he chose to reenact?"

Nick had spent a good deal of the night pondering that same question. "Whoever is attempting to get my attention wouldn't deviate from the original MOs unless he has a point to make."

"How can you be certain he didn't just make a mistake? He may have failed to anticipate Fern would be home or that Manning would have company."

"Weller would never choose a novice. His minion would be very detailed and precise. There would be nothing haphazard or spontaneous about his work. He would know when and where as well as how to strike."

"Maybe he was in a hurry," Bobbie countered. "He may have a tight deadline."

"Weller has waited this long," Nick argued. "Why rush now? True predators are supremely patient and will wait for the perfect opportunity."

"Point taken." Bobbie shook her head in frustration. "I could go back to Weller and demand answers."

"Do you really believe the FBI will allow you to see him again?" One of Nick's sources inside the FBI assured him that Weller was on lockdown—no one would be getting in anytime soon. Even if a visit were permitted, he did not want Bobbie anywhere near Weller again.

She set her hands on her hips. "First thing this morning I'll brief the team on the part I've been holding back. Will that be a problem for you?"

Despite her dedication to the job, she had withheld information for him. To protect *him*. Deep in his chest he felt an ache he had no right to feel. *Just keep digging that hole deeper, Shade*. He was already in way over his head.

"No," he said. "It won't be a problem."

No matter that he had come to Montgomery because of the murders, he'd wanted to come well before there was a reason. He'd wanted to see her. He wanted...

She abruptly reached into her back pocket and withdrew her cell. "Gentry."

What he wanted was irrelevant. All he had to do was stay close until this was over. Whoever had come for him would be watching Bobbie, anticipating Nick's appearance.

He would stay under the radar until he identified the source of the threat. Generally this step would be a fairly simple one...except there was Bobbie. Weller had positioned her squarely between Nick and that threat, handicapping his efforts. Weller was banking on the idea that Bobbie meant a great deal to Nick.

Regrettably for all involved, Weller was right.

Thirteen

They had shackled him to the gurney and strapped his arms and legs firmly in place. A plastic mask covered his nose and mouth directing oxygen into his starving lungs. His heart was beating irregularly. He felt weak and too tired to even raise his head. He made a sound, the urgency lost to the plastic mask. His chest felt tight and heavy.

His symptoms were classic.

Beneath the foggy mask Randolph Weller smiled as the guards rushed him toward Medical. The prison had its own doctor, a man far more interested in making love connections than offering an accurate diagnosis. Thankfully there was Anita. Dear Anita. The registered nurse had joined the woefully inadequate medical staff last year. She had gone out of her way to take care of Randolph.

Locks clicked open and the gurney was ushered into the facility. The beige walls, shelves and cabinets had grown shabby with time. The medical equipment was outdated and far from the best. The rooms—cells actually—were filled with patients with long-term illnesses, like cancer. The federal funding for those patients was higher, so those in charge ignored potential compassionate release options in order to keep the cash rolling in. After all, money made the world go round.

Randolph was grateful for the oxygen mask so that he wasn't forced to endure the smells of antiseptics and deteriorating flesh. The moans and howls of certain mental health patients echoed like a haunting overture, setting the tone for what was to come. Death was so very close for many of them.

But not for Randolph.

Today was a good day for him. He quickened his breathing and moaned softly, playing the part of the doomed protagonist in a fatal opera.

Far too often those who attempted to dissect him accused him of not having a heart. What a great irony that it was his heart that would change everything.

Fourteen

Mark Hanover's home was a reflection of the man—attractive but ostentatious. The problem was on the inside where those driving past couldn't see it was cold and empty. Not empty of things, but empty of all that mattered: heart, soul, joy. The emptiness echoed through Bobbie as if someone had shouted into a canyon.

"What the hell are we doing here?" Devine asked as he paced the floor of Hanover's study. "We've been waiting for what? Fifteen minutes?"

This time upon their arrival, the housekeeper had shown them to a more intimate space. Hanover's study was half the size of Bobbie's entire house. Rich mahogany shelves lined with books about finance and economics covered the walls. A broad desk sat in the middle of the room, flanked by overstuffed wingback chairs. The window beyond the desk looked out over manicured gardens and an infinity pool. Maybe Hanover wanted them to have plenty of time to take in all the details. The man certainly liked showing off.

Bobbie gestured to the chair next to her. "You should relax, partner. We're here because Mr. Hanover called with what he feels is a significant update to the statement he's already given. Let's give him a few more minutes." It wasn't like they had any other leads. Hanover was the closest thing they had to a suspect. For Fern's and Vanessa's sakes, they had to keep prodding any and all possibilities.

Devine exhaled a big breath of frustration. With visible reluctance he settled into the seat next to her. "He's probably bored and wants to yank our chain."

Bobbie turned to the younger detective. In the month they had worked together she had never seen him so rattled. The mounting tension between him and Hanover during their last meeting had been palpable. So she asked him again, "Are you certain you don't know this guy?"

"Why would I know him?"

That Devine looked away as he answered, that his jaw was as rigid as stone suggested otherwise. If she found out later that he was keeping anything from her, he would regret the decision. Being partners was a solemn arrangement of complete trust with one another's lives. It was immensely important that they trusted each other completely and had each other's backs in any situation.

Like you never lied to your partner.

She dismissed the idea. The things she had avoided telling Newt had been deeply personal and not relevant to their safety on the job.

There you go lying to yourself again.

"Did he give you any idea what this update is?" Devine looked directly at her now. "New evidence? Something he recalled from a meeting with Parker?"

"He didn't say."

She and Devine had been scheduled to meet at ten to start interviewing more of the folks who were involved with the Parkers and Manning. Holt and Bauer were doing the same with Fern's and Vanessa's friends. Unless either of them uncovered something significant, they would compare notes and update the case board on Monday. Bobbie had called Lieutenant Owens on her way here. She'd passed along the rest of the conversation she'd had with Weller. Owens wasn't happy about Bobbie's delay in reporting the details and had said as much. She'd assured Bobbie they would revisit the issue again when this was over. By now Holt and the chief would know. Both would be pissed. As soon as the three recovered from the initial irritation at Bobbie they would realize the FBI had left those same details out of their briefing, as well.

Before the day was out she would hear about it from one or all. Maybe anticipating that was the reason a headache had started deep in her skull.

Devine tugged at his tie. "I'm thinking this guy has something to hide and he's overdoing the 'I'm cooperating' card."

Bobbie rubbed at her forehead with the tips of her fingers and wished the damned ache away. As for her partner's conclusion, it happened. A perp would feel compelled to pretend to help the police. He was typically driven by guilt or by pleasure. For some, the idea of flirting with the possibility of being caught was like a drug. For others, it was a way to feel important or heroic. Hanover didn't strike her as the type who needed his ego stroked. His ego appeared to be plenty healthy.

Bobbie straightened her lapel as she relaxed in the seat once more. For a man in such a hurry to meet with them, Hanover was taking his time. She'd rushed to get dressed before Devine picked her up. Shade had promised he would be around. He'd patently avoided her question about what he planned to do.

Unless he took off to Atlanta and demanded to see Weller, what could he do?

You are the only connection to this killer.

No doubt he intended to watch her just like he had last time. He'd walked D-Boy before daylight and did his coming and going through her back door. She had yet to figure out where he parked his vehicle—a Chevy truck instead of the Ford sedan he'd driven last time. His precautions suggested he wanted to keep a low profile from whoever had drawn him to Montgomery as well as from anyone else. Staying under the FBI's and the MPD's radars was no doubt a top priority. Nick Shade did not like answering questions about himself or his intentions.

His presence was something else she was keeping from her team. *You really have this trust thing nailed, Bobbie.*

The towering pocket doors abruptly slid open and Hanover breezed in. "I apologize for keeping you waiting." He closed the doors and hurried over to where they now stood. He thrust his hand toward Bobbie first. "Detective, thank you for coming." He barely grazed Devine's palm and said nothing to him.

Oh yeah, these two definitely had some sort of history. Why would Devine lie about it?

Hanover moved around his desk and sat down. "Have you narrowed down the suspect pool at all?" He turned his hands up. "Your chief is keeping a tight lid on this one. I haven't seen the usual press releases from the department."

"Actually," Bobbie said, "we have to filter our press releases on this case through the FBI."

He surely knew this considering he'd lost millions in the Parker Ponzi scheme. Nigel Parker had been under investigation and all over the news for months. Hanover also no doubt knew that he was at the top of the feds' persons of interest list. Sometimes a killer grew annoyed that his work wasn't getting the media attention he'd expected. Bobbie wasn't convinced Hanover was guilty of anything beyond playing games.

"Of course." Hanover leaned back in his chair and said nothing else.

Next to her, Devine shifted. Her partner had reached the end of his patience. Bobbie said, "Mr. Hanover, you invited us to meet with you for what you called a significant update to your statement."

"Oh, yes." He shook his head as he leaned forward. "Please forgive my inability to stay focused. I'm still reeling from the notion that I may have been able to prevent this tragedy."

Now he had their attention. Bobbie's instincts went on point. Devine stopped his fidgeting.

"You recall my home was burglarized recently."

"We confirmed your statement about the stolen dagger, yes." Bobbie had intended to call him today anyway. "Do you have photos—for insurance purposes—of each item in your collection?"

"I do." He frowned. "Did I not provide the officer who came about the break-in with a photograph of the missing dagger?"

"It's not on file." Bobbie had checked. There had been no recent activity on the case. No new leads. No leads at all, in fact. The detective who'd caught the case had followed up. He'd interviewed Hanover's neighbors, checked with the local pawnshops and on cyber sites like eBay. Basically that was as far as the investigation had gone. Unless there was a tip, what else could be done?

"I'll round up a photo for you and have it sent over to your office right away."

"You said you have something new," Devine snapped.

Bobbie mentally cringed, not happy with the tone. Devine was an experienced detective, he was well aware you attracted more flies with honey than with vinegar.

Hanover held Devine's gaze for a moment. "I'm certain you have work to do and shouldn't be wasting your time with me." He turned to Bobbie then.

"However, this may be quite significant to your case. Much more significant than hounding my friends." He shot a look at Devine when he said this.

Bobbie looked from her partner to Hanover. "We appreciate your cooperation, Mr. Hanover."

"Very well." Hanover turned to the large-screen computer on his credenza and typed a few keys. "This is my security system. My technician was here late yesterday to adjust a glitch and he found a clip I had missed entirely."

As Bobbie watched the live feed on Hanover's backyard sped backward until he reached September 29 and stopped. The break-in had been reported around that time.

"I believe this is the man who broke into my home and took my dagger."

He hit Play and the darkness on the screen turned to light. The camera angle was from the roofline looking down on the rear yard. The time stamp read September 30, 6:00 a.m. Bobbie felt herself leaning forward as an image stepped into view, his back to the camera. The person would have come out of one of the home's rear doors, crossed the veranda and stepped onto the grass, moving toward the back of the property. He was visible on the feed for maybe five seconds and then he was out of view.

"Do you have this area on any other camera?" Devine asked. "It's hardly useful and certainly not significant if we can't see the perpetrator's face."

"Unfortunately," Hanover said, "this is the only

camera that was working that morning. Another glitch. Even the best systems have them from time to time."

"Play it again," Bobbie said. As the image came on the screen once more, she watched carefully. Definitely male. His stride was confident. Dark jeans, jacket and sneakers. He wore a skullcap, black in color, pulled down over his ears and concealing his hair. *Why couldn't you look back just once?*

"Where were you on September 29 and 30?" Devine demanded.

Bobbie turned her attention to Hanover and waited for his answer.

"I was in New York as I frequently am. On business, of course," he added. "I'm certain that's in the report I filed."

"No one stays here when you're gone?" Bobbie asked. Made sense to her that he would want someone taking care of his property.

"No, no. My staff comes in at eight. With the elaborate security system I have, I never imagined I needed the house guarded day and night." He shook his head. "I'm stunned he was able to slip past the security system."

"Does your system keep a log of the time and codes used to disarm it?"

Bobbie had to give Devine credit, his tone had evened out and he was asking the right questions.

"It does," Hanover said. "Whoever came in that morning used the access code. I can only assume he possessed some sort of code breaking electronic device. My technician tells me such devices exist."

"Have you shared the code?" Bobbie doubted an amateur would have been able to crack such an elaborate system and surely a professional would have taken more than one dagger. Not to mention all the other marketable goods lying around this house. Not even an amateur would take only one knife unless it was for a specific purpose...*like setting someone up.*

"I regret to say that I have shared it on occasion." Hanover sighed as he folded his hands on top of his desk. "Most recently with my two latest lovers, both of whom assure me they told no one."

"What about your staff?" Bobbie asked. Certainly they had the access code. He'd just said they came on at eight and he wasn't home on the dates in question.

"They do," Hanover allowed, "but I trust my staff with my life. If anyone shared the code it was one of my *friends*."

"Why haven't you changed the code?" Devine asked, his tone returning to one of utter impatience.

He and Bobbie really were going to have to talk.

"I should have." Hanover turned his hands up. "Rest assured, it was changed after the dagger went missing."

"We'll need the names and contact information for your two friends." Bobbie stood. "Also, have your technician download that clip for me."

Hanover smiled, strangely pleased with the idea. "I'll have him do so today."

"Thank you." Bobbie reached a hand across his desk. "We appreciate the call. You never know when a single detail might break a case."

Hanover shook her hand, held it a moment longer than necessary. "I almost forgot." He released her then and reached into the middle drawer of his elegant desk.

Bobbie looked to Devine who was staring at her curiously. She shrugged.

"Remember I told you I knew your mother." Hanover passed her a large envelope, the kind used to mail standard-size letters without folding them. "I found these photos and thought you might want them."

Bobbie accepted the envelope, her pulse racing at the mention of her mother's name. She'd worked hard to dismiss his odd insistence that he knew her mother. It shouldn't have bothered her. Her mother had been born and raised in Montgomery County. If she were still alive she would be around the same age as Hanover. It was far more likely that they knew each other than not.

"Thank you." She would not look at the photos or pursue the subject with Devine staring at her. She could feel his scrutiny, sensed the barrage of questions he would launch when they got in his car.

Hanover showed them to the door, he kept a running monologue going but Bobbie hardly heard a word he said. The envelope held her full attention. She tried to rationalize her overreaction to the package...to the man. It wasn't the concept that he had known her mother that got under her skin, it was the subtle insinuation in his tone when he spoke of her mother that bothered Bobbie.

Once they reached the sidewalk, she set her personal feelings aside and asked her partner, "What was he talking about when he mentioned hounding his friends?" Better to keep the conversation on the investigation rather than give Devine the opportunity to dissect Hanover's alleged relationship with her mother.

"Bauer and I questioned a few of his close friends." He paused at the driver's side of his Porsche. "We may have been a little more aggressive than necessary with certain ones."

Bobbie exhaled a lungful of frustration as she settled into the passenger seat. Bauer knew better. Her partner should, as well. "That's never a good idea, Devine."

He grunted what he apparently considered a response.

To his credit, he held questions she knew would be coming until they had driven away. "Your mother knew Hanover? Have *you* met him before?"

"He says he knew my mother." She had no intention of discussing the subject with him. "I met him for the first time when we came to interview him about the Parker murders."

"Strange."

"Your aunt doesn't know him?" she challenged. "If she grew up here, chances are they've met."

"She's never mentioned him." He stared straight ahead. "You said you hadn't met him before and you grew up here."

Bobbie didn't bother arguing that the man was far older than her and she wasn't rich like his aunt and Hanover. Instead she stared straight ahead while he drove. The silence grew suffocating. No matter how hard she tried to move past the idea, she couldn't. Finally she said, "Hanover clearly wants me to think he knows you. Why do you suppose that is?"

"You think if I knew him I wouldn't have mentioned it already?" He answered without answering at all and without so much as a glance in her direction. "You've asked three times already."

"I noticed the tension between the two of you yesterday, then again just now."

Devine tugged at his tie. "I try to be accepting," he admitted, "but the truth is I'm a little more homophobic than I care to admit. The way that guy looks at me makes me want to get as far away from him as possible."

"He probably does it on purpose just to make you sweat." A high-level businessman like Hanover would know how to make anyone he perceived as an adversary or a challenger uncomfortable.

Devine scrubbed a hand over his face. "He did a hell of a job and all for nothing. That damned security clip was a joke. What kind of system is set up to capture the back of anyone leaving?"

Bobbie agreed with him there. She thought of the dark clothes, the hat. Other than parts of his hands, nothing identifiable about the intruder was exposed on the video. Maybe Andy could blow up the image and find something. Andy Keller was a damned good evidence tech. If there was something to be found on the clip, he would find it.

"What's the next address?" Devine asked.

Bobbie set the envelope aside and pulled out her notepad to check her list. They had a lot of second interviews to do. No matter that they'd narrowed down the list considerably, there were still a hell of a lot of names. Business associates of the Parkers were listed first, friends and family next. If Weller had set these murders in motion, every step they had taken so far was irrelevant.

A person never knew what or who would be the end of him.

She wondered how many times Weller had considered that his own son had been his downfall. Bobbie could imagine how many times Nick had wished he'd killed the son of a bitch.

There were some sins that couldn't be forgiven.

Fifteen

"You're sure he isn't home?" Asher asked. He had no desire to piss the guy off. The bastard would only take it out on his wife and then Asher would have to kick his ass.

"Tricia saw him leave for work," Holt said. "Let's go."

They had enough on their plate already. Taking on the situation with Holt's neighbors was something they really didn't have the authority or the time to do right now. But Asher couldn't say no when Holt asked. He climbed out of his Mustang and met Holt in front of the vehicle. Since she'd been at home when she called, he'd driven by and picked her up. The Sheltons lived a couple houses down from her. Holt and her wife heard them arguing all the time.

"So—" Asher walked up the sidewalk next to his sergeant "—since Tricia had the baby I guess that makes you the husband. Does that mean you're usually the one on top when you have sex?"

Holt shot him a look. "Fuck you, Bauer."

"No, really." He kept time with her movements as they climbed the steps to the porch. "I'm just trying to wrap my head around the relationship." He'd been giving Holt a hard time about her being gay since she and Tricia married. She had to know he was kidding around. Hell, he'd attended their wedding and bought their baby a hell of a gift card from Babies "R" Us.

Holt ignored his question and knocked on the door. While they waited for the lady of the house to answer, she glanced at him and muttered, "Ass-hole."

Asher grinned. "But you love me anyway."

Holt grunted a noncommittal response.

They both came to attention when the double dead bolts on the door snapped. The rattle of the security chain was next. All that to keep the bad guys out, when the real bad guy lived inside. Asher shook his head.

The door opened a narrow crack. "What do you want?"

The wife, Olivia. She sounded as small and afraid as she did each time they came to visit her. This time was different, though. None of the neighbors had called the police after hearing her scream or the asshole she'd married shouting profanities at her. This was the first time the baby who lived here wasn't crying at the top of her lungs. This time was off the record.

"We know he left for work," Holt said. "We'd like to talk to you for a few minutes."

"The baby's sleeping," Olivia Shelton said, her voice shaking. "We're fine. I don't know who called you, but we're fine. Y'all need to stop bothering us."

"Let us come in and see for ourselves, Olivia, and we'll be on our way," Holt said, taking another tactic.

Shelton hesitated for a long moment, and then she relented. "Just don't wake the baby." She pulled the door open wider, staying in the shadows behind it.

Inside was dark. The blinds on the windows were drawn tight. The only light was in the hall that led to the three bedrooms. The smell of sausage and biscuits lingered in the air. Shelton had probably been up since dawn cooking and cleaning for the piece of shit grease monkey she'd married.

"What do you want?"

"We need you to turn on a light," Holt insisted. "We can't do this in the dark."

It wasn't completely dark, but damned close. Asher could make out the woman's outline as she moved across the room and turned on a lamp. The dim glow did little to light up the room but it gave a clear picture of Shelton's face before she could move away. Both eyes were swollen practically shut. Her lip was busted and turned inside out. Cheek was bruised.

Fury rushed through him. He wanted to kick

her no-good husband's ass. "When did he do this to you?"

She jumped. He hadn't meant for the words to come out in a growl.

Holt held out a hand. "We're here to help, Olivia. You're not helping yourself or your child by protecting him."

The damned woman refused to file charges against the bastard or to get a restraining order. She swore her blacked eyes and bruised face were her fault. She fell or walked into a door. Asher bit his lips together and kept his fists balled at his sides when he wanted to rail at her for being such a fool.

"He's not a bad person."

Asher rolled his eyes. What the fuck? "Will he be a bad person when you're lying dead on the floor?"

She flinched.

Holt shot him a look.

He ignored her. "Listen to me," he said to Shelton. "He's going to kill you. That's what guys like him do. You might not die today or tomorrow, but he will kill you. Could be as sudden as him slamming your head into something or could be as slow as breaking your nose and a few ribs, smashing your face over and over while you die a little bit more on the inside every day. Is that what you want for your daughter?" Asher nodded when she only stood there staring at him, her skinny bruised arms hugged around her body. "She'll grow up seeing this and believe it's normal. The next thing you know she'll marry some guy who'll do the same thing to her. Is that really what you want?"

Silence swelled in the room, growing bigger and bigger with each passing second. When another ten seconds elapsed and she didn't say a word he shook his head. It was bad enough for the woman to live in this nightmare, but it was just plain fucking sickening for her to wish it on her kid.

"How can I stop him?"

Asher's head came up. He and Holt shared a look.

"First," Holt said, "we need you to take out a restraining order so he has to stay away from you and the baby. You should also press charges. Our hands are tied unless you take action."

"They won't try to take my baby from me?"

Asher wouldn't touch that one.

"The truth is, Olivia," Holt explained, "if you don't do something they're more likely to take your baby to protect her."

"What do you mean?" Shelton drew back a step, her entire body trembling now.

"Police officers have an obligation to report these incidents to Child Services," Holt said. "How many times has someone from Child Services been here already? It's only a matter of time before they decide your decision to continue living in a home with an abusive man is a danger to your child."

Tears spilled down her pale, bruised cheeks. "I told 'em I would never let him touch her."

Asher restrained his frustration and went for the gentlest tone he could summon. "You won't be able to stop him from hurting her any more than you can stop him from hurting you."

"If I get a restraining order or press charges he'll kill me," she whispered, her voice desperate.

The three of them stood there in the crushing quiet once more. The woman wasn't going to do the right thing. She was too afraid.

"Let us take you and the baby to a family shelter," Holt offered. "Pack a few things and we'll take you there right now. Then you can get a restraining order and go from there."

Shelton looked from one to the other. "I…I can't."

The finality in her words reverberated in the silence that followed. There was nothing else they could do. Not legally, anyway.

"I need to see the baby," Holt said, resignation settling in her tone. "You know the routine. I have to confirm she's unharmed."

Asher waited in the living room while Holt followed Shelton down the hall. Guys like Wesley Shelton should be dragged into the street and publicly beaten to death. How could a guy treat any woman—especially the woman he supposedly loved—like this? Sick bastard. One of these days he would get his. Asher just hoped he was around to see it.

Once Holt confirmed the baby was okay, she tried one last time to talk Shelton into going to a family shelter. She refused.

As they exited the dark house, the sun made Asher squint. The need for a drink nudged him

Debra Webb

but he pushed it away. He wasn't going to fuck up his life with alcohol anymore. If he stayed on that doomed path he would be just as hopeless as Olivia Shelton.

"I was impressed by what you said to her," Holt said as she settled into the passenger seat of his Mustang. "I've told her that before, but she didn't listen. I'm hoping this time will be different."

"She just needs to kill the son of a bitch and be done with it."

Holt fired him a look. "I'm glad you didn't say that kind of shit in there."

Asher shrugged. "It's the truth. You know he won't stop until one or the other is dead. Have you ever seen one of these cases end any other way?"

Holt didn't answer. Instead, she put through the call to Child Services for a follow-up visit to the Shelton home. Didn't matter if she answered him or not. She knew he was right. You take a man that obsessed with a woman and that filled with violence, he wasn't going to change.

Asher hoped Olivia Shelton realized that sad fact before it was too late.

Sixteen

Chief of Police Ted Peterson parked in front of the house that had been his home for more than half his life. He'd brought his young bride here forty years ago—they'd share life's joys and tears in this home. After her illness began he'd taken care of her here…until he was no longer capable of adequately providing for her needs.

This grand old historic house had been Sarah's dream home. She'd worked for years to restore it to its former glory. Though they hadn't been blessed with children of their own, that sad fact never stopped Sarah from hosting graduation parties, wedding showers, baby showers and too many other events to recall in this big old house. Now she was gone. He'd laid her to rest in the place she'd chosen before the Alzheimer's stole her from him completely. He'd ensured she was dressed in the pale pink two-piece suit she'd picked out when they were first married. Money had been so damned tight but she'd fallen in love with the suit that was reminiscent of her favorite first lady's style and he would have sold his soul to buy it for her. The matching gloves and shoes completed the ensemble that had been her favorite. She'd worn that dainty hat and those elegant wrist-length gloves to church once a year, to celebrate their anniversary, every single year of their life together. The pink suit she'd worn only on very special occasions, like to Bobbie's wedding.

His sigh filled the emptiness in the car. Now it was time to sell the house to a new family. To others who would love and cherish the memories they built here as he and Sarah had. It was time, as his wife had told him on one of her rare lucid days, for him to move on and start making new memories.

Yesterday, Joanne, his Realtor and Sarah's sister, had posted the for sale sign. Ted's heart still felt heavy. It was the right thing to do. He was almost sixty-three. He no longer had the time or the desire to take care of this big old house and the three-quarter-acre yard.

It was time to let go.

Dorey's car pulled up behind his and Ted smiled. He watched as she exited her vehicle and strode toward his. His pulse sped up. She was so beautiful. They had worked together for years. As the commander of the Major Crimes Bureau, Lieutenant Eudora Owens was as tough as she was beautiful. Their affair had started from afar but many months passed before they became lovers. Those stolen moments had deepened into the kind of relationship he'd thought he would never again have.

She opened the passenger-side door and got in. "Sorry I'm a little late. So—" she gazed out at his home "—you listed the house."

Ted smiled, still feeling a little sad about the decision. "I did. Joanne says it will sell quickly. She's already had numerous calls."

Dorey searched his face, her smile understanding. "It's a lovely home. I'm not surprised at the interest."

The quiet settled around them as she fastened her seat belt. Ted started the engine and pulled away from the curb. He pushed the bittersweet past away and looked forward to the future.

"I close on the Lockwood Place town house next week." He rested his arm on the center console and tried to relax. The next subject he intended to broach was a sensitive one. He'd been waiting for the right moment to speak with her about *their* future. This morning he had decided he wasn't waiting any longer.

"I think you'll be very happy with your choice." She placed her hand on his. "It's a charming place. Manageable and comfortable."

He glanced at her and squeezed her hand. "I'm glad you like it."

"I love the outdoor fireplace. The courtyard is so private. I can imagine sitting by a roaring fire with a glass of wine." She nodded. "Very nice."

"If your calendar is clear next Saturday, you

could help me with the artwork choice the interior decorator has prepared."

The gesture was slow in coming, but she finally nodded. "I can do that."

"Good." His courage slipped a bit. God knew they had a lot on their plates at the moment. Three dead, two missing. But even cops had to eat. "I thought we'd have lunch downtown today."

"We can discuss the homicide and abduction cases." She shrugged. "Make it official business. Apparently Agent Hadden was just as in the dark about the things Weller said to Bobbie as we were."

No one was more annoyed at the news than Ted, but he didn't want to talk about any of that right now. Dorey, on the other hand, always looked for a proper explanation for their time together in public. He wanted that to change. *Now.* "I don't want to discuss business."

Her hesitation lasted far too long. His chest ached with insecurity. He was far too old to feel this uncertain in the presence of the woman he loved.

She shifted in her seat so she could look at him. "What're you saying, Ted?"

"I've decided to retire."

His heart stumbled as the words echoed in the car. He had been thinking about it for months now. He hadn't worked up the courage to take the necessary steps. It wasn't until this moment—when she came up with a legitimate excuse for their lunch—that he made the final decision.

"Are you certain that's what you want to do?"

Though her tone was firm, it wasn't about her

not being happy with his announcement. He knew Dorey too well. What she didn't want was for her happiness to be the compelling reason for his decision.

"I'm certain. I want to get on with my life. I can't do that and remain chief of police."

"I could transfer," she offered. "Sheriff Young could find something for me."

Dorey had made this offer before. He would not have her sacrifice her career for his. His career had reached its pinnacle and he could retire with the knowledge he had accomplished all he could possibly hope to. He had the necessary time in grade, he was set. Dorey, on the other hand, was still climbing. She was immensely intelligent and hardworking. Hell, she was still young, just fifty-two. She had earned the right to rise in her career in the years to come. She deserved the very best and he intended to see that she achieved her heart's desire, personally and professionally.

"Absolutely not." He shook his head to emphasize the words. "I'm ready to retire." The fact was he'd been ready for a while now. "I've made no secret that I'm considering that step. Stella says she's ready to do the same."

Stella Jernigan had been his administrative assistant since he took the office of chief. She had turned seventy this year. She swore she was only waiting on him to retire so she could. She claimed she couldn't trust anyone else to take proper care of him. Ted was lucky she'd stayed on all these years.

"Why don't we talk about it more tonight,"

Dorey suggested. "You should consider what you'll do next before making such a monumental decision."

Her insistence on playing devil's advocate irritated him. "I plan to fish and play golf and maybe a little volunteer work with troubled kids, but my primary focus will be on enjoying my life and my *wife*."

The catch in her breath sent a thrill through him. Though he'd suggested they should make their relationship official on numerous occasions, he had never formally asked her to marry him. He supposed today was as good a time as any.

"Ted," she said, her voice trembled just a little, "you buried your wife of forty years last month. You need to breathe a little before you decide to marry again. There are steps that need to be taken."

"I don't want a prenup." She'd mentioned that before, too. "What's mine is yours."

"You have Bobbie to think about," she argued. "She has always been like a daughter to you and to Sarah. Sarah would want you to ensure Bobbie benefited from the prosperity the two of you enjoyed during your marriage."

He didn't have an argument on that one. She was right. He hadn't stopped to consider the full implications of not taking certain legal steps before remarrying. Of course he wanted to contribute to the financial strength of Bobbie's future. God knew she was more alone in the world than he was. At least he had Dorey. Bobbie had no one. "I'll draw up a new will. That'll take care of Bobbie."

His goddaughter would be the first one to say she wanted no part of his estate. She was fine. James had left her well cared for. That was her stock answer for every damned thing. The ache in his chest deepened. For the past forty-eight hours he'd struggled with not posting another surveillance detail on Bobbie. She reminded him often that she could take care of herself, that she should never be treated any differently than any other cop in the department. More often than not Dorey backed her up. Then he'd learned that she'd left out a significant portion of her conversation with Randolph Weller. As had LeDoux. Ted had called the bastard first thing after Dorey gave him the news. LeDoux had insisted he hadn't been authorized to pass along that part of the conversation.

"I think drawing up a current will is a good idea," Dorey agreed, prompting his attention back to the present.

"What about marrying me?" He braked for the intersection and set his gaze on hers. "I'm serious, Dorey. I want you to be my wife."

"If you won't take some time," she reasoned, "then give me some."

"Are you saying you don't want to marry me?" He hadn't intended for the words to sound so harsh.

A horn blasted behind them.

"The light's green, Ted."

He clamped his jaw shut to hold back his frustration. Had he misread her? How could he have been so certain and be so wrong?

"I didn't say I didn't want to marry you," she

said, releasing his heart from a stranglehold. "I said I need some time to consider the plan you've made."

"Very well." His fingers tightened on the steering wheel. "My decision is made." He had spent the past two years watching his wife die a minute at a time. Last year he'd gone to a crime scene and identified the body of his goddaughter's husband as well as her child. Two months ago he'd buried one of his best detectives and dearest friends. Life was too short. He wasn't going to waste a single day of whatever time he had left. "I'm retiring at the end of the year."

If he was lucky, Dorey would agree to a wedding on some tropical island where the ugly things one human could do to another were someone else's problem.

Seventeen

Bobbie left Devine waiting in his car in her driveway. He usually stuck to her like glue, probably a
direct order from the chief. She'd used the excuse
that she needed to grab a tampon and he'd smiled
and said he'd wait in the car. Still, if she lingered
too long he might decide avoiding the awkwardness was not as scary as angering the chief. She
had to hurry.

In the spare bedroom she moved aside a couple
of boxes, finding the one she wanted. She sat down
on the floor and opened the box. Hanover's insinuations would not stop eating at her. She needed to see
if he was in any of the photographs from her parents' life before she was born. This particular box
held the family albums her mother and father had
created. There were five albums that predated her
mother's death and only two that came after. Her
father hadn't been quite as good at putting memories onto the pages. As a teenager she'd helped him

for a while, and then she'd gone off to college and the only photo albums were the ones on her laptop and cell phone.

She picked through the albums until she found the one that contained photos of her mom's life from high school through the first couple of years of marriage. Her parents had married the day after she graduated high school. Her father, being seven years older, had already finished college and the police academy. He wore his newly issued dress blues for their wedding.

Mary Jane Fleming had been beautiful. Both her father and the chief had always said Bobbie looked just like her mother. Not in Bobbie's opinion. Her mother was much prettier. Bobbie peered at the photos of her mother's friends from school. There were only a few group photos. Mary Jane never attended college. She always said she'd gone straight from her parents' home to her husband's. From solving calculus equations and writing essays to preparing dinner and eventually changing diapers. She'd sworn that it was the best decision she'd ever made. The memories made Bobbie's heart glad.

Her smile fading, she reached for the envelope Hanover had given her. She removed the four photos he had tucked inside. Her mother was pictured in each one, but none of her other friends were with her. The people in the photos were complete strangers to Bobbie. Looking at this piece of her mother's past made Bobbie oddly uncomfortable. She shoved the photos back into the envelope.

Was Hanover suggesting he and her mother had a more intimate relationship than that of mere acquaintances? Her mother appeared to be older in the photos. Her hairstyle had changed since her high school days. Bobbie reviewed the photos from her parents' first years of marriage. They'd been married almost five years before Bobbie was born. She decided those early years were the time frame in which the photos Hanover had given her were taken.

Why was her father not in any of the photos? Had Hanover taken the photos? He wasn't pictured in any of them, either.

She made herself look at them again. The group, four women and two men, weren't in a house or school. The place looked more like a club. One of the photos had captured part of what appeared to be a jukebox. She squinted to read a sign on the wall: Rusty Fiddle. Bobbie didn't recognize the name. Had her mother been going out with these people while her father worked? Her dad had told her many times that his working the night shift had made their marriage pretty miserable those first few years.

Bobbie packed the albums back into the box. She tossed the photos Hanover had given her on top. She knew Hanover's game. He was trying to unsettle her. As he had with Devine, he had succeeded.

The real question was why did an innocent man need to put them off balance?

There was only one answer.

Hanover was hiding something that might incriminate him.

A knock on her front door made her jump.

"Damn."

She'd lost all track of time. She got to her feet, straightened her jacket and adjusted her Glock. So what if her mom had known Hanover. That didn't mean anything. He was using the vague connection to throw Bobbie off her game. She had two missing women and at least one murderer to find.

Another knock on the door echoed as she reached it. She checked the viewfinder. *Devine.* She opened the door. "Sorry. It took longer than I expected."

"I don't mean to rush you," he apologized, "but the lieutenant says the Parker boy's aunt needs to see us as soon as possible."

Sage Parker was tucked away with a security detail at the Renaissance Hotel downtown. If they were lucky the boy had remembered something that would help their case. "Let's roll."

Bobbie set the security system and locked up. They could use a break and she damned sure needed something to take her mind off Hanover and his innuendoes. Maybe she would discuss his insinuations about her mother with Nick. Hanover hadn't stated they had a relationship and the pictures could have been taken by anyone, but it was in all the things he didn't say...the way he looked at Bobbie and the tone of his voice.

Mark Hanover wanted her to believe he knew something she didn't.

Renaissance Hotel
2:15 p.m.

Two FBI agents and one MPD officer, all females, waited outside the suite where Sage Parker and his aunt were sequestered. Chairs and a table had been provided for their comfort. The officer stepped forward as Bobbie and Devine approached.

"Ma'am," Officer Springer, according to her name tag, acknowledged Bobbie and then nodded to Devine. "Mrs. Lowery asked that you come in alone, Detective Gentry."

Bobbie glanced at Devine. "No problem." She had explained to her partner how the boy had reacted whenever a man came into his hospital room. Obviously that fear hadn't subsided.

Devine gave a nod. "Why don't I stand in for you, Springer, while you have a break."

One of the agents stepped forward. "I'll need to see your ID, Detective."

Bobbie showed her badge and while Devine and Springer chatted, she knocked on the door. Marla Lowery opened it and welcomed her inside. The living area of the suite was spacious and well appointed. A television inside an armoire was set to a channel that displayed the security detail outside the door.

"They wanted me to be able to see whatever was going on outside the door." She gestured to the television. "If I see anything that concerns me I'm supposed to call 9-1-1."

"Standard procedure. Try not to be overly concerned." Bobbie looked around, didn't see the boy.

"Any news about Fern?"

The hopeful expression on Marla's face made Bobbie wish she had better news. "Nothing yet, but we're doing all we can."

Marla nodded, her hopeful expression shifting to one of despair. "Agent Hadden said the same thing when he came by this morning."

Bobbie understood that time was moving incredibly slowly to Marla. Her family and home were in Nashville. Maybe they would catch a break today. "I was told Sage wanted to speak with me."

"He's in his room playing video games." Marla indicated the bedroom on the left. The suite had two, one on either side of the living area. "I've been talking to him and trying to help him see that the sooner we figure out who hurt his family, the sooner this person can be caught and his sister can be found."

Bobbie appreciated the aunt's efforts. "Has he remembered something?" They should be so lucky.

Marla made a face. "He won't tell me. He insisted he had to speak with you. I'll get him for you."

Bobbie sat down on the sofa while Marla spoke softly to the boy in the other room. The sound of his video game hushed and then the two of them joined Bobbie. Sage offered a quick smile and a vague wave.

Bobbie patted the sofa next to her. "Why don't you have a seat and tell me what you've been up to, Sage."

He glanced at his aunt. She picked up on the

cue. "I need to call my daughters and see how everything's going."

When she'd disappeared into the other bedroom, Sage looked up at Bobbie. "I dreamed about...*that* night."

Bobbie gave him a sad smile. "I'm sorry. I know this is really hard."

He stared at his hands, one of the game controllers still clasped there. "I miss them."

Bobbie resisted the urge to drape her arm around his shoulders. He might not appreciate the gesture. "I sure missed my mom after she died. I was about your age."

He exhaled a big breath. "How long does it last?" He looked up at her again.

"A while," she admitted. "I wish I could tell you it's fast, but it's not. At first it's really hard every day, all day."

"Nights are the worst," he said. "I can play my games and do my homework and not think about it in the daytime, but when I try to go to sleep it all comes back."

"Eventually, it won't hurt as much. You won't think about it as much." Bobbie was halfway through the next school year after her mother died when she realized she didn't think about her every minute of every day. That realization, too, had come with some measure of sadness. "You'll do other things. Make new memories."

He nodded. "I have to make all new friends. New teachers." He exhaled another big breath. "A new family with three more girls. One was bad enough."

Bobbie laughed. "I'll bet your sister is your hero."

He peeked up at her, his eyes glistening. "Sometimes."

"I know she can't wait to give you a big hug. She loves you. Your parents loved you very much. Never forget that."

He nodded, his face clouded with sadness.

"Did you remember something you wanted to tell me?"

Sage looked around the room as if he wanted to be sure no one was listening. His gaze stumbled on the television screen where Devine and the agents were standing around making small talk.

When the boy sat silently staring at the screen, Bobbie offered, "Would you like me to turn that off or close the door to your aunt's room?"

He shook his head, then stared up at Bobbie. "I saw the man."

Bobbie's heart thumped hard against her sternum. Was he talking about the dream? "When?"

"Not the first time when I heard him saying the bad words. *That night.* When my mom and dad…" He shrugged those skinny little shoulders. "I didn't want to tell you. I was afraid he'd find out I saw him and come back and get me. Like in that movie I watched with my sister. She said the witnesses get killed most of the time."

Bobbie nodded. "I won't lie to you and tell you that never happens, Sage."

His eyes grew even rounder.

"But," she added, "we're keeping you safe until we catch him so you don't have to be afraid. The truth is, you can help your sister by telling me the whole truth about that night."

He blew out a big breath. "I woke up. It was quiet so I figured everyone was asleep."

Bobbie held her breath and waited for him to continue.

"My parents weren't in their bed. I went to my sister's room and she wasn't in her bed, either."

"Did you go looking for them?"

He moved his head up and down. "It was dark upstairs, but I could hear the TV in the living room. I thought maybe they were watching a movie. Sometimes they watched movies real late, especially if it was one I wasn't supposed to see. I made it to the stairs and that's when I saw him."

"Where was he?"

"In the living room." He swallowed hard. "He was carrying my mom." He shrugged. "She was asleep or something."

Cold seeped deep into Bobbie's bones. "Did he see you?"

Sage shook his head. "He didn't look up."

"Did you see his face?"

"Not at first, he was wearing a mask." Sage turned the video game controller over in his hands. "He stopped for a minute. That's when he pulled off the mask and wiped his forehead like he was sweating or something. He almost dropped my mom doing it." Sage shuddered. "Before he went down the stairs he looked over at the back door and then at the front. I guess the siren outside surprised him or something."

"Siren?" Bobbie tensed. "You heard a siren outside?"

He nodded. "You know, the ambulance kind of siren. Like there was an accident or somebody sick."

"I know what you mean," she said hoping to urge him on.

"The man," he said, "he held real still until the sound went away. I couldn't move. I felt like I was frozen. I knew if he looked up he'd see me."

Bobbie forced in a breath. "Can you remember what he looked like?"

Another nod bobbed his head up and down.

Adrenaline ignited hard and swift. She needed a sketch artist right now. Bobbie reached for her phone. "I'm going to call someone to help us draw his picture."

Sage peered up at her, his eyes wide with worry and uncertainty. "I can show you what he looked like."

"Okay." Bobbie lowered her phone. She looked from Sage to the newspaper and magazines on the table. "Show me."

Rather than pick up one of the magazines or papers as she'd expected, he got up and walked across the room to the armoire that held the television. He pointed to the screen. "He looked like that."

Blood roaring in her ears, Bobbie pushed to her feet and made her way to where he stood. "Like what?"

He pointed again. "Like him."

Sage Parker pointed at her partner... *Steven Devine.*

Eighteen

His back to the wall, Nick watched a drop of sweat slide down the longneck bottle of beer. The dimly lit bar was packed. Then again, what had he expected on a Saturday night? Bodies were crammed against the bar and overflowing the booths lining the graffiti-filled brick walls. Nick had arrived early to claim a booth in the corner farthest from the entrance and the bar. The location wouldn't escape the noise but it was unquestionably private.

Most of the day he'd followed Bobbie around. When she'd returned to CID at four, he'd decided to meet the unexpected source who had contacted him. Nick was suspicious by nature, but the call had raised all sorts of red flags. At best, he could obtain a good deal of information in one fell swoop; at worst, he was wasting his time. Seemed like a decent risk to take. And, frankly, he was curious why the man would call him. He no doubt had a self-serving agenda. The question was whether or not his agenda would prove beneficial to Nick's own. The sooner the assassin sent to take Nick out was found, the sooner innocent people would stop dying. The part that bothered him the most was the two missing women. There was little he could do about the murder victims since they were dead before he arrived. But the two missing, there was still a chance he could save them.

A waitress arrived with two more beers like the one Nick was still nursing. "Your friend said he'd join you in a moment."

Nick scanned the crowd. No one broke from the swarm of bodies or even looked his way. The possibility that this was some sort of setup nudged his instincts. A bar stool turned and the man seated there stood. It wasn't until he met Nick's gaze that he was sure it was LeDoux. Apparently the special agent had arrived even before Nick. Half-empty beer bottle in one hand and a four- or five-inch stack of magazines in the other, he strolled over to the booth, bumping everyone he passed as if he'd had a few too many already. Tonight LeDoux was evidently incognito. He wore faded jeans, sneakers and a pullover sweater that was either from a local thrift store or was his longtime favorite, along with a baseball cap.

He plopped down in the booth and placed the magazines on the table. "Your beer is hot." He abandoned the empty bottle he'd been holding and reached for a fresh one.

Nick pushed his half-full bottle aside and picked up the cold one. "I didn't know you were a car buff." He gestured to the stack of hot-rod magazines.

"Everyone needs a hobby." He drew down a slug of beer, then slid the stack to Nick's side of the table. "Even a hunter like you."

"When did you get into town?" Nick kept his gaze on the man, looking for tells. He wasn't the least bit nervous, more resigned. He sat back in his seat, shoulders down, face impassive.

"As soon as I learned Bobbie had visited your old man."

Nick didn't give him the satisfaction of a reaction. "What do you want?"

They might as well get to the point. He preferred not to have Bobbie out of his sight for too long. He'd added tracking software to her phone. The best hacker on the planet had taught him how to break into any brand of smartphone. Occasionally it was the only way to accomplish the desired result.

"To help."

Nick laughed. "I don't mean to sound skeptical, but I am." He leaned forward. "Skeptical, that is." LeDoux had not been assigned to the Nigel Parker case or the abductions. The FBI was involved, yes, but not LeDoux. Nick didn't have the whole story since his source at the FBI was suddenly mum on the subject but something was going down with LeDoux. "What do you want?" he repeated.

LeDoux held his gaze. "I think Weller is up to something."

"You go to all this trouble—" he gestured to LeDoux's getup "—and you can't come up with something more original to say?" Of course the bastard was up to something.

"He's been keeping tabs on Bobbie." LeDoux downed another slug of his beer and then wiped his mouth with the sleeve of his sweater. "Did you know that?"

"Did you notice this before or after she paid him a visit?" Nick met his unflinching stare and asked what, in his opinion, was the bigger question, "What are *you* up to?"

The stare-off lasted another ten seconds. "Maybe the same thing as you," LeDoux confessed.

So Special Agent LeDoux was watching Bobbie, too. "How's the wife?"

This time LeDoux flinched. "My ex-wife is just fucking awesome. She's already engaged to a former friend of mine."

"That's too bad." Nick sipped his beer and decided to do a little digging. "Things must be slow in the BAU if you're in Montgomery without an assignment."

"Who says I'm not on assignment?" LeDoux waved down the waitress and ordered another beer.

He wouldn't meet Nick's gaze now, which was telling enough. "Whatever the reason for your visit, I prefer to work alone."

"That might not be such a good idea this time." The waitress placed another beer in front of LeDoux. He thanked her. "Besides, you worked with Bobbie."

And he hadn't been able to get her out of his head since. "She gave me no choice."

Bobbie Gentry had proven to be the most stubborn woman Nick had ever met. No matter that she'd lost everything, she'd refused to give up on finding the bastard who'd stolen her life.

"I can keep the Bureau off your back."

The statement surprised Nick. He knew the feds watched him. They had since he turned in his father. They'd never given him any reason to be concerned or taken any steps to prevent him from going after the next name on his list—until the Storyteller. Now, for some reason, he was under new scrutiny.

"Why would you do that?"

"Because I believe in what you're doing." This time LeDoux looked straight at Nick when he said the words.

"Isn't what I do undermining your job security?" After all, Nick accomplished the same goal at a meager fraction of the cost.

"That doesn't matter to me."

LeDoux looked away again. The words had sprung from bitterness. Somehow the agent had become disillusioned with the job. It happened. FBI agents, especially profilers, were like doctors: they had enormously high divorce and burnout rates. But why his sudden appearance in Montgomery? And why keep an eye on Bobbie—unless it was a personal interest?

"I'm afraid," Nick warned, "you'll have to convince me this arrangement would be mutually advantageous."

"Before you make up your mind—" LeDoux

tapped the magazines "—a little reading material you might find interesting."

Nick pulled a couple of bills from his pocket and tossed them on the table. He stood and picked up the stack of magazines. "I'll be in touch."

He melded into the crowd, zigzagging through the throng of bodies until he reached the front entrance. His grip tightened on the magazines as he surveyed the street. He wasn't entirely convinced this meeting wasn't a setup.

When he reached his truck without incident, he climbed in and locked the door. Rather than have a look at what LeDoux had given him, he drove away from the crowd and the lights of the city. He wound around until he was certain no one had followed him, and then he drove to Bobbie's neighborhood. He rolled into the carport of the house two streets over from hers. The house was deserted and the carport looked shaky at best, but it kept his vehicle out of sight.

Before getting out, he turned on the flashlight on his phone and flipped through the pages of the magazines, one by one. A smile tugged at his lips as he shook his head. Case reports had been slipped between the pages. Each one roughly outlined Nick's involvement in the takedown of a serial killer. The reports dated as far back as nine years but many were missing. These reports, he suddenly realized, only covered the hunts where the target chose to take his life rather than face justice. No question the FBI was building a case against him. It wouldn't be difficult for the reports to be altered to indicate the targets that had opted for suicide had been murdered instead.

At the bottom of each report the sources used to compile the data were listed. One name stood out on each page.

Randolph Weller.

All this time the FBI had been following Nick's work, he'd assumed it had been about him being Weller's son. He had been wrong. It had been about feeding Weller's sadistic need to monitor his activities. What else had the FBI given him to keep their pet monster satisfied?

Nick gathered the magazines along with his backpack that contained the material he had already collected and made his way through the dark yards until he reached Bobbie's. He unlocked her backdoor and D-Boy greeted him. Nick silenced the alarm and locked the door. He needed to build his case map.

The second bedroom was empty save a few boxes. He set his materials aside and arranged the boxes like a table in the far corner of the room. He separated his materials into individual stacks and then he began. He taped each report and photograph on the wall, building a history for each victim.

Each step took him on a journey—like a map—into the life of a victim.

The more he knew about the victims the better he would understand the killer.

Nineteen

They sat in her driveway saying nothing for a good ten minutes.

"It feels like everyone is looking at me differently now."

Bobbie turned to her partner. "He was trying to explain what the killer looked like the best way a ten-year-old can. You were the only male around. You have dark hair like the man he saw carrying his mom. You probably have a similar build. This is good. Now we know we're looking for a Caucasian about your size and age with dark hair. This could provide the break we need to find Fern and Vanessa alive."

"The way he looked at me." Devine shook his head, the movement barely visible in the dark. "When you opened that door, he was terrified that I might come in the room."

"He would have been terrified of any male coming in the room," she reminded him. "He's scared and confused. His whole life has been stolen from him."

Bobbie knew a little something about how that felt. The pain that accompanied the memories of her lost life was different now, duller, deeper, but it was still there. Like she told the Parker boy, it would take time for the worst to pass.

"Bauer and Holt." Devine heaved a big breath. "They were just beginning to be friendly, like I was a real member of the team."

"That's about Newt." Bobbie had experienced those feelings in the beginning. She felt guilty about liking or respecting Devine. It was as if she had accepted that Newt could be replaced so effortlessly. "Losing him is still so new. Watching you step into his place and do a good job is difficult. Embracing you is like we've forgotten him." She met Devine's gaze, hoping he could see the smile on her face. "You've made it too easy to like you. Being a damned good cop doesn't hurt, either."

"I appreciate you saying so, Bobbie."

"Enough already. No one believes Sage Parker saw *you* in his house. Think about it, now we not only have a general description of our killer, we also learned about the accident EMS responded to just before midnight on Wednesday. That helps narrow down the time frame the killer was in the house." She reached for the door. "It's all good. Now go home. You'll feel better tomorrow."

"Would you like me to walk you to the door?"

Bobbie laughed. "I know you didn't just ask me that."

"It's late." He shrugged, looking away. "My parents raised me to be a gentleman."

"I'll be fine." Bobbie got out. "Good night, Devine."

He called good-night to her as she closed the door. Before she reached the hood he'd already started the engine and turned on the lights, giving her a well-lit path. She unlocked and opened the door, the absence of the security system's warning told her Nick was already here. D-Boy bounded to the door to greet her. She locked up and gave his head a rub.

She tossed the small leather shoulder bag she carried onto the sofa and went in search of Nick. He wasn't in the kitchen. As she moved toward the hall she spotted the light on in the spare bedroom. Her pulse reacted to the anticipation that seared through her veins. Nick was here and she was responding to his presence as if he were a potential lover rather than a resource on this baffling case. *Just plain dumb, Bobbie.*

He looked up from his work when she paused at the door. "You're home."

No matter that she knew he didn't mean *home* in its usual sense, his announcement tugged at her on a very basic level. She resisted the impulse to shake her head. Where was her mind?

"I am." She surveyed the room. The boxes she'd stacked haphazardly now sat neatly on one side of the room.

Her gaze swept over the wall where he'd created his case map and her breath stilled in her lungs. Like the one he'd built in his room at the Economy

Inn two months ago, photos and reports lined the wall. He'd started with the Parkers and all he had found on the family as well as names and background info on anyone who might have motive to commit the murders and abduct their daughter. Next up were Slade Manning and Vanessa Olson. Bobbie crossed the room, again stunned at the depth of the information he had collected. His case board, or *map* as he called it, was considerably more comprehensive than the one she and Holt had built.

She turned to him. "Will it do me any good to ask how you got your hands on these?" She indicated an FBI report and then another and another. "I would think by now you know you can trust me enough to share."

"I don't reveal my sources." He taped a final document on the wall near the Parker collage. "You've been looking for this."

Bobbie moved closer and had a look. It was tox screen results. Both Heather and Nigel Parker were positive for fentanyl. "Where did this come from?"

"The feds stepped in and put a rush on the results. Your department should have it tomorrow. Since the feds have no interest in Manning, his results aren't in, but we can safely assume the same will be found."

She shook her head. "You're not going to tell me who gave this to you, either." It wasn't a question. She knew he wouldn't. Nick Shade had not found and stopped dozens of serial killers by operating fast and loose. He had rules and he never deviated.

Except with you, Bobbie. And even his small lapses with her were guarded.

He'd told her that he never allowed himself to get close to anyone. Yet, here he was in her home. She wasn't the only one who felt something growing between them. Maybe she would never know what that something was, but it was there. A single, fragile thread that tethered them by tragedy and loss… a lifeline in emptiness. It was need, she decided. The fundamental need all humans felt that neither of them, no matter how hard they tried, could deny.

Rather than answer her, he stepped closer and her foolish pulse reacted. "You're tired."

She was. It had been a long day. "I didn't tell anyone you're here, but I did brief the lieutenant about Weller's warning."

"You did what you had to do."

Frustration edged into the weariness already overwhelming her. It annoyed her to no end that she was having trouble quantifying their *relationship* or whatever this was. Particularly when they were alone like this. "Where's your truck? I don't even know where you park. I come home and you're just here."

The irritation in her voice made her cringe. She was ready for this day to end. Between Hanover jerking her chain and Sage Parker throwing her partner for a loop, she was ready to shut off her brain for a few hours.

"A couple of streets over. There's an abandoned house with a carport."

She gave herself a mental kick in the ass. "I

know the place." She had no right to take out her frustrations on Nick. None of this was his fault.

Shifting her attention back to the case, she considered the photo of Hanover. "I don't think he's our killer." She moved to the far side of the wall and studied what was obviously Hanover's professional bio pic probably found a dozen places on the internet. "He's far too self-absorbed to put himself at risk for a kill that wasn't essential to his survival."

"This is the face he wants you to see," Nick said. "You might not recognize the face he shows others."

This was true. She told Nick about the useless video clip he'd insisted she and Devine see. "Why draw so much attention to himself?" She didn't want to talk about Hanover's references to her mother. Not yet. It felt too personal.

Bobbie almost laughed at the thought. Nick Shade had seen every inch of her scarred, damaged body. He knew her deepest, darkest secrets. Even if she wanted to, she couldn't possibly hide anything from him. It was only a matter of time until he knew exactly what Hanover was doing to her.

"He makes you uncomfortable."

See, Bobbie, you can't hide from him. "Apparently, he knew my mother."

"He's done his homework."

"What do you mean?"

"Everyone knows what happened to your husband and child. Hanover wanted more shock value than that common knowledge would convey so he went deeper into your background looking for another tender spot."

"Apparently he did know her." Bobbie went to the boxes and found the one she needed. She passed the envelope to Nick. "I'm sure you'll recognize my mother."

She watched his hands as she removed the photos. The memory of those hands moving so tenderly and chastely over her body made her look away.

"You look like her. Exactly like her."

Bobbie cleared her throat. "That's what my dad always said."

"Do you know where this photo was taken?" He turned the one with the jukebox around for her to see.

She shook her head. "I thought I'd ask Uncle— the chief. He might remember where the photos were taken."

He passed the photos back to her, their fingers brushed. "Hanover's not in the photos. He could have gotten them anywhere solely for the purpose of making you uncomfortable. This doesn't mean he knew her the way he appears to want you to believe."

Bobbie returned the photos to the box. "You're right. I'm letting him get to me for no reason. He's doing the same thing to Devine."

"Never trust a man who uses the past to lead you in a different direction."

Bobbie smiled. "Good advice."

Nick moved closer to her. He reached out and tucked a wisp of hair behind her ear. "He's playing a game on the backs of the victims in this case. A man who'll do that is capable of ugly things, no matter the face he shows you."

They stood staring at each other for a minute or more after he stopped speaking. She wanted to touch him. To feel the strength of his arms around her. There were things she wanted to say. To ask. But it was late. She was tired. Being tired made her vulnerable.

Still, there was one question she couldn't deny. "What face are you showing me?"

He didn't answer for what felt like another minute. He reached for her hand, placed it against his jaw. His skin felt hot. The hint of beard stubble set her fingers on fire. "The one you want to see."

And there it was. The elephant in the room. He would never allow her to know him completely. His self-preservation instincts were far too strong. He would not risk the pain of opening himself up to her or to anyone else. His father's betrayal had wounded him far too deeply. She was no better. Beyond her medical needs, no one had touched her in almost a year—no one but Nick Shade, and his touch had been about helping her through tragedy and nothing more.

They were two damaged people frantically attempting to survive without suffering further injury.

An impossible goal.

For one endless moment she wanted to draw away and then she understood that was exactly what he wanted her to do. He would never dare to touch her this way or have her touch him except to push her away.

Instead of pulling back, she said, "Show me more."

He held utterly still for two beats and then he tunneled his fingers into her hair and kissed her. His lips were softer than she'd expected but the rest of him was as hard as stone. By the time he released her she was gasping for air.

"Careful what you ask for, Bobbie."

She tucked her trembling hands under her arms. "I'll bear that in mind in the future."

"If you want an apology—"

"I don't." She steadied herself. "I'm glad you kissed me. I…" She licked her lips, savored the taste of him. "We should do that again sometime."

He held her gaze a moment as if he might say something, but then he looked away.

"So." She turned to his case map. "If Hanover isn't our killer. Then who?" She cleared her throat and moved closer to the wall of information. *Get your act together, Bobbie.* She tapped the photo of Sage. "He saw the killer." She set her hands on her hips and mulled over all that Sage had told her. "He said the man looked like my new partner. Devine's all torn up about it."

Nick joined her, keeping a safe distance. "You said Hanover makes Devine uncomfortable?"

Bobbie nodded. "I think he's flirting with Devine. It makes him furious. Hanover is a real piece of work." She stared at the photo of Sage again. The boy desperately needed something good to happen.

Please let us find his sister alive. "Devine is rattled. I wouldn't be surprised if he decided he wanted to go back to Birmingham after this. I don't think he's accustomed to being doubted."

She bit her lip, wishing she could just go to bed instead of trying to figure out this crazy puzzle and the man. But this puzzle was the reason Nick was here. The other—the kiss—was nothing more than a way to relieve the pressure from this building attraction or whatever it was. Stressful situations did that sometimes. Normal human reaction.

"Hanover has basically the same build as Devine," Nick noted. "Dark hair. The boy may not have noticed the scattering of gray. It's possible he's the man he saw. Why do you believe Hanover isn't the killer?"

"Besides having an alibi?" Hanover's assistant had happily explained that the two of them had worked until well after midnight both Wednesday and Thursday. "He's too cocky. As if he wants us to suspect him. The idea of it thrills him."

"He's toying with you. Pulling your strings, watching you react. Your initial instinct is probably right."

Which meant they still had nothing except a vague description that could fit a large portion of the city's male population.

Twenty

The doorbell chimed, the Westminster notes resonating through the cavernous entry hall.

Mark Hanover stalled in his retreat toward the stairs. A frown furrowed his brow. An unexpected guest at this hour could only mean misfortune. If there was an abrupt drop or gain in the Asian stock market he would have received notification. The European market was hardly worth worrying about these days and the US market grew more volatile every day.

Perhaps luck was with him tonight and his ex-wife had run off to Vegas to wed her latest lover. The sooner she was married again or dead—either would be quite acceptable to him—the sooner she would stop running through his money. He despised the contemptible bitch. The only thing he loathed more than her was the alimony he was forced to pay. He should have taken care of her already.

Then again, perhaps he had. He'd paid her latest boy toy a small fortune to keep her distracted. A wedding contract came with a sizable bonus.

Mark checked the small monitor next to the front door. *Steven Devine*. He smiled. He'd wondered when this moment would come. Frankly he was surprised Bobbie Gentry wasn't with him. Steven stood on the other side of the door, the landscape lighting illuminating the anger and frustration radiating from every delicious inch of him.

Mark hesitated only a moment before disarming the security system and unlocking the door. Since he had nothing to hide from the handsome detective, the fact that he was ready for bed was of no significance. He drew the door open. "Well, well, what have we here?"

Devine took one look at him and turned his head.

Mark smiled. He always slept naked. After a rigorous workout each night he showered and didn't bother with clothes until he readied to go into the office. Annoyed the hell out of his ex-wife. Apparently his unexpected visitor wasn't pleased about it, either. "If you're planning to come inside, I'll find a robe if that makes you more comfortable."

Devine still refused to meet his gaze. "I'll wait here until you do."

"Very well." Mark turned his back and started for the staircase once more. He took his own good time. When he reached the landing his penis was fully erect. He wasn't ashamed of his aging body. He went to great lengths to keep himself fit. Not one lover had ever complained about his physique. As for sexual prowess, Mark had never been better.

He walked across his bedroom and into the closet. He fingered through the choice of silk robes until he found the one he wanted. He donned the exquisite royal blue robe and made his way back downstairs, anticipation sizzling along his nerve endings. Steven Devine had grown into quite a handsome man. But then, Mark had known he would. His gaze rested on the other man's as he descended the final step. His mouth was as perfectly shaped, his lips as lush as ever.

The detective, still dressed in his sharp suit, stepped into the foyer and closed the door behind him. His stare was menacing. The blue of his eyes burning through Mark like laser beams. He shivered with delight.

"I don't know what you think you're doing," Steven said, his voice a low growl, the sound making Mark even hornier, "but it won't work."

Mark laughed softly. "It appears it has already worked." The French clock he'd found years ago in a little place in Avignon began its deep resounding count of the midnight hour. "You're here, aren't you?"

Steven sprang like a panther, shoving Mark into the nearest wall and moving in so close he could feel the anger humming through the younger man's body. "I will not let you get away with this."

Mark's heart raced with the deep growl of his voice and the underlying threat of physical harm. "How could you possibly hope to stop me?"

The muzzle of his weapon was suddenly shoved against the soft underside of Mark's chin. He shuddered with the excitement of it, his cock throbbed against the silk fabric of his robe, nudging the other man.

"You ruined my childhood," Steven warned. "You will not ruin this."

"I gave you what you wanted," Mark whispered, his mouth yearning to taste the saltiness of his skin, the sweetness of his tongue. He was ready to explode with need.

Steven encircled his throat with the long fingers of one hand. "You raped a child, you son of a bitch."

Mark closed his eyes, remembering how tight Steven had been. He drew in a deep breath, smelling the last traces of the cologne Steven had applied that morning. Dear God, he could eat him alive. "When did you ever complain?"

Steven's handsome face was twisted with the fury coursing through his lean body. Mark had never wanted to fuck anyone as much as he wanted to fuck Steven right now.

"She sees what you're doing," Steven cautioned. "And we are going to get you."

Mark laughed, loving this more than he ever imagined possible. "You don't scare me. I will never be caught and you're not going to be the knight in shining armor who charges in and changes that fact. I'm untouchable. I always have been."

"You're interfering with an official investigation," he said through gritted teeth. "She'll back me up. Wait and see."

"She," Mark said, "is as helpless as you are. I could destroy you with one simple phone call."

Some of the anger drained from his face. Mark smiled. Oh, yes. This was worth whatever the cost…whatever the risk.

Steven drew back, lowered his weapon and visibly attempted to calm himself. "This is your final warning, back off."

Mark laughed long and deep as Steven stormed out the door. He wasn't concerned in the least about the spitfire who'd worked so hard all these years to turn himself into a well-respected detective who fought crime and sought justice for the innocent.

Mark knew his deepest, darkest secrets.

Twenty-One

Atlanta Federal Prison
Sunday, October 23, 9:15 a.m.

"Turn the cameras off."

The guard named Malcolm appeared startled by the request. "Agent LeDoux, you know we're not supposed to do that unless Mr. Zacharias visits him. The warden—"

Tony leaned closer to the man. "Unless you want the warden to know about your arrangement with Shade, you should do exactly as I say."

Malcolm's eyes widened. "I...don't know what you're talking about."

"You shouldn't use your personal cell phone if you want to keep your communications secret." Tony gave a half laugh. "Now turn off the video and the audio."

"Yes, sir." The guard went to the control box and did as Tony asked.

Malcolm unlocked and opened the door to the corridor leading to the interview room. The two guards who had escorted Weller there waited as per protocol. Tony opened the door between the two and entered the room where Weller waited. Behind him the swoosh of the door closing was followed by the definitive sound of the lock turning.

"My, my." Weller smiled. "So many visitors in one week. Aren't I the lucky one?"

Tony dragged out the lone chair on his side of the table and dropped into it. Weller was shackled per regulation. There was always something revitalizing about seeing psychopathic killers like him in chains. Personally Tony would much rather see them dead but this was the next best thing.

"I hear you're having trouble with the old ticker." Tony scrubbed at his chin, made a mental note to shave on the way back to Montgomery.

"They tell me I'll live," Weller assured him.

"That's too bad." Tony cleared his throat. "I met with your son last night."

Weller smiled, his evil eyes gleaming. "Is that so? How is my dear son?"

Tony allowed several seconds to pass before responding. He wanted the bastard to worry. Funny, he decided, how a man who ruthlessly murdered and butchered so many could worry about another human. Three or four times Tony had watched each interview in which Weller's son was mentioned. In each instance the bastard's expression and posture changed so subtlety it was nearly impossible to note. Unless you watched and watched and watched. This vicious monster had one Achilles' heel. In whatever way his black heart worked, he cared for his son.

How fucking unbelievable was that?

"He's determined to get himself killed just to prove he's nothing like you," Tony said bluntly. He'd figured out what drove Shade. "Frankly, I don't see how he stands the idea of who he is long enough to get up each morning. Maybe he'd be happier if he didn't."

The fury that lit in those fathomless eyes abruptly extinguished and a slow smile spread across his thin lips. "Watch yourself, Agent LeDoux, you're sounding more and more like the very *monsters* you profile. Oh, wait." He pursed his lips a moment. "That's right. You don't do that anymore, do you? You're being reassigned. Didn't you get the memo? Your erratic behavior has become a liability to the prestigious BAU. Perhaps you'll land in North Dakota or some other godforsaken place more suited to your skill level."

Tony kept his jaws clamped together for a full ten seconds before he dared to speak. "I guess that puts us in—" he shrugged "—a similar situation. You're stuck here—" he gestured to the room at large "—and I find myself at a not so happy place in my career. What I need is a big sensational splash to get my career back on track." He cocked his head and smiled at the bastard across the table. "I think I'm going to help your son prove you ordered the murders in Montgomery just to lure him into a trap. You know how badly the Bureau wants to prove he's not what he seems. I can make sure that effort fails."

"What a clever man you are, Tony." Weller's eyebrows hiked up. "Too bad your speculation is nothing more than exactly that—*speculation*."

Tony stood and leaned over the table, bracing his hands there and putting his face in the bastard's. "Or maybe I'll really fuck with you and see that your son is framed for those murders. Wouldn't that be a shame?"

Weller looked him straight in the eyes. "Watch yourself during this difficult time, Tony. We wouldn't want your superiors to find that you are more unstable than they think."

Tony drew back, turned and walked out.

There was no reason to worry that the guards stationed outside the door had heard anything, the room was basically soundproof. Still, before leaving he checked the video and audio to ensure Clinton had done as Tony directed. At this point he didn't trust any damned body. He paused as he passed Clinton. "You tell a soul about my visit and you'll be filing for unemployment."

Clinton said nothing as Tony walked away.

Tony should feel guilty for what he was doing, but he didn't. He felt nothing except the determination to prove he could do something no one else had been able to do. He'd watched how the game was played for too long not to understand there was only one way to survive in this world. Do whatever necessary to get the job done.

To hell with the rules. He knew exactly what he had to do no matter the cost.

Find and reveal the person inside the Bureau who allowed Randolph Weller to reach outside these prison walls.

Twenty-Two

"I know it's Sunday," Lieutenant Eudora Owens began, "and we'd all rather be someplace else like church."

Bauer laughed. "No point wasting a perfectly good Sunday morning in church when you're going to hell anyway."

The LT rolled her eyes.

"Speak for yourself, Bauer," Devine challenged, "the rest of us might have different plans."

Bobbie propped her head in her hand, mostly to cover a smile. It was good to see the team interacting the way they did before they lost Newt. He would never want the team to suffer because he was gone. *Miss you so much, Newt.*

Nick's kiss nudged its way into her thoughts. She wanted to regret the moment but somehow she couldn't. She had felt the urgency in his touch. Maybe they were both a little desperate for human touch.

Desperation is never a smart thing. Distraction was even more dangerous and definitely something neither of them could afford just now.

Clearing her mind, Bobbie fixed her attention on the case board as Owens reviewed what they had so far, which was not a hell of a lot. A sketch artist had worked with Sage Parker to develop an image of the man he'd seen. The sketch had been shared with the FBI and other departments as well as the media. Devine still dropped his head whenever the sketch was mentioned. He needed to deal with it. The sketch could be an important tool in the search for Fern Parker and Vanessa Olson—that was top priority. Not a single cop in the MPD was going to relax until those girls were found.

Next to Bobbie, Holt's chair squeaked with her shifting. She hadn't said much this morning. Bobbie wondered if baby Howie was sick or if she and Tricia were fighting again. A cop's life was complicated. Throw a newborn into the mix and things could be really tough. Bobbie made a mental note to remind Holt not to take a minute with the baby and her wife for granted. *It could all vanish in an instant.*

"Unfortunately," Owens was saying, "the bites our killer took from the hearts of Heather and Nigel Parker weren't clean enough to create an impression."

Though Bobbie had heard this news first thing this morning from Carroll, she groaned along with the rest of the team. She and Carroll had discussed at length all her findings, including her conclusions about the murder weapon.

"For now," Owens continued, "we've officially linked the Parker, Manning and Olson cases. The list of persons of interest continues to grow, but we have no true suspects. The tip line has given us nothing but leads that don't pan out. We need to find the connection among these victims. We need to find it fast, people. Our friends in the FBI are working equally diligently toward that end. The chief and I sat in on a briefing at eight this morning. They're still beating the bushes just as we are."

"Hanover's dagger may be the murder weapon we're looking for," Devine said. "Dr. Carroll believes the blade in the photo he provided is a match to the pattern left in the bodies of the Parker victims."

"That doesn't make him the murderer," Owens countered. "The FBI believes this is the work of a fledgling serial killer." Everyone in the room grumbled and she raised her hands to quiet their protest. "However, I don't agree. I believe the warning Weller shared with Bobbie is what set these murders in motion. If that proves the case, we're looking at a far more cunning foe here. A killer potentially sent by one or more of the most heinous serial killers alive today. The FBI insists this so-called Consortium does not exist. They believe Weller is playing some sort of twisted game with Bobbie and his son, Nick Shade. Whatever the case, we need to stay focused and watch our backs."

"Why isn't the FBI sitting in on this briefing?"

Bobbie had wondered from the moment she entered the room why no one had shown up other than their team. It wasn't like the feds to ignore a briefing.

"Since we're only going over the limited information we have," Owens explained, "I saw no reason to include God and everyone else in this briefing. We passed along what we had to share this morning."

As true as her statement was, Bobbie had been a part of this team too long not to understand that the LT's announcement was code for someone on the FBI's team had seriously pissed her off. She was generally a gung-ho team player.

Holt said, "Late last night I received a call from Manning's sister. She and the family forgot to mention a broken engagement with a woman the vic dated a couple of years ago. Bauer and I are interviewing her this afternoon."

"Two years is a long time to wait for vengeance," Bauer said, showing his skepticism about the lead.

"Follow every lead," Owens reminded, "no matter how seemingly unlikely. Taking into consideration Weller's possible involvement, the killer is probably someone none of the victims knew, but we have to go through the usual steps until we have reason to do this any differently."

When the killer learned Nick was in Montgomery, Bobbie figured going after him would be the next logical step. Nick kept his vehicle parked away from her house. He hadn't appeared at any of the crime scenes as he had the last time they'd worked together. But she knew better than to believe he was hiding. Whatever his strategy he wasn't ready to share it with her yet.

Considering the reports he'd posted on his case map last night one thing was abundantly clear: he had at least one high-level source in the FBI. Not to mention the numerous ones he had among killers and those who studied them. His life was even more engrossed in murder than hers. She wondered if he ever took a break. Where would a man like Nick Shade vacation? What would he do for a hobby?

When was the last time you took a vacation? Bobbie had no right to point fingers. Her last hobby had been finger painting back in kindergarten.

"Keep knocking on doors," Owens said. "A neighbor or maybe a visitor of one of the neighbors had to have seen something. These murders didn't happen in a vacuum. Find a connection between Fern Parker and Vanessa Olson. Their bodies haven't turned up, so we have to assume the killer has plans for them. I want those women found *alive*." She looked directly at Bobbie and added, "Whatever you find—no matter the source—I want to hear it."

The attention in the room shifted to Bobbie. Holt had already taken her to task about not coming clean with her when she'd asked. Bobbie held up her hands in surrender. "Yes, ma'am."

Owens gave her a nod, then gathered her notes and left the conference room. When Devine and Bauer congregated at the case board to bemoan the sketch that looked so much like her partner, Bobbie moved closer to Holt. "Is everything okay? That couple down the street still having trouble?"

Bauer had mentioned how worried Holt was about the wife and kid. Watching a victim plummet toward disaster and knowing that nothing you could say or do would stop the coming crash was one of the worst parts about being a cop.

"Things were quiet for the first part of the night and then all hell broke loose." Holt yawned. "Howie's not sleeping. Tricia and I are both exhausted. I think last night was the worst."

"The one thing you can count on with a baby," Bobbie advised, "is that nothing stays the same. He may start sleeping through the night next week. He could be on the verge of a growth spurt." She smiled. "I remember when Jamie hit six months. For two or three weeks it was like I had someone else's baby. The sweet little guy who hadn't given us a minute's trouble suddenly fretted nonstop."

Holt stared at Bobbie in surprise as if she'd announced she knew the identity of the murderer they needed to find.

Bobbie opened her mouth to ask what was wrong when she realized what she'd said. This was the first time since Jamie died that she'd spoken so openly and casually about him with anyone. Getting air into her lungs was suddenly harder than it should have been.

Holt reached out and squeezed her arm. "Thank you. I'll tell Tricia we might just survive this."

Bobbie managed a jerky nod.

Westminster Drive
2:00 p.m.

Sixteen-year-old Bree Chastain could have been
Fern Parker's twin. Devine had mentioned this sim-
ilarity the first time he'd interviewed the girl. The
two had the same blond hair and wore matching
black clothes. Bree's parents, Harlan and Brenda,
sat quietly on either side of their daughter, hands
clasped. The father had called to say his daughter
might have relevant information about Fern.

"She was worried about her little brother," Bree
said. "All the trouble she'd been in lately was because of this stupid kid who was bullying Sage.
Fern never got into trouble at school until that happened."

"Did she call or text you the night she was murdered?"

Like most suspicious teenagers, Fern kept her
phone empty of evidence. Her call and text logs had
been cleared. It was possible the killer had done this
but since neither the mother's nor the father's had
been cleared, Bobbie doubted that was the case.
Regrettably it took time to get phone records and
time was something they didn't have.

Bree nodded. "I was supposed to spend the night
with her, but her parents were fighting, so she sent
me a text and said maybe we should do it another
night. I asked her to come here and she said no.
She and her brother were afraid to leave the house
when their parents fought."

"Why is that?" Bobbie asked. "Were Fern and

Sage afraid their parents would hurt each other?" There was no record of assaults, but not all were reported. Like Holt's neighbor, some people were too afraid or too ashamed to report abuse. "I know it may seem strange to you since we've already asked these questions," Bobbie explained, "but sometimes it helps to cover the same ground."

Bree nodded her understanding. "No, it wasn't like that. Their parents never did anything but yell. Sometimes their mom broke things, but nothing major. Fern and Sage were scared someone else would hurt them while they were distracted with fighting. Someone shot at their other house, you know."

Smart kids, Bobbie decided.

"They both received a lot of death threats," Mr. Chastain interjected. "We worried anytime Bree went over there."

Mrs. Chastain shook her head, her eyes bright with tears. "But how do you tell your daughter she can't spend time with her best friend?"

Bobbie got that part. Teenagers typically ran in pairs or packs. "Had anything new or different happened in Fern's life? I mean other than her parents' issues. Was she involved with a boy that maybe no one else knew about?"

Bree opened her mouth to answer but she hesitated. Devine had gotten a resounding *no* last time. Bree's hesitancy warned the answer might be different this time.

"Anything you tell us is confidential," Bobbie

reminded her. "No one will ever know the information came from you."

"She went to this summer camp back in July. Before the really big sh— crap hit the fan."

"Was this a local camp?" Bobbie readied to make notes. "Run by a church or other local organization?"

Bree shrugged. "I don't know for sure. It's a youth camp where they have rich kids helping poor kids. It's like some community outreach. Her mother signed her up for it earlier in the spring. I think maybe she went last year, too."

"All Kids Matter," Mrs. Chastain interjected. "That big nondenominational church, Life Church, sponsors it. A lot of the wealthy families in Montgomery support the effort and their teenagers sponsor less fortunate children in the community."

Devine was scribbling furiously in his notebook, so Bobbie focused on asking the questions. "You believe she met someone there she liked or looked up to?"

Another of those sad shrugs lifted Bree's shoulders. "I don't know but she mentioned it a couple of times as if it was the best time of her life."

Bobbie would look into the summer camp. "Did Fern mention seeing anyone she didn't know around the neighborhood lately? Maybe someone watching the house?"

Bree shook her head. "They had a security guard who sat in a car in front of their house but he wasn't there, like, all the time."

"Did her father say the man worked for him?"

This was the first Bobbie had heard about a private security guard. The housekeeper had insisted there was no security detail. She'd even had to take a cut in pay to stay on.

Bree shrugged. "That's what Fern said."

"Did you ever see this man?"

"Sure." She shrugged. "I didn't see him really well. His windows were tinted and he wore dark sunglasses."

"Was he white or black? Dark hair or light hair? Did you recognize the kind of car he drove?"

Devine flipped to a new page in his notepad in preparation for copying down the answers to Bobbie's questions.

"White for sure. His hair was brown or black. I never, like, stopped and stared at him. It was a big car, older I think."

Bobbie showed the girl a copy of the sketch created from Sage Parker's memory of the man who'd been in his house. "Did he look anything like this?" Next to her, her partner shifted and stared down at his notepad once more. Understandable. He was still reeling from Sage's announcement.

Bree shrugged. "I guess. Maybe. The hair is right."

"Did he ever speak to either of you?"

"Fern talked to him a couple of times."

"Do you recall when this happened?"

The girl shrugged. "I think maybe Monday or Tuesday was the last time. I can't say for sure."

"One final question," Bobbie said. "Think really

hard. Did you see him there on Wednesday?" He damned sure wasn't there on Thursday.

Bree thought about the question for a moment. "No. I don't think he was there Wednesday."

"Are you sure?" Bobbie pressed. "Could he have been driving a different car or maybe he was just parked in a different place."

"Nope. He wasn't around Wednesday morning. I would have noticed."

"Wednesday is garbage pickup," Mrs. Chastain explained. "Everyone's trash can is out at the street. It makes parking on the street difficult. I didn't notice any cars on the street that day, either."

"Did you notice the kind of car he drove?" Bobbie asked Brenda. She needed the make of that car. Her pulse was hammering with hope.

"I never noticed him," Mr. Chastain said before his wife could answer. "It's usually dark when I get home and I leave before daylight most mornings."

"One of those older Lincoln Town Cars," Brenda said. "Really old, like from the '80s. It was dark. Black I think."

"License plate?" Bobbie asked hopefully.

Mother, daughter and father exchanged glances, and then shook their heads.

"Did you get a look at him?" Devine asked the mother, speaking for the first time instead of taking notes.

She shook her head again. "I promise you I won't make that mistake again. Their killer may have been sitting out there right in front of us for days before they were murdered." Tears spilled down her cheeks. "It's just awful. So awful."

Bobbie had a bad feeling she was right about the man in the Lincoln Town Car.

Life Church
Troy Highway
4:30 p.m.

Pastor Winifred Liddell insisted on giving Bobbie and Devine a tour of the massive church before answering any questions. The church was not as ornate as some of the larger churches in Montgomery, but it was well done. No stained glass or towering crosses. According to Liddell the church dollars were devoted to bringing people together and to God. The fifty-year-old had started as a member of the church when she was fifteen. After theology school she had devoted herself to this particular church because of the good done in the community of Montgomery. All Kids Matter was one of her favorite outreach programs.

Devine seemed antsy. Maybe Bobbie wasn't the only one who didn't feel comfortable in God's house.

"I was one of those children whose family was blessed financially," Liddell confessed. "My friends and I were spoiled rotten." She gestured toward her office and then led the way. "This church was just getting off the ground at the time. My boyfriend and I were forced into service that summer. Our parents were looking for a way to be rid of us for a couple of weeks." She pursed her lips as if in thought. "Actually I think it was three weeks."

"I'm sure you remember Fern Parker," Bobbie said, ready to move past the reminiscing.

"Oh, certainly." Liddell took a seat behind her antique desk. "A lovely girl." Her face lined with worry. "It's so sad about her parents. A travesty." Her eyes rounded hopefully. "Is there any word on Fern? Has she been found?"

"I'm afraid not. That's why we're here."

Liddell looked surprised. "I see."

"We thought perhaps Fern met someone during the camp in July."

Liddell pressed a finger to her chin and nodded. "She made friends quite easily." She shook her head. "But no one in particular stands out in my mind. She was very focused on helping the other kids."

"We'll need a list of the kids who attended the camp this year and anyone Fern might have come into contact with on a regular basis. Counselors, cooks, anyone who worked during the time she was here."

"Certainly." Liddell blinked once, twice. "I hope you don't believe someone on our staff had anything to do with what happened. I have good people here. We do good work, Detective. We try to instill confidence and hope in those less fortunate."

"We're only suggesting," Bobbie assured her, "that she may have met someone who remained in contact with her. Someone who might be able to help us retrace those last hours before she went missing."

Liddell offered a dim smile. "Of course." She pulled open a drawer. "We always do a closing report each summer. The names of all involved are included with the report." She flipped through her files and then withdrew a multipage document and passed it across the desk. "You may have that copy. I can have another printed."

Bobbie flipped past the report to the names. Fifty children attended but none of the names save Fern's was familiar. The last page listed the camp workers, none jumped out at Bobbie. The final column was the names of those who provided the donations necessary to make such a big event happen.

Mark Hanover.

Pieces of the puzzle abruptly clicked into place as Bobbie passed the report to her partner. "Pastor Liddell, do you recall if a Vanessa Olson ever attended your camp?"

The pastor smiled. "Yes. She certainly did. Three summers during high school. She should finish college year after next I believe. A lovely young woman."

Bobbie's blood chilled. She exchanged a look with Devine and then said, "I'm sorry to have to tell you, ma'am, but Vanessa was abducted on Friday. We believe the same person who took Fern may have taken her."

Liddell's hand went to her chest. "Dear Lord, that's just awful. Truly awful. I've been at my sister's home in Florida for the past four days. I only arrived back home today. I saw the news about the Parkers but I didn't see anything about Vanessa."

Because of the ongoing federal case, the Parkers were national news. Vanessa Olson, on the other hand, was not. With Liddell out of town there was no reason for her to have heard about Olson. "We're hoping to find them quickly," Bobbie said. "Anything you might recall relative to Fern or Vanessa could prove useful to our investigation."

"I understand. Whatever I can do, please just let me know."

"I noticed Mark Hanover is one of your donors," Bobbie ventured cautiously. Donors such as Hanover were important to programs like the ones at this church. Liddell would be protective.

The pastor beamed a broad smile. "An amazing man. He and his father have helped with the programs for the youth in our community for decades. We're very lucky to have donors like the Hanovers."

"Would Mr. Mark Hanover have been in contact with either Fern or Vanessa?"

Liddell nodded slowly. "Certainly. He's very hands-on with all our programs." A frown inched across her brow as if she'd just realized why Bobbie asked. "Mark Hanover is an outstanding supporter of this community as well as this church."

Bobbie nodded. "You understand I have to ask."

Liddell gave another nod but her expression warned she still didn't like the line of questioning. Bobbie thanked her and stood to go. Devine followed suit. The pastor appeared more than a little relieved.

When they reached the door Liddell hesitated. "Detective Devine, are you by chance Pearl Whitley's nephew?"

Bobbie looked from the woman to her partner who smiled, the expression a pale imitation of his usual charmers. "Yes, ma'am."

Liddell gave a nod. "I thought I recognized you. Is she under the weather? She hasn't been to church all month."

"Her allergies flared up and she's feeling poorly," Devine explained. "I'll tell her you asked."

Liddell's finger went to her chin once more. "I believe you attended our camp one summer, didn't you? What was it, twenty years ago? Maybe longer?"

"Twenty-one years," Devine said. "I was just a child. I barely remember."

The two chatted a bit longer. Bobbie didn't really hear the exchange; she was stuck on the idea that Devine knew this church. He had attended the youth camp—the same one Fern and Vanessa had attended.

And he hadn't said a damned word.

Twenty-Three

Gardendale Drive
7:30 p.m.

Devine pulled into the driveway behind Bobbie's Challenger. Bobbie had struggled with the frustration and anger she felt since they'd walked out of that church. Part of her argued that she was just as guilty of holding out as her partner. She hadn't been totally honest about her meeting with Weller in the beginning and even when she had come clean she hadn't mentioned Nick being in Montgomery.

Fury belted her again. Any way she looked at it, what she did wasn't the same thing. This Consortium Weller had alerted her to had been ruled out by both Nick and the FBI. Until Nick confirmed that the MOs of the killer in the Parker and Manning murders was somehow related to him, the warning that he was in danger couldn't be concretely connected to this case. Not to mention that Nigel and Heather Parker were dead. Slade Manning was dead. Any hesitation on her part in their investigation wasn't going to change that unfortunate reality.

The youth camp, Hanover's involvement and the link between Fern Parker and Vanessa Olson could potentially affect whether those two women continued breathing. Devine had held out on Bobbie until they stumbled upon the connection by sheer accident.

He shifted into Park and sighed. "You're still angry with me."

"You're damned right I am."

"I knew Hanover when I was a kid. How could I possibly anticipate that Parker and Olson had attended the same youth camp?"

"You couldn't." Bobbie turned to him, hoped he could see her frustration in the dim light coming from the dash. "That's why we put it all out there. Everything. Anything. The second the Chastains mentioned the camp, you should have told me you'd attended." She took a deep breath and reached for calm. "I asked you repeatedly whether you knew Hanover and you lied to me every damned time. You don't get to decide what's important in a life-and-death situation, Devine."

Bobbie had called Owens and brought her up to speed. Liddell had gladly agreed to provide a list of camp participants for the past five years. She'd promised the complete list by noon tomorrow. For the better part of the rest of the day Bobbie and Devine had attempted to interview every kid who'd attended camp with Fern and Vanessa. Between interviews she had tried unsuccessfully to touch base with Hanover. He'd been away from his office and hadn't showed up at home so far.

At seven tonight Bobbie had obtained authorization to inform Hanover's assistant that if he didn't make contact with the department by noon tomorrow he would be charged with obstruction of justice. How dare the man not mention knowing Vanessa Olson, much less the up close and fairly recent contact with Fern Parker.

"It won't happen again, Bobbie," Devine promised. "You have my word. My aunt would say that a man's word is all he really has as proof of who he is."

"Your aunt would be right."

How many guys his age would move in with an elderly aunt to help with her final years of life? Bobbie liked Devine, respected him. Until today she'd found no fault in her new partner. Ultimately no matter how she rationalized it, she couldn't hold it against him since she was almost as guilty.

"We'll get past this," she assured him. "In time."

He nodded. "You giving me a second chance means a lot."

"All right." She reached for the door handle. "G'night."

"I was wondering," he said, making her hesitate. "What does your friend Nick Shade think about this case?"

Bobbie turned to him unable to keep the surprise off her face. She hadn't spoken to anyone about Nick beyond what she'd revealed regarding Weller's warning. Not once had she mentioned to

Devine that she and Nick were friends. She certainly hadn't mentioned having seen him or spoken to him.

"Bauer told me what Shade did to help you." Devine looked down for a moment before meeting her gaze once more. "I shouldn't have asked."

Why would Bauer do that? He knew how Bobbie felt about the subject. She dismissed the feeling of betrayal for the time being, but that didn't mean she was going to answer Devine's question. "When I hear his conclusions I'll let you know. See you tomorrow."

"Night."

He gave her a two-fingered salute and Bobbie climbed out and headed for her front door. The cold air made her shiver. The evenings were growing cooler. Though Alabama was known for the occasional sixty-degree day in December, the winter season often showed its harsher side with temps well below freezing. Despite a few hotter than average days, the cool nights had come early this year. Bobbie, for one, was glad. She was ready for the heat to be over. The summer had been a long, scorching one.

When she unlocked the door the alarm was silent. Nick was here. D-Boy raced into the living room to greet her as he did every night. She couldn't wait to see anything new Nick had added to the case map he'd started. She certainly had plenty to tell him. On the kitchen table stood a huge bouquet of flowers, roses, chrysanthemums and lots of other colorful flowers she couldn't readily identify. She reached for the card and read the note.

Bobbie, I appreciate all you do for our community. You might find this place interesting. See you tomorrow before noon, as requested. Regards, Mark Hanover

Bobbie looked at the book of matches he'd tucked in with the card. *Rusty Fiddle*. This was the place in the photo. Riveroaks Road. Established 1952 was stamped on the back.

"Looks like you have an admirer."

She turned at the sound of Nick's voice, startled that he was practically standing right next to her. The man was like smoke. He could be beside you before you recognized his presence in the room. "Mark Hanover."

"Playing more games, is he?"

"Apparently." Bobbie tossed the card aside but hung on to the matches. "Today I learned he's a major financial force behind a summer youth camp both our missing victims attended."

"Do you find it strange that the only potential leads you've found seem to steer right back to him?"

Nick was right. The dagger and now the youth camp. It would be easy to lean toward the idea that Hanover was their killer, but when something was too obvious it was rarely what it appeared to be. "I do."

"He's toying with you, that's a certainty." His

dark eyes searched her face. "But is he actually involved with the murders or is someone trying to distract you? Perhaps even to frame him?"

"His connection to Nigel Parker as well as to the youth camp would make him an easy target." Bobbie tucked the matches into her pocket. "How do you feel about going out tonight?"

"Why not?" He touched the petals of one of the roses. "You can tell me about your visit to the church."

So he was following her. "You got it. Give me five minutes to change."

Bobbie hadn't been out since she and James went to a restaurant downtown for their anniversary last November. Of course this wasn't a date. It was work…or sort of, anyway. Mainly it was personal. She wanted to know whatever it was Hanover thought he knew about her mother. More important, she needed to know if he had anything to do with those missing women and her three murder vics.

She shuffled through the hangers, realizing she had no dresses or skirts. She'd never expected to need one again. She'd never intended to go out—not even with friends—ever again. A pair of jeans and a sweater would have to do. The sweater was soft and pink, not her favorite color, but Jamie had picked it out for her as a Christmas gift last year. Bobbie touched the soft fabric and her heart ached. Until three weeks ago she hadn't been able to open the gifts that had sat under the artificial Christmas tree she refused to take down. She'd left every single thing in the house just as it had been that last day of the life she'd lived there. Somehow seeing the presents sitting there whenever she went to the old house had felt oddly comforting. Maybe deep inside she'd hoped she would open that door one day and find James and Jamie waiting for her.

They're gone, Bobbie.

Recently, she'd stopped allowing herself to pretend. Three weeks ago she'd sat down in front of the Christmas tree and opened the gifts from her husband and child. The present from James had been far more intimate. Silky lingerie. She smiled. He'd always bought her the non-practical things she never bought for herself. And the sweater from her baby. She smoothed a hand over the soft fabric.

Bobbie drew in a deep breath and blinked back the burn of tears. "Miss you."

Centering on the here and now, she ran a brush through her hair and called herself ready. She took the matches from the pocket of her discarded trousers and tossed them on the nightstand. Nick waited where she'd left him, in the kitchen. He surveyed her from head to toe and back as she walked across the room.

"You look nice."

"Thanks." She gave D-Boy a treat and grabbed her keys. She decided that going out was a good thing. If they stayed closed up in this house things could get even more complicated than they had last night. On some level she wanted to explore the feelings developing between them, but she had to be smart. When this was done, Nick would be leaving again. Her life was here...his was wherever the hunt took him. Her life was only now beginning to get back on track—primarily because of Nick Shade. He was important to her in ways she couldn't quite articulate. She didn't want to do anything that might damage this...whatever it was. Not quite a relationship, but something on that order.

Keep it real, Bobbie.

The club was only a few miles out of town. It wouldn't take more than ten or fifteen minutes to reach their destination. As Nick drove she told him about the Life Church. When she'd finished, he said, "Tell me about your new partner."

"He's a couple years younger than me. He cut his teeth in Major Crimes in Birmingham."

"He saw plenty of homicide cases."

"He did."

"Not married?"

"No wife, no kids. He moved to Montgomery to take care of his elderly aunt."

"Sounds like a nice guy."

Bobbie wasn't sure if he meant the observation as a compliment or was being facetious. "So far."

"You think it's the face he wants you to see."

After a bit, she admitted, "Maybe. He seems... overly anxious to prove how nice he is. Too willing to go out of the way to please." She shrugged, mostly at herself for the unexpected harsh characterizations. When had she decided to fault Devine for the traits she'd thought she admired? She was tired and frustrated, mostly at her partner and Hanover. This wasn't a good time to ask her about either. "For the most part I think he's a good cop."

"But there's something that feels off."

"Maybe. Yes." This was the first time she'd admitted those feelings to herself, much less out loud. It had started with the Parker case. From the moment they interviewed Hanover the first time Devine had turned anxious. Having the Parker kid say the killer looked like him hadn't helped. Now the youth camp business. Their relationship was a little rocky at the moment. Owens had ordered Bobbie to put her phone on Speaker when she'd called. The LT had chewed out Devine for failing to mention the youth camp and his knowledge that Hanover was involved. She'd thrown in a few shots at Bobbie for failing to set a good example for her new partner and it was true. She hadn't exactly been a stellar role model.

"He's down two strikes," Nick commented. "Keeping his knowledge of Hanover from you and then the youth camp. I'd hate to be him if he hits the third strike."

She laughed. "I might have to kick his ass."

Nick laughed. The sound startled Bobbie at first. It was the first time she'd heard him laugh—the real thing, anyway. She liked it.

After a minute or two of quiet, she asked, "Did you learn anything new today?"

"I reached out to a few of my less palatable sources and the one thing they all agreed on was that somehow Weller has been reaching outside his prison walls."

She glanced from the road to him. "How can the FBI not know about this?"

"It's not unusual for inmates to manage connections to the outside through guards and other prison staff."

"Wouldn't they watch Weller more closely?" Bobbie shook her head. "Have more rigorous checks and balances for anyone allowed to interact with him?"

"Presumably."

Bobbie opened her mouth to speak twice before she decided how to ask. "Could he want you dead? I mean, could he really have sent someone to kill you?" Weller had acted so concerned for Nick's safety. Maybe it was, as Nick said, only the face he wanted her to see.

"If it suits his purpose."

The words were spoken in such a matter-of-fact tone. She bit her lip and considered how to ask about the part that troubled her most. "Are you afraid he might succeed?"

"Death is the only true guarantee in life." He glanced at her. "Being afraid wouldn't help me stay alive."

"Good point." Even if she didn't like it much.

"The real question is how many will die before I find the killer he sent."

"Is that what you're doing when we're not together? Looking for the killer?"

"I'm doing what I always do. Watching, analyzing and researching."

"You make it seem so ordinary."

"This is what I do. Don't you feel like the routine of investigating a murder is ordinary for you?"

"But I'm not generally the target."

"You were the target last time."

He had her there.

"I'm glad you're back." Her words rang in the silence for what felt like forever. She wondered if she should have kept them to herself. Now that she'd said them the least she could do was say the rest of what was on her mind. "I wish the circumstances were different."

He glanced at her again, lingering a little longer this time. "Me, too."

She resisted the impulse to touch him. Things had gotten a little out of control last night. It was imperative they stay focused on the case. *Maybe another time.* The realization that she wanted it to happen again surprised her. Rather than resist the idea, she tucked it away for later consideration.

Nick slowed for the final turn. The parking lot of the Rusty Fiddle was empty, but there were lights on inside the long, low building. Neon beer signs were dark. A large black door served as the main entrance. A single streetlamp lit the parking lot.

Nick reached for the door before she could. "Do we know why we're here? What Hanover wants you to discover?"

She shook her head. "I guess we'll see."

He opened the door and the smell of stale cigarette smoke and beer filled her lungs. Chairs sat on top of tables. Stools lined a long bar on the other side of the room. The jukebox blared a slow country tune. Whoever was here was obviously in the back. Nick walked to the doors beyond the bar and called a hello.

While Nick spoke to the man who appeared from the kitchen or whatever lay beyond the bar, Bobbie walked over to the jukebox. This was where the photo had been taken. The jukebox was newer but the sign hanging above it was the same. Rusty Fiddle.

Bobbie scanned the place again, more slowly this time. Why would her mother be here? Had she and her friends come just to have fun? Had it even been a club back then? Maybe it had been a restaurant?

Bobbie wandered over to the bar where the man had set up a beer for Nick.

"Can I get you something, ma'am?"

"No, thanks. Has this place always been a club?"

"Sure has." He braced his forearms on the bar. "From the fifties all the way through the eighties, all kinds of bands came through that door hoping to be noticed. A lot of music scouts hung out on these very stools." He indicated the ones along the bar. "More than one country star got a start here." He gestured to the other end of the room where a small stage stood. "There's lots of photos of the groups and people who performed here back in the day if you care to have a look."

Bobbie nodded. "I'd love to."

He led the way, turning on the lights as he went. Just as he said, the back wall beyond the dance floor and the small stage was crowded with photos.

"Some of 'em are dated. Some aren't."

Bobbie scanned the framed photos, moving from one side of the wall to the other, until she reached the decade she was looking for.

Her gaze landed on a photograph identical to the one Hanover had given her. She pointed to the photo. "Do you know these people?"

He shook his head. "My old man could have told you every one of 'em's name. I can't remember the ones that far back."

"I'd like to speak to him. Your father, I mean."

"He died a couple of years ago."

Damn it. "I'm sorry to hear that."

The man shrugged. "He had a good life. Sometimes a man just has to realize when his dance is over."

Bobbie nodded as she studied the photo once more. How could her mother have performed at a club like this and she not know it?

"I should get back to work," the man said.

Bobbie thanked him, her attention still on the photo. The whole idea was crazy.

As if her concern had beckoned him, Nick was suddenly at her side. "We all have our secrets, Bobbie. Your mother was no different."

She nodded, uncertain of her voice.

"The first question you need to ask is why Hanover would want you to know it."

Nick was right. "He wants me off balance."

"Your next question should be why."

The answer to that question worried her the most.

Twenty-Four

"How're you feeling, Dr. Weller?"

Randolph smiled at the nurse peering down at him. "Better now, thank you."

She patted his chest as if he were a child. "If you keep having these episodes they're going to have to send you over to Emory for further testing."

"Did the doctor say so?" Randolph asked in the feeblest voice he could summon.

"He did, indeed." She fastened the cuff around his arm and checked his blood pressure. "Those FBI fellows want to keep you healthy." She peered at the monitor. "Still a little high."

"Shouldn't you be home by now, Anita? It's very late."

She removed the cuff and set it aside. "Then who would keep you company? I'd have to leave you shackled in here all by yourself." She touched the ring of iron encircling his left wrist. "A man shouldn't be chained up like this and left alone when he's not feeling well."

"It's certainly not comfortable." He twisted his wrist, making the chains rattle.

"Would you like some music to calm you?"

"That would be lovely, Anita."

She crossed the room and turned on the old-fashioned portable radio she'd brought to work with her. The station she preferred played that annoying pop music. Where was her taste? Her scrubs were two sizes too small and her eyeglasses were far too large even on her inordinately round face. She reeked of cheap perfume. It was all he could do to bear her nearness. But she served a purpose. One made the best of one's circumstances, did he not? Randolph recalled well the unfortunate occasion when he'd been forced to choose two homeless specimens for his inspiration. The decision had been a hasty one and hadn't served him well at all. His current circumstances were quite similar. This time, however, he'd planned far more carefully.

The attentive nurse returned to his bedside. With her back to the camera and the music filling the room, she put on her stethoscope and pretended to listen to his heart. "Everything is ready, Randy," she whispered and then giggled softly.

The only other person who'd dared to call him Randy had died soon after. He'd cut him up into tiny pieces and fed him bit by bit to the neighbor's dogs. Randolph had been young then. Young and impulsive. The ability to control his urges had taken time. He'd almost managed a perfectly average life.

Until Nicholas destroyed all he'd worked so hard to build. It was time to make his wayward son see the error of his ways.

"By this time tomorrow night," the foolish cow murmured, "you'll be free."

"Dear, dear Anita." He gazed up at her with feigned affection, something he suspected her own mother had forced herself to do. "How will I ever fully repay you?"

"Being with you is all the payment I will ever need. You've made me the happiest woman in the world." She giggled again and drew away.

Randolph watched as she made notes in his chart. Poor thing. She had no idea that tomorrow would be the very last day of her pathetic life.

Twenty-Five

As requested, Mark Hanover appeared at CID at noon. Lieutenant Owens decided to sit in. Bobbie had no problem with her second chairing the interview. She'd suggested Devine help Holt and Bauer with the long list of names from the All Kids Matter program. Every single one had to be contacted, if possible, and interviewed. Hopefully this interview would be more productive without Devine in the room to distract Hanover. The man seemed to get some sort of jollies from yanking Devine's chain. He did the same to Bobbie, but, unlike her partner, she managed to keep her reactions to herself.

"Quite frankly, Lieutenant," Hanover said, "I'm surprised the MPD would waste time harassing me. Shouldn't you be more concerned with who took those poor girls and murdered three people?"

Owens smiled. "You may rest assured that we're

very concerned, Mr. Hanover. That's why you're here."

Hanover gave her a nod as if to say "touché."

"You and your father were instrumental in making the Life Church summer youth program come to life," Bobbie said. "Thirty years later the two of you remain the largest benefactors of the church as well as its programs."

"Is it a crime, Detective, to want to serve the community?" Hanover set his elbows on the interview table and steepled his fingers. "My family has a history of giving back. Perhaps if you did your homework you'd know this already."

Bobbie smiled. The pressure was getting to the man. Where was his haughty sense of humor today? "Your support is commendable. I'm also confident you're aware we're interviewing many people associated with the church and the summer programs offered there. You shouldn't feel singled out. In fact, you've gone out of your way to be cooperative until now. Is there a reason you're suddenly taken aback by our questions?"

Bobbie had a feeling Nick was on to something. Someone might very well be trying to set Hanover up. But why? If the person Weller sent was framing Hanover, what did that make Hanover? An innocent bystander? *I don't think so.*

"As you say, I have been cooperative. There's nothing further I can add to your efforts." He sat back in his chair. "I find this attention on my philanthropic work to be most harassing. I didn't think it necessary to have my attorney present, but perhaps that was a hasty decision."

"Is that why you wouldn't return my calls yesterday?" Bobbie asked. "It was almost as if we had some sort of psychic connection going on until yesterday. As soon as I discovered your association with the youth camp you were unavailable."

Hanover smiled. "I'm an international businessman, Detective. I have meetings all over the world. Thanks to your fine detective work I have to conduct all those meetings via teleconferencing. I believe I've been more than accommodating."

Bobbie started to ask him what connection he had to the Rusty Fiddle but Owens spoke first. "Mr. Hanover, we appreciate your cooperation. If we have any additional questions we'll let you know."

They all stood and before Bobbie could think how to keep Hanover from walking out, the lieutenant had already ushered him through the door. When he was gone Owens turned back to her. "Keep an eye on him. Considering what you and Devine have told me, I don't believe he's being fully forthcoming."

"I agree." Bobbie shrugged. "I could have asked him a couple more questions."

"He needs to believe we're backing off."

Bobbie nodded, understanding where the LT was going with her suggestion. "If he believes we've moved on he might grow careless."

"And if it's our attention he wants, he'll find a way to regain it."

Bobbie smiled. "Desperation breeds mistakes."

"He'll make one soon." Owens studied her for a moment. "What does your friend Shade have to say about all this?"

That Devine had asked her the same thing just last evening gave Bobbie pause. She started to give her stock answer that she hadn't seen Nick when Owens added, "This is between you and me, Bobbie. The chief doesn't need to know."

Surprised, Bobbie answered the question to the best of her knowledge. "Weller's up to something. Nick believes all of this is a distraction. Hanover is likely nothing but a scapegoat. Someone's using him to distract us." They had discussed Hanover and his part in Weller's plan again this morning. She doubted Hanover had a clue where this was headed much less the real reason he was even part of it.

Owens nodded. "I'll talk to Agent Hadden. Put a bug in his ear."

Before Bobbie could join the rest of the team, Owens touched her arm. "Be careful. If this killer was handpicked by Randolph Weller, we're not looking at your typical hired gun."

Bobbie was well aware of that unfortunate truth. "It's been more than twenty-four hours since our killer made a move. Something's coming." She could feel it.

The downside was that they were nowhere near ready.

Owens hesitated and withdrew her cell from her belt. She stared at the screen and then at Bobbie. "I guess we spoke too soon. We have another young woman missing. Deana Venable."

Damn. "I'll grab Devine and head that way."

Owens provided the address and Bobbie rounded up her partner. Somewhere between here and there she should get word to Nick.

Fairview Avenue
4:00 p.m.

Evidence techs had rolled up shortly after Bobbie and Devine arrived. En route Bobbie had called Holt with the bad news and then she'd called Liddell. The pastor confirmed that Deana Venable had attended the youth camp the year before last. As soon as she had that confirmation, Bobbie sent a text to Nick to let him know.

As deeply convinced as she was that Hanover was not the perp they were looking for, she was as certain as she could be that he knew the person behind the murders and the abductions. Was this some sort of game to him? Maybe a man who had everything as Hanover did was bored and in need of a thrill.

Too bad he apparently didn't care that three lives were at stake.

Bobbie moved back into the living room where Deana's roommate, Erin Nesmith, waited. She'd been interviewed by Devine already. Bobbie and Newt had long ago worked out a strategy for conducting interviews. One of them would go first and then the other would follow up. Whether it was the difference in technique, the time in between to think or the reaction to male versus female, the interviewee always gave a little more information the second time around.

"How you holding up, Erin?" Bobbie settled into the recliner next to the sofa where the roommate sat.

"I can't believe this happened." Erin shook her head, eyes glistening with renewed tears. "I should have been here."

Erin had spent the weekend with her parents in Mobile. When she'd come home around noon today she'd found the front door unlocked and slightly ajar. Deana's purse and phone were in the house. Her car was in the driveway. There was no indication of a struggle. Erin swore she hadn't touched a thing other than her friend's phone. She had called their mutual friends and Deana's family and no one had seen or heard from her since the day before. Uniforms were canvassing the neighborhood but if this was the same perp, chances were no one saw anything.

"The person who took Deana plans very carefully," Bobbie explained. "He knows how to get in and get out without notice. If you'd been here you might have ended up a victim." Bobbie was beginning to think that Manning and the Parkers were murdered because of their connection to the missing women, not vice versa.

Erin searched Bobbie's face. "Is she like the others?"

The warnings had gone wide. Young women

who had attended the Life Church summer youth camp were to be on guard. Liddell wasn't too happy about that part but she understood the MPD had an obligation to warn the public. Every donor, staff member and volunteer of the camp was being interviewed.

"We'll operate under the assumption she is until we have reason to believe otherwise."

"Is she going to die?" Erin scrubbed her hands over her face. "I can't believe this. She's planning her wedding. You have to find her."

Deana was only twenty-one. She'd completed her undergraduate degree this year and was working on her MBA. Her fiancé had been in Huntsville on business for the past week. He was on his way back to Montgomery now. Deana was an adult and, with no signs of foul play, ordinarily Bobbie might suggest the woman had taken a break from her life. But, as a past participant of the same youth camp as Olson and Parker, she couldn't afford to assume anything. Frankly, anytime a person was unaccounted for and had left their cell phone behind it was a good idea to be a little suspicious.

"We're doing everything we can to find them," Bobbie offered. A missing vulnerable adult alert had been issued. "We have reason to believe Deana as well as the others are still alive."

Erin pressed a hand to her chest. "Thank you. I don't think I could face her parents if you'd told me otherwise."

"Did Deana ever mention anyone from her time at the Life Church summer youth camp?"

Erin shook her head. "I didn't even know she'd attended the camp. She never talked about things like that. We moved in together a year ago and she's been focused on school and her wedding most of that time." She hugged herself. "I'm never getting married. It's way too complicated. I told her they should go to the courthouse and do the deed and then tell their parents."

Bobbie remembered feeling that way. But her aunt and uncle had insisted on a wedding. Not to mention James's mother would have had a stroke if they'd skipped out on the big family plan. It felt like forever ago that they'd been planning their wedding.

Marrying her had cost James everything.

Bobbie pushed away the haunting memories. At least there was no body at this scene. That was something.

What in the world was this guy doing with all these hostages?

Criminal Investigation Division
7:30 p.m.

Holt added the photo of Deana Venable to the case board. As Bobbie predicted they now had two case boards. The sheer number of POIs and potential victims had taken on a life of its own. They had cross-checked all victims and determined the single common thread was the summer youth camp. The missing women were very different. Deana was about to start grad school. Vanessa was a college student and fitness coach. And then there was Fern, a high school student. Ages varied as much as five years and physical descriptions were all over the place. Deana was short and a little on the heavy side while Vanessa was tall and thin. The perp appeared to be selecting victims based solely on their attendance at the summer youth camp. The only upside so far was that there was no new homicide victim. Owens was still at the joint task-force briefing. Bobbie hoped the FBI or the Sheriff's Department had found something because MPD sure as hell hadn't found a damned thing to help find those women.

Bauer and Devine were interviewing the staff at the restaurant where Deana had dined with friends last night. Bobbie had returned to help Holt cover the rest of the names on the list from Liddell.

"Thank God this is the last one," Holt grumbled.

They had spent hours calling each name on the numerous lists to establish that the camp participant was safe and to warn her to be careful. Eventually they would interview each one face-to-face. The effort wasn't exactly going to get them any closer to the killer but the work had to be done. As with the previous two scenes, the perp had left no evidence and so far no one had gotten a glimpse of him except Sage Parker and maybe the Chastain girl. The few hits they'd gotten on the sketch had turned out to be dead ends.

Bobbie made the call to the first name on the final list. While she spoke with the woman on the other end, she watched Holt. The sergeant was on edge. Tired. Frustrated. They all were, but they didn't all have a new baby at home. Bobbie's heart squeezed at the memory of feeling so damned guilty for missing all the new things her son was doing while she worked long hours. Every day it seemed he had learned something new and grown just a little bit more. And most days during that final month they'd had together she'd felt like a zombie from lack of sleep.

Bobbie moved on to the next name on the list. She wondered if she would ever have a family again.

Her fingers stilled on the phone.

Why in the world would such a thought even cross her mind? The last thing she wanted was to put herself in the position to be hurt that badly ever again. Besides, she could never replace the family she'd had with another one. It wasn't possible. She would spend the rest of her life alone.

She closed out the thoughts and made the calls. Call after call to women who could be the next victim of a serial killer they knew absolutely nothing about and whose next murder could happen anytime, anywhere.

Gardendale Drive
11:00 p.m.

Bobbie arrived home and a minute later Nick showed up. It didn't take much to deduce he was following her. She almost laughed at the thought. There were around three hundred women out there they needed to be watching but, this time, Bobbie wasn't one of them.

When they'd greeted D-Boy and stood awkwardly in her kitchen for about two minutes, Nick finally spoke. "It's Hanover we need to watch."

Bobbie's heart skipped about two beats. "I thought we agreed he wasn't our killer."

"He's not, but our killer is connected to him. The two appear to be playing each other or feeding off each other."

"Jesus." She shuddered. "I toyed with a similar conclusion today. Owens and I discussed it. So, have you been watching him?" Every time she learned something new about Hanover, it was one more mark against him. What she really wanted was to get him in a room and make him tell the truth about the missing women and about her mother, but there were laws against that sort of thing.

"I'm watching someone close to him," Nick said. "Hanover is the true pawn, like we thought. I'm not sure he realizes what a dangerous game he's playing."

Bobbie crossed her arms over her chest and looked at Nick expectantly. "Are you going to tell me who that someone is?"

He held her gaze for a long moment before he answered. "Not yet."

When she would have launched a protest, he continued, "If these women die it's on me. I can't allow that to happen. One wrong move or word could tip the scales in the wrong direction."

As much as she resented the idea that he wouldn't trust her with whatever he had learned, she understood to some degree his need for caution. Two months ago she had been in his shoes. Each murder the Storyteller committed was one more innocent victim taken to get to her. "Is there anything I can do to help?"

"Keep looking. You're closer than you know."

They stood there in silence, the tension expanding between them. There was so much Bobbie wanted to say to him, to ask him. The urge to touch him came fast and hard. She fisted her fingers into her palms and held her breath to slow her heart. His gaze dropped to her mouth and her foolish heart stumbled.

"I should," she blurted, "I should shower and get some sleep."

He nodded and looked away.

Bobbie hurried through her shower and closed herself in her room. Staying in this small house with him night after night was growing increasingly difficult. The tension had been building exponentially since that kiss night before last. She dried her hair, wishing the blow-dryer would drown out the thoughts whirling in her head.

She stared at herself in the mirror over her dresser. At first glance she still looked like the Bobbie she had always been. Her hair was the same. There were a few more lines bracketing her eyes. The thin scar around her neck wasn't as prominent as it once was. But beneath the tee and lounge pants she wore there was a map of the agony she had suffered. Hideous scars that spoke of a vicious serial killer. The slight limp and the dull ache that burrowed deep into the bones of her right leg reminded her every day. Unbearable words were tattooed on her back. All of it told the story of pure evil. The scars on her wrists that underscored the defeat she had suffered to anyone who looked.

Yet none of it told the whole story. The true loss could no longer be seen. James and Jamie were gone. Only her memories of them remained.

Bobbie closed her eyes and thought of the man down the hall. She wanted to touch him and to know him…completely.

When this case was over he would go. Months or years could pass before she heard from him again. Maybe she never would. Her shrink would tell her that a man like Nick Shade had long ago turned off his ability to feel. They could never share what she and James had shared. All they had was this moment and it was filled with uncertainty and pain… with fear and death.

She didn't need Nick Shade and he didn't need her.

The only thing either of them really needed was to find this killer before he finished what he'd come to Montgomery to do.

Bobbie opened her eyes. It was true. That was the one unequivocal connection they shared—the one true mutual need. To find the bad guy and save those young women and head off any potential danger Nick might face before this was done.

But it wasn't all she wanted.

I want more.

She burst out of her room before she lost her courage. Nick was just stepping out of the bathroom. His hair was damp. He wore nothing but jeans and they didn't cover nearly enough to prevent her from staring at his body.

He asked, "Is something wrong?"

Before she could summon the right words, she walked straight up to him. "Yes." She would not lose her nerve now. "We need to do something about this…whatever it is between us. It's in the way. We need to…clear the air."

"What is it that you think we need to do?"

That his face—his voice—remained completely impassive made her want to scream. "I want you to touch me." She took his hand and placed it on her breast. "I want you to—"

"Fuck you," he said, his voice hard now. "Is that what you want?"

Fury whipped through her. *He wants to make you angry, Bobbie. He wants you to back off.* "No." She grabbed his face and went up on tiptoe, putting her lips close to his. "I want to fuck *you*."

She kissed him. Long and deep. She smoothed her hands over his chest, her body trembling at the feel of his. He held stone still but she didn't care. She locked her arms around his neck and wrapped her legs around his waist. Nothing he could say or do would change her mind.

Her fingers delved into his damp hair and he stopped resisting and carried her to her bedroom. She reached for the switch to turn off the light.

He stopped her. "We do this in the light. Not in the dark."

She was scarred and damaged. He knew this. Her breasts, her legs, all marked by the sadistic bastard who had devastated her life. Why would he want to see that ugliness? Was this another ploy to deter her?

She didn't care. She wasn't stopping now.

Her feet somehow found the floor and his fingers found the hem of her tee. He pulled it up and over her head. Her hair fell over her shoulders, brushing skin that was already on fire. He tossed the garment aside and reached for the waistband of her lounge pants. With painstaking slowness he peeled away the final layers covering her. For one long moment, he simply stared at her as if he wanted to memorize every inch of her, every hideous mark. Then he leaned down and kissed the jagged scar on her breast. Bobbie closed her eyes and gave herself completely over to him.

One by one he kissed each blemish, each place evil had touched and when he finally filled her, she came apart completely.

Twenty-Six

There were three now.

The last girl to join them wouldn't stop crying. Vanessa had been trying to console her for hours but she just wouldn't calm down. Her name was Deana.

Deana didn't know the man who had taken them, either, but it was the same mask-wearing asshole who'd taken Vanessa and her.

Fern bit her lip hard to hold back a sob. She wanted out of here. Her parents were probably losing their minds. Her brother was probably like Deana and wouldn't stop crying. Fern wanted to go home. She didn't want this to be real.

Her life was fucked up enough. This just wasn't fair.

She crawled to the back of their hole and dug around in the box for another pack of water. The packets of water and food were what Vanessa called rations, military packaged food and emergency water. She said whoever used this place must have been a survivalist or ex-military. Fern didn't care what it was as long as this shit kept them alive.

There was plenty for a few more days. Surely the police would find them soon.

A little voice she wanted to ignore warned they might never be found. They might starve to death in this fucking hole.

"You're that Parker girl."

Deana had finally stopped sobbing. "Yeah," Fern said.

"I heard about you—"

"You probably heard about me, too," Vanessa said, cutting her off.

Fern was glad. If the bitch had been about to say something bad about her family she might have to slap her fat face. Fern was filthy and scared. She did not want to hear anybody's shit. Especially somebody who five minutes ago had been crying like a little baby.

"He's going to kill us, you all know that, right?" Deana demanded as if she knew something everyone else didn't.

"Not if we stay smart," Vanessa argued. "There's only one of him and there's three of us."

"That's right," Fern said. "We can take him." She thought of the motherfucker and she decided she might be able to take him all by herself.

Deana laughed. "You are both so full of shit. Tell her the truth."

What the hell was she talking about? Fern wished she could see. It was completely black in this hole. Vanessa's lighter had died.

"Shut up," Vanessa snarled. "You shut up or I'll shut you up."

Fern's heart started to beat too fast. Something wasn't right. "What does she mean?"

"He killed Vanessa's lover," Deana said, "when he took her."

Shuffling sounds echoed in the darkness. "Shut up," Vanessa growled. She sounded like she was next to Deana now.

Fern was confused and scared. What the hell was she talking about? "I don't understand."

"He killed your parents," Deana snapped. "It was all over the news. He gutted them like deer."

Fern's stomach did a crazy flip-flop. "You're lying." She shook her head. Deana was just lying. She was a stupid, fat bitch. Fern had seen her big thighs when that asshole forced her into this fucking hole.

Vanessa must have punched her. Deana grunted and then Fern heard smacking sounds and scuffling. She wished she could see and she'd get a few punches in, too. Lying bitch!

The screech of metal sliding against metal shrilled above them. Fern froze. The hatch or whatever was opening.

A beam of light cut through the darkness. It was dark outside, too. "Hello there."

Fern scrambled to the ladder and stared up at the light, her eyes squinting. "I want to talk to my parents."

"I need to shake things up," he said, paying no attention to Fern's demand. "Create a little shock and awe. Who's game? I need a volunteer." He waved his gun in front of the light. "Or I can choose."

Fern reached toward the ladder. "Me," she cried. "I'll do whatever you want." She frowned. This was the first time he'd said so much. His voice sounded familiar.

A body suddenly slammed into Fern, pushing her aside. "She's just a kid," Deana said. "Take me. I can do anything you want. And my parents still have money. They'll pay whatever you ask."

The man chuckled. "I'll bet they would."

Fern started to shove the fat bitch out of the way when a hand grabbed her from behind. She tried to pull away but Vanessa jerked Fern hard against her and away from the light.

"Shh," she whispered next to Fern's ear.

Fern started to fight her but Vanessa held her even tighter.

"Well come on up here, Miss Venable. I'm certain you'll do just fine."

Fern was sure she'd heard his voice before.

Deana struggled up the ladder, the wood creaking and groaning under her weight. As soon as she was out of the hole that heavy old hatch fell closed again. The black darkness swallowed them once more and the slide of metal warned he had locked the damned thing.

Fern tore loose from Vanessa. "Why did you do that?"

"Listen to me, Fern." Vanessa's hand found her and pulled her close as if she was going to hug her. "He's a very bad man. He's not going to let Deana go. He'll do something bad to her. You're better off here with me. Maybe help will find us before he comes back again."

Fern's body felt as if it weighed a million pounds. Her stomach hurt. "She was telling the truth, wasn't she? He killed my parents."

"Yes."

Sobs rushed up into Fern's throat. "What about my brother?"

"He's okay. I saw on the news that the police found him alive."

Fern had been so mean to him. Never even told him or her mom and dad she loved them. She collapsed on the ground and let the sobs overwhelm her.

Now she was going to die and her brother would be all alone.

Twenty-Seven

11:59 p.m.

Deana had done exactly as he told her. No matter that she had wanted to run screaming into the night. He'd placed a cloth bag over her head, and then he'd taped her hands together behind her back. They had walked for a few yards in what felt like grass before reaching steps. After climbing the steps, the boards of an old porch had creaked as they crossed it. Then the hinges of a screen door had whined as he'd opened it. They'd walked through a room with old-fashioned linoleum on the floor. The floor was the only thing she could see beyond the bag if she looked down just right. As he led her forward the floor turned to wood. Not the kind of wood like her parents had in their home. This was old wood. The kind found in ancient houses. He'd sat her down in what felt like a chair and then he'd fastened her legs to it.

It took her a minute after he'd fastened her to the chair but she began to realize that he was no longer in the room. Deana tried to be strong. She really tried to think what to do. Instead, she fell apart. She moaned and sobbed when she should have been trying to get free. How could she free herself? Her arms and legs were bound and her face was covered. That was the moment when she surrendered. Urine seeped from her bladder, trickling between her thighs.

She was going to die. She should have known he would never let her go.

"Now."

He was back. Her breath caught.

He removed the bag and studied her. "Let's see what we can do."

Deana blinked. The man didn't wear a mask now. Instead he wore a shoulder-length blond wig. She stared, startled by his face. His cheeks were as red as a clown's. Heavy eyeliner and mascara made his eyes appear huge. Bloodred lipstick was smeared on his lips. The blue dress he wore was formfitting. He'd shaved his legs and arms and maybe his chest. If not for his voice and the Adam's apple she would not have guessed he was a man.

"What do you want from me?" she cried. She just wanted to go home. She was getting married. She didn't want to die.

He sighed. "I'm thinking brunette." He reached into the box that sat next to her chair and drew out a dark wig. He tugged it onto her head, then swept the bangs out of her eyes. "Perfect."

Shock held her still as he painted her eyes and lips. He dusted her cheeks with blush. She stared blankly at him. He was insane. Completely insane and she was going to die.

He pulled a skirt from the box and pulled at the stretchy waistband. "This should work." He turned his attention to her. He picked up a big knife from the counter and waved it at her. "I'm going to cut your legs loose. I want you to remove your jeans and put on this skirt. You give me any trouble and I'll slit your throat right now."

Tears blurring her vision, Deana did as he asked. She sat perfectly still while he cut through the tape binding her ankles. She stood and let him unfasten her jeans and drag them down. She lifted first one foot and then the other. When he threw the jeans aside she ran.

Hurry! Hurry! Hurry! She had to get out of this place!

He caught her halfway across the kitchen. The cold blade of the knife pressed against her throat, stinging her as it sliced shallowly into her skin. She screamed deep in her throat. The sharp bite of the blade and the feel of the warm blood dripping down her throat sent terror roaring through her. *Oh God. Oh God.* She did not want to die.

"Be a good girl now and put on the blouse."

She held stone still while he cut her wrists free. He handed her the blouse and she tried to figure out how to pull it over her head without messing up the wig. The blouse looked too small. *Please let it fit.* She had no idea what he would do if it didn't.

"Do not mess up your makeup," he warned, those red lips flattening into a thin line.

Somehow she managed to get the blouse on. The only thing that saved her was that the scooped neck was so low it made for a wide opening to poke her head through. The damned blouse was skintight. The waistband of the bell-shaped skirt cut into her gut. She felt like an apple shoved into a deflated balloon. She couldn't breathe.

He pointed to the black pumps on the floor and she stepped into them, twisting her ankle in the process. She never wore high heels like this. She couldn't possibly walk in them. Her heart pounded so fast she felt as if it would burst out of her chest.

"Spread your legs."

Fear closed her throat.

"Spread your legs," he repeated.

She inched her feet wide apart. Her lips trembled with the need to cry. "Please."

He reached into the box once more and brought out a leather belt. Attached to the belt was a large pink dildo. A cry squeaked out of her. Holding the knife by its hilt in his mouth, he pulled up her skirt and strapped the belt around her waist, leaving the dildo up front like she had sprouted a huge penis. Unable to move, Deana stood with her legs spread, the skirt hiked up and the big pink penis thrust out in front of her.

She closed her eyes and prayed hard. *Please, please, God. I don't want to die like this.*

A ripping sound forced her eyes open. He'd torn off a piece of duct tape. He was going to bind her arms and legs again. She stood frozen while he reached between her legs and taped the dildo to her thigh.

"Now." He pointed to the tray waiting on the long dining table. "You may serve the tea."

She looked from the tarnished silver tea service up to the chandelier. It was massive and very ornate. Light reflected and twinkled from the hundreds of crystals draped on its numerous arms, the light rained over the table and the tea service like shiny raindrops. Where was she? Why was he doing this?

"Serve the tea!" he shouted.

Deana jumped. She somehow managed to walk to the table. Her hands shook, making the lid of the teapot rattle as she poured the tea. When he sat, she sat. She followed his lead and sipped her tea. She tried so hard not to allow the cup and saucer to rattle or to make a face at the bitter taste.

When she had finished the tea, she sat the cup and saucer aside. She lifted her gaze to his. He was never going to let her go. She was going to die. She saw it in his eyes.

"Come along." He stood and held out his hand, his grotesquely painted mouth smiling.

She moistened her lips, wished she could swallow. Her heart was in her throat. "Where are we going?"

He winked. "To give her what she deserves."

Twenty-Eight

Asher tossed his keys on his desk. This was way too early to be at the office. He scrubbed a hand over his face. Holt would bitch 'cause he hadn't shaved. How could he shave when he was up all night watching her damned neighbors' house? He had no business getting personally involved, but damn it he couldn't help himself. He'd run into Olivia Shelton at the supermarket Sunday evening and he'd seen the fresh bruises on her throat. She'd cried and begged him not to tell Holt.

He'd ended up promising her he would keep her secret this time. What he really wanted to do was catch that husband of hers in just the right place so he could give the bastard a taste of his own medicine. Since that hadn't proven possible so far, he spent his nights watching her house. He'd doze off after all the lights went out. The husband left every morning about six to head to the garage where he was a mechanic.

Doing this forever wasn't feasible. At some point the woman would have to do the right thing or Asher would kill the guy and then he'd be fucked. Not a good scenario for him. Why was it guys like Wesley Shelton never turned up the victims of homicide investigations? Shelton was more likely to become the killer than the victim. Being the coward he was, his victims would typically be female and far weaker than him.

"Piece of shit."

Coffee. He needed coffee bad. Between the twisted case they were working and this extra-curricular activity, he was dead on his feet. He straightened his shirt, draped his tie around his neck and proceeded to knot the damned thing as he made his way to the lounge. He filled the brew basket and then poured in the water. He had no idea how long it would take to brew the pot. Coffee was always done when he came in.

The older guys preferred to make the coffee. They swore the younger generation didn't know how to make good coffee. This morning Asher felt anything but young. He felt as old as hell.

When the machine stopped dripping he poured a cup and took a sip. He groaned as the hot brew slid down his throat. "Oh yeah." Now, that was a cup of coffee.

He headed for the bullpen. Might as well get started reviewing the list of POIs they needed to interview again. At this point it felt as if they were repeating the same steps over and over and getting nowhere. They hadn't found anyone who'd seen or heard a damned thing beyond the family who'd noticed the old Lincoln Town Car and that lead had turned up nothing so far. Holt and Owens insisted they had to interview the whole damned list of names again. And again.

How many times and ways could they ask the same questions?

He stalled before he reached his desk. Devine was here. Asher started to say good morning and to ask him why he'd come in so early but his jaw locked. Devine was going through Bobbie's desk. It had taken Asher and everyone who worked at CID a couple weeks to get used to the new guy. Even now, some mornings Asher walked in and expected to see Newt making the rounds. He'd be wearing the blue suit he loved so much and sporting that damned flattop he'd worn since he was fifteen. Not once had Asher ever caught Newt pilfering through Bobbie's desk.

Devine looked up and spotted Asher. He smiled and said, "Morning, buddy. You're mighty early."

For a split second Asher didn't respond. The smile was right, Devine's voice was right, but that moment he'd hesitated between seeing Asher come through the door and smiling had missed a beat.

"Pulled an all-nighter outside a vic's home." Asher walked to his own cubicle and set down his coffee. "I just made a fresh pot of coffee."

"You're a braver man than me." Devine laughed. "The last time I tried to make a pot I thought the desk sergeant was going to shoot me."

Asher smiled. "Yeah, some of these guys are a little territorial."

Devine held up an evidence bag. "Finally." He closed what sounded like a drawer. "I came in early to take this back to the lab for Bobbie and I had a hell of a time finding it." He breezed past Asher's cubicle. "I'll be back in a few."

Asher gave him a nod and turned back to his coffee. Evidently he was jumpy this morning, seeing trouble everywhere he looked. He needed a good night's sleep.

"Bauer!" Devine shouted from the corridor.

"Fuck." Asher set his coffee down again and hauled his weary body out of his chair. "What the hell is it?"

"There's a guy in the parking lot taking a big-ass wrench to your car."

Asher pushed past Devine and bolted out the front door just as his windshield shattered. "Motherfucker!"

The guy swung the tool again, taking out the passenger window. When he drew back once more, Asher grabbed him by the arm and twisted. The wrench hit the ground.

Wesley Shelton.

"You just made a big mistake, pal." Asher shoved him backward.

Shelton regained his balance and charged Asher.

Asher hit the asphalt. The air burst from his lungs. Shelton straddled him and pounded a fist into his face before Asher could react. His jaw absorbed the blow. His lip cracked and the taste of blood filled his mouth.

Fingers curled into a tight fist, Asher plowed his right hand into the bastard's face. Then he bucked, throwing him off. In the next second Asher was on top of him, his Glock shoved into his face. Fear widened Shelton's right eye, his left was swiftly closing from the blow Asher had landed.

"You're under arrest, asshole."

"Stay away from my wife." Shelton went for another punch.

Asher blocked the blow with his left arm and shoved the muzzle of the Glock into his throat. "You do that again and my finger might just slip, you piece of shit. The only person who needs to stay away from your wife is you."

Shelton sneered up at him.

"Uniforms are on the way," Devine said.

Asher got to his feet and wiped his mouth with the back of his hand. "Read him his rights. I don't want to mess this one up. This dumbass assaulted me." He looked at his Mustang and groaned. "God damn it."

Shelton kept his mouth shut as Devine cuffed him and recited the Miranda. Asher had to walk away. He couldn't believe the dumb fuck was stupid enough to show up on city property at the damned Criminal Investigation Division and try something like this.

Bobbie's Challenger rolled into the lot. She parked and jumped out of the car. Asher looked

300 *Debra Webb*

back at his car and groaned again. "Shit." He'd just gotten it back from the shop.

"What's going on?" Bobbie hustled over to where Asher stood staring at his damaged vehicle. She glanced over at Devine who was making sure the uniforms took care of Shelton.

Asher jerked his head in that direction. "He's the husband who beats Holt's neighbor." He set his hands on his hips and shook his head. "Thought he could scare me, I guess."

"Why would he want to scare you?" Bobbie had that look. The one that said she suspected Asher had done something he shouldn't.

"I've been watching their house at night." He shrugged. "Just to make sure she and the kid are okay. I guess he noticed."

Bobbie smiled. "Wait. I thought you weren't a nice guy?" She punched him on the shoulder. "Didn't we have that conversation?"

"Whatever."

"Come on." She wrapped her arm around his. "I'll help you clean up that handsome mug."

He looked back at his car and growled. "I should just get a new car."

"That might not be a bad idea," she said.

Bobbie ushered him into the ladies' room and sat him down on a toilet seat.

"This is weird." Asher shuddered. "I shouldn't be in here."

Bobbie laughed. He liked the sound. It had taken her a long time to learn to laugh again. She gently cleaned his split lip with a wet paper towel.

He winced and growled and she laughed some more.

"You sound awfully chipper this morning," he ventured. "Is there something you need to tell me, Detective Gentry?"

She grinned. "Actually, I do have a bone to pick with you."

He kept to himself the crude remark about the bone he could give her. He respected Bobbie too much to say shit like that. Still, it crossed his mind.

"So pick," he told her.

"You told Devine about Nick Shade."

His first instinct was to deny the charge. "If I did I didn't mean to."

Bobbie frowned at him. "Explain what that answer means."

"The first week after he transferred in we might have had a few beers together." He shrugged. "It's possible I mentioned things I shouldn't have. That was before I started AA," he tacked on.

She exhaled a big breath. "Don't let it happen again."

He held up two fingers, then remembered it was supposed to be three. "Scout's honor."

Bobbie smiled. "I'm proud of you, Asher."

He stood and pulled her against his chest in a hug. "I'm proud of you, too."

They stayed that way for a long time. It wasn't often that either of them let their emotions show.

Maybe that was something else that needed to change.

Twenty-Nine

The chief had called a special briefing.

Bobbie struggled to stay focused while Holt and Owens went over the meager updates to the Parker-Manning murders and the three missing women as well as the way they appeared to intersect with Mark Hanover. There was not enough evidence to arrest Hanover for anything. As he had pointed out numerous people supported the summer youth camp. But he was the only one who'd had a dagger stolen that might have been used as a murder weapon—*might* being the operative word since the weapon had not been recovered. And he was the only one who kept insinuating himself into the investigation. At least until recently.

Since Nick insisted it was someone close to Hanover, she and Devine had made a list of Hanover's closest associates. As soon as this briefing was over, they would start plowing through those names.

As hard as she tried to pay attention, images and sounds from last night kept invading. Nick hadn't left her bed as she'd expected he would. He'd held her tucked against his body the rest of the night. She'd fallen asleep that way and roused to the feeling of him extracting his arms from around her. He'd taken D-Boy for a walk. She'd wanted to lie in bed and cocoon herself in the smell of him on her sheets. Instead, she'd hit the shower and made coffee. When he returned the awkwardness she'd feared hadn't come. They'd shared a quick breakfast and discussed details of the case like normal people.

Except you aren't normal, Bobbie. And neither is Nick.

Owens said something and gestured to their visitor. Bobbie blinked and reminded herself that Special Agent Anthony LeDoux had shown up for this unscheduled briefing. Maybe the briefing had been his doing. She didn't know why he was here rather than the agent from New York, but it appeared he was taking over and wanted to be more involved in the MPD's investigation. He'd thrown in that Vincent had been called back to the Big Apple. Really it didn't matter as far as Bobbie was concerned. A fed was a fed—her history with LeDoux notwithstanding. Still, it seemed unusual considering Vincent had been from the White Collar Crimes Division while LeDoux was from the Behavioral Analysis Unit. Evidently the FBI had decided that the murders had less to do with Nigel Parker's Ponzi scheme and more to do with a potential serial killer recruited by Weller. Maybe. Possibly. Jesus they needed a definite lead.

Whatever LeDoux's reason for gracing them with his presence there wasn't a hell of a lot to pass along in the way of updates. Every name on the list of known business associates, wronged investors and clients, family members, classmates and friends of the victims had been interviewed twice. They had absolutely zero true suspects. The Life Church connection and the dagger put Mark Hanover at the top of the persons-of-interest list. The man had an alibi for the murders and the abductions as did everyone else they could find who had ever threatened or been involved with one of the victims.

The case was back at square one except for the news she'd received shortly before the briefing about the video clip. Andy had called to say the clip Hanover provided had been altered. Part of the actual video was missing. Now, why would the man offer up a clip from his security video to supposedly help with the case if he was going to alter it? The reasonable conclusion was that he had something to hide.

There was just one thing to do: go at Hanover from a different angle.

Lieutenant Owens took the floor while Holt passed out the profile LeDoux's team had provided. Bobbie surveyed the report. White male, twenty-five to thirty-five. Introverted. OCD. Well if they'd had this profile a few days ago they could have saved themselves a lot of time. Not a single one of the business associates or wronged investors of Nigel Parker's, or friends and coworkers of Slade Manning's could be called an introvert and most were older than the profile suggested. They could have ignored all the female friends and fellow students or coworkers associated with the three missing women. Hanover would have been eliminated, as well. Wow. She rolled her eyes.

"Check in with your sources," Owens was saying. "Someone out there heard or saw something. Interview the neighbors one more time. Call on the POIs at the top of your lists again."

Holt added, "Bauer is still going through the list of older Lincoln Town Car owners registered in the tri-county area."

Bobbie glanced at Bauer. His jaw was bruised and his lip was split but he'd fared a hell of a lot better than the asshole who'd taken a wrench to his car. Bauer winked at her and Bobbie smiled. He'd been right about her feeling chipper this morning. She did a quick inventory and realized she didn't feel the guilt she had expected, either. Maybe she'd turned that corner the shrink was always telling her about. *A brighter day is just around the corner.*

Maybe. Too early to tell, she decided.

"We have," Owens said, dragging Bobbie's attention forward once more, "three witnesses who saw a man in a Lincoln Town Car watching the Parker home. We need to find him. Whether he's our killer or not, he may have seen something he doesn't realize is relevant."

Owens took her seat and LeDoux pushed back

his chair and stood. Bobbie stared at him, hoped he noticed how much she disliked him at the moment. He'd lost weight, she noticed. Evaluating him rather than listening to him gave her a ridiculous sense of glee. Back in August when he'd returned to Montgomery to lead the task force on the Storyteller case, he hadn't been wearing his wedding band. He still wasn't. Evidently he'd lost his wife to the job. In addition to the weight loss, he looked as if he rarely slept. Basically he looked like hell. She recognized the face, she had looked at it in her own reflection every day for months.

As much as she wanted to hate him and blame him for his part in the loss of her family...of her life, she couldn't. He'd lost a hell of a lot himself. More than most knew. She wondered if he'd ever told anyone what really happened in that dilapidated shack two months ago?

She had kept his secret as promised.

He droned on about all he and the Bureau were setting in motion in an effort to help MPD find the killer or killers responsible for these murders and the abductions, repeating the mantra that they must find the killer or killers before anyone else died. He highlighted the points Owens had already made.

Bobbie shifted in her seat. The chief had cast several glances at her the past few minutes. Maybe Owens had told him Nick Shade had contacted her. No, Bobbie decided, Owens wouldn't do that. He'd likely come to that conclusion all on his own. Maybe they could talk after the briefing. She had plenty to discuss with him, but they would need privacy for her questions. Could her mother have really been friends with a man like Hanover? She'd tried to put the concept out of her head. To chalk up Hanover's comments as nothing more than the game she knew it to be. Somehow she couldn't.

"We're looking more closely at the possibility that Randolph Weller is behind the events happening in Montgomery," LeDoux was saying.

Bobbie snapped to attention. What had she missed? "Do you have evidence he's involved?"

All eyes turned to her. She ignored the stern look from Owens and stared at LeDoux. She wanted an answer to her question.

"We're working on that," LeDoux said. "Unfortunately—"

"Did he provide a name?" the chief asked, appearing as surprised as Bobbie at the news.

"As I was saying," LeDoux went on, "unfortunately we never got to those questions. Weller suffered a cardiac episode and had to be transported to Emory Hospital. He'll be questioned again as soon as the doctor gives the okay."

Bobbie's ability to breathe failed her. Nick needed to know this news ASAP.

"It is our belief," LeDoux continued, "that the unknown subject you're dealing with is not your run-of-the-mill killer. Your department should be on high alert."

The chief said, "I'll expect the FBI to keep us fully informed. It's imperative that we neutralize this threat as quickly as possible and bring those women home safe."

"What's Weller's condition," Bobbie asked as soon as the chief paused to take a breath.

LeDoux glanced at her but quickly looked away before saying, "Cautiously optimistic."

"We have work to do, people," Owens said. "Though our primary focus will be on the missing we still have three murders on our plate. Keep that in mind while you're out there, but do not lose sight of the goal—we must find these women before they become homicides."

If Weller died, would the killer he'd sent abandon his mission? Weller had looked healthy when Bobbie saw him. Every instinct warned her that this was wrong. She glared at LeDoux. She would wager there was more he wasn't sharing.

"That's all for now," Owens announced.

Bobbie and LeDoux continued the stare down as chairs scooted away from the conference table. LeDoux was the first to look away.

Shake it off, Bobbie. She had questions for the chief. Then she would find Nick. She wasn't going to waste her time trying to make LeDoux talk.

As soon as LeDoux was out the door she stopped her uncle before he could do the same. That he would have left without giving her the usual warning to be careful showed how badly this turn of events had shaken him.

"I need to ask you something." She glanced around to ensure the room had cleared.

He looked at her with the long-suffering patience she had stretched to the limit on far too many occasions. "I don't have a lot of time. LeDoux and I are having a conference call with the special agent in charge of the Weller situation."

"My mother used to sing in a club over on Riveroaks called the Rusty Fiddle."

He appeared taken aback by her statement. "Where did you hear this?" He shrugged. "Had to be thirty-two or -three years ago."

So it was true. Jesus. "Mark Hanover showed me photos of her at this club."

The chief held up a hand. "We'll have to talk about this another time, Bobbie."

"Was she having an affair?" As much as she hated voicing the question, she couldn't let this go until she understood whether her mother and Hanover were more than acquaintances.

The chief's eyebrows reared up. "Your mother wanted a career in the music industry." He shrugged. "She had a beautiful voice. She was a beautiful woman. Her dreams of breaking into country music put a strain on her relationship with your father. That's true. Hanover must have seen her sing at that club. To my knowledge she hardly knew the man. They weren't friends and certainly weren't in an intimate relationship. Making a career in the music industry was just a fleeting dream before you were born."

The realization of what his words meant hit Bobbie hard as she did the math and put the time frame together. "She gave up her dream because she got pregnant with me."

"Yes."

The word hung in the air like an ax about to fall.

She had stolen her mother's dream. Why had she never mentioned it? Why hadn't she gone on to pursue her dream after Bobbie was born?

Because some people put their child before their careers...but not you, Bobbie.

"We'll talk about this again," the chief assured her. "For now, understand that Hanover is a vile man. He's made it his mission in life to find the vulnerabilities of those he targets and then he crushes them. He's a person of interest in this complicated investigation. He's toying with you, Bobbie." His brow furrowed with worry. "Perhaps you should allow another detective to pursue his involvement in this case."

"LeDoux's waiting," she reminded him. No way was she letting this go with Hanover.

When the chief was gone Devine appeared at the door. "You all right?"

She exiled the old memories and the new hurt. Whatever choices her mother had made, didn't matter now. "I'm great. I just need to use the ladies' room. Give me a minute."

Bobbie didn't wait for his response. She hurried to the bathroom and leaned against the door inside. Hands shaking, she called Nick's number. She waited through two rings, her heart racing.

"Hey."

Just hearing his voice was oddly reassuring. "There was a briefing. LeDoux was there." She took a deep breath and said the rest. "Weller suffered what he called a cardiac episode and they moved him to Emory Hospital."

For a moment Nick said nothing. "They should've let him die."

Before Bobbie could decide how to respond he said, "I have to go. Be careful."

She stared at her phone. Would he go to Atlanta to see Weller? The idea of him leaving tore at her. She put her phone away. *Focus, Bobbie.*

She had three missing women and a killer to find.

Bobbie exited the bathroom and found her partner. "Let's go see a man about a dagger."

"We're going to see Hanover again? I thought Owens wanted—"

"I have more questions for him," Bobbie said, cutting her partner off.

Devine shrugged as they moved toward the door. "He hasn't exactly given us anything useful so far."

"That's because we've been asking the wrong questions."

Thirty

She and Devine had been waiting for twenty minutes in a private lobby outside Hanover's office. According to his assistant, he was on a conference call. Bobbie didn't care how long she had to wait she wasn't leaving without talking to him. Devine, on the other hand, paced the floor. He didn't see the point in another meeting with the man. The last time Bobbie had met with Hanover he'd insinuated he thought it was time to call his lawyer. He might refuse to see her.

It was a chance she had to take.

Like his home, Hanover's business accommodations brandished his wealth. According to her research he'd purchased this three-story historic building twenty years ago. The article claimed he'd taken the derelict piece of history and turned it into a showplace fit for a businessman of his stature. The first-floor main lobby had marble floors and decadent artwork reminiscent of the time when parts of the building were purportedly used as a high-class brothel. From the carpet to the chandelier, even this private lobby on the top floor was elegantly appointed.

What was all this beauty and elegance hiding? Could he possibly know that someone close to him was a murderer? Was framing him? Were the two of them playing a game or were they both involved in the murders?

Three people were dead, three more were missing. This was no fucking game.

Devine finally sat down in the tastefully upholstered chair next to her. The ridiculously expensive bottles of designer water the assistant had brought sat unopened on the table between them.

"He's making us wait to get under our skin."

"Probably," Bobbie agreed.

"What do you make of LeDoux's announcement that Randolph Weller may have actually orchestrated these murders?" Her partner shook his head. "I've heard about the friends of inmates doing their bidding, but a serial killer following orders? The entire concept is over the top."

"Maybe it's not so over the top. He's a serial killer. Why wouldn't he have friends who were killers, too?"

"I suppose it makes a kind of sense," Devine allowed. He frowned. "So you believe we've been asking Hanover the wrong questions?"

"We've focused on Hanover's relationship with Nigel Parker and with his show of philanthropic deeds. We're moving past all that and focusing on what he expects to gain from being a part of this investigation."

Devine nodded slowly but his expression told her he didn't get it.

"If he's not our perp there's a reason he keeps inserting himself into the situation. Our goal is to find his motive."

"He's a certified weirdo, if you ask me." Devine looked around the room as if he hoped Hanover could hear him.

Bobbie wouldn't argue the point.

Devine leaned toward her, his face turned to her profile. "So what's the deal between you and LeDoux?"

When had her partner become such a busybody? She turned her face to his, forcing him to draw away a few inches. "I think all this time you're spending with your aunt is turning you into a nosy old lady."

A smile spread across his lips. "You might be right about that." He shifted his attention forward. "Be that as it may, I saw the way he looked at you. He's got a thing for you, Detective Gentry."

"I think what you saw was frustration. LeDoux and I don't see eye to eye on much of anything."

It was true. Although last year she had worked hard to impress him. The Storyteller case had been her first big case working on a joint task force with the FBI. Her first time working with some-one as high up the food chain as LeDoux period. For months after she escaped the Storyteller, she had hated LeDoux for allowing her to be a part of the investigation. She fit the bill perfectly of the Storyteller's preferred victim. LeDoux had recognized this immediately and had chosen Bobbie for the task force because of it. But the truth was, she had quickly realized exactly why LeDoux had picked her. Rather than back off, she'd dedicated herself that much more to the investigation. In the end she hadn't hated LeDoux nearly as much as she'd hated herself.

To some extent she had come to terms with the decision she'd made, but she would never forgive herself. Understanding was one thing, forgiveness another one entirely.

"Perhaps," Devine acquiesced. "Frustrated or not, he's like you."

Bobbie looked to her partner once more. "I'm afraid to ask what that means."

Devine met her gaze. "My aunt says we all have demons, but there are demons and there are *demons*. You can always spot the folks who battle the worst demons, the burden of the war is written in their eyes."

"Your aunt's a smart lady." She knew a little something about the demons that haunted LeDoux. She also understood that you couldn't analyze the kind of criminals his team profiled without damaging your psyche.

"You're a good cop, Bobbie." Devine gave her a nod. "Not just anyone could survive what you endured and get up every morning to face the possibility of a similar risk over and over."

She decided it would be best not to mention that

it was always easier to take a risk when you had nothing to lose.

Hanover's assistant, Prentice, stuck her head into the room. "Mr. Hanover can see you now."

"'Bout time," Devine grumbled under his breath.

He followed Bobbie from the room and down the corridor behind the attractive assistant who looked barely old enough to have finished college. Bobbie mentally skimmed through the names of those who had attended the Life Church summer youth camp. No Prentice that she recalled. As they crossed the assistant's office space to the grand doors leading to Hanover's office, Prentice paused. "Can I offer you anything else? Coffee, soda?"

"No, thanks." Bobbie was ready to talk to Hanover. They'd wasted enough time.

When Prentice shifted her attention to Devine, he shook his head.

Finally, she opened the double doors. Hanover stood behind a desk, a wall of windows overlooking downtown Montgomery serving as a backdrop.

"I apologize for your wait." He gestured to the chairs in front of his stylish desk. "Please, make yourselves comfortable."

Bobbie took the seat to her left. Devine sat in the remaining one.

"Can I assume you've had a break in your case since yesterday?" Hanover settled into the luxurious leather chair behind his desk. "I've been following the progress on the news and there's been no arrest. In fact, the only news is that you have another young woman missing."

"Then you should have recognized her name. Deana Venable attended your pet project at the Life Church." When he said nothing, she went on, "We've also learned that your missing dagger is most likely the weapon used to murder at least two people."

Hanover frowned. "I suppose that's good news for your investigation, if rather unsettling for me."

"The dagger was stolen from you," Devine offered. "You had no control over what the perpetrator did with it after he stole it." Her partner's gaze narrowed. "Did you?"

Hanover didn't exactly smile but his lip twitched. "You are a clever detective."

"There's a problem with the video clip you provided," Bobbie said, drawing his attention back to her.

"Problem?" Rather than look surprised, he looked intrigued.

"The clip was altered," Bobbie explained. "Part of it had been edited out. Did your security company do that?" From the corner of her eye she saw Devine glance at her in surprise.

Hanover flared his hands as if he had no idea. "I will certainly pose that question. I have no idea why they would do such a thing."

"For the record, Mr. Hanover," Bobbie said, "I don't believe you killed Nigel Parker and his wife. Or Slade Manning. I don't even believe you kidnapped a single one of those girls."

Hanover's expression closed. "Well that's certainly good to hear. Considering me a suspect simply because I lost the most money to Nigel's scheme is ridiculous. What I lost was of little consequence to my overall wealth. Others who lost far less suffered considerably more."

"We're well aware of your net worth, sir," Devine pointed out. Though he'd recovered from the surprise she'd failed to share with him quickly, she recognized the irritation in his voice.

"As your partner said," Hanover said to Bobbie, "the dagger was stolen from me. Clearly I couldn't have been the one to use it." He shrugged. "If I'm not a murder suspect, then I suppose you're here simply to harass me. It's a shame such hardworking detectives as yourselves can't find something more relevant to do."

"Interfering with an investigation is against the law, Mr. Hanover," Bobbie said. "I believe the video clip you provided was a waste of resources and time, which you must know could be interpreted as hindering our investigation and ultimately obstruction of justice."

He laughed. "Now what would I hope to gain by interfering with your work, Detective Gentry?"

"Attention. Notoriety." She shrugged. "I've been wondering the same thing. Why would you try to hinder this investigation? What could you possibly know that you want to hide if you're as innocent as you say? Or maybe someone close to you is attempting to frame you and you're having so much fun with us you've failed to notice the seriousness of the situation."

Understanding or something on that order settled across Hanover's face. "I hear you and a friend took a little road trip. Did you find what you were looking for, Detective Gentry? I'm just full of information about those days. We could talk about it if you like? I have lots more photos that might interest you."

Fury rumbled through Bobbie, she wrested it back. "You see what I mean, Detective Devine. We're here to discuss a multiple homicide case that includes three missing women and Mr. Hanover tries to mislead us." She glanced at her partner. "I think he's doing this on purpose, trying to keep us off balance in what he obviously sees as nothing more than a game."

"I believe you're right." Devine leveled his gaze on Hanover. "Sir, it's abundantly clear that my partner has lost patience with your impertinence. If there's anything you're hiding related to these investigations, now would be the time to share that information."

Anger darkened Hanover's face. "I think we've all said quite enough." He stood. "If you'll excuse me, I'm running behind on my next appointment."

The assistant appeared to escort them to the elevator as if she'd overheard her boss's last statement. More likely he had alerted her via a private intercommunication system. Bobbie sent one last look at Hanover before leaving. Prentice led them out of the suite of offices and to the elevator. She watched until they were onboard and headed down.

When her partner would have spoken Bobbie put up a hand to keep him quiet. She didn't want to say a word until they were out of and away from this building.

Two minutes later they were in her Challenger. She started the engine but waited before pulling out into traffic. "I'm sorry I didn't tell you about the video clip but that unexpected briefing put me off track."

"Understandable." Devine gave her a nod. "I'm thinking we've pushed Hanover into a corner."

Bobbie agreed. "He knows something he doesn't want to share. It might not lead us to our perp, but it's relevant."

Devine stared at her a long moment. "Do you really believe he knows the killer?"

"I hope for his sake he doesn't because a smart killer never leaves loose ends."

Thirty-One

Boultier Street
5:30 p.m.

Nick had waited on LeDoux to call him back since Bobbie gave him the news. The agent had finally sent a text half an hour ago with a time and location. As soon as LeDoux slid into the booth, Nick demanded, "Tell me he's secure."

"He's secure." LeDoux motioned for the waitress and ordered a beer.

"Who gave the authorization for him to be moved?" According to his medical records Weller had no health issues. Nick had checked on more than one occasion in hopes of learning the bastard had developed cancer or some fatal heart condition.

"The prison doctor." LeDoux looked him in the eye. "I don't like this, either, but it happened. The prison has an obligation to provide medical care. I'm certain you've heard about the lawsuits over inadequate health care in the prison systems. And we both know the Bureau wants to protect its asset."

Nick shook his head. The feeling that the other

shoe was about to drop wouldn't go away. "This is a mistake. You must have realized by now that Weller is behind these murders and possibly the abductions. He's planning something. This sudden cardiac episode is no doubt part of his plan."

"We have him contained." LeDoux let his own frustration show. "He has more guards than he had in the prison. He isn't going anywhere."

Nick wouldn't waste any more time arguing with him. "Have you looked into the man, Mark Hanover, Bobbie has been investigating?" Nick didn't generally share sources with the feds or anyone else but they were running out of time here. "Or her partner, Steven Devine?"

"Hanover is no one. As for Devine, what's the problem, you jealous that he's Bobbie's partner? The guy is a decorated veteran cop. The whole team around Bobbie is top-notch."

Nick ignored the fact that LeDoux had gotten one part a little too right. But Weller…holy hell. Nick couldn't shake the feeling that the worst was yet to come. "I think you should have a second look at Hanover and a nice long one at Devine and you'd damned well better remind your people to watch Weller closely. Whatever his plan, it will happen soon. He'll make a move. Count on it."

"We have the situation under control." His beer arrived and LeDoux downed half the glass in one long swallow.

Nick had given LeDoux a heads-up. There was nothing else he could do.

LeDoux frowned and reached into his jacket

pocket. He removed his cell and stared at the screen a moment before taking the call. He listened for several moments, his complexion going pale. "I'm on my way."

When he put his phone away, he set his gaze on Nick. His tone as well as his expression warned the news was bad. "How did you know?"

Nick searched the other man's face for some indication of what he meant. "Know what?"

LeDoux shook his head. "Half an hour ago Weller walked out of the hospital. He's gone. They're locking down the city in an effort to catch him. You knew this was going down."

Outrage and too many other emotions to name hardened in Nick's gut. "Any damned fool should have known." He pushed out of his chair and gave LeDoux a final warning. "They won't be able to stop him."

"You better hope you're wrong."

After all that had happened LeDoux still didn't understand. There was no force on earth that could change how this was going to play out.

Thirty-Two

Athens, Alabama
6:00 p.m.

Randolph Weller inhaled deeply of the fresh air.
He closed his eyes and lifted his face to the sun. It
had been so long. The feel of the warm rays was
like a lover's caress. He would love to stand like
this for hours. Alas, he couldn't quite afford the
time just now, but soon, very soon.

He opened his eyes and surveyed the yard that
spread out into rolling pastures. He smiled. He
wished he could be in Montgomery to see Bobbie's lovely face when she received the news. Oh,
and Nicholas. If only Randolph could be a fly on
the wall when Nicholas was informed that his father had escaped. He drew in another deep lungful
of the fresh, country air. It was good to be free. He
couldn't wait to meet Bobbie again without all the
formalities of guards and shackles. He so wanted
to know her better. Beyond the fact that she had
somehow captured his son's attention, she intrigued

Randolph. Rare was the soul who could manage such a feat.

Soon all who had poked and prodded at his brain within the esteemed FBI would hear the horrifying news about Dr. Randolph Weller's stunning escape. The whole lot of them would desert their trivial activities and focus on finding him. Not one would sleep for fear of him coming to make them pay for what they'd done to him.

Pathetic creatures. Try as they might, they would fail because Randolph would never make the same mistake again.

He made his way back to the house. He resisted the impulse to remove his shoes and feel the grass beneath his feet. He had one final matter to which he must attend before he completely relaxed.

The screen door screeched as the cow stuck her head outside. "Randy, you want some lemonade? I just made a fresh pitcher."

He produced a broad smile as he reached the porch. "You are too good to me, Anita."

She blushed. "Come on in here. I have some family albums I want to show you. My grand-mamma died last year and left this place to me. I didn't tell a soul back in Atlanta. We'll be safe here for a while."

"You amaze me," he said as he approached the door where she waited.

She took him by the arm and ushered him inside. "I'll always protect you, Randy."

"You're far too thoughtful."

When she turned to prepare his glass of lemonade, Randolph reached for the cast-iron skillet sitting on the stove. He swung it hard against the back of the cow's head. She plummeted to the floor like a felled oak, the glass pitcher shattering in the sink, lemonade splattering the counters.

He knelt next to her and leaned down to speak into her ear. He wanted her to hear his words before she drifted off into unconsciousness. "I'll be right back, dear. I need to run out to the barn and fetch that ax I saw. You stay here now," he added in that sickening Southern accent that made her every word so immensely exasperating.

Randolph left her twitching and jerking on the floor. Perhaps he'd hit her harder than he'd intended. Oh well, what was done was done. He would enjoy the work to come whether she did or not.

Adrenaline rushed through his veins. It was good to be back.

As soon as Nicholas heard the news he would understand what came next.

You will not be able to stop me this time, son.

Thirty-Three

Deana Venable's family would no longer have to wonder if their daughter would be found. Pastor Liddell had discovered her body as she prepared for the Tuesday night Bible study class. Two uniforms had been posted at the entrance to the church parking lot to turn away the folks who showed up for the canceled class. Yellow crime scene tape fluttered in the breeze that had kicked up as the sun disappeared.

An evidence tech snapped photos of the woman's body where it lay sprawled across the steps leading up to the altar. A river of blood had made its way down those same steps, fleeing the depraved scene. The victim wore a brunette wig and clown-like makeup, otherwise her mutilated body was nude. Her breasts and labia had been cut away from her body, and lastly her throat had been slashed. Besides the blood, something putrid was smeared on her thighs.

"Jesus Christ," Bobbie repeated for the umpteenth time.

The coroner was en route. Reporters would be right behind her. What better way to make headlines with the ravaged body of a homicide victim than to find one in the house of God?

Bobbie dropped her head. "I'm sorry I couldn't find you sooner." *Please let me find Fern and Vanessa before this sick bastard can do this to them.*

Bobbie stood and joined Devine where he was finishing up with Liddell's statement. Questions whirled in her head. Why murder the last victim he abducted rather than the first? Could this mean Fern and Vanessa were already dead? If they were alive, was he providing food and water to keep them that way?

Damn it! She wanted to find those women alive.

Seated on a pew, Liddell dabbed at her eyes with a tissue and peered up at Bobbie. "I have to tell her parents." The pastor shook her head. "They can't hear this anywhere else."

"Just a few more questions and we'll take you to Deana's parents." Bobbie sat down beside her.

Devine took his cue and stood. "I'll see if Dr. Carroll has arrived."

Bobbie peeled off her gloves and tucked them into her pocket. "Forgive me if Detective Devine has already asked you some of these questions."

Liddell shook her head. "Ask whatever you need to. Anything I can do… God have mercy." She closed her eyes and started to pray again, her lips moving urgently.

When she'd opened her eyes once more, Bobbie asked, "When were you last here—before you found her?"

Liddell dabbed at her eyes again. "Yesterday. I'm usually here several hours every day, but today I had hospital visits." A faint smile trembled across her lips. "Then I hurried home to bake the cookies for tonight. I like to prepare something special for the ones who make the extra effort to come to the Bible study after a long day at work."

Bobbie waited for her to continue. Outrage swam in her veins. She wanted to get this guy. She wanted to go to Atlanta and shove her Glock in Weller's face and demand some answers.

"I was taking the cookies to the kitchen." She gestured to a side door that led to the corridor that joined the church to the fellowship hall. "I always come through there." She laughed, the sound feeble. "The fellowship hall was only added a few years ago and I just never changed my way of doing things."

The broken platter and scattered cookies lay at the far end of the main aisle separating the pews, confirming the pastor's story.

"Does anyone else have access to the church when you're not here?"

Liddell frowned and then nodded. "The church doors are always open." She gestured to the side door. "That door is locked when I'm not here. Most things a thief would consider marketable are in the fellowship hall." Fresh tears welled in her eyes.

"Anyone can come into the church to pray whenever they like."

"I haven't seen any cameras," Bobbie said. "Do you have any sort of security system?"

Liddell shook her head. "The only security I depend on is God."

Some days it felt like God wasn't watching. Bobbie looked toward the altar where Deana Venable's body had been staged in the most debauched way. Today was one of those days.

"Ma'am, I know we've discussed this before," Bobbie ventured, "but please bear with me, it's imperative that we cover all bases."

Liddell nodded, the movement jerky.

"Is there anyone associated with the church or any of its work who has ever given any indication that he or she is capable of something like this?"

Liddell dropped her head and began to sob. Bobbie struggled for patience. Finally, the pastor composed herself once more. "There was a girl years ago." She shook her head. "Decades ago. She was twelve and she claimed Mark tried to rape her but—" Her gaze collided with Bobbie's. "No one believed her. You have to understand that it's my duty to support this community through the church. The Hanover family gives the kind of money we couldn't hope to get anywhere else."

Fury twisted through Bobbie as she glanced toward the victim. "Do you think Hanover's money will matter to the Venable family?"

More of those hiccuping sobs came. Bobbie had

no sympathy for the woman. "The girl recanted her story."

"I'll need her name." If she could get the girl—woman now—or her family to make a statement, that was something she could use against Hanover. It was too late for the family or the victim to seek criminal charges but justice could still be found if they could tie Hanover to these murders. And there was always civil action.

"The family moved away after that and the girl died. Leukemia I think." Liddell swiped at her face with the wadded tissue. "The rumor was that Mark's father gave them a hefty sum of money to go."

Bobbie held back the hurtful words she wanted to say. Even if Liddell had been more forthcoming sooner they still might not have been able to save the woman. Hanover's sick sexual appetite didn't make him a killer, but it was one more link to the murders and the missing. There was no question, Hanover had to know the killer.

"Excuse me, Detective Gentry."

Bobbie looked up at her partner who'd appeared at the end of the pew. Had the killer made a mistake this time? "I'll be back in a moment." Bobbie couldn't look at Liddell as she stood and walked away. This was a regret the pastor would have to live with for the rest of her life.

Devine ushered Bobbie to the entrance doors, well out of hearing range of anyone in the church. "Owens called."

Bobbie automatically checked her cell. She'd put

it on vibrate when she'd arrived but she hadn't felt it go off. Sure enough she had a missed call from the lieutenant. "We need to find Hanover." She tucked her phone back on her belt and shook her head. "Liddell just told me—"

"Bobbie," Devine interrupted, "a nurse from the prison in Atlanta is missing. They think she helped orchestrate the escape."

Devine's eyes were wide with disbelief or shock but Bobbie didn't have a clue what he was talking about. "What're you talking about? What escape?"

Her partner made a face that said he was even more surprised by her answer. "Owens called to tell you Randolph Weller escaped."

Gardendale Drive
8:00 p.m.

Devine dropped Bobbie off at her house. She had tried to call Nick but he hadn't answered and he hadn't called her back.

She and Devine had been to Hanover's home and his office. The housekeeper, the assistant—no one knew where the hell he was so a BOLO had been issued. Bobbie felt sick at the very core of her being. Carroll had called to say the creamy gunk smeared on Venable's thighs was decayed human tissue. The corpse the tissue came from was likely in its putrefaction stage. Thankfully Carroll had found no indication that Deana had been sexually assaulted. But where the hell had the dead tissue come from? Bobbie shuddered at the grotesque images that came to mind. Carroll would conduct additional testing and get back to her.

Bobbie unlocked her front door and stepped inside. She could only imagine what Nick was feeling. The man who murdered his mother and dozens of others was out there somewhere planning God only knew what. She flipped on a light and stalled. Her heart plummeted when the alarm's incessant warning finally penetrated her thoughts.

He was gone.

If he'd been here he would have shut off the security system. She entered the code to silence the damned thing, closed the door and locked it, then tossed her bag on the sofa. Of course he was gone. He would want to get on Weller's trail as quickly as possible.

She had wanted to say goodbye.

Wait. A new tension coiled inside her. Where was D-Boy?

The thought had barely filtered into her weary brain when the sound of the back door opening echoed.

"Good boy."

Nick's voice.

Bobbie went to the kitchen. Nick released D-Boy from his leash and the animal bounded to her, almost knocking her over. She rubbed his head but she couldn't take her eyes off Nick. "You're still here."

For a moment they stood there staring at each other. Bobbie spoke first. "I was afraid you'd left already."

"I can't go yet."

No matter that the killer Weller had set in motion was still out there, she was surprised Nick hadn't gone after his father. *Doesn't mean he stayed for you, Bobbie.* "What're you going to do?"

"You know what I have to do."

She did. He felt a responsibility to the people here. "Any word on Weller?"

"They found the nurse's body in Athens." His voice was distant, hollow. "LeDoux is headed there now. I need to meet him at the location. See if Weller left anything that will help with the hunt for him, but I'll be back before dawn. Can you stay with Holt or Bauer tonight?"

No way was she letting him do this alone. She headed for the door, grabbing her bag and her keys en route. "I'm going with you." She paused, hand on the knob. "You ready?"

He held her gaze as he moved toward her. "You sure about that? You might be needed here."

"We can't find Hanover. We don't have a single solid lead. I think I can slip away for a few hours."

Something flashed in his eyes, relief maybe.

He took the keys from her hand. "Thanks. I could use the company."

Bobbie imagined that was the first time in his adult life that Nick Shade had said those words. She was glad he'd said them to her.

Thirty-Four

Tony walked out the back door, the wooden screen door slapping against its frame behind him. *Breathe.* He needed to breathe.

The scene inside the farmhouse was definitely Weller.

When he'd cleared his lungs enough to draw in a few deep breaths that didn't reek of death, he walked back inside. The Limestone County sheriff and two of his deputies watched in disbelief as the crime scene techs he'd summoned photographed the gruesome scene. Tony had given the sheriff a hand as to how to proceed. The man had never been faced with a scene like this one. It was classic Weller.

Anita Meyers's body had been chopped into eleven pieces. The legs and arms as well as the head had been severed from the torso with an ax. Then the legs had been separated at the knees and the arms at the elbows. Finally the torso had been severed at the waist. The dismemberment had taken place in the kitchen. The old wood floor bore the hack marks of the ax and was soaked in blood.

Once Weller had finished taking the body apart, he'd cleared a spot in the living room and spread a white sheet on the floor. Piece by piece he'd reassembled the body in a grotesque manner. Laying the arms and legs at impossible angles. The work wasn't up to his usual standards but he'd obviously been in a hurry.

"So, you say," Sheriff Dennis Copeland said as he moved over to stand by Tony, "Anita there helped this Weller guy escape."

Copeland had explained how the farm had belonged to Meyers's grandparents. Meyers had moved to Georgia after high school and as far as the sheriff knew she hadn't come back to Athens often until after her grandmother passed away last year.

"She did," Tony said with all the patience he could drum up. At this point they suspected she had been providing Weller with medication that caused him to present with a heart condition. The details weren't firm, but likely her assistance had been the key to him being moved to Emory Hospital. Anita had facilitated his escape there. The security cameras told that story well enough. "You need to make your deputies aware that Weller is no common killer."

Copeland was a short man probably only a couple of years away from retirement. He pushed his glasses up his nose and stared at Tony. "Is that so?"

Tony had already explained that Weller was a serial killer but the man didn't seem to fathom the magnitude of the situation. "Yes," he said, "Weller did this—" he gestured to the mess on the floor "—to forty or so other victims before he was captured. If he isn't found soon more will die."

Copeland set his hands on his hips and looked Tony straight in the eyes. "Well, if catching him is what you want, you'd better hope he gets out of Alabama real fast. Because if we find him he won't be captured, he'll be shot dead."

The FBI wanted to recover their asset, but Tony was with the sheriff. He hoped like hell the bastard was shot on sight.

A set of headlights bobbed as a new vehicle arrived on the scene. Tony recognized the car immediately. He walked out to meet Shade and Bobbie. She had sent him a text letting him know they were only a few miles away.

The driver's side and passenger's side doors opened at the same time. The spotlights the county had set up around the house highlighted Shade's tall form and Bobbie's smaller one.

"Was he here?" Shade asked.

Tony blew out a breath. "Yeah. He killed the nurse who helped him escape." Tony had no fucking sympathy for the ignorant bitch.

Shade walked past him and headed for the house. Tony had advised the sheriff that a detective and a *consultant* from Montgomery were en route.

"How the hell did they let this happen?" Bobbie demanded.

"You watch the news," he grumbled. "She was

desperate for attention and he gave it to her. She thought she was in love. Now she's dead."

Bobbie shook her head and followed the path Shade had taken.

Tony trailed after her. No need to rush. He'd seen all there was to see. When they reached the porch the three deputies who'd been inside shuffled out. The sheriff had apparently ordered his men outside. Or maybe Shade had. Bobbie went in first, Tony right behind her. Shade was in the living room staring at his father's work. Off to one side the sheriff watched as if he'd tuned in to the movie of the week.

Feeling the two-day stretch without sleep, Tony tucked his hands into his pockets and joined Shade at the edge of the sheet. He said, "We'll see a hell of a lot more than this if we don't find him."

Shade continued to stare at the dismembered corpse. "I'll find him." He glanced at Tony. "This time I'll finish what I started."

Thirty-Five

The hole opened again.

Vanessa pulled Fern behind her as they stared up at the stars. It was night again which meant Deana had been gone maybe twenty-four hours and no one had come for them.

Deana was dead. Vanessa knew it.

When her body trembled with the need to cry, she squared her shoulders. Slade was dead. Fern's parents were dead. How the hell were they supposed to survive this? The need to curl into the fetal position was almost overwhelming. No. She had to be strong for Fern. She was just a kid. This bastard was not going to hurt her.

Fern had told her she'd thought she recognized his voice. She thought maybe he was the security guy her father had hired to watch their house. She'd cried and told Vanessa how she'd made out with the guy a couple of times. Most likely he'd used the girl to get into her parents' home. Sick bastard.

A click sounded and then the beam of a flashlight blinded them.

Vanessa backed up a couple of steps, keeping Fern behind her. She squinted up at the light.

The man flashed the gun again. "Good evening, ladies."

The blinding light prevented Vanessa from seeing his face.

"I need another volunteer. Who would like to get out of this dank hole tonight?"

Fern bolted away from Vanessa and toward the ladder. Vanessa dragged her back and muttered in her ear. "Remember, we talked about this."

"I want to go," Fern whispered, her words frantic. "I need to see my brother. To tell him—"

"He won't take you to your brother," Vanessa growled against her cheek.

"Come on now," he warned. "Don't make me come down there."

"I know it's—" Vanessa cut off the accusation Fern intended to shout at him.

"Shhh." Vanessa's heart stalled as she waited for Fern to decide what she was going to do. For this to work they had to stick together.

The poor girl nodded, a keening sound escaping her.

Vanessa almost wilted with relief.

"I'm waiting," he singsonged.

Vanessa ushered Fern all the way against the back wall of the hole or cellar or whatever the hell it was. Then, she summoned her strongest voice. "If you want us, come and get us."

They had no weapons. They were scared and weak, but if the bastard came into this hole they would charge him. They might end up dead, but maybe he would, too.

They were going to die anyway.

She was banking on the idea that he wouldn't take the risk.

"Come up here now!" he roared. "If you want to live," he said more calmly, "if you want to go home, do as I say."

Feeling Fern's thin body quaking against her, Vanessa held her ground. "Come and get us, motherfucker."

The flashlight went out.

Vanessa held her breath.

Endless seconds ticked off in the silence.

The iron door slammed shut, closing out the night stars. The grating sound of metal against metal announced he'd locked it once more.

Vanessa's knees gave out and she sank to the ground. Fern went down with her. They hugged and sobbed. She had been right. He wasn't about to risk getting injured or worse coming down here after them.

Maybe they would live a little longer. And maybe the cops would find them before he came back.

Thirty-Six

"I'll contact you once I arrive."

Mark didn't have time for explanations. His longtime friend and overpaid attorney, Sawyer Eddington, tried again to convince him to stay.

"They have nothing, Mark. Conjecture. Hearsay."

Winifred had called Mark and informed him that in a hysterical moment she had told the police what he did all those years ago. She'd threatened to tell even more if he dared to withdraw his funding from the church. Mark had laughed at her. He'd already paid for that mistake once. Sawyer knew this. Now the police did, as well. Mark was ruined. Even after the dust settled from all this drama, coming back was hardly an option.

"This will blow over," Sawyer was saying. "They have no evidence against you. You haven't done anything wrong. The past is merely hearsay. The girl is dead."

His friend could be utterly naive at times. Or perhaps he simply didn't know Detective Bobbie Gentry. She would never let this go. She would poke and prod until she learned about all the others. Bobbie was too pure of heart just as her mother had been. Mark had wanted her so badly. He'd gone to the club and watched her sing again and again. No matter what he'd offered her—the fucking world— she would not betray her husband. Mary Jane Fleming was the one woman he had loved more than himself. No matter how he tried, she chose her no-body husband over Mark. What a fool. She could have had everything.

"I have to go. I can't risk being anywhere more than a few minutes." He'd only returned to the house to get his extra hidden passport. An alterna-tive ID was a must. Money in various banks around the world under that alternative ID was sheer bril-liance.

After enduring a final warning from Eddington to stay calm Mark ended the call and shoved the phone into his pocket. He took a breath. Grabbed the passport and credit cards from the safe in his closet and—

"Hello, Mark. I've been waiting for you."

He froze. There was no mistaking that voice. All the things he had intended to do with the rest of his life flashed before his eyes. A sad smile tugged at his lips. Mark had known this time would come one day.

"I'd planned to bring you a gift, but—" he made a sound, something like a laugh "—there were no volunteers and the time got away from me. You know how it is."

Mark turned slowly to face his destiny.

No man could cheat fate forever.

Thirty-Seven

Commerce Street
Wednesday, October 26, 7:00 a.m.

Bobbie pulled to the curb at Bauer's building. She sent him a text to let him know she was there. She'd managed a couple hours' sleep on the way back from Athens. She hadn't meant to doze. She and Nick had gotten back to her place just after four. She'd headed for the shower. Nick made coffee and asked her about her agenda for the day as if his father weren't out there somewhere planning God only knew what. He was way too calm under the circumstances.

At some point on her drive to Bauer's place, she'd realized why Nick had been so damned calm. He already had a plan. Last night he'd said he couldn't leave yet, and then this morning he'd dodged her questions about where he'd be today. At some point in the past two or three days he'd warned her that he suspected the killer was someone close to Hanover.

He knew who the killer was. She would bet every

damned thing she possessed that he was out there trailing the killer right now. He would know exactly how to approach his prey without giving the first hint he was close.

"Damn it." She hoped like hell he kept in mind that Weller could be closer than anyone suspected. This wasn't like Nick's other hunts. This was personal. The idea of what Weller might have in store for his son and countless others, including her, was unfathomable. She'd seen and felt Nick's concern last night when he'd stood over his father's latest victim.

No, not just concern. *Fear.* She'd seen a fleeting glimmer of fear. Or maybe it was her own fear she'd seen reflected in his eyes.

Athens was less than three hours from Montgomery. They had to be on their toes. If Weller was headed this way or already here…

Jesus Christ. Things were only going to get worse.

If they didn't find Vanessa and Fern soon chances were the two would end up like Deana. Sage was counting on Bobbie. She had to find his sister alive.

And somehow she had to help Nick.

Bobbie checked the time on her cell. Where the hell was Bauer? With a quick tap of his name she waited through four rings. The call went to his voice mail. If he'd gone off the wagon last night she was going to kick his ass. She emerged from her car and went into the building, bypassed the elevator and took the stairs.

By the time she reached Bauer's door she was a little irritated and her leg was aching from the climb. If she could get up every morning and face the day without wanting to kill herself, he could damn sure do it without a drink.

She pounded on his door.

No answer.

"Shit."

She pounded again, a little harder this time.

Still no answer.

Frustrated, she grasped the knob and gave it a twist.

To her surprise the door opened.

Bobbie stilled. The anger and frustration vanished. "Bauer?"

She reached for her Glock. "Hey, man, it's time to go to work. You up?"

Silence.

Gripping her weapon, ready to fire, she pushed the door open with her right foot.

The metallic odor of blood hit her like a punch to the face.

Heart thundering, she felt for the light switch to the left of the door. Lights came on in the main living area. No movement. She eased into the apartment. "Bauer, you up?"

It was in that next second between the words leaving her lips and her eyes surveying the room that her brain registered what lay on the floor beyond the dining table.

"Bauer!"

Bobby rushed across the room. She slipped in

the blood and fell to her hands and knees. Her weapon slid across the floor.

She stared first at her hands.

Bauer's blood.

Her gaze dropped to the floor where he lay face-down in a massive puddle of his own blood. The back of his head was a swollen, oozing pulp.

Shit! Shit! Shit! "Bauer?"

She turned him over and instinctively checked for a pulse. He was gone. Her heart broke into a million screaming pieces as she pulled him into her arms. "Nooo."

She reached for her cell and yanked it free of her belt. Her fingers shook so badly it took three attempts to get the numbers right. Blood smeared the screen.

"Nine-one-one, what is the nature of your emergency?"

"This is Detective Bobbie Gentry." She drew in a shuddering breath and gave the address. "Officer down."

The phone slipped from her fingers as she read the words written in blood on the floor three maybe four feet away from where she sat holding Bauer.

This one's just for you, Bobbie.

She screamed so long and hard her lungs ached from lack of air.

Then the fury came. She stared down at the man she loved like a brother. "I'm so sorry." She kissed his bruised jaw and lowered him back to the floor.

Think like a detective, Bobbie.

She'd already contaminated the crime scene. Not that this fucker ever left any evidence behind. But this scene was different. It was a mess. It spoke of emotion. Of rage.

She rubbed the blood from the screen of her phone and called Devine. "Find Holt. Bring her to Bauer's apartment." She took a deep breath, shook all over as a fresh wave of hot tears blurred her gaze. "It's bad."

Her next call was to Andy. She wanted the best they had here. Andy was the best.

She clipped her phone back on her belt and surveyed the room. "No indication of a struggle," she said aloud, her voice wobbling. "No forced entry." Adrenaline exploded in her chest. *He knew his killer?*

Legs feeling rubbery, she started to move and realized her shoes were covered in blood. She removed them, scrubbed her hands on her slacks. Her blouse and jacket were saturated with blood. God damn it!

Forcing her mind to work, she walked around the blood, picked up her Glock. Didn't care that it had Bauer's blood all over it, too. She checked the bedroom and bathroom. She should have checked the rest of the apartment when she first came in.

Clear.

The sirens were wailing outside now. She came back into the main room. *Inventory the details, Bobbie.* Blood was thick and pasty. His arms had felt slightly stiff. He'd been dead several hours.

Carroll. She should call the coroner. On the floor partially hidden by the sofa was a large metal object. She could only see part of it. Looked like a wrench. The murder weapon, she presumed. The idea that the wife beater—what was his name?—could have hurt Bauer flittered through her head. No way. He wouldn't know to leave the message.

Think, Bobbie. She needed Carroll and those techs here now.

"Bobbie."

Her head shot up. Nick was at the door.

She held up a hand. "Don't come in." She wiped her face with the back of her forearm. "Bauer's dead." Her voice shook so hard she wasn't sure he would understand what she said.

Nick stepped back for the uniformed officers who rushed up behind him.

"Talk to the neighbors," she said in a relatively steady voice. "See if anyone heard or saw anything. Call the building manager and get access to any video surveillance they have." She took a moment to compose herself. "This is one of our own."

Holt appeared at the door next. "Is he…?"

Bobbie nodded. More of those damned tears slid down her cheeks. "Whoever did this… Bauer must have known him."

The sergeant crossed the room, Devine right behind her. She knelt next to Bauer. Her body shook with her quiet sobs. Bobbie dropped to her knees next to her.

Holt gasped.

Bobbie followed her gaze to the message written in Bauer's blood. She turned to Bobbie. Fury tightened her lips. She shot to her feet and strode out of the apartment. Bobbie dragged herself up and went after her.

Her partner's blood smeared on her clothes, Holt drew her weapon on Nick. "This is about you."

Bobbie put her hand on her arm. "This is not about any of us. It's about a fucking sadistic killer who doesn't give one shit about anyone."

Nick didn't flinch. Despite the profound sadness she felt, Bobbie abruptly wondered if he cared whether or not he lived beyond this point. Two months ago she wouldn't have cared if she died as long as the Storyteller died first. Was Nick doing what he could do until his heart stopped beating? His existence couldn't be considered living.

Holt lowered her weapon. "Get out of here. I can't look at you right now." She turned to Bobbie. "Go home." Her voice faltered. "Wash off Bauer's blood and then find the son of a bitch who did this."

Bobbie held her ground. "As long as Devine stays with you."

"What the fuck ever," Holt growled.

Bobbie pulled Devine aside. "Do not leave her no matter what she says."

He nodded his understanding. "I called the LT. She's notifying the chief and then coming straight here." He glanced at Nick before asking Bobbie, "You'll be okay?"

"Yeah." Bobbie dragged in a breath. "Thank you."

She looked back once more before heading for

the stairs. She could feel Nick behind her but she couldn't look at him or speak to him.

Not because she believed this was his fault.

This was her fault.

She had let the Storyteller into her life last year and that one mistake had stolen every single thing she cared about.

She'd had enough. If Weller and whoever he'd commissioned to do his dirty work wanted her, all they had to do was come and get her.

She sat down in her car, blood smearing on the black leather seats, and suddenly realized she had left her shoes in Bauer's apartment. Her socks were soaked in his blood.

Bauer was dead.

He was dead because of her. She laid her head against the steering wheel and cried.

"Maybe I should drive."

She looked at Nick standing in the vee made by the open door. She hadn't even closed the door. Without a word, she crawled over the console, leaving a trail of blood, and drew herself into a ball. She buried her face in her knees and wept like a child.

She wanted all the emotion to drain from her body. All the hurt and agony. All the sadness. The loss. She wanted it all to go.

And then she was going to beat the truth out of Mark Hanover.

Thirty-Eight

Nick had done everything short of picking Bobbie up and hauling her away from Hanover's office. He couldn't make her see that nothing she did was going to stop what was coming.

This was between him and Weller.

He shouldn't have come back to Montgomery. He'd fallen right into the bastard's trap. Now he had to keep Bobbie clear of the fallout. He had allowed her to become an increasingly dangerous weakness and now Weller was using that weakness against him.

How would he ever protect her?

"I'm sorry, Detective," the assistant said. "Mr. Hanover isn't here. He didn't come in this morning. I haven't seen him since day before yesterday."

"If you know where he is," Bobbie warned, flashing her badge just in case the woman had forgotten who she was, "you'd better talk now or you'll end up a potential accessory to murder."

The assistant continued to plead her case. She had not seen or heard from her boss. Nick watched Bobbie put her badge away. While she had showered, Nick had cleaned the blood off her phone, badge and gun. He didn't want her to have to do it. He'd put her bloody clothes in a bag and tossed them into the trash can outside her house. She never needed to see those clothes again. Then he'd cleaned her car as best he could.

Owens had called and told Bobbie the wife beater who lived down the street from Holt had an airtight alibi. The guy had taken a large wrench to Bauer's Mustang the day before. Though a lawyer had quickly gotten him released after assaulting Bauer yesterday, Shelton had gone straight home, knocked his wife around and then gone out and gotten shitfaced. Prattville PD had picked him up on a driving under the influence charge and he'd spent the night in jail. Was still there. The only good news was that the wife had obtained a restraining order and filed charges. She and her daughter had moved to a shelter for the time being.

Shelton was facing serious prison time for assaulting a police officer in addition to the charges his wife had filed. Though a similar wrench had been used to bash in the back of Bauer's head, it was nothing but a diversion. The message to Bobbie showed the killer was deteriorating. Why leave a distraction to throw the police off and then leave the message that conclusively tied the murder to previous scenes? The killer had murdered five people, up close and personal, and abducted three in a mere six days. He had to be running on empty, starting to screw up. The end was near.

Nick was ready. The evidence in Bauer's apartment—the lack of a struggle or forced entry—confirmed his latest assessment about the identity of the killer.

The chief of police had called Bobbie twice. For a change he seemed grateful she was with Nick. A turn Nick hadn't expected.

"I swear I have no idea where he is," the assistant said again. "Have you spoken to his attorney, Sawyer Eddington? He will probably know where he is."

Bobbie took the attorney's number and wheeled around to exit the office. Nick followed.

"He could be on his way out of the country by now," Nick warned. If Hanover was even remotely involved, he no doubt had realized that he was in way over his head.

Bobbie said, "We'll check his house."

Nick didn't argue. While he drove to Greystone Place, Bobbie called Eddington who, like the assistant, swore he had not seen or spoken to Hanover. Bobbie sent a text to Owens requesting a warrant for Hanover's and Eddington's phone records.

At Hanover's house Bobbie rang the doorbell four times before she gave up and walked around to the side yard. Nick's senses shifted, making the hair on the back of his neck stand on end. They checked the side door. Locked. No sound came from the house.

"We should proceed with caution," he advised.

Bobbie removed her weapon from its holster and made an agreeable sound.

When they reached the rear courtyard, the French doors stood open. Nick stepped in front of Bobbie. Before she could stop him he crossed the threshold into a den or keeping room near the kitchen. They moved soundlessly through the house.

Nick spotted the blood on the marble entry floor first. He held up a hand and pointed in that direction. They moved along the center hall and the bloody mess near the staircase came fully into view. Organs lay in a pile in the circle of thickening blood with the heart crowning the mound.

Naked and sprawled on his side on the cold marble floor was Mark Hanover. He'd been gutted in a similar manner as the Parkers without the suturing and cleanup. On top of that, he'd been castrated the same way as Manning. From where Nick stood he could see that a pink dildo had been crammed into his anal canal. The severed penis had been tucked into his mouth.

"Stay back," Bobbie cautioned.

No matter that he didn't want to, he deferred to her request. He understood he shouldn't contaminate the crime scene.

Bobbie held her left forearm in front of her nose. The smell of coagulating blood and feces was heavy in the air. "I need to call this in and ensure the house is clear." She reached down and retrieved her backup piece and handed it to Nick. "Stay put."

He took the weapon and walked around the pool

of blood. "Call it in. I'll make sure the house is clear."

She wasn't happy about it but she let him go.

He bounded up the stairs and moved from room to room. As long as he could hear Bobbie's voice as she spoke on the phone he was okay with her being out of his sight. Once she stopped talking he couldn't get back to her fast enough.

"Upstairs is clear." He moved toward the dining room to help her check the rest of the downstairs rooms.

The killer had obviously deviated from Weller's agenda into his own. He'd grown desperate and sloppy. He was unraveling.

"Evidence techs and the coroner are on the way," Bobbie told him when they returned to the entry hall.

She stared at Hanover's body as if she hoped he would give her the answers she sought. Even in death the bastard was still playing with her head.

"He's either tying up the loose ends," Nick said, "or he's gone completely off the rails. This is an emotional kill." The killer had wanted Hanover to suffer. Nick would wager there hadn't been any drugs used in this kill.

Bobbie rubbed a hand over her mouth. "Jesus Christ I don't want Fern and Vanessa to die."

Nick wished he could give her some hope but chances were the women were dead already. "I'll check the exterior perimeter."

She nodded, her gaze still on the dead man. Her

cell rang as Nick moved into the kitchen. He heard her answer.

"Where the hell are you?"

At the sound of her demand Nick turned around to find Bobbie had followed him into the kitchen.

Her eyes were wide with disbelief. She tapped the screen, putting her cell on Speaker.

"Before we get to the reason I called, there's something I'd like to say to you, Bobbie."

Weller. Son of a bitch!

Nick's body hardened with fury. He battled the need to snatch the phone from her and to tell the bastard he was coming for him. As if Bobbie had read the need on his face she pressed a finger to her lips.

"I'm startled by how much I respect you," Weller said. "I admire such determination and dedication to the job, especially after all you've been through."

"I'm sure you didn't call to compliment me on my work ethic. What do you want?" Bobbie's own fury was written all over her face.

"Right now you may feel as if things can't possibly get worse, but you have my word that I've only begun. What you've seen so far is merely a prelude. Every ounce of courage and tenacity you possess will be required to survive what's coming, Bobbie. Remember those words if you remember nothing else."

"Where the hell are you?" she demanded. "If you give yourself up now maybe you won't end up dead."

"You needn't worry about me, Bobbie. I'm quite adept at taking care of myself."

When she said nothing in return, he continued, "My son is there with you, isn't he? I don't need your confirmation. I can sense his presence in the sound of your voice."

"I will find you," Nick warned. "This time I will kill you."

Weller laughed, the piece of shit. "I look forward to that day, son. Remember what I said, Bobbie."

The call dropped off. She and Nick stood there staring at each other until the wail of sirens shattered the silence.

"He wants you to come after him," she said, her voice soft and filled with the worry he saw in her eyes.

Nick had no choice in the matter. Weller had made the first move. He was waiting for Nick to make the next one. But he couldn't leave until this—he looked at the dead man on the floor—was done.

The bigger picture cleared for Nick.

Weller had planned his escape carefully. He had known he would need a head start. If there had been any lingering doubts about his involvement in all this, there were none now. The killer he'd sent to Montgomery had nothing to do with stopping Nick or hurting Bobbie. Not really.

Six people were dead and two were still missing—all to distract Nick long enough for the bastard to escape and to gain a head start on this cat-and-mouse game.

Thirty-Nine

Lockwood Place
1:10 p.m.

Where was Joanne? Ted checked the time again. He should have canceled this damned walk-through. One of his detectives had been murdered this morning but Joanne had insisted that half a dozen other buyers were chomping at the bit to get their hands on this place. He had to take the time to do this. Even the chief of police deserved a quick lunch break whether he bothered to eat or not.

He glanced at the street. She had promised it would only take a few minutes. Where the hell was she?

Frustrated, Ted climbed out of his vehicle and walked to the door. He put in a call to Joanne to find out what the holdup was. When she answered, he said, "I thought we were meeting at one."

"But your office called to say you couldn't meet until after three," she argued. "My secretary gave me the message an hour ago."

"Who called?" He hadn't even mentioned the

walk-through to Stella. He'd only told her he was taking a quick lunch break.

"I'm out of the office right now," Joanne said, "I'll ask my secretary when I get back. Are you at the town house? I was headed to a showing near Lockwood so I'm only a few minutes from you. I can be there in five or so minutes."

Ted puffed out a breath. "I'm here. I suppose we might as well get this done."

Joanne apologized and assured him she was on her way. His irritation mounting, he tucked his phone back into his pocket. He cupped his hands around his eyes to peer through the glass in the door. He hoped that one cracked tile in the entry hall had been replaced. When he leaned against the door it swung inward.

Well, damn. It wasn't uncommon for vandals to break in and destroy newly built homes. As secure as this community was, there could still be trouble. An angry subcontractor who'd been let go, or just a rebellious teenager with too much time on his hands and too little supervision. Ted pushed the door open further and stepped inside. All appeared to be as it should including the broken tile. It had been replaced. He breathed a little easier.

Ted palmed the .22 he carried in the holster under his jacket. He preferred not to wag around a larger weapon. Dorey would say it was the politician in him and he would argue that he wasn't a politician, but the truth was some degree of political finesse was necessary to do the job.

He moved from the foyer to the side hall and

checked the master bedroom first. All was as it should be. Seeing the serene blue on the walls that Dorey had helped him select made him smile. He couldn't wait to start the rest of his life here. He returned to the family room and moved into the kitchen. So far so good—he drew up short. The glass in the window of the rear door had been smashed.

"Son of a bitch." He reached for his cell with his free hand. A report would need to be filed for insurance purposes. He should check upstairs, too.

Pain pierced his back. Deep inside something burst and he couldn't catch his breath. His fingers tightened on the phone. He spun slowly around and dropped to his knees. He stared at the leather shoes only a step or two in front of him. His gaze traveled up long legs and to the face that peered down at him.

"You," he gurgled.

"I'll tell your goddaughter you said goodbye while I watch her die."

With the last of his strength Ted tried to reach for the bastard. He missed and crumpled to the floor. The tile he'd painstakingly selected with Dorey's help felt cold against his jaw.

He couldn't draw in a deep breath. He tried to make his fingers work to call 9-1-1 but he couldn't.

Bobbie.

He had to warn her.

His eyes closed and he stopped thinking.

Forty

Bobbie stood beneath the spray of water, her eyes closed in an attempt to shut out the world. She had to have another shower. She couldn't get the stench of Hanover off her body. Hurt twisted through her.

Bauer was dead.

He'd died because of her. His killer had said as much. The others—the Parkers, Manning and Venable—were dead because of her. If those other two missing women died, it would be her fault, too. No matter how her shrink tried to convince her or how she'd fooled herself into believing that nothing that had occurred during the past year was her fault, it was a lie.

Tears brimmed past her lashes and she turned her face up to wash them away. She shook her head and took a breath. *Pull it together, Bobbie. You need to be out there finding this son of a bitch.*

Steeling herself, she backed from under the spray of water and shut off the faucet. She climbed out, scrubbed the towel over her scarred body and dried her hair as best she could without bothering with a blow-dryer. With a pair of jeans and a sweater on, she put her wet hair in a ponytail. She strapped the .22 and its holster to one ankle and her knife in its sheath to the other before shoving the Glock into her waistband at the small of her back. Weller was out there and he wanted Nick. Based on his phone call, he intended to use Bobbie to get to him.

She hoped she got the chance to save Nick the trouble by putting a bullet between Weller's eyes. He was the one who'd set all this in motion. He would pay. Fury charged through her. Whatever it took, she would help make that happen.

She opened the door and stepped out of the steam-filled bathroom. The fury and fight seemed to dissipate from her the same way the steam did as it met the cooler air in the hall. For a moment she tried to steady herself. After a couple of deep breaths she put one foot in front of the other until she found Nick in the room where he'd built his case map on the wall. None of it mattered. They had lost this battle already. *But they could not lose the war.*

He turned to her and before either of them could speak pounding on her front door jerked Bobbie's attention in that direction. Another pound followed by "Detective Gentry!" echoed through the house before her weary body could react.

Nick brushed past her, reaching the door first.

Two uniformed officers, one Bobbie recognized, Officer Delacruz, now stood in her living room.

"Sorry to barge in like this, ma'am."

"What's going on, Delacruz?"

"Lieutenant Owens told us to pick you up and bring you to her location."

Bobbie looked from the young officer to Nick. Had they found Fern or Vanessa's body? Damn it she hoped not. "What's her location?"

"She's at the ER, ma'am."

Worry tore at her. "What happened?" Even as she made the demand, she grabbed her bag and stepped into the shoes she had abandoned at the door when she'd come home.

"That's all we were told, ma'am."

"I'll follow," Nick said.

Bobbie understood he didn't want to let her out of his sight, but he needed to be focused on finding the killer Weller had sent, not to mention Weller himself. "No. You stay. You said you were watching someone close to Hanover. Keep doing that. We need a break. Soon."

Nick nodded and she was out the door. If Holt or Devine had been…

She couldn't think about that right now.

Baptist Medical Center
3:00 p.m.

Bobbie hurried through the sliding doors. She spotted the lieutenant immediately. She sat alone in one of those damned uncomfortable preformed plastic chairs. She looked up and the devastation on Eudora Owens's face told Bobbie two things. It was bad and it was personal.

Uncle Teddy.

"What happened?" Bobbie sank into the chair next to Owens. Blood roared in her ears as if her head was under a waterfall. No, this couldn't happen. He was the only family she had left. Flashes of those moments in this same ER when Newt died had her heart pounding harder.

"He took a quick break to sign off on the walk-through of his new town house. The Realtor had told him it was imperative he do it today." Owens's lips trembled and tears rolled down her cheeks. "I guess he was waiting for him there."

Wait. "The Realtor is a woman." Joanne Rogers, Aunt Sarah's sister, who was anxious to list Bobbie's former home.

Owens blinked and dabbed at her eyes with a tissue. "That's right. Mrs. Rogers received a phone call saying their appointment was canceled so she didn't go until the chief called her to ask why she wasn't there. If she hadn't gone straight over to the town house…" The LT shook her head. "He wouldn't have made it."

Bobbie's chest constricted. "Someone was waiting in the house for the chief?"

"The perp had broken in through the back door." Owens drew in a shaky breath. "I have uniforms talking to the residents at the community. There's video surveillance in most of the gated communities. I'm hoping we'll find something. We believe he was still there when the Realtor arrived. She said she heard something like glass crunching as she entered the front door. The perp likely heard her come in and call out to Ted and then he ran." When she stopped rambling, she turned to Bobbie. "It's bad, Bobbie. Really bad."

Bobbie struggled to keep the fear and anger out of her voice. "Will he make it?"

The longer the LT hesitated before responding, the harder Bobbie's heart slammed against her rib cage.

"He's in surgery. The dagger punctured a lung. There's internal bleeding. He's lost a lot of blood." She swiped at her cheeks. "But he's strong." She finally met Bobbie's gaze. "He has to make it."

Bobbie put her arm around the other woman's shoulders. "He'll make it."

Owens was right. *He had to make it.*

Dagger? "Did you say 'dagger'?" Bobbie asked.

"Holt believes it's the murder weapon we've been looking for." Her voice broke on the last.

Jesus Christ. Bobbie's cell phone shuddered in her back pocket. The vibration reminded her that she needed to check in with Devine. If Holt was at the scene where the chief had been stabbed, Devine should be with her. Why the hell hadn't anyone called her about the security footage at Bauer's building? And now the killer had struck again? Devine should have let her know about the dagger. What the hell? They had to get this guy contained…unless there was more than one, which might explain how he was working all around them as if they were standing still.

Bobbie dragged her cell from her pocket. She didn't recognize the number.

"Gentry." She gave Owens's arm a squeeze as she stood and moved toward the doors. Reporters were already gathered outside like vultures waiting to pick the bones. Off-duty cops were there, too... waiting to hear news on their chief and prepared to do whatever might be needed, like donating blood.

Bobbie closed her eyes. How had her one misstep last December culminated in all this?

"Hey, *mami*, you okay?"

The sound of Javier Quintero's voice set her teeth on edge. "What do you want, Javier?"

"See I can't even talk to you without you getting all bitchy and shit. You owe me, *mami*, have you forgotten?"

She did owe him. As much as it pained her to admit. "What do you want? I'm at the ER. This is not a good time."

"I heard your *jefe* got a knife in the back."

How was it a piece of shit like Quintero could already know the details?

"I'm hanging up." She didn't have time for this.

"Hey, hey," he shouted before she could tap the end call button.

"What?" He had five seconds.

"I was calling to see if you was okay 'cause that beast of yours is out running around the street barking like crazy."

"D-Boy is loose?" Had Nick accidently let him get out? Doubtful and D-Boy certainly wouldn't run from him. If the dog was running around loose,

Nick was not at her house. He would have rounded D-Boy up before there was any trouble.

"Yeah. He's acting all crazy. One of my boys almost had to shoot him but he ran off."

Shit. "I'll be right there."

Gardendale Drive
4:20 p.m.

Bobbie had borrowed the lieutenant's car. She'd tried to reach Nick but got no answer and then she'd called for backup to meet her at the house… just in case. The radio kept playing the news about the chief over and over until Bobbie had to shut it off. Every available member of law enforcement in Montgomery County was reporting in to help find the perpetrator who dared to kill one of their own and to take a knife to the chief.

Bobbie wheeled into her driveway. Two officers were already there.

"The door was open like this when we arrived," the older of the two told her.

Bobbie drew her Glock and went inside. She listened carefully, analyzing any sound. It was quiet. She drew in a deep breath and sorted the scents of her home. The faint smell of lavender still lingered in the air from her shower. Living room and kitchen were clear. Hall was clear. Bathroom was clear. The door to the second bedroom was open. She moved through it.

The research Nick had gathered for his case map was exactly as it had been when she'd left not two hours ago. No sign of a struggle anywhere in the house unless something had happened in her bedroom. She started for the door and one of the officers appeared there.

"The other bedroom is clear, ma'am. No indication of a struggle or a hurried search."

Nick was probably following the lead he'd spoken about but why would he leave the door open? Why wasn't he answering his phone? Had someone come into her house after he left? She checked the alarm system keypad. *Unarmed.* Didn't make sense. Nick would have set the alarm when he left.

She heard D-Boy coming before she saw him. He barked madly. Bobbie hurried past the officer and found the other one cornered by D-Boy in the living room.

"You know this animal?" he asked, his hand already on the butt of his weapon.

"It's okay, boy." The dog trotted over to her. "Go on outside," she told the officers. "I'll lock up and be right there."

When they were outside, Bobbie checked the back door and walked the house once more to ensure they hadn't missed anything. She checked his water bowl and gave D-Boy a treat before going out the front door and locking it.

"I'd like the two of you to check with the neighbors. Find out if anyone was seen near or going in or out of my house."

When they set off to do as Bobbie ordered, she loaded up in her Challenger and drove two streets over to the house where Nick had been parking his truck. She pulled into the driveway and her heart dropped to her stomach.

His truck was parked under the carport.

Bobbie's cell vibrated and she checked the screen hoping it was Nick.

Holt.

"Yeah." Bobbie held her breath, bracing for what might have happened now.

"Where the hell is your partner, Gentry? Bauer's building manager said Devine picked up the surveillance video. If he's ID'd the killer and gone rogue on us, I'm blaming you for setting such a bad fucking example."

Bobbie tried to think. How many hours had passed since she'd talked to Devine? Jesus. He was supposed to stick close to Holt. "I don't know where he is, but don't worry I'll find him."

"I want both of you reporting in within the hour."

Holt was gone before Bobbie could rally a "yes, ma'am." She put a call in to Devine. When he didn't answer she left a voice mail. "Where the hell are you?"

As she backed out onto the street her cell sounded off again. Anticipation buzzed through her. Hopefully it was Devine.

The Boss. If Owens was calling...

"Is he out of surgery?"

"Not yet, but the nurse who came out to update me said he's holding his own. I knew you'd want to know."

Bobbie barely held her tears in check. "Thank God."

"I'm certain you'd rather be here," Owens said, "but I really need you in the field. I beefed up the security detail on Sage Parker. I'm worried our killer is cleaning up."

"I think you're right. You take care of the chief," Bobbie urged. "We'll take care of business."

Owens thanked her, her voice wobbling a bit. Bobbie tucked her phone away. Now if she'd hear from Nick with word that he was okay…and her partner, damn him. Jesus Christ it was all happening at once.

Forty-One

When Steven Devine had showed up at Bobbie's house, Nick understood the detective wasn't there because he needed to find her or because he was worried about her. He was there for Nick. Nick had been expecting him. With Bauer's murder, Nick had sensed the big finale was near. Devine had drawn his weapon and ordered Nick into the trunk of his car. Attempting to fight him would have been pointless.

Sometimes the only way to accomplish the desired goal was to surrender to the inevitable. Nick had spent twelve long years doing all within his power to hunt down the serial killers no one else seemed able to catch and to ensure their reign of terror ended. Though he had studied psychology, it wasn't necessary to be a psychologist to understand his motives. Each time he stopped a serial killer he was making up in some small way for not being able to stop his father…for not recognizing sooner that his father was the sort of monster bad movies were made of.

This time, however, wasn't about any of that; it was about Bobbie.

He had not been able to stop thinking about her since the day he'd made her that promise to find the Storyteller. He had kept that promise and in keeping it, he had lost the ability to move on and never look back. He wasn't sure he could live the way he had for the last decade. Existing in the shadows and moving from one hunt to the next. He needed to know she was safe. He needed to be able to hear her voice and to see her from time to time. He couldn't give her anything more than he already had and he expected nothing. Every part of him roared in denial of the assessment, but he would not allow sheer need to rule him.

He would not permit Weller or anyone else to hurt her to get to him.

Eventually the car stopped moving and Nick was taken through a pasture to a barn. He'd been bound and left on the floor in what might have once been a large storeroom but was now a secure, however rustic, prison. He'd been here an hour or more. Too long.

He'd expected company by now but no one had come to check on him or to torture him. It was possible the room was equipped with cameras or audio. Devine had used duct tape to secure him. Stretching to loosen the binding took time, but it could be done. Slow, tugging movements were required to gradually lengthen and loosen the strips.

The creak of a door opening drew his attention over his left shoulder. A single bare bulb clicked on overhead, blinding him with the sudden brightness. He squinted, tried to make out the man standing over him.

Devine.

He dragged a stool from the other side of the room and placed it in front of Nick. He sat down to study his hostage. "You know I wasn't supposed to touch you." He laughed. "I was only commissioned to get you to Montgomery and keep you distracted." He gave his head a shake. "There's just one problem. I can't let you go the way he told me to. The opportunity to kill the hunter—the son of the great Randolph Weller—is far too incredible to pass up."

Rather than look at him, Nick assessed his prison while he had light. The walls were rough-cut lumber but the floor was dirt. Shelves lined a far wall. A couple of old boxes sat in one corner. His gaze shifted back to the table about six feet away. Long, rustic wooden table. An array of torture instruments was arranged across the top.

"I didn't want to rush," Devine said, noting his attention on the table. "I wanted to take my time and savor the moment, but, unfortunately, I don't have as much time as I had hoped. Hanover's stupidity pushed up the timeline."

Nick stared at him, wanting so badly to burst loose and tear into him. "Why kill your friend? Hanover could have been a valuable asset. His money would have secured a clean escape."

"Friend? Hardly." Devine leaned forward a bit. "The bastard raped me as a child. He knew what my aunt and uncle were doing to me every summer and instead of trying to help me, he joined in the fun." He laughed. "He had the upper hand when I was a child, but no more. I knew all his dirty little secrets."

Sick bastard. "Your little game of one-upmanship cost lives."

Devine laughed. "Three of those lives was the cost of getting you to Montgomery, but who's counting?" A shrug lifted his shoulders. "I had my first kill when I was only ten. I pushed my uncle down the stairs. The old bastard took his sweet time dying. I actually had a stiff one by the time his body stopped twitching." He sighed. "As your father would say, once I'd had a taste there was no going back."

"Now you've lost your scapegoat," Nick reminded him. "Hanover is dead."

"Sadly, I'm afraid you're right."

"You have me," Nick suggested. "You don't need Bobbie or those other women. I can take you to Weller, then you can kill both of us. Imagine how celebrated you'll be."

Devine shook his head. "The other two are irrelevant and I'm afraid Bobbie can't be spared. I've wanted to hurt her since the day I laid eyes on her. I might even let you watch her die."

Nick was the one who laughed then. "Mark my word, Devine, you're the one who's going to die."

Forty-Two

Bobbie had called Nick's phone at least a dozen times. She'd even called LeDoux and left a voice mail asking if he'd heard from Nick. *Where the hell are you?*

The sun had set when she parked in front of Pearl Whitley's home. The house was one of the few grand plantation homes left in Montgomery County. The once green paint had faded to a sad gray. The slave quarters still stood in the backyard, a sad reminder of that part of the South's history. According to Devine, his aunt's home had been part of a huge farm at one time, but much of the land had been sold off as she grew too old to take care of things. He intended to help her manage what remained for the rest of her life.

If he was still alive.

She had called Devine almost as many times as she'd called Nick, with no luck. Coming here was a long shot and she might not have done so if Pastor Liddell hadn't called again. She was worried about Devine's aunt. Liddell had tried calling and dropping by to no avail. With Hanover's murder the pastor was worried that other longtime donors to the church were being targeted. Maybe the pastor's concern about the aunt was nothing, but considering both Devine and Nick were MIA, dropping by felt like the right thing to do. With Bauer dead, the chief gravely injured and still in surgery as well as two vics still missing, the chances of finding her partner lounging around the house were pretty slim. Wherever he was, this was definitely not the time for him to be out of reach. Something was wrong. Nick's questions about Devine nudged her. So maybe that off feeling she'd had about him wasn't so off.

Don't sell him out yet, Bobbie. Devine could be dead or dying somewhere. Damn it.

She stepped up on the wide porch and closed the distance to the door. Would Nick have come here looking for Devine or his aunt? She glanced around the yard. How would Nick have gotten here? His truck was still parked a few blocks from her house. None of this made any sense.

After a couple of bangs on the towering slab of ornate painted wood, Bobbie leaned closer and held her breath so she could hear better. Beyond the door was as quiet as a tomb.

She glanced around to ensure no one was watching before gripping the ancient knob and giving it a turn. The door opened. These old houses were bad for that. Breathe on a door too hard and it creaked open.

Drawing her Glock, she stepped inside. "Ms. Whitley, are you home?"

The house was as grand as she had expected it to be. The towering three story—complete with a turret—was in need of a coat of paint inside, too, but the faded colors didn't detract from the overall beauty. Antique furniture was interspersed among the more modern pieces, though nothing was newer than 1950, she decided. The entry hall spread into double front parlors with a grand staircase between them. Bobbie slid a finger along the graceful mahogany table standing in the center of the enormous entry hall. No one had dusted, she noted the dust bunnies parked against the baseboards, or vacuumed in months. Mrs. Whitley was well into her seventies, but Bobbie would be genuinely surprised if she didn't have a staff, a housekeeper at least. She moved beyond the stairs, past the dining room. A silver tea service in serious need of polishing sat on the massive dining table. Could have been sitting there for months. The dust on the table around it was disturbed as if someone had recently sat there to have tea.

She moved into the kitchen and an odor made her cringe. The smell reminded her of the open grease trap at a restaurant kitchen where she and Newt had once worked a homicide. The Whitley kitchen was filthy. Dirty dishes were piled in the sink. Pots and pans were scattered over the stovetop, remains of prepared food molding inside. Cupboard doors stood open. A swarm of black flies crawled on the panes of the window above the sink.

Had Devine stopped staying with his aunt? He

hadn't mentioned moving but he surely wasn't living in this filth.

Bobbie walked back through the kitchen and into the entry hall. "Ms. Whitley?" She hesitated at the bottom of the staircase and called again.

Still no answer.

Tightening her grip on her weapon, Bobbie made the slow climb up the stairs. At the landing an octagon-shaped seating area on the left provided the turret shape. A long hall stretched in either direction. Six doors lined the hall. She went left first. The two bedrooms and bath were well appointed like the rest of the house but no sign of the elderly aunt. The larger of the two was apparently the room Devine used. Those fancy suits he wore lined the closet along with about a dozen pairs of shoes. How could he allow the house to fall into this condition? The only room that was halfway clean was his. The rest was a damned health hazard. She hesitated before exiting the room. There wasn't a single photo on the wall or anywhere else in the room. Expensive cologne and other toiletries stood in a neat row on the dresser, but not one other thing that could be called personal.

Weird.

Bobbie moved back into the hall and toward the other end. "Ms. Whitley?" First bedroom was clear. Bath, too. "It's Bobbie Gentry, Steven's partner."

She paused at the door standing at the far end of the hall. "What the hell?"

The door was covered with plastic, white duct tape sealed the edges. Bobbie pulled at the tape, it fell away fairly easy as if it had been removed and reattached repeatedly. She peeled the plastic aside far enough to open the door and the odor of rotting flesh hit her in the face. She gagged. Across the room what looked like the corpse of an elderly woman was chained to her bed. Forearm across her nose, Bobbie approached the bed. The woman's hair was long and gray. Her eyes had sunk into her head and her lips had pulled away from her teeth, making them appear too large for her face.

Bobbie leaned closer wishing she had turned on the overhead light. A decaying cat was curled up next to the woman's remains.

"Shit."

Bobbie drew back. The victim had been dead a couple of weeks. Maybe three. Her body had blackened, the skin and fingernails were loose. Cracks in her skin had leaked fluids into the linens. The fabric gag that had kept the woman, presumably Ms. Whitley, from screaming was loose now as the flesh sagged away from her face.

Jesus Christ.

At some point her legs had been spread apart, her ankles secured to the bedposts with a rope. Her pelvis region was hardly more than mush. Bobbie's stomach turned as she realized this could very well be what the creamy substance found on Venable's thighs was.

Swallowing hard to prevent heaving, she moved around the room, taking in the discarded wigs and dresses. Sticking out from under the pile was a large pink dildo not unlike the one found at the

Hanover scene, only this one was attached to a belt. Pieces of duct tape were stuck to it along with more of that creamy gunk. Oh, hell. She turned back to the bed. Fury bolted through her. Liddell had asked Devine about his aunt and he'd said she had allergy issues.

Bobbie shuddered. "Allergies, my ass."

Where was that son of a bitch? She yanked her phone free of her belt and started to call in the scene. *No service.* Damn it! She hurried back through the bedrooms, no house phone. She bounded down the stairs and checked the downstairs rooms. In the kitchen a phone hung on the wall but it was dead. The line running from the baseboard had been cut. Swearing under her breath, Bobbie walked out the back door and off the porch to see if she could pick up at least one signal-strength dot.

No service.

God damn it!

She moved around the yard trying to pick up enough service to at least get a text through to Holt. *Nothing.* She had to hand it to Nick. His hunch that the killer was connected to Hanover was on the money. *Son of a bitch*!

How the hell had she worked with Devine for a month and not seen what he was?

Exhaling a breath of frustration, she took a moment to calm herself. Shadows were quickly overtaking the landscape. If Devine was part of this—on some level she still resisted the idea—Nick could be here... Fern and Vanessa could be, as well. Squawking drew her gaze to the darkening sky. A flock of blackbirds circled, dipped and then disappeared into the trees.

You gotta hurry, Bobbie.

The yard was bordered with crepe myrtles and other shrubbery. A detached garage sat thirty or so yards away from the house. Her attention hung there even as she considered that she should go out to the road and see if she could get service there. If necessary, she would drive a mile or so down the road.

Maybe she'd check out the garage first. Her instincts were buzzing. If Devine had anything to do with these murders or those missing women she would kill him herself, by God.

If? Denial was no place to be right now. Devine's dead and decomposing aunt was chained to a bed. The house he'd clearly been living in was in chaos. He was definitely involved.

Could he have killed Bauer?

Red-hot rage roared through her. Bobbie steadied herself. She had to focus. Had to find those women. Had to get this bastard. *Stay cool.*

Keeping an eye on her surroundings, she started toward the garage. How could Devine's record be so spotless? Fury crashed through her all over again. She gritted her teeth to prevent screaming in frustration. *Focus!* She had to do this right for Bauer and all the others.

Muffled sounds, like pounding, echoed on her left. Bobbie jerked in that direction. *Clear.* She scanned the massive yard. There were too many shadows for her liking but nothing moved. With all that shrubbery a small army could be hiding from her.

Fuck!

More muffled sounds brushed her senses. Voices. *Female.* Bobbie moved toward the barely audible noise. She edged around a group of crepe myrtles. She squinted in the growing gloom, spotted the pipe jutting from the earth first and then she saw the heavy iron door in the ground. It wasn't that large, maybe three feet square. Pounding echoed again. Bobbie's heart lurched. She fell to her knees next to the rusty old door. There was no lock, just an iron rod that slid through loops of metal effectively barricading the opening. She slid the rod back and struggled to lift the door. When she threw it back against the grass, she peered into the dark hole that was likely an old storm shelter. It was as black as pitch down there. She turned on her phone's flashlight app and looked again. Damned thing was like a big-ass grave.

A face appeared in the narrow beam of light. *Vanessa Olson.* She stood at the bottom of an old wooden ladder.

Suddenly another face peered up at Bobbie.

Fern Parker.

Thank God.

The women started to talk and cry at the same time.

The sound of a car engine snapped Bobbie's attention back toward the garage. She held up her hand and then stuck her finger to her lips to quiet the women. She listened. Didn't hear anything. She showed her badge and then gestured for them to come up and wait next to her. The crepe myrtles provided some amount of cover from the house and the garage. She peeked beyond the row, scanned the yard. The shrubbery bordered the yard all the way to the road. She turned back to the women who appeared uninjured. She imagined they were hungry and dehydrated but they were alive. Obviously they'd had some source of water and food.

"Stay down." She gestured to the shrubs. "Stay behind those and make your way to the front of the house." She passed Vanessa the fob to her Challenger. "Drive toward town. As soon as you have service call 9-1-1 and tell them an officer needs assistance. I have to find out who's here." She glanced back at the garage. "Remember to stay behind cover until you're as close to the car as possible, understand?"

Heads nodded.

Bobbie passed her cell toward Vanessa. Fern snatched it from her. "I have to call home."

Bobbie's heart sank.

A car door slammed.

No time for this. Bobbie grabbed Fern by the arm. "Go," she growled. "Someone is here and I'm betting it's not help." Slumping with defeat, Fern passed the phone to Vanessa. "Call for help as soon as you have service," Bobbie repeated.

Vanessa nodded and then urged Fern toward the road.

Bobbie watched until the two were out of sight, keeping low behind the shrubs. She tightened her hold on her Glock and made her way toward the garage. The sound of a door closing had come from that general area.

The garage doors were open but it was essentially dark beyond them. The sun had set and night was coming fast. She held a position next to the doors and listened for a full minute. No sound. Weapon held in both hands, she swung around and stared into the garage. Nothing moved.

She entered the garage and checked all sides of the vehicle parked there to ensure no one was hiding behind it. Then she opened the driver's-side door and the interior light came on. There was no one inside. The car was old, from the '80s or '90s. It smelled bad, like the aunt's bedroom. She couldn't decide if the odor was just that moldy, musty smell or if it was something dead. The upholstery was stained but the dark color of the fabric made it impossible to tell in the dim light if the stains were blood. There could be a body in the trunk.

As she straightened away from the door the emblem on the hood snagged her attention. *Lincoln.* A black Lincoln Town Car, older model, like this one, had been seen outside the Parker home. A man with dark hair had been behind the wheel.

He looked like that.

Sage Parker's words slammed into her brain.

"Put down your weapon, Bobbie."

Devine. She'd had plenty of clues and she hadn't wanted to see it. She'd chalked every damned one up to coincidence. What a fool she'd been.

She turned around slowly. She could barely see

him in the dim glow coming from the interior of the car but she knew his voice. "You."

He smiled. "Me."

"Why?"

He laughed. "I've studied Weller and all the other greats. I even visited him once when I was in college. Of course I used an alias. We kept in touch over the years. You'll never know just how much leeway the feds give the old bastard. We became great friends. It made me enormously happy to impress the famed Picasso Killer. When this opportunity presented itself, I saw a way to capitalize on it. What better way to show the master who's best than by killing his enigmatic son, and you, of course?"

Her fingers tightened on her Glock. "Where's Nick?"

"Not to worry. I'll take you to him." He gave her a pointed look. "As long as you behave, *partner*."

Renewed agony welled so fast inside her that she trembled with the force of it. "You killed Bauer."

"Drop the weapon, Bobbie."

She would not. She would die first.

"Unless you do exactly as I say Nick will die. I'm sure you don't want that, do you?"

Like he wouldn't kill them both anyway. She repeated her question. She wanted to hear him admit what he'd done. "Did you kill Bauer?"

He eased a step closer. "Drop the weapon now. I will not tell you again."

"What's to keep you from shooting me either way?"

"I have very specific plans for you. Now, be a good girl, Bobbie. Your friend is waiting. If I have to tell you again he's dead."

She tossed her Glock on the ground.

"The cell phone and the backup piece."

She would kill him right now except then she might never know where Nick was. He could be locked away someplace the way Fern and Vanessa had been. If she didn't find him he would die. This was the only way. "I dropped my cell in the yard."

She prayed he would buy the story as she lowered into a crouch and removed the backup piece, leaving it on the ground. If she could keep him talking just a few minutes maybe help would arrive in time.

Devine smiled. "I'll bet you tried to call for backup, didn't you? Cell service out here sucks."

"You're a sick piece of shit, Devine. How could you do that to your aunt?"

His laughter boomed in the small building. "She was an insane old bitch who should have died a long time ago. Her own housekeeper and gardener hated her. They were only too happy to retire last month. With a hefty bonus, of course. The only living thing that was loyal to her was that fucking cat." He gestured to the open door. "Let's go."

Bobbie stepped out of the garage and into the yard. It was completely dark now. She hoped Fern and Vanessa had made the call for help.

"Behind the garage," Devine prompted.

Bobbie rounded the building. The bastard's

Porsche was parked in the grass. So this was the engine and the slamming door she had heard.

He opened the trunk. "Get in."

"I thought we were going to Nick."

"Not unless you cooperate!" He jerked his head toward the car.

She didn't move. "Why did you kill Bauer?" The loss was like a knife twisting inside her.

His sigh was audible. "I knew he didn't like me when I first arrived. So I worked extra hard to make friends. I told him stories that I've never told anyone else. I went out of my way to be a buddy to him. I actually think it was working. Until he caught me taking the video clip from your desk and though he seemed to buy my explanation he went to the chief. I knew it was only a matter of time before the two of them recognized the real me. There. Now you know."

Bobbie stalled again. "You're the one who stabbed the chief."

He laughed. "I certainly did. I'm utterly pissed he didn't die. His Realtor arrived before I could ensure he took his last breath. As you can imagine, leaving a witness forces the need to reinvent myself. Not fun. Now get the fuck in the trunk."

Bobbie was going to kill him. Whether she survived today or not, she was going to kill Steven Devine before she drew her last breath.

For now, she did as he demanded. She climbed into the trunk and he slammed the lid shut.

As the car bounced over the ground she thought of all the things she was going to do to cause him pain. A quick death was too good for him. She wanted to watch him struggle to breathe, to endure the pain the way Bauer had. She wanted him to close his eyes for the last time knowing that he had failed. That all his work had been for nothing.

But first she had to find Nick.

Devine didn't drive very far. The darkness prevented her from seeing much when he dragged her from the trunk. There were no lights for as far as she could see. Was Nick here? What about Weller? He could be here preparing for a big finale.

At least Fern and Vanessa were safe…hopefully.

This place was well outside the city. Considering the short distance he'd driven they were likely not far from the old plantation house, she decided. Maybe still on the property. The building he'd pushed her into was large, like a barn. No doubt there would be a barn and other outbuildings on the property.

Devine had left her and hadn't returned. Bobbie couldn't be sure how long he'd been gone. Half an hour maybe.

First he'd bound her hands behind her back with duct tape. Her ankles, too. Then he'd left her lying on the cold ground. Had to be a barn. What she felt beneath her was dirt and straw or hay. She twisted her hands to stretch the duct tape. She pulled her knees apart and worked at extending the strips wrapped around her ankles. Then, she slowly curled backward, trying to reach her ankles with her hands. With a little bit more time she could stretch far enough to reach beneath the cuff of her jeans. As soon as she was free the bastard was hers.

She and Devine had worked closely together for a solid month. For some reason the subject of backup pieces hadn't really come up. Most everyone knew that a smart cop wore an ankle holster with an extra firearm for a backup piece. But she never told Devine about the knife.

She thought of the first time she and Nick had met. He'd told her where she kept each of her weapons. He'd been watching her on her runs and noted her adjusting each one. She'd learned something from him and since that time she'd worn her knife and sheath strapped to the inside of her left shin. It wasn't as handy as it had been at the small of her back, but it was there. Just like it was now.

Devine was a dead man.

The beam of a flashlight moved toward her. Bobbie stilled.

"Heads-up, Bobbie. It's time."

"Where's Nick? You said you were bringing me to him." Bobbie dug her fingers between the denim and her skin, tunneling beneath the loosened tape. She could almost reach the knife but she couldn't allow him to see her efforts. She struggled to keep herself still, save for her fingers. Had to keep her face clean of the effort.

"We'll join him in a moment," Devine said. "I have to be leaving soon." He crouched down in front of her. "I wouldn't want to overstay my welcome now that my secret's out. So, get ready, partner. I'll be back in a few minutes and we'll finish this."

Bobbie had news for the guy. The only place he was going was to the morgue in a body bag.

Forty-Three

Lynette set her hands on her hips and tried her best to look authoritative when the truth was she was falling apart inside.

Bauer was dead. They'd been partners for nine years. God damn it!

The chief was still in serious condition over at Baptist Medical. And she had two cops who were fucking missing. As if that wasn't crazy enough, the two missing women they'd been searching high and low for had called 9-1-1 from Bobbie's phone and warned that she was in trouble. Both were bruised up, dehydrated and suffering from some level of shock, but they were alive. Somehow Bobbie had found them.

But where the hell was she? And where was Devine. Neither of the women could identify their abductor. Fern insisted he was the security guy her father had hired, but there was no record her father had hired anyone just before his murder.

The kid—Sage—had pointed out Devine as looking like the man who killed his parents, and judging by things around here it had to be Devine. *Bastard.* Lynette had showed Fern a pic of Devine and asked if he was the security guy who had watched their house and she'd gotten hysterical. Nothing she said after that made a damned bit of sense. Later, when she'd calmed down maybe she could make a positive ID.

The morgue attendants carrying the gurney slowly navigated the staircase. Lynette didn't see how the hell they'd moved the body with it seeped into the mattress the way it was. They hadn't bothered trying to pull the dead cat away from the woman's remains for fear of leaving part of the victim stuck to the cat's carcass. Carroll would have the pleasure. Carroll had estimated the aunt had been dead about three weeks.

Lynette had known there was something off about Devine.

Bauer hadn't liked him from day one. Lynette had assumed Bauer was a little jealous because the new guy was handsome and charming, too. Now, with the dead aunt and the black Lincoln Town Car they'd found in the garage and the two women who had been held in a hole in the ground in his backyard…*fuck*. Whether Fern Parker ID'd him or not, it was pretty fucking clear Devine was their killer.

"I should have listened to you, partner," she muttered, her heart breaking all over again.

A uniform hurried to where Lynette stood in

the entry hall. "Ma'am, we haven't found Devine or Gentry or any other bodies so far."

Where the hell were they?

Lynette ordered, "We need more spotlights. Maybe there's another hidden cellar around here." These old plantation homes were full of secret spaces, not to mention all the outbuildings.

"Yes, ma'am."

"Sergeant Holt, have we found our missing detectives?"

Lynette turned to find Owens striding through the door. "No, ma'am. Only Devine's dead aunt. According to the coroner she may have been left to starve to death." Carroll wasn't ready to commit to the other travesties that had been done to the woman and how much of it was postmortem. "The Lincoln Town Car's upholstery is stained with blood and there are bags of bloody men's clothing in the trunk. I think it's safe to say it's the vehicle we've been looking for."

Owens shook her head. "Are you telling me that Detective Devine is in some way responsible for this clusterfuck?"

"That's what I'm telling you." Lynette shook her head in disgust. "Anything back on the BOLO on Nick Shade?" She figured he was with Bobbie. She hoped like hell they weren't dead already. At this point she didn't really give a shit if Devine was dead.

"Nothing yet," Owens said wearily.

Through the open door Lynette saw three sets of headlights bouncing up the driveway.

"Did you order more bodies to help with the search?" She looked to Owens, who was also staring at the new arrivals. The spotlights that had been set up around the house showed three unmarked sedans come to a stop in front of the house.

"I did not."

Owens headed out onto the porch, Lynette followed.

Special Agent Michael Hadden as well as half a dozen other feds marched toward the house.

"Have you found Detective Gentry or Nick Shade?" Hadden demanded.

Lynette deferred to the lieutenant. She had never liked Hadden. She liked him even less right now.

"We have not. How can we help you, Agent?"

"We want Nick Shade. We believe he may have information on the whereabouts of his father."

Forty-Four

Bobbie listened intently for Devine to return. She'd tugged at the tape until it was loose enough to get one hand out, and then the other. She stretched down and dragged her knife from its sheath and used it to cut through the tape around her ankles—in the back where Devine wouldn't be able to see unless he turned her over.

The fingers of her right hand tightened around the handle of the knife. *Come get me now, asshole.*

So far she hadn't heard any sounds to indicate there was anyone else nearby. If Nick was here—and alive—he was bound and gagged. Was Devine keeping him at a different location?

Fear twisted in her belly at the idea that Weller could be coming. What if this had been Weller's plan al! along and she'd played right into it?

She did not want to be the reason Nick died. Too many people had died because of her. Her jaw tightened. It was going to end—one way or the other—today.

The beam of a flashlight neared and Devine

crouched down, holding the light close to her face. Bobbie squinted at the brightness of it.

"It's time, Bobbie."

She tuned out all other thought and focused on the monster in front of her. *Distract him. Put him off balance.* "You know, Devine, I get why you murdered the Parkers and Manning. You had to lure Nick here." She made a dismissive face. "I even understand you wanted to hurt me when you killed Bauer and tried to kill the chief. But what did your aunt or Deana Venable ever do to you? Or Mark Hanover for that matter?"

He exhaled a big breath. "Bobbie, Bobbie, Bobbie, how can you still see the world through those rose colored glasses after what Gaylon Perry did to you?"

She laughed. "I see. A tough guy like you doesn't want to share his dark and dirty secrets. What'd your aunt do? Make you clean behind your ears? Wash your mouth out with soap?"

A smile twisted across his face. "Mostly she loved to watch, but there were plenty of times when she joined in."

He didn't speak for half a minute and Bobbie feared she had pushed the wrong button. She could not screw this up. *Focus. He'll see your fear.*

"Dear old Aunt Pearl always wanted a daughter. She was quite bored with her nephew, so she dressed me up like a little girl and we had tea parties." He made a sound of dismissal. "She even taped my penis against my balls so it wouldn't show through the cute little silky panties she bought me.

It all seemed quite innocent if uncomfortable to me. I was just a child after all."

Bobbie tightened her fingers around the handle of her knife. *Keep talking, you bastard.*

"But then the Colonel noticed what a pretty little girl I was." Fury tightened his lips. "He did things to me." Devine cleared his throat. "And she never lifted a finger to stop him. I waited a long time to show her just how much I appreciated her looking the other way."

Bobbie braced to make a move. Devine grabbed her arm. "Now, let's go have some fun with your friend before I put him out of his misery."

Her heart pounded with a burst of adrenaline as he hauled her to her feet. When he would have dragged her from the room she jerked at his hold, simultaneously swinging her free arm around and thrusting the knife at him. The blade swiped across his arm, piercing fabric and skin.

He growled and grabbed her forearm, holding back the knife before she could stab him in the chest. She pushed harder, roaring with determination but he was stronger than her. He forced the blade back toward her.

"Do you really think I'm going to let a bitch like you best me?"

She kicked at him. Tried to head-butt him but he dodged the move. With one arm bracketed around her waist holding her tight against his body, he forced the knife to her throat with the other hand.

Bobbie froze, her fury drained away and the survival instinct seared through her.

"I could kill you right now," Devine whispered in her ear, the blade pressed against her throat. "But I want to fuck you first just to see what Gaylon Perry risked coming all the way back here for."

"Just look how that worked out for him." She spat the words at Devine.

The blade drew away from her throat and he shoved her to the ground. He tossed the knife behind him. When she would have scrambled away he drew his weapon, taking aim at her head.

"No one's coming to save you this time, Bobbie." He got down on his knees, straddling her waist. He placed the flashlight on the ground so that the beam shone on her face and torso. "I'm sure you've noticed that I'm a lot smarter than Perry was." He reached for her sweater with his free hand, his right keeping the muzzle of the weapon pressed against her cheek. "Let's see some of those scars I've heard so much about."

He shoved the hem upward, revealing her bra. One finger slipped into a cotton cup. She shuddered in revulsion. He ripped her bra loose and squeezed her breast. Son of a bitch she wanted to kill him!

"Hmm. Not bad." His hand trailed down her torso until he reached her waistband. He unfastened her jeans and she went stiff and utterly still. His disgusting fingers inched farther and farther downward. "Are you always this hot, Detective?"

"Get off me, you piece of shit!" She grabbed his right arm and tried to move the weapon away from her face.

He laughed. "Don't make me pull this trigger,

Bobbie." He leaned closer. "I'll still fuck you even with half your head blown off."

She twisted her body and pushed with all her might to get that gun out of her face. He snatched his hand from her jeans and rammed it against her throat, cutting off the air to her lungs and pinning her to the ground. She pushed harder. Had to... She managed to lift her head just far enough to clamp down on his right hand with her teeth.

He screamed and jerked away from her, the barrel shifting from her face. But his left hand stayed locked on her throat.

She punched him in the balls.

He backhanded her and the gun flew from his grasp.

Bobbie grabbed for his neck but he shot upward out of her reach. The flashlight rolled away.

She kicked at him but he moved up and away too quickly. It was then that she realized he wasn't moving of his own volition. His feet dangled in the air, the beam of the flashlight spotlighting the bizarre struggle.

Bobbie scrambled for the weapon. She palmed it and groped for the flashlight while Devine struggled with whoever had hauled him off her.

"I give up!" Devine screeched between gasps for air.

Bobbie got to her feet, the weapon leveled on the sound of his voice. She turned the beam of the flashlight in that direction.

Devine held his hands out to his sides in a surrender position. His head was cocked back as if someone had him by the hair.

Bobbie spotted her knife. The blade was pressed against Devine's throat.

Nick.

The light settled on Nick's profile.

Relief rushed through her. He was alive.

"I give up," Devine repeated. "Tell him, Bobbie. I'm surrendering. I have a burner phone in my back pocket. Call it in."

Bobbie took a step toward him. "Keep your hands up." She looked to Nick. "You okay? You can put the knife down. I've got him."

Nick met her gaze, his eyes black with rage. He didn't respond and uncertainty trickled through her.

"We've got him," she repeated. "Put the knife away."

Her heart bumped harder and harder against her sternum. Finally the blade eased away from Devine's throat and she could breathe again. Her own throat ached from where the bastard had nearly crushed her windpipe.

They had him now. The son of a bitch wasn't getting away. She relaxed marginally as she reached toward Devine to get the burner. "Put your hands on top of your head and get down on the ground, you piece of shit."

"Whatever you say, *partner.*" The bastard started to reach upward and then he grabbed for the weapon.

The knife ripped across his throat.

Hot blood spurted across Bobbie's face.

Devine's hands went to the gaping wound. Blood spewed between his fingers.

He dropped to the ground.

Bobbie fell to her knees next to him, his blood oozing down her face.

Devine twitched once, twice and then the spurt of blood stopped and he stilled.

Her heart thundering, she shifted the beam away from his body until the light landed on Nick. Blood dripped from his hands, from the blade of the knife he still clutched.

There will come a day, soon I fear, when he will be forced to kill. When that time comes he will learn the deep, dark secret he has denied for so long.

Weller's words echoed through her. Had he set all of this in motion in hopes of the events culminating in this moment?

The bloody knife fell from Nick's hand.

Once he has experienced taking a life, he will not be able to resist killing again and again.

Forty-Five

It was well after dark when Lynette got home. No matter that thirty-six hours or so had passed since she held her dead partner in her arms, she couldn't get the smell of his blood off her. She stood at the back door and closed her eyes. God, could she do this without him?

She'd been a damned cop for fourteen years. She and Bauer had been partners for nine of those years.

How the hell was she supposed to get past this?

She went into the house through the side door and locked it. With a weary breath she toed off her shoes and left her utility belt on the floor next to them. Out of habit she placed her weapon on the top shelf above the washing machine.

The unit had lost two of its best. First Newt and now Bauer.

Rage boiled up inside her when she thought of Devine. It was a damned shame she hadn't gotten to cut his fucking throat herself. She hoped he burned in hell for all eternity.

She peeled off her jacket and blouse, and then her slacks. Tonight, for the first time since she'd graduated training, she hated being a cop.

Taking care not to wake anyone, she padded quietly to the nursery. Tricia slept when the baby slept so she was likely already in bed. She had called Lynette several times to check on her since she hadn't been home since before Bauer was murdered.

She couldn't possibly come home until his killer was found.

At the door to Howie's bedroom Lynette paused to relish the sweet baby scents. How was it this world could be so damned cruel and yet something as precious as a child come from it?

She went to the crib and peered down at her sweet child. The bunny rabbit night-light provided a gentle glow that highlighted his rosy cheeks and those little pink lips. He was mostly bald save for a fine scattering of red hair. Lynette loved that he would have her red hair.

A smile tugged at her lips and she fought hard to hold back the tears. They streamed down her face anyway. Major Crimes would never be the same. Her life would never be the same.

She smiled at her sleeping baby and promised, "I'll get through this for you."

Arms encircled her and she turned to face the woman she loved with all her heart. "Didn't mean to wake you."

Tricia kissed her cheek and took Lynette's hand in hers. "I wasn't asleep. I was waiting for you." She drew Lynette from the room, down the hall and into theirs.

Lynette heard the water in the tub running before they entered the bathroom. The only light inside came from the dozens of lit candles all over the room. Steam rose from the hot water filling the tub. Tricia unfastened Lynette's bra and slipped it off. Then she knelt next to her and drew her panties down her legs.

Tricia stood and urged her to the tub. "Relax. I'll pour you a glass of wine."

All Lynette could do was nod. If she opened her mouth to try and speak she would fall completely apart.

Yes. She would get through this terrible time with the help of the people who loved her.

Tomorrow they would start to rebuild the Major Crimes Unit.

Forty-Six

Criminal Investigation Division
8:50 p.m.

Bobbie couldn't shake the headache. Her head had been throbbing all day. Lack of sleep, dehydration, there were plenty of reasons.

Weller had not been spotted. Airports, bus stations and rental car agencies had all been checked. He was simply gone. This conclusion had come from Owens since between the feds and the department Bobbie and Nick had been sequestered in separate interview rooms for hours.

"Debriefed" the feds called it.

So far everyone agreed that the kill in the Whitley barn was clean. It would be days before their official findings were passed along to the chief in a final report. Nick's actions were clearly carried out in self-defense to save both their lives.

Deep down she wondered if he had dropped the knife when she'd first asked him to if things would have played out differently. Whether it would have or not, she would take those details to her grave.

Steven Devine got what he deserved. She would never betray or second-guess Nick.

The Parker and Manning cases were now closed. Sage Parker and his sister had been reunited and would go to Nashville with their aunt to heal and be raised in a loving family. Thankfully the chief was expected to fully recover. Lieutenant Owens had left a few minutes ago to go back to the hospital. As soon as Bobbie got something for this raging headache she was going to see him. She'd spoken to him by phone and he had insisted he was fine but Bobbie needed to see for herself.

First she had to talk to Nick. They hadn't had a moment alone until now.

They were both free to go although Holt told her the feds had a hard-on for Nick and intended to continue their investigation into his activities, particularly where Weller was concerned. It wasn't fair but it was the way things worked sometimes.

Right now they needed to talk. *Alone.*

He glanced at her as the corridor cleared, leaving just the two of them for the first time since they had left that barn. His expression was impassive as if he felt numb. She was still waiting for the numbness. Strangely it refused to come.

Bobbie drew in a deep breath. "You ready to go?"

He shifted his gaze from hers but nodded in answer to her question.

They walked outside together. Her heart beat faster and faster. Devine was Nick's first kill. She remembered that sickening feeling. No matter that the vic was a total scumbag, it still changed you inside in ways that were difficult to articulate. The idea that forcing Nick into that exact situation had been Weller's goal from the beginning wouldn't stop nagging at Bobbie. Eventually she intended to broach the subject with Nick. But not today.

They climbed into her Challenger. She had no idea who had brought it here but she was glad.

"You feel like eating?" She couldn't remember the last time she'd eaten. Not that she was actually hungry, but he might be.

Nick shook his head.

As she drove she tried to think of something reassuring to say.

"You'll feel better after a shower." She'd cleaned up in the ladies' room. Her clothes were bloody but at least her face and hair were no longer sticky with the bastard's blood. She glanced at Nick, hoping for a response.

He said nothing.

Rather than continue trying to encourage a conversation, she let the silence fill the space between them. Ten minutes later they parked in her driveway. It wasn't until that moment that she realized how very tired she was. She walked to the door and unlocked it. Nick followed her inside. D-Boy rushed to greet them. It all felt so ordinary. But it wasn't. Everything had changed.

Randolph Weller was free. The balance Nick had fought so long to maintain was disrupted. His ability to avoid bloodshed had been taken from him.

Nothing would ever be the same again.

She understood that place and the reality that there were no words that would give him solace just now. She asked, "You want to shower first?"

He remained by the front door.

"I could order pizza," she offered, her pulse picking up. He was leaving. Before he uttered a single word she felt him drawing away.

"I should go. LeDoux sent me a text. He thinks he has a lead on Weller."

"You could stay here tonight. Leave fresh in the morning." He had to find Weller. She got that. "If LeDoux is planning to help you, the offer will still be good tomorrow."

"I killed a man," he said, his voice low and raw, defeated.

"You're not your father, Nick. You did what you had to do. It's not the same. Devine would have killed me and probably you, too, if you hadn't stopped him."

His gaze met hers and the pain she saw there punched a hole in her heart. "We both know what happened."

"No one else will ever know those particular details."

"I know."

The ability to breathe deserted her. "What does that mean exactly?"

"I have to go." He looked away. "I won't be back."

"Nick." She moved closer. Searched for the right words to change his mind.

He held up a hand to stop her. "I can't be here with *you*."

"So you'll leave and never look back."

"It's what I do."

For a moment she mentally tallied all that she'd lost this last year. Her husband, her child, her partner, her aunt and then Bauer. She didn't want to lose anyone else.

But she had no choice. She had to let him go. "I understand."

"Goodbye, Bobbie."

She couldn't say goodbye. It felt too final.

He reached her door and she blurted the words she would not allow him to leave without hearing. "I'll be here if you find yourself out this way again."

He hesitated but he never looked back.

The door closed and then the silence echoed around her.

Bobbie pressed her forehead against the door and squeezed her eyes shut to hold back the damned tears. Every part of her hurt. How was one person supposed to survive losing so much? She held her breath, listened to the insistent pounding in her chest. And yet she just kept on living.

Maybe she wasn't supposed to have a whole life again. Maybe being a cop was supposed to be enough.

Something Weller had said abruptly ricocheted through her. *Every ounce of courage and tenacity you possess will be required to survive what's coming, Bobbie. Remember those words if you remember nothing else.*

She raised her head. "Son of a bitch."

He had something bigger planned for Nick and it somehow involved her. He would never have said those words to her otherwise.

Determination seared through her veins as she tugged her cell phone from her pocket and made the only call she could. When Owens answered, she said, "I need some time off. I'll call you when I'm ready to come back. Give Uncle Teddy my love."

Bobbie ended the call before her LT could question her.

She had to go after him.

Nick couldn't do this alone.

* * * * *

Watch for the next SHADES OF DEATH *novel,*
THE COLDEST FEAR, coming soon from
Debra Webb and MIRA Books. Did you miss
the beginning? Look for the series prequel,
THE BLACKEST CRIMSON, and the first book,
NO DARKER PLACE!

The Sandy Shore Killer.

"What are the odds…" Josh continued in that deep
voice of his "…that in this sleepy little town, there
would be not just one sadistic killer…but two?"

She licked her lips. "Considering how rare serial
killers are…I'd say those odds should be astronomically
low. But then…you're FBI. You should know better
than I do."

"They are astronomically low. Coincidences like
this one don't happen." *Flat.*

"But…it is happening."

"Something set this guy off. Something brought
him here…" His head turned and he gazed at the hotel
behind her. "Can't help but wonder…if it was you."

She backed up a step. *He knows. He dug into my
past. He dug too deep. He found out what I did—*

"You and all the reporters," he continued as his
hazel gaze slid back to her. "He didn't like the fame
that Theodore Anderson was getting, so he decided to
steal the spotlight. And you and your buddies—with
your twenty-four-seven news coverage—you just fed

his beast. You made him more determined to get the attention he wanted."

Casey shook her head. "You think this guy came here because of the reporters? Is that the theory the FBI is running with?"

His hand lifted and his fingers curved under her cheek. "We're off-the-record. Way, way off…"

His fingers were faintly callused, a little rough against her skin.

"As I said, it's highly unlikely we'd have two serial killers in the same town. That just doesn't happen. Serial killers are rare to begin with and this…it isn't by chance. Your 'Sandy Shore Killer' was drawn here for a reason."

"Have the victims been connected in any way?" She had to press for more details.

"You know about the victims already. Attractive women in their twenties, all single, all visiting the area—no close personal ties here. And that's all I will say about them now."

His hand dropped away from her cheek and curved back around his handlebar. He revved the engine again.

Right. He was leaving. "Thanks for the ride."

His gaze raked over her. She wondered…did he feel that odd, thick tension between them? The heated attraction that seemed to fill the air?

His hazel stare burned.

He did.

"Good night, Casey."

Don't miss HUNTED,
available July 2017 wherever
Harlequin® Intrigue books and ebooks are sold.

www.Harlequin.com

INTRIGUE

EDGE-OF-YOUR-SEAT INTRIGUE, FEARLESS ROMANCE.

Save **$1.00**
on the purchase of ANY Harlequin® Intrigue book.

Available wherever books are sold, including most bookstores, supermarkets, drugstores and discount stores.

Save $1.00

on the purchase of any Harlequin® Intrigue book.

Coupon valid until September 30, 2017.
Redeemable at participating outlets in the U.S. and Canada only.
Not redeemable at Barnes & Noble stores. Limit one coupon per customer.

52614835

5 65373 00076 2   (8100)0 12280

® and ™ are trademarks owned and used by the trademark owner and/or its licensee.

© 2017 Harlequin Enterprises Limited

HICOUPCE0617